# THE TROUBLESOME OFFSPRING OF CARDINAL GUZMAN

Louis de Bernières' novels are *The War of Don Emmanuel's Nether Parts* (Commonwealth Writers Prize, Best First Book Eurasia Region, 1991), *Señor Vivo and the Coca Lord* (Commonwealth Writers Prize, Best Book Eurasia Region, 1992) and *The Troublesome Offspring of Cardinal Guzman*. The acclaimed and bestselling *Captain Corelli's Mandolin* won the Commonwealth Writers Prize, Best Book, 1995. The author, who lives in London, was selected as one of the twenty Best of Young British Novelists in 1993.

Louis de Bernières

# THE TROUBLESOME OFFSPRING OF CARDINAL GUZMAN

VINTAGE

Published by Vintage 1998

2  4  6  8  10  9  7  5

First published in Great Britain in 1992 by
Martin Secker & Warburg Limited

Published by Minerva 1993

Vintage
Random House, 20 Vauxhall Bridge Road,
London SW1V 2SA

Random House Australia (Pty) Limited
20 Alfred Street, Milsons Point, Sydney
New South Wales 2061, Australia

Random House New Zealand Limited
18 Poland Road, Glenfield,
Auckland 10, New Zealand

Random House South Africa (Pty) Limited
Endulini, 5A Jubilee Road, Parktown 2193,
South Africa

Random House UK Limited Reg. No. 954009

A CIP catalogue record for this book
is available from the British Library

ISBN 0 7493 9857 4

Papers used by Random House UK Ltd are natural, recyclable products made from wood grown in sustainable forests. The manufacturing processes conform to the environmental regulations of the country of origin

Printed and bound in Germany
by Graphischer Grossbetrieb Pössneck GmbH

This book is dedicated to my family,

for their unfailing faith and enthusiasm;

to Caroline, for her fund of stories

and her luminous presence; and to all those who are

persecuted for daring to think for themselves.

# Contents

# Prologue

These events transpired just after the time when the most powerful soft-drinks company in the world pulled off the greatest feat of advertising in modern history.

Fired with the spirit of corporate enterprise, enthused with the idea of refreshing the whole of mankind, and not content that their famous logo was scrolled in neon from Red Square to Tierra del Fuego, they bought into a joint Russian/American space shot, and proclaimed themselves from the heavens in a manner unknown since God Himself set his bow in the sky.

They launched two satellites, one at each pole, to project their name upon the eternal snows so that it was visible in the telescopes of distant races and strange civilisations, who accordingly changed their name for our planet. In the Arctic there evolved new species of red polar bears, foxes, and seals, which were then too conspicuous to leave their boundaries of light and venture into the whiteness, and in the Antarctic the same effect was observed upon emperor penguins.

But this message was as nothing compared to their transformation of the moon. Hundreds of silver-suited workers with post-graduate degrees in astrophysics and low-gravity hydraulics drove their specially designed paint-spray vehicles between hundreds of kilometres of carefully placed markers, until below upon the earth could be seen the company name resplendent, fluorescent, and unmistakable.

Anthropologists set out in droves to the remotest corners of mountain and rainforest in order to gather data upon the effect of this lunar metamorphosis upon primitive thinking, and returned disappointed. Even the Navantes, the Cusicuari, the Kogi, the Acahuatecs, were familiar with the logo that could be found hanging from trees in areas presumed to be unexplored, that could be seen above the doorways of brush huts and painted upon the rocks of Mount Aconcagua.

But with the passage of time even the specially formulated paint could no longer stand the conditions of our satellite. Sprayed with lunar dust, battered by meteorites, expanded and contracted by extremes of temperature, the writing began to break up until it appeared that the face of the moon was smeared with blood. People would look up at the sky of night, and shudder.

# Part One

Hoy, sin miedo que libre escandalice,
puede hablar el ingenio, asegurado
de que mayor poder le atemorice.

En otros siglos pudo ser pecado
severo estudio, y la verdad desnuda,
y romper el silencio el bien hablado.

Francisco de Quevedo y Villegas (1580–1645)

('These days, without fear that his freedom
will offend, an intelligent man may speak,
safe from the intimidation of the more powerful.
   In other centuries rigorous criticism,
the naked truth, and the eloquent man's breaking
of silence, could have been crimes.')

# 1 *His Eminence, Tormented By Demons, Resolves To Save His Soul*

Once again, Cardinal Dominic Trujillo Guzman felt a pang like that of childbirth spear him in the belly, and he doubled over, clutching himself and moaning. As always when this happened, his only thoughts were of the guilt of his life. In his anguish it was as if ancient coffers opened before his eyes, but instead of overflowing with gold doubloons, louis d'or, silver crucifixes encrusted with rubies, there spilled out demons.

His Eminence knew all his parade of demons by heart; they were an infernal pantheon that, as he lay there upon the stone floor gaping with anguish, passed before him in a monstrous parody of a Holy Week procession, mocking him for his faults and rejoicing.

At the head of the diabolical rout was the creature with the two contending heads in loud dispute. The necks were indeed swanlike, but their length and flexibility merely made it easier for those vile mouths to dart and bite at each other, as with kisses grown too passionate. 'Vatican Two, Vatican Two,' one of the heads was screaming, and the other was shouting, equally shrill, 'Tradition, tradition,' as though that was all there was to that time in 1968 when His Eminence had attended the very first conference of Latin American bishops in Medellin. He was a powerful man even then, and he had gone away in disgust, determined to do away altogether with the influence of Liberation Theology in his own episcopacy. To be sure he had tried reason, persuasion, and the quoting of precedents, but that did not prevent his priests from abandoning their worldly goods and disappearing into the backlands with only a donkey and a wooden crucifix to stir up the discontent of the poor, fill their minds with economic theories that had nothing to do with the maintenance of churches and cathedrals, and everything to do with dispossessing those very rich people whose generosity it was that ensured that the Virgin should be represented by silver statues. 'Nothing is too good for God,' His Eminence would say, only to have some parish priest retort without respect (and employing some nauseatingly stereotypical formula), that, 'Loving one's neighbour is a matter of praxis.' His Eminence recalled without nostalgia the bitter arguments that had so often degenerated into unecclesiastical personal insult as he had dismissed a poor priest as a 'slogan-monger' only to be dubbed in return 'an oligarchic parasite whose fat belly is full of the bread of the lowly'.

He remembered his early years when life in the Church had been one of tranquillity and routine, a kind of dreamlike state perfumed with incense and lulled with chant. He remembered how he had, one by one, got rid of his turbulent clergy. There had been that one who had left anyway, and had got killed in a skirmish when the National Army had surprised a party of Communists; and there was Don Ramón, who he had browbeaten in repeated interviews until he had forced a promise that he would never again allow a political opinion to pass his lips.

Nowadays there were no parish priests with donkeys and wooden crucifixes. Instead there were plump, jolly priests who drove land-cruisers, who wore gold rings inlaid with the cross, and everything was to his satisfaction, except that when he suffered agony like this, the other side of the argument always presented itself to him, and he recalled that in many villages there were no priests at all anymore. In those places people made a cult of the Black Virgin, begging her intercession even in the most un-Christian projects, and there was no sanctioned marriage; men got women pregnant and then disappeared, leaving behind them improbable matriarchies with no conception of the Fatherhood of God. It was at times like this that His Eminence felt the burden of all the contention that had sundered his ministry and which made him wonder if in his certainties he had not been altogether too inflexible.

After the Contending Heads came the leathery creature with five legs that he knew as the Hinderer, tripping everybody up, raising instantaneous and invisible walls that all the others crashed into, so that the dreadful procession compressed itself into a concertina of flailing limbs and obscene imprecations.

Skilled as he was in the redaction of his horrifying visions, His Eminence remembered as if by reflex the machinations in which he had involved himself in order to close down the village schools.

It was not that he was opposed to true education, where one

6

learned the catechism by heart, the multiplication tables, the lives of the saints and national heroes, the basics of literacy, and the story and meaning of the Passion of Christ. To these he was not opposed at all. What he opposed was the brainwashing of the poor by thin and virtually secular missionaries who were poisoned by the insidious ideas of Paulo Freire, who prattled about 'liberating the illiterate masses from their culture of silence', preaching 'struggle' and 'participation in the historical process'. His Eminence could concede the good intentions of such idealists, but how could he tolerate the idea of the nation's young growing up without an education that would arrange in advance an eternal place at God's Right Hand in Heaven?

These pitiful youngsters with such an 'education' would surely be condemned forever to the limbo of the heathen, or the purifying flames of purgatory, or perhaps the everlasting torture of hell, tormented by demons such as these very demons, except that the demons of hell were even worse. Why did he feel guilty, when his reason told him that he would be saving them from spending eternity on fire without being consumed, with tridents twisting in their entrails? Why worry about it when they would have been saved by him personally from being violated everlastingly by the twin organs of Lucifer, one up their backside and one up their vagina (if they were women, that is, which they mostly were, since women were the greatest tempters after Satan himself)? Did those defenders of the underprivileged understand that the Devil's two penises were toweringly huge, rougher than corn husks, and ejaculated semen burningly cold in such quantities that the condemned split repeatedly apart before being miraculously mended in order to be dually raped all over again? And yet His Eminence felt dejected about all those schoolhouses that were now pig-sheds and brothels, as well as about the careers of all the priests he had blighted, and also about the time when he had won promotion by falsely declaring in the relevant ears that his main rival for the post was homosexual.

And here was the demon he knew as the Concealer, who was a furtive character indeed. He was praising the Cardinal with a sarcasm and irony so adept that all the demons were squealing with swinish and delighted laughter. 'He is honest,' said the Concealer, raising one finger in the air, so that His Eminence was reminded of the time when he had sold the cloisters of a cathedral to a supermarket chain, and had kept half the money for himself. 'He is chaste,' proclaimed the Concealer, and he burned with the shame of having impregnated Concepcion, his kitchen maid. He was reminded that once he had gone to a brothel in disguise, but the whore had recognised him and he had been obliged to have her killed, and then the killer had tried to blackmail him, and so he too now lay in unhallowed ground where his soul cried continually for light and for revenge in the crepuscular world of the Cardinal's nightmares.

'He honours his mother and father,' said the Concealer, grinning whilst the demons sniggered and pointed, and the cleric recalled how he had left his own mother to die a lunatic in the filth of an asylum rather than house her in the palace and thereby let it be known from her appearance that he had Indian blood in his veins.

'He loves his neighbour, he is full of compassion,' smirked the Concealer, so that the vision of a ghastly mistake returned to him once more. It had been in the time of the disappearances, which he had not believed to be truly occurring, thinking the stories to be the propaganda of subversives. He had given away to the Army the hiding place in the sanctuary of a Marxist priest, and had had to look on in horror as they had filled him up with bullets and carried him away in the St John's Day altarcloth, which he had later received back, freshly laundered, but dark with perpetual and reproachful stains.

And the whole congregation of these skeletal monsters, the Smiters, the Flaming ones, the Litigators, the Dispersers, the Falsifiers, danced around him as he lay upon the flags, panting and groaning. He gazed up at those leering eyes with their sepulchral squints, their skin like that of corpses, stretched tightly over the sharp angles of their bones (reminding him, forgive him the blasphemy, of the dried body of a saint), their copious genitals flapping and waving with a rustling like vultures' wings, and he turned over on his back, still cradling the terrible pain in his entrails.

He closed his eyes and concentrated. '*Domine Deus*,' he began, his voice cracking with grief. '*Agnus Dei, Filius Patris, Qui tollis peccata mundi, miserere nobis; Qui tollis peccata mundi, suscipe deprecationem nostrum, Qui sedes ad dexteram patris, miserere nobis.*' With peace descending upon him he added, '*Kyrie, Eleison. Christe, Eleison,*' and then he confessed to Almighty God, Blessed Mary ever-Virgin, Blessed

Michael the Archangel, Blessed John the Baptist, to the Holy Apostles Peter and Paul and all the saints, that he had sinned exceedingly in thought, word and deed. He struck his chest in penitence, as at mass, and the twittering demons faded from the room at the same time as the appalling pain in his guts diminished to the remains of a suggestive throb.

Concepcion came into the lectorium and found him struggling to get to his feet. 'The pain again?' she enquired. 'You must take yourself to a doctor, my cadenay.'

'I accept it as a just punishment,' he said, looking up at her through the tears of his terrible affliction.

Concepcion was a mulatta, his kitchen maid, with one child of his to her credit, and in truth he loved her in her carnality more even than he loved the Virgin in her sexless spirituality. She put her arms around him to give him comfort, and, later in the night when she had slipped into his chamber, she solaced him with the musky familiarity of her nakedness.

But when he got up at three o'clock in the morning to go to relieve his bladder he could not resume his sleep because the cohort of the devils was back again, parading around the room, swinging from the lightpull and the tapestries sown by widows that depicted the Stations of the Cross.

Worst of all, the Obscene Ass was there, with his donkey's head and his donkey's member which one minute was so erect that it bounced along the ceiling leaving a trail of glistening fluid, and the next was trailing flaccidly along the floor like some praeternatural gastropod from a cheap horror movie.

His Eminence left the bed and rushed in a frenzy to the chapel, where he kissed the altar and fell upon his knees whilst the demons cavorted and gibbered even upon the Christus Rex that reigned upon the wall. '*Munda cor meum*,' he prayed, '*ac labia mea, omnipotens Deus, Qui labia Isaiae prophetae calculo mundasti ignito . . .*' And they shrieked and turned their backsides to him, farting sulphurously and contemptuously before disappearing amid a chorus of '*Diabolus tecum, diabolus tecum*'.

After their gales of ribald laughter had faded into the furthest corners of the palace, His Eminence prayed for a very long time and, finally, by way of atonement, promised faithfully with his hand upon the reliquary that he would without fail use his office well to bring the light of the truth of the Church to the entire nation. He would send out the Dominicans to detect errors and defeat them with the aid of the copious logic of Saints Anselm and Aquinas, to evangelise the heathen, to save his own tainted soul by ensuring that before he died a million other souls would have been pointed heavenward with all the foolproof precision of a gringo missile.

## 2 *Ena And The Mexican Musicologist (1)*

Sometimes ignorance can be most beneficial; were it not for my ignorance I would have nothing of what I have today, which in fact is considerably more than I ever could have expected, and is also considerably more than I deserve.

In the first place, nothing of all this could have occurred if I had been a native of this country, rather than what I was, which was an itinerant and not very successful musicologist, specialising in folk-tunes of the Andes, which I used to collect and publish in anthologies. I think that the only people who bought them were probably superannuated Western hippies who formed groups, all dressed in ponchos and sombreros, which played in the student unions of West Coast universities and could not even pronounce a proper Castilian 'o' on the ends of words.

I was travelling in this country looking for charango tunes that used the pentatonic mode, when I passed by a church in Ipasueño, where there was being held the funeral of a policeman. Out of curiosity I went and stood by the door, which is how I first heard the 'Requiem Angelico', which is now so famous that there is no need for me to describe it. It was being played by a small group of musicians playing mandolas, quenas, and the harmonium, and even in that form it moved the whole congregation to tears, myself not excepted.

Assuming that the piece was traditional, I wrote it down immediately in my manuscript notebook with a feeling of the greatest excitement imaginable. As I travelled on through the sierras it fermented continuously in my mind, until one morning I awoke with an arrangement of it for string quartet almost wholly formed in my imagination. I wrote it down in a great hurry before it slipped away, and when I reached the capital I lost no time in posting it to my publisher in Mexico City.

All the rest is history. The success it enjoyed there caused it to spread into the United States, whence it spread to France and the rest of Europe, where it became the theme of a Rumanian film that won at the Cannes Film Festival, probably only because of the music. The consequence of all this was that I became immensely wealthy because of the royalties, and you can easily imagine my alarm and distress when it transpired that the music was not traditional at all, but had been composed by the famous Dionisio Vivo of Cochadebajo de los Gatos. There was a spectacular panic in the legal department of my publisher, and eventually I travelled all the way to Cochadebajo de los Gatos with the company lawyer in order to sort out any problems before they arose.

It was an horrifically arduous journey, taking four days through the sierras on muleback, and when we arrived at that extraordinary city populated entirely by eccentrics, it seemed at first that it had been a wasted journey. This was because Sr. Vivo himself had been quite unaware that his melody, and he himself also, were famous all over the world. He seemed to be very surprised, and had nothing more to say upon the subject than that we sould simply divide the proceeds half/half, since although he had composed the tune, I had made the arrangement. When he showed me his own arrangement I was astonished to find that it was in any case remarkably similar to my own, except of course that it was scored for different instruments. My lawyer jumped at the chance to come to so amicable an agreement, and Sr. Vivo even said that he did not mind if it was not retrospective, which meant that I could keep all the royalties that I had thencefar earned.

Having spent some days in that wonderful city with its proliferation of tame black jaguars, its Inca buildings, and its population who practise the most enlightened and congenial religion I have ever come across, I fell ardently in love with the place and resolved to stay there despite its isolation from the rest of the world.

I chose a small house on the edge of the city, and dug out the alluvial mud with the help of several cheerful characters who said that they came originally from Chiriguana, a settlement that was destroyed in a flood some years before.

It was an ideal place for me, because I wanted fresh mountain air, space, privacy, a place where one could palpably feel the presence of ancient gods and the spirits of nature. But also it was a place where, when in the appropriate mood, one could find spectacular revelry and good humour.

The house was merely an empty shell, but I chose it because it was on the sunny side of the valley, high enough to have a good view over the town, with a sufficient breeze to diminish the occasionally stupefying heat. It took me a good year to make the place inhabitable.

The first thing that I did was to dig out the well at the side of the house, which had caved in on itself and was full of mud and rocks. I was helped in this by a Frenchman named Antoine, a man of considerable culture who had chosen to live here because he was attached to the people, with whom he had arrived in the original immigration. Like most Frenchmen, he was extremely fond of philosophising about women, and was married to someone called Françoise, who had apparently been cured of a foul cancer by indigenous methods.

It took us two months to dig out the well and rebuild its walls, and at the bottom I found the skull of a baby, which I assume to have been left there as a sacrifice in times past. I keep this tiny skull on my bookshelf as my own Renaissance-style memento mori, and I frequently speculate as to the nature of the story of its tragedy. There was fortunately still water at the bottom of the well, and I remember that when I remarked to Antoine that it was strange that water should flow beneath the side of a mountain, he observed, 'I can think of many stranger things.'

We repaired the walls and roof of the house, and painted the rooms completely white so that they became suddenly clean, bright, and spacious. Antoine and I managed, at some danger to ourselves (I feel in retrospect), to install electricity by connecting up a cable to the faltering system invented by a teacher. This man was Profesor Luis, who had set up a row of windmills to generate power; this was perfectly adequate for lighting, but was somewhat feeble when high amperage was required, so that the electric cooker that I had flown in by helicopter turned out to be of more use as a storage cupboard.

It often happens when setting up a house that one finds quite suddenly that there is an urgent need for some item overlooked during the last expedition. The track down from my house was a deeply pitted one that served as a watercourse each time that it rained, and although I have stabilised it since, it was to begin with only negotiable on foot or by mule, or by Antoine's ancient three-wheeled tractor. This tractor had been half-buried in the mud of the flood at Chiriguana, but Sr. Vivo's father, who is in fact General Hernando Montes Sosa, governor of Cesar, had it dug out and brought in slung under a vast helicopter gun ship, at his son's request. It is commonly said in this country that General Sosa is the only member of the military hierarchy who ever does anything useful.

There was at the far end of the town a tienda that sold goods brought in by mule-train from Ipasueño, and so every few days I would find myself rattling and bumping my way to it on Antoine's formidable old tractor. This shop was owned by a middle-aged couple who left the running of it to their daughter, a girl of twenty or so years whose name was Ena, as I discovered by overhearing the father asking of her the price of a bottle of Ron Caña.

Ena was small and strongly built; usually she wore a plain, faded blue dress, and her feet were always bare. Sometimes I used to think that her head was very slightly too large for her, but she had an appealing and serene face framed by her long black hair. She reminded me forcibly of a Greek girl with whom I had once been in love, for she had the same smooth and soft olive skin, and big brown eyes beneath eyebrows almost heavy enough to meet in the middle. On her forearms were the traces of soft black downy hair, which, to be frank, is something that has always driven me crazy, and her fingers were slim and elegant.

The best thing about her, however, was her elfin spirit; she had an air of quiet amusement, a semi-concealed puckishness, an innocent devilry, that gave her the aura of having existed from all eternity, and of being able to see the funny side of virtually everything. I perceived that she had a streak of mischief in her, as was to be revealed when I discovered how it was that she had kept me for so long in ignorance.

I had found in Sr. Vivo an inexhaustible library of Andean tunes, and he had also taught me to play the guitar, pointing out that it was a perfect instrument for arranging on, as it had the capacity for three different voices at once. It was my custom then, as it is still, to spend a part of every evening during and after sunset learning and practising new pieces sitting on the doorstep of my front door. The acoustics of the quiet air of the mountainside were absolutely perfect, and Antoine used to say that I could be heard clearly all over the town. 'Listen,' the people would say, 'the Mexicano is playing again.' Sometimes I would stop and hear the crickets setting up their own ragged symphonies, and, as I have unnaturally sharp hearing, I could listen also to the conversations of the bats.

One evening I was playing 'El Noy de la Mare', which is a particularly lovely folk-tune from Catalonia. It is quite difficult to play because its variations are very subtle, and I still play it often to remind myself of the gratitude I feel for what it helped to bring about.

I thought I saw a shadow move in the darkness behind the wall, and then disappear. I was puzzled, but thought no more of it, and began to play the arrangement for guitar of the 'Requiem Angelico' that Sr. Vivo and I had made between us. To me it seemed exquisitely tender, and I became wholly lost in it. When I had finished something made me look up, and again I saw a shadow move, except that this time it detached itself from the darkness and then came towards me. The tune had made me think of the earth goddess that they worship around here, Pachamama, and for some reason I momentarily felt an awed panic that it was Pachamama herself that I had evoked. But it was Ena.

She stood before me, and I saw that her huge brown eyes were brimming with tears. We looked at one another in silence for a few moments and then, with all the natural grace of a little girl, she sat down cross-legged in front of me and said very gravely, 'That was so beautiful. I have never heard such saudade. Please play it again.'

'I do not play it too well,' I said. 'You should hear Sr. Vivo play it.'

'Play it again,' she said, 'except for me this time, and not for whoever it was that you were thinking about.'

I was a little startled at this, and I laughed at her percipience. But as I began to play it I realised that I wanted to play it especially well for her, and that I was trying too hard. I fumbled a few notes and then forced myself to stop thinking, so that I could enter into the music.

When I had finished she reached forward with a wondering expression and tenderly brushed her hand across the strings. Then she leaned back and sighed very deeply. 'I wish I could do that,' she said at last.

'Perhaps one day you will.'

'No, never. For that one needs a lot of sadness. I do not have enough sadness.' Then she laughed and cut me a sideways glance. 'Now tell me, who is the one you were thinking of when you were playing before?'

'She lives in Mexico City,' I confessed, much to my own surprise. 'She is younger than me, and older than you. Unfortunately she does not love me, and so . . .' I shrugged, '. . . I play sometimes for someone who never hears.'

'You should play only for those who listen, and love only those who love in return. That is what I would do.'

'You are wiser than me, I think.'

'Obviously. Now play me some Spanish ones, real Spanish ones, with duende and gracia.'

The only variety of flamenco with which I was aquainted was the soleares, the solea, and soledades, because that was all that Sr. Vivo himself had learned when he had once visited Andalucia. One can play these pieces quite slowly, because their theme is the melancholy of solitude. I played four in a row, during which time she sat with her head cocked to one side watching my fingers attentively. At the finish she said, 'Your hands are like spiders. I think that you should learn the tiple and the charango as well.' Then she stood up and straightened her one blue dress, saying, 'I think that I shall return tomorrow. This is a good way to break a paseo.'

'Ena,' I asked, 'why is it that sometimes your parents call you "Ena" and sometimes "Lena"? I have often wondered.'

She laughed lightly. 'If that puzzles you, I will tell you. It is because when I was very little I could not say "Lena", so I said "Ena" instead. So now I have both the names at once.'

'A very simple explanation. Be careful how you walk, out on your own,' I said.

She glanced at me over her shoulder as she walked away, 'Do not trouble yourself, this is not Mexico City.' I watched her vanish into the darkness, turning to wave before she disappeared, and I was left alone with the cicadas.

# 3 Of The New Restaurant And The New Priest

He arrived on the day when Dolores the whore was giving Doña Constanza her last lesson in the indispensable art of making chuño. At school Doña Constanza had learned only how to make canapés and vol-au-vents, these being the only skills appropriate to a lady of her oligarchic status, who would be presumed always to have teams of cooks at her beck and call. But now that she had demoted herself to the position of campesino's lover, exiled forever to this settlement in the sierra, she was ashamed of her idleness and was embarrassed that Gonzago did all the cooking in their household.

Dolores the whore, on the other hand, had learned to cater for squads of children by different fathers, and had decided to diversify her economic activities. 'I am certainly forty years old or thereabouts, and all this squeezing and moaning has worn me out,' she said. 'And after all this time I deserve a break from constantly dripping. From now on I am a whore only on Friday and Saturday nights.'

What gave her the idea of opening a restaurant was reading a book which she had bought from Dionisio in return for a bracelet that he intended to give as a present to Leticia Aragon. Dionisio had assured her that it was 'un libro muy romantico', and she had bought it in good faith, expecting it to be all about princes and princesses or perhaps a blonde and blue-eyed victim who is gallantly rescued by a Captain of the Dragoons who turns out to be her long-lost cousin, and so they can marry after winning with difficulty the permission of his parents, and do not have to elope after all.

But it turned out that Dionisio's conception of a 'very romantic book' was a little different from hers. She read it impatiently, chewing the soggy cigar between her teeth, and waiting for the entry of the princess. Being unused to literary effort, she did not know how to recognise which were crucial parts of the story, and found herself most fascinated by the incidental recipes. The book was *Doña Flor And Her Two Husbands*, and she decided to open her own restaurant, resolving to call it 'Doña Flor's'.

The enterprise was not without its difficulties. In the first place she was obliged to dig a new building out of the mud, which had by now drained itself very effectively and become adamantine. Her life as a whore had given her a great love of her freedom, but at this time she felt the lack of a helpmeet. 'Ay, ay,' she would say, 'if only there were some man to come and dig,' and she would mop the sweat from her face with the hem of her skirt before resuming her labours. She greatly regretted that her oldest sons had disappeared to look for diamonds in the jungle, that her two eldest daughters had traipsed away to Valledupar to take up their mother's profession, and that the remainder of her brood were only old enough to carry away the bricks of spoil and could not help with the digging.

But one day when she was working she sensed a presence behind her. Her heart leapt, and she turned and beheld Fulgencia Astiz. Dolores suffered from what in learned circles would be called an 'abnormal surprise reflex', and she stood paralysed with her arms outstretched and her mouth wide open. Everyone who knew her was used to this, and often the little children would creep up on her, bang a saucepan next to her head just to see her gaping, and then run away screaming with laughter before she could recover. But Fulgencia had never seen this before, and she was puzzled by this extraordinary reaction to her presence; it looked as though Dolores had been frozen in the act of being about to give her a hug, and she stepped back and left quickly.

But later on Dolores sought Fulgencia out, and, to put it in short, they soon found that they had become friends. Fulgencia had been the leader of Dionisio's women in Ipasueño; she was a Santandereana, and there was nothing she liked more than to become involved in heroic feats, preferably entailing the risk of death or, failing that, a little bloodshed. She was constructed in the good peasant fashion, with a broad flat face and high cheekbones. She wore her hair in the same manner as Remedios, in a black ponytail, and many a man had at one time or another realised by the force of her blows to the side of his head that she was a strong woman, not to be fooled around with. She fetched ten more women who had been in the camp with her at Ipasueño, and they dug out Doña Flor's in no time at all, thatched it in two days, and buried a llama foetus in the floor to ensure the fecundity of Dolores' new business.

But Dolores was a wilful proprietor. She did not see why her own mealtimes should be disrupted, and so she closed the restaurant at breakfast, midday, and seven o'clock in the evening, and she would not open during the hours of siesta on the grounds that she needed one as much as anyone else. This meant that she was only open for trade in the mornings after everyone had departed for their labours, and in the evenings when everyone had already eaten. This was a good arrangement in only one way, which was that she hardly ever had to do any work.

Having passed this stage, and having decided to open at saner times, she then displayed a side of her character which had been hitherto undisclosed to those who knew her. It transpired that she was an obsessive experimentalist. In trials with aji sauce she developed one that was so indescribably hot that it became instantaneously famous. It was the kind of aji sauce that is tasteless for the first few chews, and which then seizes the back of the throat and sends one into a kind of frenzied dementia where one clasps the throat with one hand, half gets out of the chair, sinks back into it, waves the free hand about, emits strangled noises, gasps for water, drinks it in one swig, discovers that water only makes it worse, and then rushes out to throw oneself in the river, from which one emerges dazed and dripping with sweat, smiling sheepishly.

Dolores made a lot of money out of this dish; she served it up with braised chicken and called it Pollo de un Hombre Verdadero. This Chicken of a True Man was taken up as a challenge by all the men of the city who prided themselves in their machismo. One after the other they were brought in by their compadres and challenged to eat the whole meal without so much as a grimace. Anyone who succeeded was immediately raised to the élite in the machismo stakes, and it was a common thing to hear it said of someone, 'What? He is no man, he could only eat a little of Dolores' chicken,' or 'Did you hear about Hectoro? He ate two of Dolores' chicken one after the other without even taking a drink. ¡Qué hombre!'

But nobody truly enjoyed this ordeal, and the men began to suspect that Dolores had found a subtle way of mocking them. They started to avoid coming to the restaurant in case somebody challenged them to trial by chicken, and so Dolores began her next flurry of experimentation. She tried Fish with Forty Cloves of Garlic, which did not prove popular, and which proved to be tedious on account of having to do so much peeling. She tried a confection called Woman's Revenge, which consisted of testicles afloat in a tapioca sauce of suggestive appearance, but discovered that it could only be a seasonal dish, since the steers were rounded up and corraled for gelding but once a year. She invented a dish consisting of several layers of tortilla with something different between each layer, depending upon what was available, which she called Bocadillo Improvisado; it turned out to be very popular with women, who have, as it is generally conceded all over the world, more adaptable and exploratory appetites than men.

At the end of her fantasia period Dolores began to serve up standard favourites, such as picante de pollo, arepas, chiles rellenos, carnitas, salpicon, and esquites, but we should not fail to mention in conclusion her final major experiment, which was with frijoles refritos. She discovered that refried beans could be made to be quite phenomenally carminative by beating eggs into it and using several different kinds of beans all in the same mash. It was this that she served to people upon whom she wished to exercise her sense of humour, and it was the very same one that caused a temporary falling out between Felicidad and Don Emmanuel, this latter having grown extraordinarily fond of it.

When Doña Constanza wished to learn the secrets of culinary success, it was natural that she should apprentice herself to Dolores, who at first was suspicious of the former's motives. She made Constanza swear on the apachita, the little pile of stones upon which Aurelio sacrificed coca leaves to the spirits of the hills, that she was not about to open her own restaurant, and that every time she served a meal she should accompany it with the words 'This is a recipe of Dolores, who makes it better than I do'. The first thing that Dolores did was to take advantage of her quite shamelessly; she made Constanza help with preserving her huge pile of potatoes, under the pretext that it was essential for every cook to know how this was done.

First she made Doña Constanza separate out the 'llallahuas', the potatoes considered to be sacred on account of their shape, and then she made her fill a large cauldron with water brought from the river. She sent Constanza away, and then fetched her after a week, telling her to carry all the potatoes up to the frost line so that they could be alternately frozen at night and heated by day for ten days. She sent the puzzled Constanza away again, only to tell her after the ten days had elapsed to go and stamp on the potatoes until there was no more moisture in them. This she did in a state of perplexity and resentment, which grew worse when she was then instructed to leave them for another month before the next lesson, which consisted of carrying them in sacks down the mountainside and stacking them at the back of Doña Flor's. 'There you are,' exclaimed Dolores, disappearing behind a pall of smoke from her cigar, 'we have made chuños.' Doña Constanza looked dubiously at the hardened desiccated vegetables and said, 'But Dolores, I wanted to know how to cook them, not how to turn them into nuts.'

'With cooking,' replied Dolores, 'preparation is everything.'

This was something that Doña Constanza could understand; her face brightened up and she said, 'It is just the same with making love.' Dolores' experience of men was that mostly they stood in a queue getting drunk, spitting on the floor and shouting to the present customer to hurry up. When it was their turn they just dived in with most of their clothes still on, their boots leaving mud on the sheet, and then they tried to leave without paying. She looked incredulously at Doña Constanza, and drawled in her rum-laden way, 'Amiga, what man is there who would go to any trouble? They are all like horses, they sink their teeth into your neck to hold you still, and then they go after another mare.' She spat on the ground for emphasis, leaving Constanza too intimidated to explain to her that Gonzago was not like that.

It was at this point that a gaunt but insouciant figure strode past the door, and the two women looked at one another in surprise. They could have sworn that a priest had just walked by, a priest who was not Father Garcia. They popped their heads out of the doorway, and without a word to each other, decided to follow him to see what he was up to, only to find that everyone else in the street had had the same idea. There was a crowd of folk following the new priest at a respectful distance, including Father Garcia, whose territorial instincts were struggling with his better nature. He was arguing fiercely with himself as to whether or not he should welcome this new priest or tell him to go away, since the parish was already spoken for. He resolved to bide his time.

In the plaza the tattered cleric mounted the plinth of an obelisk and gazed distractedly into space as though gathering his holiness together into a point of light. Garcia recognised his own familiar technique for rendering people curious and silent, and he began to enjoy the occasion for its theatrical professionalism. He was able to look at the priest more closely now, and he realised that there was something strange about him. Everything was right, but at the same time it was wrong.

Look at that hat for example; it was the correct shape, but it was a vaquero's sombrero punched out and painted black. It had been daubed very thickly to give the impression of smoothness, but one could still see the weave of the straw underneath. And what about that dog collar? It was the right size, and it was white, but it most definitely had the look of carefully torn cardboard. The black robes seemed to be made of unecclesiastical material; they were too diaphanous, too loosely woven, like cheap curtains dyed to black and cobbled into shape. Father Garcia strained forward and noted that the stitches were large and clumsy, the kind of stitching that little children achieve in their first attempts.

The new priest made the sign of the cross with his right hand, the people fell silent, and he announced, 'Brothers and sisters, I come to bring you salvation. I am but a poor wandering missionary of the Order of St Haematoma the Blessed Martyr, and I earn my bread by the hearing of confessions and the granting of absolutions. For only twenty pesos I will give you peace of mind and the assurance of eternal bliss, guaranteed by this Most Holy Relic that I carry, which is the rib of St Necrophobia herself, who miraculously ascended into heaven in the year of Our Lord one thousand nineteen hundred and fifty-four, taking with her her carapace of flesh and leaving only her bones behind.' He waved a yellowed bone that Pedro recognised instantly as having been taken from a dog.

At this many people crossed themselves, and the priest continued, 'I am to be found at the first jaguar obelisk at the entrance to the town. Be silent for the blessing.' He bowed his head and intoned, '*Non (ita me Di ament) quicquam referre putaui utrumne os an culum olfacerem Aemilio, nilo mundius hoc nihiloque immundius illud. Amen.*'

The people reiterated the amen, and the priest departed with dignity towards the place appointed by himself for his ministry.

Smiling with delight, Father Garcia turned to Dionisio and said, 'Do you know what he just said?' and the latter replied, 'My Latin is not too good, but it certainly didn't sound right. What was it?'

'It was Catullus,' said Garcia. 'It was "I believed (Gods help me) that it made no difference whether I smelled Aemilius' mouth or anus, the one being no cleaner, the other no dirtier."'

'He said that?' Dionisio was astonished. 'What kind of blessing is that?'

'It is the blessing of a false priest who is concerned to make a living,' said Garcia. 'I am going to go at once to confess to him so that I can hear more Catullus.'

He came back with a spring in his step, having been absolved in Latin with the words, 'You shit less than ten times in a year, and then it's as hard as beans and lupins and if you rubbed it between your hands you would never soil a single digit.'

He had also formed the beginnings of a firm friendship with the false priest, who was none other than the wastrel and rapscallion younger brother of Cardinal Dominic Trujillo Guzman. He had studied at the same seminary as Father Garcia, and had been thrown out on account of his absorbing interest in scatological classical literature. His name was Don Salvador, and he knew all the obscene and lascivious passages by heart. Like Father Garcia, he strongly believed in salvation through good times and fornication.

# 4 *Ena And The Mexican Musicologist* (2)

During the weeks that followed Ena used to appear regularly at dusk, and I very quickly noticed that she had a protean quality about her. On some days she appeared to be slightly plumper than upon others, and I believed that her eyebrows were on some days heavier than upon others. But that was not all, because almost everything about her could be seen to be changing from one day to the next. I found that she would forget things that I had told her the day before, yet remember them weeks later, and often she would ask me the same questions. One day she would take delight in a tune I was playing, and the next she would be dismissive about it and claim that she preferred another which previously she had disliked. Always, however, she would sit cross-legged before me, and study me with her unwavering brown eyes. 'Ena,' I asked one day, 'why do you change so much all the time?'

Instead of expressing surprise at my question, as I had expected, Ena giggled into her hands and said, 'Everybody says that. I think it is very funny.'

'I find you most mysterious.'

'O bueno, I like to be mysterious.'

The next day she brought me two jaguar kittens in a straw basket. She handed them to me by the scruff of the neck, saying, 'You will never be a real inhabitant of this city unless you have Cochadebajo cats as everyone else does.'

Normally I detest cats because they make me sneeze, and moreover they detect my dislike and come to sit on me on purpose. I was horrified at being given two of them which would one day grow to be enormous black monsters, but I confess that when I looked at them my heart softened a little, and in any case I was glad of a pretext to kiss Ena upon the cheek in token of gratitude. She blushed momentarily, and her eyes seemed briefly to catch aflame. She put the back of her hand to her cheek where I had kissed it, as if to feel the kiss again, and I felt obliged to rescue her from her confusion by saying, 'What shall I call them?'

'O,' she said, 'I think that they are both girls, so you will call them Ena and Lena, no?'

'Ena and Lena it is, then.'

Of course the cats rapidly turned my house into a battlefield resounding with squawks and yowlings, and they played incessantly a game which consisted in chasing each other around the rooms without touching the floor, dislodging in the process everything that was upon the shelves and tables. Naturally I did eventually grow to be very fond of them, even when one of them turned out to have been male, and impregnated his sister, so that I ended up being taken over completely by a squad of furry little storm-troopers that grew to be so large that I was obliged to build an extra room onto the house to accommodate them.

One night I was playing to Ena when I remarked to her, 'You know, you have completely stopped me from composing,' and a look of dismay passed over her face.

'O,' I exclaimed, 'please do not look so horrified. It is simply that I am so anxious to keep you entertained by learning new pieces, that I no longer spend any time writing music myself.'

She had a piteous expression as she said miserably, 'I am so sorry. I did not mean to be a nuisance. I believed that you liked me to come. But if you wish, I will not come any more.'

It was a very bright night because there was a three-quarter moon, and the Southern Cross was clearly visible, and I was astonished and moved to perceive that her eyes were filling with tears and that her lips were quivering like a little girl's. Instantly I felt overwhelmed with guilt at my insensitivity, and without thinking about it I went down on my knees before the place where she was sitting, and put my arms around her. I hugged her, patted her consolingly upon the back, and rocked her back and forth as my own mother had used to do. 'Ena,' I murmured, 'you must not cry. I like it that you come here, because it makes a big difference to me. I am never lonely any more.'

She sobbed upon my shoulder a short while, and then lifted her head. We looked at each other a moment, and I kissed a tear from her cheek. She moved forward, closed her eyes in exactly that fashion so often depicted in romantic movies, and kissed me very shyly and very softly upon the lips. I felt the familiar old knot in my stomach, and soon, of course, the kisses became more passionate, and the embrace more horizontal. There came a point when I knew what to say, knowing that I meant it: 'Ena, I have just realised that in all this time I have grown to love you.'

'I knew it,' she said. 'Or at least I thought I did.'

'What did you think that you knew? That I loved you or that you loved me?'

She pouted, and said, 'Both, of course. But please do not send me away.'

The next evening when Ena arrived I very naturally put my arms around her and kissed her. Or rather, I tried to kiss her. She pushed me away and hit me so hard that I honestly believe that I could not have been more greatly stunned by Muhammad Ali in his prime. I tottered on my feet, and, feeling much aggrieved, I said, 'Ena, you spent two hours last night kissing me. Now why should I not believe that you would like it just as much tonight?'

She seemed very surprised. 'Did I?'

'You know very well that you did.'

She paced back and forth with her fingers to her chin, as though she were deciphering a recondite code, and then she giggled mischievously, came forward, put her hands on my shoulders, and whispered very sexily, 'Did you like my little joke? Kiss me all you like.'

'Most amusing,' I said, still feeling offended, and we began to kiss. On this day she seemed much surer and more expert than she had been the night before, and once more I was astounded and confused. 'Why do you kiss differently from yesterday?'

'I have a different kiss for weekdays,' she said. 'Yesterday was Sunday. And I have been practising.'

'What?' I expostulated, feeling violently jealous. 'Who with?'

She smiled again. 'With no one. I have been practising by forcing my tongue between the segments of an orange.'

'You are a liar,' I said, 'but kiss me some more, according to the correct kiss for the day of the week.'

Naturally, one thing leads to another, but I did not go to bed with Ena for another two months. It was not because she was a frightened little virgin; in fact she seemed very interested in ceasing to be one at all. It was because I needed to be sure in my own mind that I really preferred to forget about my unrequited love in Mexico City, and accept Ena with the proper dedicated enthusiasm that one owes honourably to a virgin who is in good faith. Furthermore, I earnestly wanted to enter into this at the right pace, so that it was all unrushed, perfectly romantic, without unfair pressures, so that we would have the opportunity to hone our emotions to the finest point of intensity.

It was Ena herself who, one evening when we were talking by the lights of the hurricane lamps, stood up and took the cigarette from my mouth. She crushed it in the dust and proffered me her hand. I took it and she led me to my bed. In the darkness she slipped with one deft movement out of her shabby blue dress, and put her arms about my neck, embracing me tightly. Even in the darkness I could see that her eyes were glowing luminescently, with that force and brilliance of which I believe that only young women are capable. She kissed me gently and murmured, 'Now is the right time.'

A little clumsily in the dark, she undid the buttons of my shirt one by one, and slid her cool, slim hands about my chest, tangling the hairs in her fingers. She took me by the shoulders and pulled me onto the bed, at which point we discovered that it was fully taken up by a tangled bundle of somnolent cats. This broke the romance completely for a few moments, as we had to turf them off, no easy matter when they weigh so many kilos and are so reluctant to move on account of the natural inertia of feline voluptuousness.

Ena's body was a rich kingdom; it possessed the perfect generous curves of a young girl, and it had the intoxicating mustiness of a woman born for unmitigated love. Her skin was both smooth and soft, and, as I explored her with my own body, her simultaneous innocence and sensuality provoked in me a sensation that I had last felt when I first saw the Andes; my heart felt as though it had displaced itself to the region of my solar plexus, as though it was constricting my throat and depriving me of breath. I was so numb with wonder that I almost omitted to feel the shards of delight that she was sending darting through my body with her own tentative explorations.

# 5  *The Sermon Of Father Garcia To The Jaguars From The Top Of An Obelisk*

Brothers and sisters in Christ, fellow ex-Marxists and disillusioned followers of Mariategui, campesinos, whores and guerrilleros, I will speak to you of the revelation that has been unravelling itself within my spirit during the long and arduous days of our perilous journey through the mountains, from Chiriguana where we feared for our lives, to this blessed city of Cochadebajo de los Gatos, where we inaugurate a better world and a new way of life amongst the stained stones of a civilisation long immersed beneath the waters, miraculously and opportunely drained through the intervention of Our Lord in the form of an earthquake.

The revelation of which I speak is of the utmost reasonableness, and cannot be refuted either by lawyers trained in casuistry, who labour day and night to do as little as possible except swindle and confound with impenetrable jargon in order to augment to bursting the entire vaults of banks which contain their unmerited accumulations; nor may it be refuted by common sense, since it is based upon it, and nor may it be refuted by philosophers who doubt even the meaning of the words in which they express their doubt; and nor may it be refuted by the monstrous nitpickings of the Doctors of Theology who foolishly deny that cats such as yourselves possess immortal souls, and who relentlessly cavil about the mediaeval preoccupations of St Anselm and the sexuality of angels. Moreover, my friends, they create abundant schisms and contentious wranglings by their interpretations of biblical texts and the contradictions so easily to be found therein, leading one plainly to conclude that their energies would be better spent increasing the earnings of pimps and whores and discussing the number of testicles to be found within the body of a fish.

The truth is that almost none of the Bible is true, and if anyone should know, I above all should know this because I am a priest, albeit unjustly unfrocked owing to the allegations of an importunate and deluded female parishioner. But in the eyes of God I am not unfrocked for I am a true servant to whom He has delivered His Revelation, which, to put it plainly, is that the greater part of creation is a mistake and an oversight which God heartily regrets.

For is not God good and wise, surpassingly? We have only to look around and recall the events of the immediate past in order to see with absolute clarity that this creation is a work of malice. I was unfrocked because a parishioner falsely accused me of her seduction, and was believed. A party of soldiers arrived in our late village and attempted to violate Farides, the cook, before killing several of us with a hand-grenade. Doña Constanza then foolishly decided to divert into her swimming pool a river which supplied us all, whereas in a benign creation she could not have decided such a thing. And then the soldiers came back to persecute us once again, and we beat them away because we were inspired by God to cause Felicidad, the impetuous and desirable little whore, to infect all the officers with common gonorrhea and Barranquilla syphilis. And then the soldiers returned yet again so that we were forced to defend ourselves and bloodily massacre almost every single one of them, which in a good world would not be possible, so that we were obliged to leave the pueblo for fear of reprisals unprecedented in the history of our country except for during the time of La Violencia when 300,000 political assassinations took place, give or take a few to allow for the roughness of the estimate and the proliferation of unmarked graves in our benighted land.

Furthermore, we live in a world where there is theft and murder, rape and disrespect in all its many manifestations; where women deceivingly simulate orgasms and men walk around deluded that they are more of a stallion than Don Emmanuel's horse; in which our urban youth poisons itself with basuco and alcohol, for which they will lie and kill; in which there are so many orphans that one would think that they are the result of the congress of the Holy Spirit and a million invisible virgins; in which children are sold into prostitution in order to pay off debts and little boys are sodomised in secret by bishops, four-star admirals, and undeservedly famous playwrights.

Moreover, quite apart from the malignancies of human actions, we see that nature itself is against us, with its floods and hurricanes, coral snakes and scorpions, earthquakes and shipwrecks, unfathomable diseases and discomfitures; its reprehensible conjunctions of the sun and moon so that in some places people go unaccountably mad and in others there are disastrously high tides that leave fish stranded upon the sides of mountains. Above all it seems to me that nature is so designed that all that we can rely upon is the ephemerality of love.

What does this mean? How do we fathom it? May we look at the world and say 'God is Good'? No, we cannot. We look around and see a world specifically designed for our inconvenience, so that we get an itch in a private place at exactly the time that we are having an audience with someone important and therefore cannot scratch it; we find that in the sierra it is too cold and on the llanos it is too hot; in the jungle which is so beautiful one is bitten to shreds by poisonous insects, and the sea is too deep for a mariner to walk safely away from a shipwreck. One goes to bed with a desirable whore and comes away infected with diseases whose cures are too horrible to contemplate, and before the symptoms show themselves one has had time to infect numerous others to whom one then owes embarrassing explanations. No, my friends, one looks about the world and decides that some of it was built according to mischievousness and the rest according to malice.

Therefore one concludes that Satan was the architect of this cosmic prank, and God had nothing to do with it because He was resting fast asleep on the seventh day. And nor did God create Satan, because God is incapable of the perpetration of evil, which proves that Satan is co-existent and sempiternal with God, and, who knows? perhaps he is just as potent. I will tell you how it happened.

When God was asleep, Satan, jealous of His Ineffable Creativity, slipped away and created the sun, the moon, and the stars and everything material, because God created only spirit. Then Satan made a man and tried for thirty-two days to breathe life into him, but nothing happened because the clay kept drying out in the sun.

Then God sent down the angel Adam, saying, 'Hey, hey, I want you to check up on what this Satan has been doing, but don't fall asleep while you're down there, because Satan might try to put your soul inside that lump of clay.'

So the angel Adam went down to the earth and looked around and thought, 'Humm, this is interesting,' and then Satan comes up and Adam says something like, 'Nice place you've got here, what are you going to do with it?' And Satan replies, 'Nothing special. Are you staying for a while? Do you fancy a cup of infernal ambrosia?' And Adam says, 'Why not? Let's see if it's better than the celestial kind.'

And very soon they are roaring drunk together and already they are old friends, but Satan is on the lookout for his opportunity, and Adam sees his shifty glance, remembering not to fall asleep. 'I'll sing you a song,' says Satan, and he begins this epic song composed by himself impromptu in perfect alexandrines, all the spondees and dactyls and what-have-you falling perfectly into place with the kind of immaculate precision that you get when making love for the first time with the love of your life. This rhythm was perfectly designed to lull one to sleep, but Adam was determined not to fall asleep, and so he listens to the song, whose words are so beautiful and seductive that they gave Adam a hard-on and made him cry at the same time. He feels embarrassed about the erection in front of Satan, and so that helps him not to fall asleep.

Now Satan sang this song for forty-three years, making it up as he went along, without using the same word twice, now composing in couplets and now in quatrains, and now dividing it up into petrarchan sonnets and two-line epigrams. One minute it is an Horatian ode and the next minute it's in blank verse with heroic similes that last for six months, until finally the ambrosia begins to have an effect and the angel Adam falls asleep.

Immediately Satan says, 'Ho hum,' and jumps up and seizes Adam's soul and stuffs it through the ears of the clay man, and when Adam wakes up he is imprisoned.

Then God sent down the angel Eve to find out what was going on, and the same thing happened to her. After that, God became wise as to what was going on and he sent the archangel Michael down to give Satan a good bashing around the head for his impudence, and to punish Adam and Eve he said, 'I am going to let them stay imprisoned in those bodies for a while before I make the bodies fall apart, and that will teach them to fall asleep whilst on duty.'

And so the truth is that we are all imprisoned angels, the descendants of imprisoned angels, living in a world created by Satan and not by God, from which it follows that all of the Old Testament is not the Law of God but the Law of Satan, except that Satan cleverly mixed some good laws in with the bad ones to make the imprisoned angels think that he was God. And then the angel Jesus

31

came down to put things right and give us the real Law of God, which he did, except that he failed because no one has ever bothered to follow his law, which is why the world is still a mess and full of evil.

For centuries the imprisoned angels have suspected that all was not well, for they were suspicious of matter and thought that the flesh was wicked and not to be indulged. I myself thought this for a short while and forbade people to reproduce or to eat meat, since this would interfere with the inscrutable mechanisms of metempsychosis.

However I have come to understand that finally God has chosen to become interested in this material world and allow us to do battle on equal terms with the forces of evil that are locked up in men's bodies along with the imprisoned angels.

Thus it was that God arranged for us to defeat the soldiers not once but three times. The first time He whispered to Hectoro and Pedro and Consuelo the whore to go and prevent Farides from being raped; the second time we were inspired to piss and shit and drop a dead steer in the river to poison them, and we frightened them by putting animals in their sleeping bags, and Felicidad was given divine force to go and infect all their officers with common gonorrhea and Barranquilla syphilis. The third time we were given tactics that enabled us to massacre them without one loss of life amongst ourselves.

But that is not the most miraculous, for when we left the village He provided an earthquake that simultaneously emptied the lake in this valley so that we can live in it, and also poured the water into the Mula valley so that the soldiers could not follow us. Then our prodigious cats, provided by God, brought us food as we travelled. In addition He provided an avalanche that revealed the bodies of the conquistadores subsequently unfrozen by Aurelio to help us build the city where we now live harmoniously like the angels that we are.

From this it is to be concluded that God wishes us to flourish and to be the vanguard of the capture of this world by the angelic nature within us, purifying matter until it too becomes spirit. For when it is spirit Satan will have no more dominion over it, since his dominion is solely over the grossly material. It is our solemn duty to God, therefore, to reproduce and to populate the world with others such as ourselves, so that we may overwhelm the world with our convivial beneficence. Between ourselves, it would be no surprise to me if one morning we all woke up and discovered that we had got our wings back and could mate by mingling our bodies entirely.

But until that time, let us fortify ourselves with good food, including meat, and fornicate munificently so that no one will sleep at night for the mewling of babies and the necessity of changing shit-laden garments. Let mothers be sleepless from suckling and maidens sleepless from copulation. *Deo gratias*. *Dominus vobiscum*. Amen.

# 6 *Ena And The Mexican Musicologist (3)*

When I awoke in the morning I found that Ena had slipped away, and that I was sharing the bed only with the sybaritic bundle of cats. When I finally managed to get them off in order to rearrange the sheets, I found a little spot of blood where Ena had joyfully disposed of her virginity.

That evening Ena arrived at the usual time, and as she sat down I produced a little box and presented it to her. She opened it to reveal my grandmother's engagement ring, and I said, 'Ena, will you marry me? Please?'

She sat there looking at the ring, and her face seemed to go quite pale; 'I would love to,' she said, 'but I think the fact is that I cannot.' I thought that she looked miserable.

'If you want to, then you can. What reason is there against it?'

'It is for a reason that I cannot tell you yet, but when I do tell you, I think that you will understand.' Her face brightened up, and she said, 'But I can just live with you, if you would like it.'

Perplexed, I exclaimed, 'But I would rather marry you.'

'And I would rather marry you as well, but it would be unfair.'

'To whom? Your parents?'

She became agitated, and said, 'O no, but I cannot explain that either just yet. But I promise that I will tell you tomorrow, I promise it.'

Bemused, I said, 'Bueno, but you will come and live with me?'

She smiled coyly. 'O yes, indeed.'

I leaned over and kissed her on the forehead, saying, 'Now come to bed with me.'

She appeared to be absolutely shocked, and reiterated, 'Bed?'

'Yes, bed. Last night was so delicious that I have been unable to think of anything other than making love with you again.'

'Last night? Again?' She appeared to be perplexed.

'Are you telling me that you have forgotten? Is this another of your little jokes?'

She remained motionless, and then said, 'No, of course I have not forgotten, but is it not a little soon?'

I laughed at her innocence. 'Come now, Ena, one can do it as often as one likes.'

She looked very dubious, pursed her lips, and said, 'O, I do not think that I am ready yet.'

'Yes, you are,' I said, remembering the successful decisiveness of that man in *Gone With The Wind*. 'And if you are not, you very soon will be.'

That night Ena was quite different from the previous one, demonstrating once again her protean quality. She begged me repeatedly to be kind and simpatico, and at first seemed unable to relax, but eventually things proceeded just as sweetly as they had the night before. This time she stayed with me all night, waking me in the morning with a tinto, a lingering kiss, and the words, 'I do love you.'

Come and live with me, and we will say those words each morning.'

'I will come back this evening, and we can sort everything out. Right now, I am going to wash.'

She returned with her flesh glowing and her hair straightened out, and I said to her, 'Querida, how did you manage to lose your virginity twice?' I pointed to the second small blot of blood upon the sheet.

'How odd,' she exclaimed, but then added, 'I was still a little sore from the first time, and I thought that I had not healed up. That is why I said that I was not ready.' She was not looking at me, and I thought that she was trying to hide a smile and a blush, but I thought no more of it. I am no expert upon the technicalities of virginity, since a virgin these days is a very rare thing, and was quite outside my otherwise fairly extensive experience. I asked, 'How does one get blood off sheets?'

'O, just soak it and put salt upon it, or something.'

'Well, it is not important. Perhaps I will keep it there for a keepsake.'

She patted me upon the cheek and said, 'You will have all of me as a keepsake, and not only my blood.'

That night, two shadows detached themselves from the darkness, and walked arm in arm towards where I stood leaning against the jambs of my door. I had been having a mock wrestling-match with one of my cats, and was covered in dust because the animal had decided that for once it would not let me win. I thought, 'Now who has Ena brought with her?' I realised that she was with another girl, and I speculated that she might have brought a friend with her.

But when they emerged into the light of the hurricane lamps I was transfixed with astonishment. Speechless, I sat down heavily and reached like an automaton for a cigarette. My hands were shaking so much that I dropped my fósforos on the floor, and sat there so ridiculously with the unlit cigarette dangling from my lips, that both the girls burst into giggles. At length one of them said, 'Does this explain anything?'

'Two?' I asked, stupidly. 'Two? There were always two?'

They both nodded, and the one on the right said, 'I am Lena, and this is Ena.'

'Say that you are not angry with us,' said Lena in a wheedling tone of voice. She sat on the floor and rested her chin on my knee so that she could tease me by looking up at me in mock-penitence with those big brown eyes, and Ena came beside me and ruffled my hair. They then began the infernal double act which has been the bane and the joy of my life ever since. Lena said, 'No, do not be angry. This all started as a piece of fun to tease the Mexicano. You know, everyone thinks that Mexicanos are stupid, so that it seemed to be a good joke.'

'But,' continued Ena, 'we both liked listening to you, and then we both fell in love with you, and suddenly everything became very serious. And then it was too late.'

Lena added, 'And part of the game was not to tell each other what had happened, to give you a chance to guess, but you never did.'

All I could do was repeat, 'Two? Two?' in an idiotic tone of voice, as everything suddenly became clear, and the secret of 'Ena's' protean nature was revealed.

'We have always shared everything anyway,' said Lena.

'We decided not to fight over you,' added Ena.

'And now you know why marriage would be a problem, so we are both coming to live with you. If you still want us to, of course.'

'Two?' I repeated, miserably, 'How can I cope with two?'

'We love you,' said Ena. 'And you love us,' said Lena, 'and we will try not to be jealous and have fights.'

They both nodded in agreement with each other, and said, 'We promise.'

'And do you promise,' I asked, 'not to get your own way all of the time just because there are two of you and only one of me?'

'O no,' laughed Ena, 'this is a democratic city, and each of us has only one vote, so you will never win.'

'You do not have a chance,' said Lena. 'And anyway, monogamy was an invention of men who wished to reduce the power of women over them. We intend to put that right.' They began to giggle again.

'What about your parents? I have no wish to be shot.'

'They think that you are rich and famous, and in any case they do as we tell them. Profesor Luis taught us to read and to calculate, but they are ignorant, so really we are in charge of them, and they are our children.'

'And the constitution of the city says that in matters like this you can do as you like. Hectoro has three wives, Dionisio Vivo has scores of them, and Consuelo and Dolores have every man in the town sooner or later, except that they are not going to have you.'

'Ever.'

'Or else.'

'I am tired,' announced Lena, 'let us all go to bed.'

'Me too,' said Ena, pretending very archly to yawn. They laughed at me as I stood, rigid with trepidation, and I said, 'I need a strong drink.'

It was one year later, and in fact we had all got married, because Father Garcia said that identical twins were made from a single split egg, and that therefore Ena and Lena were, scientifically speaking, and therefore in the eyes of God also, only one person. He also said that in his opinion, which was informed by personal encounters with angels, God did not really give a damn about how people organised their sexual lives, as long as all that they did was motivated by love in one of its infinitely varied forms.

I was walking with my friend Antoine, and was talking with him about these extraordinary events. I asked him, 'How did they fool me? And how did no one else know either?'

He put his arm around my shoulder, and replied, 'My friend, love has no eyes. You know, we all knew all of the time. On the one hand we were all very happy for you, and on the other hand it is always amusing to play jokes on Mexicanos.'

'How did you know, you old goat? Come on, tell me.'

He tapped the side of his nose knowingly; 'Around here everybody talks, and you know, cabrón, those two were not the only ones who used to sit up here and listen to your music. I come up a great deal myself, though I have to say that I think it is about time that you learned some new pieces. That is advice from a good friend, or maybe you will begin to lose your audience.'

'A good friend?' I exclaimed. 'And anyway, I do not have much free time these days, with seven giant jaguars and two women to exploit my time and my goodwill all simultaneously.'

'And soon you will have even less time,' said Antoine.

I must have shown my puzzlement, because he added, 'You mean that they have not told you? Always the last to know? How wonderful. But I am not going to be the one who tells you; you had better ask them.'

I managed to extract a confession from Ena and Lena that same evening, and I remember exclaiming, 'What? Both of you at once? O, Santa Virgen.'

They nodded sweetly, and Ena took a cigarette, lit it, and put it into my mouth, saying, 'We were going to tell you tomorrow.'

# 7 *The Submission Of The Holy Office To His Eminence (1)*

I will state my case against my people
for all the wrong they have done in forsaking me,
in burning sacrifices to other gods,
worshipping the work of their own hands.

Jeremiah 1:16

Your Eminence, we honour in this report your sapient decision to reconstitute the Holy Office in this land and to employ it upon the redoubtable task of examining in secret the state of belief of the nation. To this end one hundred monks of the order of St Dominic were dispatched to every corner, to the stupendous and forbidding heights of the Andean mountains, to the frozen and inhospitable altiplanos, to the torrid zones of the llanos, and to the sodden and unforgiving forests and jungles of the Amazonas. Not only did they penetrate to all these areas and the cities contained within them, they also fulfilled their instruction to examine not only the superstitions of the poor, the animism and polytheism of the savages amongst whom our devoted missionaries strive to bring the light of Christ, but also the educated middle and upper classes, infiltrating themselves even into the highest echelons of secular power. This they did by what Your Eminence has so aptly described as 'Godly subterfuge', it being clear that if they had not been disguised as vendors of bamboo whistles, mule traders, herbalists, clairvoyants, egregious Protestants, birdlimers, snake-catchers and chicken-sexers, they would not have had as much success in determining the real state of people's hearts as they have in fact had. The report which you now find yourself examining is our condensation of these reports, which Your Eminence may examine in full and at his pleasure simply by requesting us to forward them to his palace.

We divide our report into three sections, beginning with the sorrowful matter of the spiritual health of our own clergy. We are

39

most sorry to report that if Your Eminence were to read through the reports of the proceedings of the Council of Evreux (1195), the Council of Avignon (1209), and the Council of Paris (of the same year), he would obtain a very accurate picture of what still obtains nearly one thousand years later in our own country.

There are priests who either sell indulgences, trade them for sexual favours, or grant them to the dying in exchange for their patrimony. We have come across the case of a bishop who sold the last joint of the little finger of St Teresa of the Infant Jesus to a pious widow (for fifty thousand pesos), when the real item in fact resides on public view in the cathedral of Bayeux in Normandy. This was the worst example of trade in relics, real and supposed. We have come across numerous samples of the True Cross which are plainly made of Brazilian rosewood, mahogany, Amazonian balsa, quebracha, and even painted clay. There are numerous shrouds of Christ displayed in various churches, there are nails from the hands and feet of Christ made of stainless steel ('miraculously unrusted despite their antiquity'), there are thorns from the crown of Christ, taxidermised birds (all of them tropical), which have had the benefit of attending the sermons of St Francis of Assisi. There are bones of Christ (contrary to the doctrine of the Resurrection), and a priest in Santander displays a head of St John the Baptist which bears a startling resemblance to the shrunken heads made by the Cusicuari Indians and sold by them in profitable quantities to North American tourists. These are in addition to the relics of so-called 'popular saints', such as Pedro of Antiochia, who could produce frogs out of people's hats and specialised in the blessing of mules and llamas. Many of these uncanonised 'saints' have a considerable priestly following, the worst case being that of a church dedicated to Lucia the Innocent, who is reputed to have given birth to twenty-two rabbits despite her virginity.

We have come across cases of monks gambling at dice for penances in monasteries in order to while away their idleness. In Santander several taverns have been opened by clergy, hanging outside of which can be seen signs depicting clerical collars, stoles, eucharistic ciboria and chalices, and even a paten upon whose stem can clearly be seen fauns in a priapic condition. In these ungodly establishments may be found their proprietors, usually in a state of inebriation at all hours of the day, with their vestments rolled up and tucked into their belts, trading scatological stories with their customers and allowing the use of backrooms and cubicles for immoral purposes.

We have discovered that licentious living is rife. In one city it is widely known that nuns organise dissolute parties and wander the streets at night. Members of religious orders, both male and female, live in a state of open concubinage, the progeny of such unions being popularly known as 'anticristos', and on whose behalf much nepotism is exercised. We have uncovered gambling, drunkenness, and a great predilection for hunting and violent sports. There are two monasteries in Asuncion which regularly organise football matches between themselves. In these games the entire monasteries turn out, meeting at a place equidistant from each. The football is sometimes of the orthodox variety, but is sometimes another object, usually a calf's head or a coconut. The object of the game is to be the first team to hurl the ball over the opposing monastery's wall. There are no rules in this game; there is much kicking, punching, brawling, hairpulling, and a torrent of obscene language such as would disgust even a stevedore or one accustomed to work with the deranged. At the end of the game there is no one who has not shed blood or had his habit torn; the cost to the monasteries concerned in terms of replacement and repair can only be imagined. It can be considered a matter of relief that the contestants do not resort to the use of arms, since we have established that up to ten per cent of the rural clergy bear arms, ranging from small revolvers to sawn-off shotguns, which are easily concealed beneath their robes. This practise is partly an understandable reaction to the prevalence of brigandage, and partly a perverse enterprise in winning admiration for machismo, which in this country is acknowledged to be a cult all to itself.

We have established that in the matter of orthodoxy of belief, our clergy matches almost precisely the general doctrinal confusion characteristic of the nation as a whole, which prompts one to question the efficiency of our seminaries. We will deal with this aspect, namely, the varieties of Christian belief, in part three of our report, part two being concerned with aberrant and diabolical practises amongst the people. We conclude this section by noting that in his inaugural speech to the Fourth Lateran Council, His Holiness Pope Innocent III declared that the vice of the laity was caused directly by that of the clergy.

# 8 How Love Became Possible In Cochadebajo de los Gatos

It is an almost invariable fact of experience that consuming passions may arise only when there is time and energy for them; love asserts as its precondition a degree of social organisation and economic stability that allows for leisure, and in this fallow field the seeds of desire, blown in by the winds, germinate, take root, and grow rampant as the orchids of the jungle.

Of course, many loves were already established at the time of the migration from the region of Chiriguana; that of Profesor Luis and Farides had grown naturally in the village now buried in silt, Doña Constanza and Gonzago had conceived their passion in the indolence of the encampment of the People's Vanguard, as had Gloria and Tomás, and the ghostly love of Federico and Parlanchina had blossomed in the infinite leisure of death.

It would be tempting to describe the efflorescence of love in Cochadebajo as a plague, a plague as beneficent as the great plague of cats, except that the word would seem inappropriate when signifying what was in truth the bloom that springs inevitably out of the loam of civilisation.

At first, the people had concerned themselves solely with the business of survival, when there was nowhere to live and food was scarce. The task of digging out the ruins of the ancient Inca town took many months, and during this time the people were buffeted by the rains and baked by the sun. Most of the houses were intact, excellently constructed, with stones so perfectly shaped that a piece of paper could not have been slipped between them even though they were mortarless. But the old palm roofs had long ago rotted to slime, and an abysmal dankness hung about the place that it seemed no amount of air and sunshine could dispel. To begin with they huddled together at night in the Palace of the Lords or in the Temple of Viracocha, warmed by each other's bodies and the musky heat of the cats.

During the day they laboured fitfully, digging the mud out in

42

blocks that were passed up the human chain to reconstruct the andenes that were eventually to circle the city and provide it with potatoes, quinoa and beans, giving the mountainsides the appearance of having been made into staircases for Titans. Others laboured to make adobe to patch up the places where stones had rotted away from buildings, and others still disappeared into the sierra to hunt meat or to go on relentlessly arduous treks in search of palm to thatch the houses.

The people grew thin with labour and lack of food, but toiled on in the faith that one day they would rest unmolested in their remote city, leading uneventful lives, growing a little fat, glad that the excitements of war would pass them by. They hoped that history would forget them and carry on by itself in other places. This hope sustained them, as did the guinea pigs, viscachas and vicuñas brought in by the stupendous cats and by the hunters, along with the mule-loads of bananas, lemons and almonds traded with the Indian settlements scattered about the sierra. As their clothes fell into shreds from constant toil they were replaced by garments woven by those same Indians, until eventually one would have had the impression that here was an intact pre-Columbian settlement, were it not for the black and mestizo faces replacing the calculatedly expressionless Indian faces that one might have expected to see above those bright red and black stripes. Neither were Indians so tall; here were Misael and Pedro, both nearly two metres in stature, and here was Felicidad, slim and dark like those who dance the siguiriyas in Andalucia, quite unlike the squat indigenous women with their small mouths, heavy thighs, and their multiplicity of petticoats.

It was when they were levering the remains of the natural dam over the edge of the precipice in order to complete the drainage of the city that Misael leaned over and realised that three hundred metres below there stretched a site ideal for agriculture, if only one could reach it easily, without walking forever to get there roundabout. The great cascade of water from the breaking of the lake had flattened the forest below, covered it with a thick layer of fertile soil, and supplied it with a river flowing through it for irrigation. Most of the work was done. 'Hijo de puta,' he exclaimed, grinning from ear to ear, 'am I or am I not a genius and the saviour of the city?' He strode off to find Profesor Luis, who was building another windmill to turn a lorry

43

dynamo that would raise the voltage of part of the town to twenty-four. Luis was contemplating his work and wondering whether it could be transformed to a yet higher voltage without losing too many amps.

'Hola, cabrón,' said Misael, 'this is indeed a fine machine.' They stood together watching the two halves of an oil drum rotating in the breeze, and Misael put his hand on Profesor Luis' shoulder. 'I have a big challenge for you, the biggest of your life.'

'A bigger one than getting my way with Farides?'

'An even bigger one, viejo. Come and see.'

Gazing out over the plain below them, already green with the encroachment of nature, but its trees shattered to matchsticks, Misael was elated with his plan and Profesor Luis was inebriated by its grandeur. 'It will be our estancia, our latifundo, it will be the best farm in the world.'

Profesor Luis shaded his eyes with his hand and squinnied against the light. 'We will grow everything,' he said, 'We will grow rice in the damp parts, we will grow avocados and bananas, we will grow cattle where the land is fallow, we will drown in milk and cheese, we will flounder in an orgy of oranges.'

'Maybe so,' replied Misael, who was suspicious of poetry on all occasions except for this, 'but you will have to construct a machine to help us up and down. It will be the biggest machine of your life, it will be a machine to make your windmills toys.'

'I will make a machine,' said Profesor Luis, 'such as has never been seen.' And he went away and lay down in the dark for two days with a blanket over his head until the germ of the machine wafted in on the mountain wind, settled in the silt of his imagination, broke its carapace with the force of its first sprout, developed tap roots and hair roots, budded with branches and the intimate details of flowers, and turned into a machine more magnificent than the system of the heavens. Profesor Luis went to eat picante de pollo in Dolores' restaurant, wiped his mouth, sat back, and mentally prepared his exposition of the machine to the natural leaders of Cochadebajo de los Gatos.

'Give me a place to stand and I will move the earth,' he proclaimed grandiloquently, but the first great feat of Archimedean leverage to be performed was not the gathering of wherewithals, but the persuasion of the people to undertake the colossal task in the first place. It seemed crazy to almost everyone that when they were still digging out the city, still remaking roofs, and scratching for food, someone should propose the diversion of labour into the construction of a giant lift.

'You are more loco than Father Garcia,' said Josef, his speech a little indistinct on account of the wad of coca in his cheek.

'It is a wonderful idea,' said Father Garcia with an expansive gesture, 'we could have it raised and lowered metaphysically with the aid of angels. If I could be sure of the infallibility of levitation, I would operate it myself.'

'We have too much else to do,' said Remedios, 'and if you think about it, we have just emigrated from the plain. Why should we want to go back down to it when here we are safe?'

'But it is not the plain, Remedios, it is a plateau, and it is better for agriculture than the plain ever was.'

'To me,' said Remedios, 'it is the plain,' and she went back to cleaning her Kalashnikov and keeping an eye on the Conde Pompeyo Xavier de Estremadura, who was nostalgically drawing a diagram of a Landsknecht sword in the dust of the floor.

'Bugger that,' exclaimed Don Emmanuel when Profesor Luis outlined his plan, 'I am already more worn out with labour than a Panamanian whore. This is a scheme for lazy times. Look how my belly has shrunk from digging the andenes.'

Profesor Luis scrutinised the proffered belly, tight as a drum and decorated with ginger hairs. 'You exaggerate, Don Emmanuel,' he said.

Hectoro puffed hard on his puro, squinting against the smoke and patting his horse's neck. 'Will I be able to descend on horseback?' he enquired.

'Undoubtedly,' replied Profesor Luis.

'Then maybe and maybe not,' said Hectoro, who believed that the fewer words a man said, the more of a man he was, and the more of a man he was, the less he got off his horse.

It was true that Misael was in favour of the plan, since it had been his idea, but even he was now a little less enthusiastic about it because he had had several nightmares in which people hurtled to their deaths in a large wooden cage, and he was worried that it was a premonition.

'We will hold a candomble to get the lift blessed by the saints,' said Profesor Luis, 'and then we will get Father Garcia to bless it, and then Aurelio will bless it with the Aymara gods and the Navante gods, and then it can never crash.' That made Misael feel better about it, but left Profesor Luis a little guilty about having played upon his superstitious susceptibilities.

Profesor Luis was disheartened, but over the next few days it was noticeable that many people were going to the edge of the cliff and gazing out over the plain. Hectoro went, and had visions of an horizon of cattle grazing on lush grasses. Don Emmanuel saw groves of avocados, reminding him that back in the village the little boys used to steal his fruit and then try to sell it back to him. Remedios saw that indeed it was a plateau, and conceived of it as a line of self-defence in the event of attack from the east, and as a place of tactical withdrawal if the assault were from the west. Doña Constanza and Gonzago went out there in the sunset, and dangled their legs over the edge. 'Gonzito,' she said, 'there is a lot of privacy down there. Remember how we used to make purple earthquakes under the trees and behind the waterfall?'

'Fine days,' replied her lover. 'One day we will go down there and find a place with no ants to chew our backsides, and not under a tree either, so that we are not shat upon by birds, and we will make purple earthquakes all over again, and shout as much as we like.'

'I am sick of falling out of the hammock,' she said, 'even though it was amusing to begin with.'

'One day we will make a decent bed, and one day we will go down there and have no need of one.'

And so it was that, much to his gratification, Profesor Luis found that people were coming to him and asking, 'What do you need for this machine?' and an improbable stockpile of heterogeneous articles began to accumulate at the edge of the precipice, some found lying about inexplicably in the mountains, some scavenged from abandoned mine shafts, some prised away from the Indians in exchange for goats and teaspoons. There were huge iron hoops with pinchbolts, lengths of cable, steel wheels, pieces of crashed military helicopter, nuts and bolts with reversed threads in old British Standard sizes, a vast windlass that had to be transported by four bulls harnessed together, pitprops so old that they had turned to stone, beams from those brontosaurial machines that once crushed ore with the motion of nodding donkeys, together with their gearwheels, antique block and tackles made of polished rosewood with toledo rivets embossed with coats of arms, and a separate pile of unidentifiable objects that 'might come in useful for something'. 'All I need now is three thousand metres of rope as thick as a man's arm,' announced Profesor Luis, 'and lots of wheels from cars, with the hubs and bearings if possible.'

The latter was easy if arduous. All that one had to do was send out long expeditions to the places where there had been roads through the mountains in more prosperous times, or even to Ipasueño. At the bottom of precipices, down below hairpin bends, hidden beneath scrub, half-immersed in cataracts, were the innumerable wrecks of the vehicles of the inebriated and the unbraked. There one could find cars, trucks, lorries and coaches of all vintages and in all states of decay, many of them complete with skeletons picked clean by grateful birds, all of them inhabited by pumas and margueys, coral snakes and iguanas, except for the ones in the rivers colonised by fish and kingfishers.

It was all made easier by Doña Constanza, who, after a fierce fight with her conscience, went to Profesor Luis and coyly held out a small elongated green book. 'I still have my chequebook,' she said, 'and I would like to help you to buy what you cannot find.'

Profesor Luis went with Doña Constanza and Gonzago to Ipasueño. It was just before the time when Dionisio Vivo killed Pablo Ecobandodo, and it was not a pleasant place to be, what with the addicts stopping the cars under the bridge and killing the occupants for money, and the motorcycle assassins roaring through the streets cutting policemen in half with bursts of explosive bullets. They came away with two mule-loads of spanners, hammers and wrenches, prodigious bolts, and heavy-duty hacksaws complete with spare blades. They had also been to see the manager of the State Mining Corporation's Iron Ore Extraction Plant, and ordered a titanic reel of rope, to be delivered to the tiny pueblo of Santa Maria Virgen. It was the first time he had ever been bribed by a cheque from the disappeared wife of a multimillionaire. He waited for the cheque to clear, and contemplated not bothering to deliver the rope. But then he remembered that Mexican-looking young man who had been with her, and how he had promised to come and castrate him personally if he reneged on the deal, and he went out with orders to the driver of the largest transporter.

As it turned out, the transporter could not get as far as the pueblito, because it could not turn the corners. The enterprising driver reversed for three kilometres until he could find a place to turn around, to the fury of a tractor driver who had the misfortune of being behind him, and who therefore also had to reverse. The transporter then reversed as far as it could in the direction of Santa Maria Virgen, and dropped the gigantic reel on the road, in a place that was as level as one might expect to find in that country of avalanche and chasm. Mercifully the reel did not take it in mind to go gleefully on its own way to some place of greater gravitational rest, and the driver proceeded on foot to the village.

In the village, in those days in the grip of basuco, he found only the incoherent victims of addiction leaning listless and bleary-eyed in their doorways. He got no sense from anyone at all, and suffered the eerie impression that he was talking to skeletons long dead, which just happened to be stretched with skin and the appearance of life. Mystified, and remembering his mother's adage that 'it was not given to us to understand', he was on the point of leaving when Profesor Luis came down the path of the mountain and hailed him. The two men walked back down the road, and Profesor Luis was horrified by the dimensions of the reel. It was taller than three Misaels and wider than two Pedros. He left it where it was and went back to Cochade-bajo de los Gatos.

What followed was the greatest feat of co-operation and determi-nation in the history of the entire department. Almost the whole population trekked out to Santa Maria Virgen, their mochilas bulging with provisions, their eyes steely, their muscles flexing with antici-pation. With them went a vast herd containing every mule, every horse, every cow, steer and bull, and, as though impervious to the solemnity of the expedition, a frolicking horde of the pet jaguars of the city. They carpeted the slopes with velvet black, darting after viscachas and birds, perching on the backs of bulls, patting at rocks and starting small avalanches, ambushing each other and rolling away in flurries of dust.

It was a journey as heroic as the original emigration; by day the sierra reverberated to cries of 'burro, burro', and 'vaca, vaca, vamos';

the people encouraged the animals in that soft falsetto beloved of drovers, and the animals lowed in the mildest of protest, resigned to their fate as the willing victims of incomprehension. Their hoofs slipped upon the rocks, and only the mules maintained a sure footing. By night the people bivouaced on the punas, and the hobbled animals ate ichu grass and emptied their minds of memory in order to meet the next day even more like themselves than they had been the day before.

It was on this expedition that Felicidad realised that she was in love with Don Emmanuel, because under the stars, wet with dew upon the blanket and between her thighs, she dreamed repeatedly of the eloquence of his nether parts. She dreamed that his polla, famed charger that it was, leapt out of a cupboard and winked at her. Its eye changed to a mouth and smiled knowingly. It hopped across the floor and sprang into her lap, rubbing itself against her palm as a kitten rubs its ears, and its purring was the same purring as the somnolent snores of the jaguars asleep amongst the people. Then suddenly she was afloat in a creamy sea of vanilla-flavoured sperm with the moon above her transforming the sea to silver, and a dolphin vaulted out of the ocean, changing in mid-arch into Don Emmanuel's pink appendage. There was a moment of terror in case it was a shark, but then she was born aloft upon it and rode towards the gap between the stars that the Indians call 'the pig'. In the morning Don Emmanuel approached her and said, 'I had a dream of you,' and she knew that when the expedition was concluded she would embark upon a voyage of love ordained.

When they passed through Santa Maria Virgen the inhabitants showed no interest; they watched with empty eyes. Only the little children, malnourished and filthy but as yet unpoisoned by basuco, clapped their hands with excitement or ran indoors for fear of the great bulls and the prowling cats. A pall of dust was raised, which settled onto the neglected houses and the leaves of the almond trees, and irritated the lungs of the addicts too apathetic to cough.

The people were abashed by the size of the reel; 'Ay, ay, ay,' they exclaimed, 'this is the grandfather of all reels, this is the one final historical reel forever. How can we move this?' Everyone stood in silence, until the squint-eyed man who used to be the policeman and the mayor of Chiriguana, and who loved his goats so much that he had even brought them on the expedition, pointed to an electrical pole and said, 'There is our axle, amigos.'

It was a tall stout pole of tarred pine, a relic of the Norwegian electrification programme funded by the United Nations. It leaned over, as though it had been awaiting the chance to jump out of its hole and do something useful, and no wires hung from its ceramic bobbins.

There was a magnificent ceibu bull named Cacho Mocho that belonged to Don Emmanuel. It was the king of all the bulls, and had been the only one permitted to eat the flowers in Don Emmanuel's garden; he had had to stop putting gates on his fields because Cacho Mocho, despite his broken horn, knew how to lift the gates off their hinges and lay them gently on the ground. It had been Cacho Mocho who had led the cattle during the emigration, and he who had led them during this journey. His testicles were so heavy that men would wince to see them swing against his legs and crash into rocks.

Tomás shinned up to the top of the pole and fastened a stout rope to it whilst Hectoro and Misael put the harness onto Cacho Mocho and fastened the other end of the rope to it. When Tomás was down, Pedro whispered a secreto in the ear of the bull and patted him on the flank. Cacho Mocho plodded forward. The rope tautened and the bull's muscles knotted and flexed beneath his skin. There was a brief moment of equilibrium when it seemed as though nothing would happen, and then the pole toppled, tearing the soil away at its root. Cacho Mocho fell forward onto his shins, bellowed with triumph, and stood up. Everybody cheered, and the bull feinted proudly with his single horn.

They lifted the pole above their heads and fed it through the hole at the centre of the reel. From then on it was a three-hour labour to harness together all the cattle, the horses and the mules, to take ropes from the axle, and to begin the formidable journey back to Cochadebajo de los Gatos with Cacho Mocho in the lead.

Even though Aurelio had established the quickest and least precipitious routes, it was a fortnight of impediments and temptation to despair. Never has there been so much yelling and cursing, so much dust clogging the eyes and throat, and never has mankind laboured so fiercely in absolute equality with its animals. The paths winding through the mountains were useless because they were scarcely ever more than a metre wide, having been established in the first place by the navigational instincts of wild goats, and so the people went directly, Indian-fashion. They cleared scrub, heaved away boulders, forded rushing torrents, descended and ascended vertiginous slopes, grew gigantic blisters that repeatedly burst, and held always in their minds' eye the vision of their plateau of plenty. Sometimes in descent they had as many cattle behind as they had to the fore, and always the colossus of a reel bumped and rolled, occasionally appearing to be on the point of running away on its own or getting stuck forever. Great pits appeared on its rims as they abraded away, and by the time that they finally rolled it into Cochadebajo de los Gatos they were worn completely and the outer layer of rope was scuffed and filthy. The people took to their hammocks and slept for three days whilst the animals went unsupervised, shaking their withers with an inexpressible feeling of freedom and release. When the town awoke, it was in the certain knowledge that they were a people of conquerors to whom nothing was impossible. They erected the axle-pole in the plaza, and to this day one can see where the ropes ate away their grooves. Every year somebody climbs to the top to nail there a fresh sombrero, and people hold hands with it between them to plight their troth. If they are unlucky they do the same thing later on in order to vanquish infertility.

Every day Profesor Luis and Misael did a little something towards constructing the machine; there was no point in rushing because improvisation calls for reflection and a great deal of scratching at one's chin and hairline. It calls for sitting down and smoking cigars whilst awaiting inspiration; it calls for copas in the whorehouse, and it requires fixing one's eyes on the middle distance and visualising pulleys and gantries. Now and then it required departing with a team of bulls to fetch more telegraph poles, or trunks of mahogany to saw into planks.

They built a platform with sides that folded out, big enough to take a tractor should they one day acquire one. It was reinforced with hammered strips of steel bolted around the planks, which were in turn bolted into an interlocking lattice of beams.

Away from the cliff's edge they constructed a vast framework that would angle out over the chasm. The two sides were built first, lying flat on the ground, and then they were hauled by straining teams of citizens into upright positions whilst they were joined crosswise by beams of quebracha. Huge notches were cut, holes were burned and drilled, pegs as thick as a child's thigh were hammered through and lashed with ropes, and then the cage was suspended in place beneath a system of pulleys made out of car wheels. Each pulley had so many wheels that Profesor Luis maintained that even a child could haul the cage up on its own, using only one finger.

At this point muletrains were despatched to Ipasueño along with Doña Constanza and her chequebook. They returned burdened with sacks of cement, gravel, and sand, and the manager of the mining corporation found himself once more unexpectedly better off. In the meantime Profesor Luis and Misael had finished the lever-operated friction brakes and had dug out of the rock a vast hole in which to set the spindle of the windlass.

It was a pharaonic spectacle. The whole town turned out to move the immense contraption to its place above the chasm. Teams of workers, stripped to the bare minimum save for those that were naked, hauled and shoved in unison to the beat of the bata drums normally used at the candomble to summon the gods. The machine creaked and swayed as it inched along the rollers, and Cacho Mocho was brought in to lay his massive head against the rear beams and strain with all his power along with the people. When it was finally in place it was time for bringing relays of water in leather buckets from the river that flowed through the city and cascaded over the cliff, to mix the concrete and mortar that would hold the windlass in place, that would glue the cairns of rock set around the trestles of the base.

At last the day of reckoning arrived and everyone gathered at the site of the greatest machine that anyone had ever seen. It was time for the squint-eyed ex-policeman and mayor to make a speech. He fired his pistol in the air to call for silence, and an expectant hush fell upon the crowd. He made good speeches, worth listening to.

'Compañeros,' he began, 'when I married Profesor Luis and Farides in Chiriguana, I stated that a good man is like a good he-goat, full of machismo, and a good woman is like a good she-goat, full of gracia . . .'

'With you everything is compared to a goat,' interjected Sergio, and the members of the crowd nudged each other and laughed.

'Nonetheless,' he continued, 'you will remember that I wished them the fertility of goats. What we see here is not the child of loins but of brains and sweat, the sweat being our own and the brains being those of our distinguished Profesor Luis, unsurpassable initiate of the mysteries of electricity and mechanical effects, educator of ourselves and of our children. Viva, viva Profesor Luis . . .'

Here they echoed 'viva' *con brio*, and the ex-alcalde raised his hands for silence: 'How like a beautiful goat is this stupendiferous device. Witness its grace and machismo. See how the cage is like a head suspended between two soaring horns. See how it overlooks the precipice as a goat perches on a crag and contemplates the infinity of space. See how it has a rope that ties it to the windlass as a goat is tethered for milking. We have yet to see how this goat will bring abundance as we milk the fertile plain below, but be assured that infallibly this behemoth, this notable juggernaut, this leviathan of a monster of a mammoth, this exaggeration of an elephant, will bring to this magnificent and companionable city of cats a munificence of plenty such that it will be a pitiful child who does not here grow fat and strong. Let the gringos boast that they have gone to the moon; what grows there? Let us boast that we have gone to the plain. Viva Misael and his angelic inspiration; viva Profesor Luis and his synthetico-analytic intelligence, viva!'

He bowed to the applause, and then Misael and Pedro drove Cacho Mocho onto the platform and closed up the side. 'Buena suerte, Cacho Mocho,' they cried, and the leaders of the city laid their hands to the windlass. It was enough to wind the heavy rope only four times around it to gain sufficient friction to set the cage in motion. It creaked loudly, and breaths were held, but then it slowly began the descent. Profesor Luis gazed over the edge, and after what seemed like an age dropped his hand as a signal that the mighty bull that had lent his strength to make the project possible had arrived at the bottom. A universal sigh of relief went up to the heavens, and then a new team took over to wind the cage all the way back up to the top.

As a reward for Cacho Mocho they draped him with flowers and shut him into a corral full of heifers. As a reward to themselves they held a fiesta that continued day and night for a week. Many were the god-saints that attended and blessed the machine in dance and song, many were the jaguars splattered with unanticipated spouts of chichareeking vomit. Father Garcia summoned Sandalphon, archangel of earth, to be guardian in perpetuity of the great contraption. The False Priest blessed it with purportedly mystical gestures and the words, '*Non tam latera ecfututa pandas ni tu quid facias ineptiarum*,' which is to say, 'You would not display such utterly fucked flanks if you were not doing something foolish.' In secret Aurelio called down the blessing of Viracocha, of Pachamama, of Tunupa, and in this way Profesor Luis' brainchild became the personal concern of a veritable pantheon, plus the benign ghost of the earthy Catullus.

The plateau grew rich within a year; it was at exactly the right altitude to grow virtually everything without fear of frost or desiccation. Soon there were other means of descent as ropes were angled out over the plain and fastened to trees so that baskets of papaya and mango, guava and lime, melons and cassava, could be hauled to the heights. Some intrepid souls sped downward like commandos on straps and wheels, and eventually smaller cages were made to carry people more safely by the same route. In the end the original machine was used only for heavy loads, and it was wound up by the same huge diesel engine that was to generate electricity for the whole town.

But all this was in the future. In the meantime a special order of merit was created so that Profesor Luis might be the first recipient of it; it was called 'The Supremely Elevated Order Of The Apparatus'. The ex-alcalde made another speech comparing Profesor Luis to a he-goat, and in the torchlight of the plaza Felicidad, feeling shy for the first time in her life, took Don Emmanuel's hand and squeezed it.

# 9 *The Submission Of The Holy Office To His Eminence (2)*

Hear the word of the Lord, O Israel;
for the Lord has a charge to bring
against the people of the land.
Hosea 4:1

Your Eminence, we consider that there are two varieties of lost sheep in this country; those who ought to know better, and those who cannot in good faith be blamed. In the first category we would find, for example, men of the cloth who take concubines and use their office to create wealth for themselves.

We intend to deal, however, with the second category first. We point out that in the last ten years (a period corresponding with your own tenure of office, but we do not say connected with it) the evangelisation of the heathen and of the uninformed has come to a precipitate halt.

There are in the sierra and in the jungle numerous groupings of indigenous Amerindians who live without the light of Christ. These can be divided into two categories also, the first being those who have never had the opportunity to hear the Word, and who therefore cannot be reproached for not living by it. There will be no prospect of improvement in this situation until adequate funding and support can be made available for missionary activity. We further point out that considerable inroads are being made by various Protestant evangelical North American sects funded by powerful organisations of undoubted idealism, but, in our opinion, of misguided fervour. You will be aware of the agreements that we have made with our government over the years, that our missionary activity should not be unduly disruptive of indigenous cultures, and confine itself to programmes of literacy, agronomy, and hygiene. This was in fact the *de facto* situation already obtaining, as, ever since the early Jesuit missions in Paraguay, pastoral care was more prominent than conversion. Your Eminence will note that forcible conversion used to be the policy of the secular authority rather than of the temporal, and that even in the time of the Inquisition in Peru, Amerindians were not held accountable for their beliefs since they were not considered to be fully human. Many of our own Catholic missions have now closed down, leaving the field open to those enthusiastic sects whose presence in remote districts has led to what can only be described as cultural disaster. The prevailing attitude of converts in those areas is that baptism leads to superior social and material status, and tribes devote their time to the manufacture of souvenirs of diminishing quality for sale abroad. Thus there are those in the mountains who still worship Viracocha, Pachamama and so on, and in the jungles are numerous animistic religions worshipping jaguar and tapir gods and living in mortal fear of demons which they believe will take away their virility or their health; and there are those who have been converted superficially by those whose creeds we consider, even in these ecumenical times, to be either false or deleterious, or both. These innocents are not to be blamed.

Nor, furthermore, do we consider blameworthy those amongst the general population both urban and rural who have either never heard our beliefs coherently explained, or who have fallen from grace through the trials of circumstance. In the first case we establish the cause to be the withdrawal or silencing of priests and nuns whose opinions were thought to be 'political'; no one has taken their place. In the second case we include those whose dire need, often but not always coupled with ignorance, has diminished their freedom of choice and of action to such an extent that they cannot be considered responsible.

Such, Your Eminence, would be the numerous population of the capital's sewers. Most of these are juveniles; they are homeless and jobless, and therefore turn to larceny, scavenging, and prostitution. Their average life expectancy is eighteen years. They succumb invariably to disease such as cholera, typhoid, puerperal fever, yellow fever, and their general level of health is so low as to make them vulnerable to measles, and to the alligators which share the sewers with them, and which have been known to carry off infants in their jaws. In this category we also include the majority of prostitutes; these are underemployed women faced with no alternative, who only practise the trade at times of extreme financial distress. Additionally we include amongst the blameless the countless hordes of those living in squalid conditions in the favelas that ring our major towns, who are the victims of rural mechanisation and the ill-advised reorganisation of encomiendas by irresponsible landlords. We are of the opinion that the spiritual advancement of such people is impossible until such a time as circumstances cease to oblige them to be wholly preoccupied with the material business of daily survival. Additionally there has been much discussion amongst ourselves as to whether or not we should include in this category the victims of the trade in cocaine.

As you will know, Your Eminence, there has recently developed a policy whereby a proportion of the cocaine production has been refined into a cheap but highly addictive confection named 'basuco', and pumped into the domestic market. The coca caciques appear to be using this as an insurance against losing foreign markets. Addicts desperate for supplies are prepared even to kill, and there has been a marked increase in crimes of theft and violence in basuco areas, as well as corruption at all levels of society there. The majority of us at the Holy Office believe that this drug satanically removes the free will granted to us by God, and we have concluded that therefore such people cannot be held accountable. Your Eminence will note that the stand against the coca cartels has been taken by judges, mayors, some police chiefs, and by such people as the famous Dionisio Vivo. This latter is a secular philosopher, and we consider it very damaging to the Church that so far no effort has been made by us to join the moral leadership against the robber barons. We consider it a priority that no priest should consent to become chaplain to one of these men, and that churches should steadfastly refuse to accept donations from them. The late Pablo Ecobandodo was a liberal patron of the Church, and churches in the Ipasueño area became dependent upon him for such things as refurbishment. Such churches are no more than whited sepulchres.

Your Eminence, we move on at this point to the first variety of lost sheep, namely those who can be blamed and would no doubt be found guilty upon the Day of Wrath. We provide the caveat however, that in between these two categories lies a very large area that can only be described as neither one nor the other.

We begin by drawing to your attention the disturbing fact that there are literally millions of people who are Catholic to all outward appearance, but in fact practise the ancient polytheism of West Africa. This polytheism was carried to our shores in the slaveships, and is known as 'santeria'. There is no hierarchy over and above that to be found within individual groups, and therefore the religion remains surreptitious and inconspicuous, managing to prosper extraordinarily despite past attempts, such as those in Brazil many years ago, to discourage it and to educate people out of it. Superficially the cult appears to be the worship of saints, but the fact is that, for example, St Barbara is really a male god by the name of Chango, and Nuestra Señora de las Mercedes is construed as Obatala, Father of the Gods. The adherents of this religion hold wild revels where sacrifices are made, idols are venerated, possession occurs, magic is performed, and there are great scenes of lewdness, drunkenness and overindulgence. Even worse than this, there is a deliberately demoniac variety known as 'brujeria', 'palo monte', or 'palo mayombe', which involves enchantments cast with truly revolting ingredients, almost invariably for nefarious purposes. It is noteworthy that there is a god named Eshu who is said by some to correspond to Satan, and who is always the god invoked first. We execrate this religion in particular because it masquerades as Catholicism, but uses Holy Water and The Host for magical purposes. Its adherents have an enviable knowledge of the saints, and therefore can only be accused of cynicism.

We excoriate also the surprisingly common phenomenon amongst the faithful of perceiving their religion as a form of magic, and priests as magicians and sorcerers. We find that some priests even collude in this delusion, as for example the case of the priest in Santa Maria who gives the Host as security against loans, saying that this will automatically bring in sufficient money for the redemption of them, without him having to do any other thing. We find that women believe that if they kiss someone with the Host in their mouth, then that person will fall in love with them; that it is believed that possession of the Host prevents drowning; that baptism is a sure cure for gout. There is a feverish collecting of talismans that is only too often encouraged by priests who willingly bless them. We find that the number of superstitions current amongst supposed Catholics would exhaust the resources of an encyclopaedia the size of an entire monastery. These superstitions are mostly concerned with the warding off of misfortune, and we believe that they may only be abated by a diminution of the precariousness of life in this country, whilst at the same time we condemn those Catholics who should know better than to believe in them.

We particularly express concern, however, about what appears to be transpiring amongst the educated and affluent in our society. We believe that amongst these most powerful people some terrible sicknesses are becoming enracinated. We cite for example the indubitable fact that amongst high-ranking members of the Armed Forces, freemasonry is now so widespread as to be almost obligatory. We find this paradoxical, since this class has traditionally been the most conservatively Catholic; but the fact is that this class shares with all the others an extraordinary ability to believe in incompatibles without perceiving any contradiction. We realise that the military have always shown a predilection for arcane rituals, the proliferation of strange honorifics and unearned medals, and we realise that they are enamoured of secrecy and hierarchy. But at the same time it seems to us that the cosmology and ritual of freemasonry is incompatible with the faith, and is really a form of occultism.

Occultism proper appears to be widely practised in the citadels of government. Your Eminence will be aware that in the past many prelates and popes have succumbed to its attractions, and that in modern times many Cubans have attributed Fidel Castro's political longevity to the practise of magic. We have sources in the government that suggest that both His Excellency, President Veracruz, and the Foreign Secretary Lopez Garcilaso Vallejo are involved in a form of occultism which involves impersonating various pagan gods, Chaldean, Egyptian, Norse, Roman and Greek. Thus disguised they perform sexual intercourse, and at the moment of crisis they vividly make a wish, which they then expect to come true. The Minister of Finance, Emperador Ignacio Coriolano, is reputed to employ oral stimulation to the same purpose. His Excellency is said to practise Rosicrucian alchemy, the Foreign Secretary has published numerous books on the occult ('dictated by the Archangel Gabriel') under a pseudonym at public expense, and the Minister of Finance apparently dowses with a pendulum over maps of the country in order to locate the mythical city of El Dorado, at His Excellency's behest. We find

59

all this deeply disturbing in a country where the constitution explicitly states that there is a right to practise all religions which are 'not contrary to Christian morality or subversive of public order'.

Lastly we report to Your Eminence that the Islamic faith is growing rapidly in this country. For some reason everybody refers to them as 'Syrians'. They do not proselytise, but gain converts on account of their upright behaviour and their lack of hierarchy. Constitutionally their position is unassailable, but historically the Church has always regarded their faith as heretical. In the third and final part of our report we deal fully with the issue of heretical belief.

In order to become more truly himself, Dionisio Vivo gave up teaching at Ipasueño College; 'If anyone wants to learn anything from me,' he said, 'they can come and ask.' With the aid of Misael, Pedro the Hunter, and a recua of five mules, he moved all of his possessions to Cochadebajo de los Gatos, with the exception of his ancient automobile, which he left at the Indian village of Santa Maria Virgen, the nearest pueblo supplied by a road. There it was lovingly tended by the two chola girls whom he had once found abandoned in his front garden, battered and raped by the coca thugs, and whom he had succoured and returned to their village.

The two girls memorised his instructions, and every week they topped up the radiator, inspected the level of oil on the inspection stick, and filled with dew the battery. They dusted it with feathers, washed it with water from the stream, and on feast days polished it with their own hair. Because people said that it was so old that it could run only on magic, the two girls crossed themselves before ministering to its needs, and would rub the bellies of their hens upon its shabby paint in order to make them more fertile. They kept it behind their choza in its own garage of palm, and charged ten pesos to anyone who wanted to come in and see it. In this way they managed to attain the ambition of every poor peasant, which is to install a concrete floor and a septic tank. Like most people they referred to Dionisio Vivo as the Deliverer, because he had killed Pablo Ecobandodo.

Dionisio himself was unsusceptible to his own myth for the very good reason that to be himself was merely normal. To him it seemed that the events of the recent past were an inscrutable reverie, from which he had not even yet entirely returned to consciousness. The sensation that he felt was the very same as one feels when something bizarre happens during a lucid dream, and he was perpetually astonished.

It was as though Eshu had played tricks upon him and turned the world upside-down and inside-out. He had been merely a teacher of secular philosophy in a provincial town, convinced of nothing except his own scepticism, and resigned to spending the rest of his life discussing Kant's ideas about the *a priori* Forms of Intuition with febrile post-adolescents who were confused by their loss of faith in their parental Catholicism. He had been an averagely sensual man who compensated for slack periods in his romantic life by taking to the arms of Velvet Luisa in Madame Rosa's whorehouse; he had been merely another morsel of flesh destined to live out his little span and then return unremarked to the Andean soil, his grave marked by a cross and small pile of stones that would have diminished as they were stolen by relatives of other dead to build up other graves.

But he had been caught up in the tidal wave of anarchy set in motion by the coca caciques; the woman he loved above all others had been butchered by the worst of all of them, and he in turn had found himself the executioner of the culprit. He had discovered inside himself a deep well of violence and hatred, and a praeternatural ability to survive the wiles of conspiracy and fate. He had found himself the father of dozens of children by different mothers, all of them unaccountably individual and extraordinary, and his philosophy of life had shrunk to the two certainties that all that mattered was to oppose barbarism and to foster that common bond of love that binds each to each.

His eyes were so forcibly blue that that was all that many who met him could remember afterwards in a land that was brown-eyed almost to the last citizen. 'His eyes see God,' they would say, and it was true that he never seemed to be looking at the ground for his next foothold, that his eyes did not flick from one thing to another, did not blink, did not seem to reflect his moods. In truth what his eyes saw was the vision in his imagination of a brief time when he had known a kind of happiness that could poison a life for its impossibility of repetition. Everywhere he saw Anica; he saw her honey mulatta skin, her legs so long that they seemed to end in the heavens. He saw the green shirt knotted below her breasts, and the soft flat expanse of her stomach. At the edge of his eye he saw her creeping up on him as she had used to do when she wanted to playfight. He wore her ring upon his little finger and sometimes would sit and contemplate the refractions of the stone as it caught the sunset or the light of noon. It was as if she were somewhere inside that tiny but infinite space, and he was imprisoned forever in the wide world.

Dionisio Vivo wore his hair quite long these days, in memory of Ramón Dario who used to cut it for him in the days before he too was tortured to death by Pablo Ecobandodo's assassins. He carried Ramón's police pistol stuck through his belt, and like Ramón, always carried a slim cigar in the barrel to give away as a present to anyone who showed him a favour or took his liking. Apart from this he habitually wore only a long-tailed shirt, and Acahuatec sandals made with leather thongs threaded through a sole sliced out of a car tyre. It was commonly said that he walked like an Indian, talked with the tongue of an angel, made love like an incubus, and slept with the clarity of wakefulness. It was also known that he was a brujo of stupendous power, equal perhaps to Aurelio and to Pedro the Hunter, but not the kind of brujo who cures warts and locates lost lovers and goats. Dionisio was only capable of the spectacular.

It had been his extraordinary 'Requiem Angelico' which had enabled him to give up his post, for the piece had become so popular that it brought him a steady income to supplement that from the weekly page that he now wrote for *La Prensa* upon any subject that took his fancy. It would be without exaggeration to say that he was now the most celebrated journalist in the country on the strength of this page and on account of the series of letters that he had once written to the same newspaper during the time of the coca war. It would also be true to say that his journalism did not in the least reflect the legend that he had become; it was cogent, humane, and urbane in the manner of the serious press in Europe or in Colombia, and there was not a trace in it of the suprarational world he had come to inhabit.

He quickly became a familiar sight in Cochadebajo de los Gatos. This was not on account of his two enormous pet jaguars, for in that city there were many such cats roaming free, all of them entirely tame. It was more on account of the natural manner in which he seemed to enter the life of that part of the people who had assumed leadership with common consent but without election; Pedro the Hunter, with his pack of silent dogs and his clothes made of animal skins; Father Garcia, with his gentle conscience, his wild metaphysical ideas, and his appearance of a depressed hare; Misael, with his

63

honest black face and his love of revelry; Remedios, with her Kalashnikov and her gift of military acumen; Josef, with his ability to find compromises that accommodated everybody's plans; Hectoro, who had three wives, never dismounted from his horse except to drink or make love, and looked every inch a conquistador; Consuelo and Dolores, the two whores who reminded the men that they were not gods on account of the possession of testicles; Aurelio, the Aymara Indian who crossed the veils between this and the other worlds and seemed to be in every place at the same time; and General Fuerte, who had deserted the army by faking his own death, and who logged in his notebook everything that was to do with lepidoptery, ornithology, and the mores of the people.

But it was with none of these that Dionisio first made friends. He was drawn naturally to the teacher, Profesor Luis, a gifted improviser of pedagogical techniques, who knew how to make infallibly right-angled triangles with three pieces of string and who could explain everything in the world with the aid of what he found providentially upon the mountain slopes and in the gutters. It was Profesor Luis who made the windmills that generated electricity to fill the car batteries which illuminated the headlamps hanging from people's ceilings and ran the gramophone in the whorehouse. It was he who calculated the necessary height of the levees that kept the river in check, and who used a pole and a protractor to work out how wide the terraces should be that rose up upon the slopes of the sierra, along with their best angle of inclination for the purposes of irrigation.

Dionisio spent many evenings with Profesor Luis, and Farides, his wife. She was a dedicated cook who would not permit her husband to enter the kitchen in case he infected it with disorder or uncleanliness. This caused him some distress since he was prevented from enjoying his evenings by a pervading sense of guilt that she was working and he was not. 'Men,' she said, 'contaminate everything with maleness,' and beneath the verdict of this sweeping condemnation he was obliged to spend his time hanging around in the doorway with a concerned expression whilst Farides skinned the guinea pigs and chopped the cassava.

But when Dionisio arrived with a bottle under his arm and a puro up the barrel of his pistol, Profesor Luis was able to relax and reconcile himself to an evening of companionable silences and shared opinions, oblivious to the clattering of pans that normally reminded him of his wife's contempt for a man's daubings in the art gallery of cuisine. The two friends would sit with their feet on the table, furtively removing them if there were any sign of Farides being about to enter, or they would loll in hammocks slung from the posts that supported the roof. It was on one such occasion when they were unsuccessfully trying to work out how one blows smoke rings, that Dionisio remarked, 'What this town needs is a tractor and a library, or maybe a bookshop.'

'Indeed,' replied Profesor Luis, 'I am very proud of the fact that I have taught almost everybody to read.'

'I have noticed,' observed Dionisio, 'that there is such a thirst for reading matter that people walk along reading the writing on cigarette packets over and over. I think I could very easily get hold of some books.'

'And as for the tractor, which would be a miracle indeed, those of Don Emmanuel and Antoine remain buried in mud in the village of our origin. But I do not think it would be possible to get them here. Even if we repaired them on the spot, which we could not, they could be incapable of crossing the mountains as we did on foot.'

'I know how to do it,' said Dionisio.

'Then we will. Look, I have blown a smoke ring.'

## 11 *The Submission Of The Holy Office To His Eminence (3)*

> I said, You shall call me father
> and never cease to follow me.
> But like a woman who is unfaithful to her lover,
> so you, Israel, were unfaithful to me.
> Jeremiah 3:19

Your Eminence, we submit this section as the third and final part of our report upon the state of the nation's spiritual health, and we take the liberty of appending an addendum, outlining what action we consider should be taken in the light of our findings.

But to commence, we examine the phenomenon of heretical belief. In order to do this we have been constrained to define our terms by delimiting exactly what is meant by the word 'heresy'. Tertullian (*De Praescriptione Hereticorum*, c. 200 AD) defines it as a doctrine that cannot be found in the original teaching of the apostles. We have consulted the *Summa Theologica* and the *Summa Contra Gentiles* of St Thomas Aquinas, noting that he was the first of the Doctors to maintain that heresy was a sin 'meriting not merely excommunication, but death also' (an opinion no more, we hope, embraced by the Church). We have consulted the Bull *Ad Abolendam* of Pope Lucius III (1184), but most particularly the proceedings of the Lateran Councils, beginning in 1215 under the pontificate of Innocent III. We noted Canon Three of the Fourth Lateran Council, which outlines the provisions to be taken against heresy, thus engendering the 'Inquisition', whose activities have proved to be the most shameful of all the shameful blots upon the history of our faith. We find in Pope Innocent's actions solely the extenuating circumstance that he shared in the commonly held terror that the six hundred and sixty-sixth year of the Beast of the Apocalypse was imminent, in the form of Islamic encroachments into Christian territories. We contend that the very idea of inquisition is itself heretical in origin, since the first one recorded was during the reign of al Mamun (813–833). His 'mihna' was an Islamic institution whose function was to extract public confession that the Koran is the 'created speech of God'. To conclude, we decided to adopt the definition of heresy as 'a doctrine or body of doctrines held in opposition to the stated doctrine of the Catholic Church'. We pass over those opinions expressed by Protestant faiths and by the various sects of Islam, concerning ourselves solely with those held by people who profess their Catholicism. We leave it to Your Eminence to decide what is truly heretical and what is merely curious.

We have discovered that most Christian heresies arise in the first place out of attempts to resolve the 'problem of evil'. This is as true in our own day as it was in the days of St Bernard of Clairvaux and Raymond VI of Toulouse. Your Eminence will, we hope, pardon the desultory manner in which this section of our report wheels and circles back upon itself; he will understand that this is because we have been constantly obliged to return to the theme of how it is possible to reconcile the superabundance of evil in this world with the omnipotence and beneficence of God. That is, *'unde malum?'*

Thus we relate different heretical opinions in the manner in which they were related to us, as stories and myths, and without expressing judgements or controverting them.

We have heard that Satan involved in his fall other angels which were to become human souls. This explains why the soul is neither earthly nor perishable. We are 'imprisoned angels, striving back towards the light'.

We have heard that when Satan was defeated by Michael, he took one third of the angelic militia to earth, along with the sun, the moon, and the stars. In some versions, it was Satan who was the creator of the earth.

We have heard that Satan was equal to God, a jealous neighbour, and that he waited for thirty-two years outside Heaven's gate in order to show the angels a woman, and this is why they left Heaven. They rained down denser than rain for nine days and nine nights.

We have heard that matter was created in co-operation between God and Satan so that they could have a ground upon which to do battle.

We have heard that Satan was God's child, and that therefore he is either (1) The Christ, (2) Greater than Christ, or (3) Christ's lesser brother; that Satan is the child of a greater, infernal god; that Satan and Christ are the children of God by different mothers; that Christ is the result of Satan's having seduced God's wife; that Satan is really 'the Laws of Nature'. We have heard that Satan is the creator god of Genesis, and that therefore the Old Testament Law of Moses is Satan's Law. The New Testament is the 'Good God's' Law. Therefore Moses, David, the patriarchs and prophets were Satan's prophets. Moses was 'an evil seducer' who mixed some good laws in with the bad ones in order to disguise the evil of the bad ones. Others maintain that the prophets deliberately falsified the law, and others still that the prophets lived in a separate world from this one, so that their laws do not apply here. Such opinions explain the remarkable outbreak of anti-Semitism in Cucuta last year.

Connected with this, we have heard that because John the Baptist was Elias, he was therefore an Old Testament prophet, and was therefore an adversary of Christ. Again in Cucuta they believe that his mother and father, as well as the angel of annunciation, were demons, and they refer to him scathingly as 'the water porter'. Additionally we have heard claims that the Holy Trinity is earth, fire and wind.

Many apocryphal texts have somehow gained circulation and credence here, and we have found copies of the Gospel According to St Thomas, the 'Interrogatio Johannis', the Vision of Isaiah, as well as an extraordinary plethora of modern 'gospels' written down by people who claim to have received them by revelation. Thus there is a Gospel of Isabel the Whore, who enjoins people not to eat beans because flatulence is deleterious to spiritual health. The Gospel of Ricardo of Rinconondo claims that Mohammed was a reincarnation of Christ, who had returned in order to lose his virginity, and the Gospel of Maria of Malaga claims that Christ was really a woman who formed the third part of a 'Holy Trinity', of whom the other two were Mary Magdalen and Mary, Mother of Jesus. Not only do such 'gospels' exist in written forms, there are also many evangels which have remained oral thus far, but which nonetheless have gained great currency. For example, there is a city called Cochadebajo de los Gatos, which does not even appear upon the maps. In this place the population practises santeria, but there is also an Indian named Aurelio in whom the people place great faith for his medical advice; much of his advice and philosophy is gained from Aymara Indian and

68

Navante Indian mythology, and has syncretised with the beliefs even of 'good Catholics'. In the same place there is a notable heresiarch, an unfrocked priest named Garcia, who leads a dissipated life and consorts with a false priest whose command of Latin extends no further than the lewder passages of Catullus and Ovid. This Garcia preaches a dualistic faith, and advocates self-indulgence and concupiscence as the means to salvation. He has gained literally thousands of followers all over that part of the sierra. In this he is not at all unique, for there are many others like him. Your Excellency will no doubt be aware of the phenomenon of Canudos in Brazil, where Antonio the Counsellor once gathered thousands of faithful who fought to the last drop of blood for their whimsical beliefs. We have the impression that there are many Antonio the Counsellors at work unnoticed in this country.

We have heard that the Blessed Virgin Mary and Jesus Christ were both angels, who merely appeared to be fleshly (the theory of the *corpus phantasticum*); that she became pregnant through her ear; that she was a sinful woman of the flesh, or even a prostitute; that she was really a male named 'Marinus'.

Of Christ we have heard that he was merely a man, of sinful flesh, because only the fleshly may come to earth; that there were two Christs, one fleshly with Mary Magdalene as his concubine, who was crucified and suffered on earth, and that the other one was without sin, neither ate nor drank, was unfleshly, and was crucified in the invisible world; that Christ's death was a scandalous defeat at the hands of Satan, who still therefore reigns here; that he reopened the path to heaven for his fellow fallen angels; that his miracles were black magic, and he a sorcerer; that he died upon the cross in each of the seven heavens; that he could not suffer or die, and therefore it was a demon that died in his place.

We have heard that earth is a penitence for fallen angels, and that when we die we are tormented by demons into transmigrating into another body, the new host depending upon one's degree of merit. They prove reincarnation on account of numerous stories such as that of someone remembering where they lost a shoe in their past life as a horse, and the shoe turning up in that spot, as predicted. We have also heard that there is no resurrection at all in the flesh.

We have heard that there is no purgatory, or that purgatory is nine times brighter than fire, that eighteen angels transport the good through it, spending one day in each of the seven heavens. In heaven there are pastures, savannahs, jungles, and birdsong. There is no hunger nor leprosy, and people don a 'robe of light' and reclaim the crowns that they wore before their fall as Satan's angels.

We have heard that there is no free will; one is an angel or devil by predestination, and therefore repentance and attempts to behave well are pointless. This doctrine is justified by divine foreknowledge, and is used to license absolute libertinism, even including incest.

We have heard that all sacraments practised by a sinful priest are null and void, and that this is backdated to all sacraments made previously. Thus people will flock to be rebaptised when they perceive that their priest has sinned.

Of carnal matters it is said that marriage is 'demoniac' and that married congress is 'legalised fornication'; this means that it is equally sinful to be married or to indulge in premarital intercourse, which justifies the latter, as one is condemned to sinfulness in either case.

People have invented strange prohibitions of their own, having found a heterogeneous collection of things to be satanic. Thus there are persons who will not eat flesh because the Devil created it, nor cheese, nor eggs, nor milk, but they will eat fish, because it is 'the spontaneous product of water'. Many will swear no oaths, citing Matthew 5: 33-37, which means that they will not get married because they will not make the vows. For the same reason they refuse to become godparents. For others, insects, fish and lice are diabolical, as are serpents, frogs, toads, lizards and mice. There are cohorts of mendicants who refuse to work on the grounds that it prospers a world made by the Devil. They become formidably parasitic upon the ignorant poor, who nonetheless support them gladly. Some of these consider eating to be work, and they starve themselves to death in order to reprove the flesh.

Amongst the more curious beliefs that we have found to be current are these: that Pontius Pilate paid interest upon Judas' forty pieces of silver; that it is very good luck to wear the Gospel of St John upon the top of the head; that only those who are perfect may say the Pater (thus most people never say it at all, and block their ears at the points in the service where it occurs); that God created evil in order to have something against which He might comprehend Himself; that one has to plunge oneself into evil in order to understand and overcome it; that Heaven will only come when the last soul is saved, including that of Satan himself.

We could exhaust Your Eminence with the continuance of this section of our report, but to put it in short, we find that there is a plenitude of heretical belief in our country. We discovered Arianism, Waldensianism, Mazdaism, Zervaism, Albigensianism, Manicheanism, Bogomilism, theosophism, Paulicianism, Nestorianism, monophysitism, and Hussism. We found numerous gnostic groups, including one that actually preached salvation through oral intercourse, and yet was composed of those who earnestly declared themselves to be Catholic. We found a nun who wandered in dishevelled condition about the countryside proclaiming that the Roman Church was 'the whore of the apocalypse, the synagogue of Satan, a monument of dead stones'; yet around her neck she wore a locket containing a picture of His Holiness which she kissed very frequently with more than religious passion. Above all we find that the prevailing practice is that of kathenotheism, by which we mean the custom of treating as the Supreme Being whichever deity one happens to be addressing at any given moment.

To conclude, we agree between ourselves that what we have discovered reveals two things. The first is that the religious imagination of the people is far from dead. We have found an extraordinary vivacity of belief amongst them; they expend great intellectual energy in constructing theologies, arguing about them, and observing the precepts that they develop. This reveals a profound spirituality amongst them which overflows into their artistic endeavours and permeates every aspect of their lives. We believe that this must be a cause for great rejoicing, because it uncovers to what extent we find ourselves upon already fertile soil.

The second thing that is revealed is that this soil is untilled, these sheep unshepherded. We point out once again that many of these beliefs are shared by clergy, which points to an appalling lack of training and pastoral support. We cannot be surprised by bizarre and heterodox beliefs amongst the laity once this is taken into account. Secondly, we state that it was a severely retrograde step to close down so many church-supported schools on the grounds that only politically radical priests and nuns were prepared to work in them.

This has resulted in widespread ignorance amongst youngsters, not only of the faith, but of everything else as well.

We firmly recommend that very large sums of money be released in order (a) to properly staff, maintain, and equip our seminaries and missions, (b) to reopen all closed missions and schools, and (c) to expand such school and missionary services all over the country, until every citizen has the opportunity to resolve issues of religion according to a conscience which is fully informed of the relevant facts and arguments. We further strongly recommend that the Church be prepared to shift its attentions somewhat away from those who at present receive our greatest attention and consolation (the pious middle classes), and go forth once more amongst the needy and the sinners, as Our Lord directed us to do. We are of one mind in believing that such money would more profit the world in this way than by remaining in fixed-interest Swiss bank accounts, or by being invested in the Ecclesiastical Mining Corporation.

## 12 *How We Brought The Tractors From Chiriguana To Cochadebajo de los Gatos*

I believe I mentioned before that during the reconstruction of my house I had the use of Antoine's ancient three-wheeled tractor, a machine ideal for negotiating the precipitous tracks of the mountain-sides, and I like to believe that I had more than a little to do with its arrival here, as the blisters upon my hands at the time amply testified.

In fact we have the use of two tractors in this place, which is indeed a miracle because the city is completely inaccessible to wheeled vehicles, however rugged. The other tractor belongs to Don Emman-uel, and it was his that we fetched first all that time ago, just after I had arrived to take up residence and just before I was seduced into my delightful captivity by Ena and Lena, who have now both given birth to daughters. I am so busy with them these days that it is yet another miracle that I am finding time to write all this down.

I could observe in passing that miracles are not a great rarity around here; I would be prepared to wager my own life that this is the only place on earth where a man may meet his own ancestor in the flesh, which is what, if I may be permitted to digress, happened to Dionisio Vivo.

It appears that during the original migration to this town there was an avalanche that uncovered the frozen corpses of an entire military expedition from 1533, at whose head was the Conde Pompeyo Xavier de Estremadura, a Spanish aristocrat who had served the monarchies of both Spain and Portugal. Aurelio the brujo somehow contrived to bring these characters, including the Conde, back to life. I understand that they caused mayhem in the town with their arrogant behaviour, until Hectoro found a way to bring them down to size. This is ironic, because Hectoro looks and behaves much like a conquistador himself, and his face is very like that of the Conde.

The Conde was, and still is, remarkably disorientated by his resurrection; he refuses to learn to read on the grounds that only monks should have the need of it, he threatens people who displease him with the vengeance of the King of Spain, and he talks about the events of the sixteenth century as though they were only yesterday. He reports that in heaven one hunts and 'goes a-whoring', a strange thing to hear from a literal-minded Catholic of that era. He is cared for by Remedios, the leader, or ex-leader, of the People's Vanguard, and I daresay that she is the only woman here with a sufficient degree of fortitude to put up with him. I have no doubt that she loves him dearly, but I remember that once when he was in an aristocratic rage about a dent in his cuirass which he alleged that she had put there by dropping it, and he was waving his rapier in her face and threatening to slit her nose 'as I did with the moor in Cordoba', she walked past him without flinching and picked up the armour. She took it out into the plaza, put it at the bottom of the jaguar obelisk, and shot four holes through it with her Kalashnikov. With her eyes blazing magnificently, and tossing back her black ponytail, she marched regally back into the house, leaving the Conde with his mouth agape, and all his rage evaporating into astonishment.

The Conde was always prone to astonishment, such as when he saw the helicopter that came to fetch the tractors, and when he first came face to face with Dionisio Vivo. The fact is that they both have the same unnervingly blue eyes, probably for the reason that I gave above, which is that the Conde is Dionisio's progenitor.

Dionisio was merely strolling down the street accompanied by his two jaguars, which are even larger than mine, when suddenly the Conde burst out of his doorway and waved his rapier in the former's face, once again threatening to split his nose 'as I did with the moor in Cordoba'. Dionisio said something to the two animals, and they leapt on the Conde, pinning him to the ground with their prodigious weight. I might add in parenthesis that this is yet another miracle, since no one else's cats pay any attention to what they are told. Dionisio waited patiently until the Conde had finished his fearsome string of archaic oaths and maledictions, and then demanded to know why he had been accosted so rudely. 'You have stolen my ring that was given to me by the King of Portugal,' announced the Conde, 'and I will have it returned or I will have you beheaded and the hands that stole it thrown to the ravens.'

Dionisio wore two rings, both on his left hand. One of them was a woman's ring that he wore upon his little finger, and the other he took off and held before the Conde's eyes. 'This ring?' he enquired, and the Conde explained, 'That ring, by God.'

'This was given to an ancestor of mine, the Conde Pompeyo Xavier de Estremadura. It was presented to him by the King of Portugal in gratitude for some disgraceful mercenary episode, and has been passed down my family ever since. It is not yours.'

The Conde adopted his usual perplexed expression, and muttered, 'But I am the Conde Pompeyo Xavier de Estremadura. I myself.'

'If indeed you are, then your portrait hangs in my father's house, wearing this very ring. However it is not a very strong likeness of you, I must say.'

'He was a dog of a painter,' said the Conde, 'and I paid him only half the crowns I owed him, the Devil rot his heart.'

However, I perceive that this digression is getting us no further towards the explanation of how we brought the tractors to the city, and perhaps I should conclude it by saying that Dionisio undertook the re-education of his ancestor, simultaneously using him as an invaluable source for obscure historical information, and for filling in gaps in the family tree. Perhaps I should add that the Conde has been recently agitating to meet Dionisio's father, being under the impression that since the latter is a General he would be sufficiently warlike for them to have something in common.

But General Hernando Montes Sosa is in truth as far from barbarity as his ancestor is from civilisation, and it is because of him that the two tractors came to the city.

As I recall, it was shortly after the Battle of *Doña Barbara*, the consequence of an ill-conceived literacy project by Dionisio and Profesor Luis, that the former announced that he could get his father to arrange for a helicopter gunship to go and dig out the tractors from the mud of the Mula basin. There was very considerable opposition to this, because no one wanted anything to do with the Army. General Fuerte and Capitan Papagato wanted nothing to do with it because they were both deserters, and the rest because they had in the past suffered inconceivable persecution by it.

Dionisio, however, insisted that his father was a democrat and that the Armed Forces were now firmly under democratic control. He pointed out that General Fuerte and Capitan Papagato could very easily go to Santa Maria Virgen for the day, and that there was an amnesty in place for guerrillas ever since the many Communist parties had been legalised. He further pointed out that nobody knew that anyone in the city had ever been a guerrilla in the first place, for the simple reason that nobody outside the area even knew that Cochadebajo de los Gatos existed. 'If you like,' he said, 'I will meet the gunship in Ipasueño, and after we have taken off the pilot will be blindfolded, and I will guide him here verbally. In this manner he will never know where he has been. I will persuade him that it is a special army exercise, and I will arrange for my father to award him a medal or some kind of proficiency certificate.

Now Dionisio's father was a man convinced that since the Army was the servant of the people it should occupy itself in peacetime by serving them. Naturally he knew nothing about the blindfolding plan, and so he agreed to what his son told him on the telephone, and agreed also that he should meet the gunship in Ipasueño Plaza, and that the pilot should be under his instructions. And that is exactly what happened.

The enormous machine landed in Ipasueño Plaza and caused an inferno of chaos as everybody scattered and their sombreros were swept away by the breeze of the blades. Dionisio and his two jaguars climbed in, giving rise to the myth (still current) that they had ascended to heaven in the fiery vehicle described by Ezekiel, and he managed somehow to persuade the pilot that part of the plan was to gain experience of flying blindfold. He came up with some wild hypothesis about how a helicopter pilot blinded in a gas attack might sometime have to fly his crew out under their spoken guidance. I should add that there were four members of the Regiment of Airborne Engineers on board also, but they were in the back of the aircraft and could not have memorised the route even if they had wanted to.

I do not know how Dionisio Vivo knew the way by air (people say that he is more than he seems), but the machine arrived in our own plaza, causing a confusion here equal to that at Ipasueño. The cloud of dust that was raised up in the noonday heat was of a peculiarly choking variety, and at least one innocent chicken met its maker in the vortex of the blades, scattering blood and feathers disproportionate to its size.

Embarking on this voyage were Antoine and Don Emmanuel, since the tractors were theirs, myself (at Antoine's invitation), Aurelio, who was taking over from Dionisio as navigator, Sergio, and Misael. Together with the four airborne engineers and the pilot, this meant that there were eleven of us armed with spades and shovels for the purpose of digging out the tractors, but there would have been space for many more of us in that vast machine of war, which was probably sold to our own government by the Yanquis in exchange for dollar bananas and emeralds.

Aurelio did not blindfold the pilot, as he asserted that at the end of the journey the pilot would not be able to remember where he had been; he smoked a vile-smelling concoction the whole way, saying that this was the purpose of it. He was, as usual, in the traditional dress of his people, complete with the long plait behind that in fact one hardly ever sees on an Aymara these days.

Don Emmanuel as usual behaved most embarrassingly, and I have the vivid recollection of him urinating out of the sliding door 'because I have always enjoyed making piss-holes in the snow'. He seemed oblivious of the fact that he was teetering above three hundred metres of empty space at the bottom of which was not a soft landing. He was shirtless, having failed to anticipate the extreme cold of altitude, and in his navel he wore a small, greying wad of cotton wool. He claimed that it was impregnated with alcohol, and that he wore it because one evening Felicidad had seen fit to explore the bottomless recesses of the aforesaid navel with her forefinger, and had pronounced it to be both smelly and full of fluff. He asseverated that he liked to conduct a campaign against 'dingleberries' of this nature, and seemed most disheartened to find that whilst he was urinating the wad had been whipped away by the slipstream, whereupon Misael remarked that he would have been spared this indignity had not his belly been so protuberant.

The journey took a mere hour, which astonished Sergio, who said that it had taken many days to travel it on foot with the cattle and the mule-trains. It was a spectacular itinerary. We flew between the peaks and at as low an altitude along the valleys as could be managed, because it was warmer and because the pilot said that it saved fuel. We saw numerous tiny Indian settlements dotted amid the pajonales, flocks of vicuñas and llamas ran wildly beneath us, and we saw the worked-out mines that had once filled the coffers of the Houses of Castile and Aragon. The vibration of the aircraft set off a spectacular snowslide in one place; from our position the cascade of snow looked all innocence, majesty and beauty, although God help anyone who might have been beneath it. A more paralysing death could not be imagined.

It became clear that Aurelio was leading us over progressively lower altitudes, because the air even in the cabin began to feel palpably thicker and more clinging, and beneath us the vegetation had grown lusher and more arboreal. We flew over a stretch of forest, and saw a thin plume of smoke, which Aurelio said was his wife Carmen smoking the rubber. It was said of Aurelio that he could be with his wife in the jungle at the same time as he was with us in Cochadebajo de los Gatos, and that no one could tell which one was the real Aurelio, not even Carmen.

Having crossed this forest we sped on over the Mula basin. Sergio and Misael were utterly astonished by what they saw, because the lie of the land had changed completely since the time that they had inhabited it before the flood; nothing was recognisable except for the roofs of buildings and even they were greatly obscured by primary growth. The jungle was reclaiming the land, and this seemed to give Aurelio great satisfaction. Apropos of this he told us that of all plants, God enjoyed making the cactus the most, and of all animals he enjoyed making the dormidera. This last is a giant black anaconda which sleeps so profoundly that its snores keep all other jungle animals awake, not only because of the reverberations, but also because its pungent halitosis militates against sleep.

Misael and Sergio recognised the roof of Doña Constanza's hacienda, and fell into a fit of laughter from which it was almost impossible to rescue them. Don Emmanuel explained to me that it was because the Mula had changed course so much that it now ran clean through Doña Constanza's swimming pool. I failed to see the humour in this.

We flew on to the site of where Don Emmanuel's hacienda used to be, and the helicopter had to hover there whilst the four airborne engineers descended on a winch in order to clear a space in the vegetation for it to land. This having been done, the craft was landed and we were obliged to hack our way to the site of the tractor shed, where we found that both tractor and shed were buried one and a half metres deep in alluvial deposits, and were completely entangled and encased in lianas.

It was midday, and down there on the plain the heat was dizzying in intensity. Add to this the infernal pestiferations of the insects, and you will appreciate that to me it was a purgatorial experience which I hope never to repeat. The only bright side of it was that we saw many animals that were unafraid on account of their ignorance of humans. We saw a maned wolf, looking exactly like a fox on stilts, and we saw a potu pretending to be a branch. We saw an ant-eater carrying its baby on its back, and a capybara, which Aurelio called 'the master of the grasses'. Apart from that we saw a boa, a whipper snake, and a teju lizard carrying a bird's egg in its mouth. The capybara made a fine meal when we all got home.

We sweated and grunted over removing the roof of the shed, and further sweated and grunted over cutting away the growth and digging out the machine. The perspiration seeping into my broken blisters was an excruciation. Altogether it took three hours to perform this task, and it seemed more like an aeon, but in the end it was worth it just to see what the pilot did to Don Emmanuel.

Don Emmanuel was, I think, somewhat depressed to see what had happened to his hacienda, and he lost his customary good humour. To begin with he was directing his picturesque curses against the tractor, the insects, and the lianas, but he finished up by cursing all of us as well. His red beard was glistening with the sweat that ran down from his brow, and his capacious belly had acquired a deep red hue.

Now the pilot was a very big black man with a distinguished bearing, and he was intelligent too; they do not allow morons to fly helicopter gunships. He was saying to Don Emmanuel, 'I think we should dig a tunnel under the tractor so that we can get the cables underneath.'

Don Emmanuel looked at him balefully and asked, 'Do you have a dog?'

'Si, señor,' replied the pilot.

'Well,' said Don Emanuel, 'your dog's your mother.'

There was a stunned silence, and then all of us except for Aurelio, who has a great respect for dogs, burst out laughing. The big pilot carried on digging for a few moments, and then he straightened up and said, 'The next person to laugh finds their own way home,' and we all fell silent on the instant. But Don Emmanuel would not desist. 'Your mother is so much of a man that she is really your father,' he said, and then he added, 'And you wear a moustache in order to be reminded of her.'

The pilot said nothing, but when we had the tractor hooked up to the helicopter by cables and were embarking, the pilot blocked Don Emmanuel's way and held out a helmet rather like that of a motor-cylist, and a thick quilted suit. 'We wear these for the extreme cold of high altitude,' he said.

Don Emmanuel looked puzzled.

'You are not coming on my aircraft,' said the pilot. 'Put these on and ride the tractor.'

Now, we could see that Don Emmanuel was about to protest, but the big pilot went up close and glared down at him, holding out the suit. He added, 'Or walk.'

Meek as an alpaca, Don Emmanuel put on the flying gear and clambered onto the seat of the tractor. He sat there clinging to the cables all the way home, whilst the pilot flew as close to the ground as it is possible to imagine. I am prepared to bet that Don Emmanuel was not only petrified but was positively congelated with cold once we got into the sierra. We were looking out of the doors, watching him frantically warding off the buzzards and alcamarini birds that hurtled towards him, and all of us swore afterwards that it was the best thing we had ever seen.

When we returned it was too late to go back to fetch Antoine's tractor, and so we decided to fetch it on the day following. But when we assembled at dawn, who should come along but Remedios, Consuelo and Dolores, all armed to the teeth, and Misael said, 'Madre de Dios, they have come to take revenge upon the Army.'

But it was not so, for Remedios said, 'You men get out of here, it is the women's turn to ride the helicopter today,' and Sergio started to protest, saying things like, 'Ay, ay, this is man's work, you pretty things go back to your pots,' and that was the worst remark he could say. Dolores swung at the side of his head with her mochila, and it cracked against his ear like a pistol shot. Dolores keeps her mochila filled with Brazil nuts in order to threaten any man who refuses her advances, but for once a ride in the helicopter was of more importance to her than one hundred pesos for a good lay.

So we men backed off, and the women brought Antoine's tractor back in good time even though Consuelo spread the story later that Dolores had enjoyed all four of the soldiers plus the pilot during breaks in their labours, and the latter spread stories about Consuelo being envious. They had a fight afterwards during the fiesta that was held to give thanks to the serviceman, interrupting the speech that Remedios was making in which she was declaring peace unilaterally on the Army and announcing the formal disbanding of the People's Vanguard. After the fight was over Remedios said that in future the Army could help as often as they liked, as long as they were from the units commanded by General Hernando Montes Sosa. Indeed, later on they arrived with a helicopter bearing ten drums of fuel for the tractors, and three mechanical engineers to dismantle them and put them into service.

As for Don Emmanuel, he made peace with the pilot at the fiesta, but just as the latter was leaving he said, with a big white smile on his black face, 'As for you, you son of a bitch, your grandmother bore you by your brother.' He was shaking Don Emmanuel's hand so hard, and gripping it so tight, that all that Don Emmanuel could think to reply was, 'Just so, cabrón, you are exactly right.'

## 13 *In Which His Eminence Makes A Fateful Choice*

His Eminence Cardinal Dominic Trujillo Guzman put the report of the Holy Office down upon his desk, uncharacteristically muttered an obscenity, and immediately crossed himself and cast his eyes heavenward, that it might be forgiven him.

He went to the window and gazed out over the city, which was sinking picturesquely into its usual short but spectacular sunset, and an vile stench invaded his nostrils, completely obliterating the momentary peace that had followed his anger. He leant out of the window and saw a dead hog floating along the river below, adorned with a king vulture that was busily engaged in trying to puncture its bloated raft. When the hog and its passenger had passed by, he noticed that there was a new smell, and that a couple were fornicating behind a bush. He saw that opposite there was the normal small knot of pious widows dressed in black, who always waited there in the evenings so that he could bless them when he appeared at the window. He raised his hand in greeting, remembering just in time to transform the casual gesture into a blessing. The women crossed themselves and rattled off at high speed a decade of the rosary before disappearing into the gathering darkness. His Eminence sniffed the air and identified the new smell.

'Don Susto,' he called, 'in here please,' and his secretary appeared. Don Susto was a small Franciscan with a perpetual sniffle, and grime beneath his toenails on account of his tenacious determination always to wear sandals. He took his vocation very seriously, and it was a torment to him to have been hauled away from his monastery in order to serve at the palace under a master whose failings were all too apparent to him. Being at an age of sixty years, worn out by a lifetime of prayer on stone floors, meagre diet, and getting up at five o'clock in the morning even when this was unnecessary, Don Susto had aged prematurely. He was shrunken and stooped, few shreds of hair sprouted forlornly from his scalp, and he was cadaverously thin. Of all his many virtues the one most valued by His Eminence was his conscientiousness, and his one solitary vice was smoking a pipe in secret with the windows of his cell wide open. He had lived forty years in the terror of being discovered by his superiors, and never confessed the sin directly until upon his bed of death. He was to die in puzzlement, having been informed by his confessor that smoking a pipe was not even a venial sin.

The faithful secretary shuffled in with a ledger beneath his arm, and His Eminence summoned him to the window. 'Identify this smell,' said the Cardinal, 'and tell me if it is what I think it is.'

Don Susto leaned over the sill and sampled the rank odour. 'I believe it is urine,' he said, 'it is unfortunately a sign of the times.'

'What times?' demanded the Cardinal. 'Is there ever a time when the river past the palace should should be so malodorous?'

'It is because of los olvidados,' said Don Susto. The Cardinal sniffed haughtily, suspecting that he was about to receive a lecture upon a social issue, and asked, 'And who are the forgotten ones?'

Don Susto tried to stifle his surprise at being asked such a question, and replied, 'They are the very poor, Your Eminence. They have set up a favela outside of town, and it is very squalid. It breaks one's heart to see them. They have no sewers, and so they go in the river even though they also draw their water from it.'

The Cardinal screwed up his face in disgust. 'They should be removed. No doubt it is a nest of thieves and prostitution.'

'But where to?' asked Don Susto. 'They have overflowed the classical ruins in the Incarama Park, and when they were removed they simply found their way back again. They are truly the lost souls of our time, and yet they are courageous, Your Eminence.'

'How so, Don Susto? They are the feckless and the indolent, nothing more.'

'It is true that they are uneducated and their morals are frequently deplorable, Your Eminence, but they are masters of improvisation. Every time it rains their cardboard shacks are washed away, and twenty-four hours later they are all built again. They make delicate stews from rats and sandal-leather, they live by swarming over the garbage tips raking them over for scraps, and in this way they are akin to Lazarus, Your Eminence. They suffer typhoid and cholera, and yet they hold the best carnivals in the capital.'

'The carnivals are a pagan abomination, Don Susto.' There was a long silence as the latter held in his feelings on the subject, and then the Cardinal asked, 'Why are they here?'

'Some are fleeing the anarchy of the cocaine regions, some are victims of agricultural mechanisation and underemployment, some are the victims of the reorganisation of the latifundos, some are fleeing the law in other regions, and some are hoping to make it rich in the big city. Most of them are cholos and don't even speak Castilian. I have been meaning to suggest to you, Your Eminence, that here is an opportunity to set up missions upon our own doorstep.'

His Eminence sniffed. 'We should get them moved back where they belong, to the care of their own priests. But there is something more urgent that I need to clarify with you.' He went to the desk and picked up the report of the Holy Office. 'Which incompetent atheists compiled this travesty of a report? And which incompetent nincompoop chose them for the task?'

Don Susto was taken aback by the anger in the Cardinal's voice, and perplexed by his vehemence. 'It was the Bishops of Cucuta, Asuncion, and La Igualdad, three most eminent men, Your Eminence.'

'What? Those crypto-Communists? Those sloppy Liberals? Who appointed them, in the name of the Virgin?'

Don Susto thought carefully about the most tactful way of admitting that he had chosen them himself. 'I consulted with Rome about who were the most eminent theologians in the country,' he said at last, 'and those were the names that they sent me. I did it in good faith, Your Eminence.'

The Cardinal was stunned momentarily into silence. He placed the sheaf of paper that he had been waving back onto the table, and returned to the window, only to retreat once more on account of the rancidity of the air. He raised his arms and let them fall to his side in a gesture of resigned despair. 'It is enough to make one into a Protestant,' he said. 'I ask for a report on the spiritual state of the nation, and what I get back is a sustained attack on the Church itself, and, by implication, against my administration. Have you read it?'

'Indeed, Your Eminence.'

'And what is your opinion?'

Don Susto sensed danger and chose his words carefully. 'It is certainly critical of the Church, Your Eminence.'

'And do you agree with those criticisms?'

The secretary hedged. 'I am not qualified to express an opinion, I have insufficient experience of our work in the field. But I do agree that there must be a connection between the spiritual state of the nation and the spiritual state of the Church. It strikes me as evident.'

The Cardinal picked up the report again and flicked through its pages, picking upon the portions that particularly irked him. 'It implies that we are seven hundred years behind the European Church, trading in relics, selling absolutions; it states that there are high officials who have mistresses – have you ever heard such a thing? Do you know of a single case of this?' He paused for rhetorical effect, and could not fail to notice that Don Susto was so wide-eyed at his hypocrisy that his mouth was actually hanging open. The Cardinal felt the flush of shame rising to his ears, and he turned away and walked once more to the window, affecting an indignant impatience. 'In the second part,' he continued, 'a connection is implied between my term of office and the general decline. It rambles on about social conditions, knowing full well that we have no remit to interfere with matters of politics, and it accuses us of accepting tainted money from criminals. It even goes so far as to attack the upper classes, who are the very bastion of the church . . .'

Don Susto could not restrain himself. 'The bastion of the Church is the Gospel,' he said, and the Cardinal glared at him icily before continuing, 'And the third part blames the proliferation of superstition upon the Church, accusing us of the misappropriation of funds for material purposes, as if we could survive without invest- ment. It is an outrage, Don Susto, an outrage.' He looked down from his superior height at the secretary, demanding with his glance the anticipated nods of agreement.

Don Susto was not a courageous man, but neither was he a man without principle. He did not nod. He stood very still, and then said softly, 'Your Eminence, I beg your permission to return to my monastery.'

'You agree with this report, don't you, Don Susto?'

Don Susto said nothing for a moment; he was saddened by how far his life had wandered from his original quest for peace and contemplation. He had not been a monk so long in order to end up in a palace arguing with a cardinal who was a business-manager in scarlet robes. 'Do I have your permission?' he asked, evading the question.

The Cardinal was weary; he placed the report back on the desk once more, sighed, and said, 'As you wish.'

The old secretary leaned forward to kiss the Cardinal's ring, and then knelt to take his benediction. He stood up, and before leaving he asked, 'Your Eminence, may I say something of a personal nature?' And the Cardinal nodded his assent.

'Your Eminence, it would ease my mind very greatly if you would consult with a doctor about the pains in your stomach. The days of hairshirts and flagellation are over, and the bodily pain merely increases your spiritual affliction.'

The two looked at one another as man to man for the first time, the panoply of office torn away. His Eminence extended his hand, and the secretary shook it. When Don Susto had gone, the Cardinal felt a choke of loneliness and unworthiness gather in his throat, and he too reflected upon how far his own life had deviated from the ideal of his youth.

Don Susto did not return to his monastery for ten years. Instead he wandered away on foot to lead the life of a mendicant and to reduce himself to a perfect point of simplicity. On his way he discovered a young faun trembling in a brake, abandoned, and he adopted it. It grew stately and graceful, following him wherever he went, and, inspired by the story of St Hubert, he hung a crucifix between its antlers. With the aid of this animal he made many conversions amongst the people of the sierra. Whilst with the Quechuas he discovered that in their language his name meant 'sickness', and so he changed it to 'Salud'. This is why in some places one can find to this day little shrines decorated with silver tinsel, in which there are crude statuettes of a horned monk smoking a pipe, referred to by his devotees as 'San Salud'. There used to be many more such shrines, but they were torn down by missionaries who took them to be pagan.

After Don Susto's departure His Eminence, pondering his secretary's advice to consult a doctor, felt the appalling pain overwhelming him once more. Instinctively he went to the window to take deep breaths of the evening air, and instead inhaled the dank putrefying stench of sewage. Violently he vomited out over the walls of the palace, and, doubled over, he sank to his knees. Sobbing with pain he prayed to the patron saint of sailors, St Erasmus, who was martyred by having his entrails wound out of his body upon a windlass. When the pain passed, and he was still breathless with its aftermath, he prayed also to St Job, patron saint of syphilitics. He knew that soon the reckless itch to visit a brothel would again overwhelm him, and he had a terror of passing infection to his mistress, Concepcion.

He sat for a little while, the report of the Holy Office in his lap, and decided to begin the next phase of his campaign. He decided that the leader of his crusade of preaching would be Don Rechin Anquilar, a man of absolutely cold intellectual certainty.

# 14 *The Monologue Of The Conde Pompeyo Xavier De Estremedura Walking In The Sierra*

A woman is the Devil's work, by God. How she angers me, and I, a man of noble birth. Never before has a woman got the better of me and made me suffer such indignity. There is a misalignment of the heavens that nature should be so upset and the natural order skewed. I say to her, 'My breakfast, woman,' and audaciously she replies, 'Get it yourself,' or she meekly makes it and then she pours it in my helmet and says, 'Eat, pig, from your trough.' Or I say, 'Come to me tonight, I wish to enjoy you,' and she says, 'I am tired,' or, 'Go to the whorehouse,' and then she comes to me, by God, and she wishes to mount me and make me play the woman's part, and she tells me, 'Do not just lie there, move it in me,' and I am reminded that when I mount her she will not stay still, but she moves her hips and moans, enjoying it most indecently, and all my intention is lost and I let loose cannonades before the walls are breached and the keep mined. And then she reproves me and I am ashamed like a boy who has fallen from a horse. I am so unmanned that betimes I reach for my sword and I say, 'I will slit your nose as I did with the moor in Cordoba,' and she laughs in my face and turns aside the blade and kisses me so that I am like a puppy who rolls over.

Remedios. She is a woman fit for kings, a woman to raise warriors of either sex. I can see her even with my eyes closed as I sit upon this rock so far from Estremedura. I will play a sport with myself and ponder what she is doing, and when I return I will ask her, 'Remedios, what were you doing whilst I was away?' She is dressed in green pantaloons, but that is not difficult, since she is dressed always as a man and a warrior to boot. She is cleaning her weapon, she has it in pieces on the table, and she furrows her brow and her eyebrows almost meet in the middle, and she is saying, 'Tchhh,' because there is a mote of dust in the barrel, and if I look down the barrel my gaze meets her fine brown eye, and with my other eye I see that she is smiling at me and she has all her teeth, most exceedingly white and fine. She ties her hair behind her head, very black and straight, and I say, 'Woman, you have a horse's rump upon your head, I will have it cut off and we will wind it into bowstrings or stuff cushions,' and she replies most boldly and without hesitation, 'Querido, I will geld you with it.' It is fine strong hair.

How upside-down is the world! I am the least of men when before I was life and death, ordering the execution of emperors and founding fair cities bulging with slaves, using gold toothpicks and having my cuirass burnished by women using donkey-piss and their own hair. And afterwards I would give the prettiest a good lancing. Those were the days. Now I owe my life to an Indian. The dishonour of it, to be lifted from death's embrace by the black arts, I, a Catholic servant of His Catholic Majesty. To be jerked from heaven to a world where women rule and even children read, their noses crammed in books like priests. It is a sacrilege, and now my armour rusts and when I kick a dog, it bites me.

I find that I have descendants who refuse me my ring, and Señor Dionisio Vivo says, 'Come, it is time to be educated in the modern world,' and I say, 'A thousand shits on your modern world,' but he takes my arm and explains the principles of flight and the abominations of democracy, as though there had been no advance since ancient Greece. And afterwards I come home and I see Remedios, and my heart lifts as she kisses my beard and says, 'Did you have a nice day at school?' and I say with all humility, 'Woman, remove your clothes,' and she takes them off, and just as I have unbuckled all my accoutrements with prodigious haste and fumbling, she slips her clothes back upon her body and says, 'Querido, it is time you learned romance,' and I raise my voice and the very mountains tremble with my oaths, and she pats my cheek and says, 'Querido, how sweet you are.' A woman is the Devil's work, by God.

## 15  *Concepcion*

Concepcion had cooked fish in dende oil, and now she was braising it in a sauce of peppers, garlic and tomatoes. It was going to be so tender that the flesh would fall off the bones, first one side, and then the other. If she was very careful the fillets would not break up at all, and she would be able to turn them over with the spatula and pick out what was left of the bones with the tip of a knife. She would purse her lips with the concentration, perhaps everything would turn out right, and then she would pick out the tiny roundels of flesh in front of the gills and eat them herself, before throwing the head and fins out of the scullery door for the stray cats. The roundels were the most delicate and delicious bits, and they were the only thing that she ever withheld from the Cardinal.

She referred to him as her 'cadenay', which in Quechua means 'my chain', and although the Indians commonly refer to their spouses in this way, and nothing should be read into it, it was in her case particularly appropriate, for Concepcion was bound to him by every link of her being.

She had been only thirteen when she had been taken on in the kitchens and old Mama Cuchara had taught her the polite way to curtsey to the Cardinal and stand behind him when he ate, waiting for his requests, pretending not to notice when the peas scattered from his fork or a morsel of food fell onto the tablecloth. It was her job to knock discreetly upon his study door in the mornings and deliver him a silver pitcher of rich coffee and the bread rolls, and to run back there when he pulled the chord of the bell to ask for a jug of water or a piece of fruit. Sometimes he used to raise an eyebrow at her scurrying and bobbing, and would say, 'Calm down, my child, it is not so important that you should wear out the palace with bustling,' and she would smile and curtsey as she had been taught, and say, 'No, Your Eminence.'

He was very handsome in those days in his ecclesiastical robes, with his greying hair and his black eyebrows, his fine European complexion and his eyes the colour of a lake on a cloudy day that always looked down at her from a height even when he was seated, and which seemed to be the filter of so much knowledge. When he patted her on the head or put his hand on her shoulder in a paternal way, it was as though for a moment a lacuna had been plugged. She had never known her own father, her mother had been crushed by a police van whilst lying drunk in the darkness of an alleyway, and that was how she had ended up with the Sisters Of Charity, who sent her to the palace to work in the kitchens. Because the Cardinal was her new father, she sometimes responded to his caring gestures in the way that a daughter would, and sometimes she allowed the physical space between them to disappear, such as when he showed her an interesting illustration in a book or together they smelled the perfume of a flower. Sometimes their faces touched, and he would feel the soft caress of her hair on his cheeks, catching the scent of a young girl somewhere amongst the odours of onions and polish. One day he stroked her cheek and said, 'You are a very sweet child; how I envy you your purity and innocence,' and with her blossoming intuition she had deduced from this that he was sad and lonely. Her heart was moved by his sorrow, and her belly stirred with the first intimations of love.

Concepcion calculated time by the passage of her menstruation. It was at the fortieth menstruation that Mama Cuchara died and left her in charge of the kitchens, and just after the sixtieth that she was in the room when His Eminence had his first attack. The Cardinal was standing by the window with his hand on the curtain chord when suddenly an expression of panic crossed his face, his breath whistled with a sharp intake, and both arms went to his stomach as he doubled over and panted. With one hand he groped for the table, and he fell into his chair with his mouth wide open and tears of pain in his eyes.

She was helpless and undecided for a moment, but then she ran to him and knelt down before him. He gasped again, and she instinctively circled him with her arms and hugged him, whispering as he rocked the words that she been used to hear from her own mother in those distant times when she had had someone to embrace: 'Tranquilo, tranquilo.'

'O, I have a terrible pain,' he said, throwing back his head, 'o, it is terrible. Concepcion, help me, for the love of God.'

She held him tightly, pressing the side of her head against his until the ratcheting breath eased and subsided. He relaxed and placed his hand on her arm in a kind of confidential gesture of appreciation, and at that point the fear of losing him and the love that had been growing in her belly combined in a conspiracy of fate, and she kissed him fully upon the lips.

When their mouths parted everything had changed. The whole basis of their relationship had been knocked aside as if by earthquake, and neither of them had any words to back away or to go forward. The Cardinal looked into her eyes and saw that the pupils were as large as moons. He saw that her young lips were moist and vulnerable, and he saw the dark little mulatta freckles upon her cheeks. It was a moment of decision, a point where he was forced to choose between the laws of nature as God made them, and the laws of the Church and a censorious world.

It was not as if he had been unaware of the covert machinations of the natural love that had been growing as imperceptibly as a tree. He had often found her slender young form materialising in his imagination as he sat at his desk pondering some administrative conundrum, or, God forgive him, when he was upon his knees praying for a sign that he would be delivered from his imperfection. More than once he had found himself speculating upon the impossibilities of this temptation; a girl one-fourth of his age, a mulatta, uneducated, probably barely a Catholic, and he vowed to chastity and a life of love directed not to this but to another world. This was no prostitute to be visited furtively and disguised, to be confessed obliquely and forgotten until the next time; this was Concepcion, who had placed her trust in him and was barely more than a child.

She took the choice away from him. She sat in his lap and hugged him with such fierce loyalty that his heart was unfathomably touched, and his hands that had been lying on his knees as though he had disowned them were suddenly raised to circle her. 'I have never been loved before,' he said, and immediately wondered why he had said it.

'I, too, am an orphan,' she murmured, and although he had not meant to imply this with what he had said, he did not deny it. He thought of his demented dead mother with her obscene collection of furs, and his father, perpetually absent, speculating in government bonds and buying one car after another, using his position to climb the ladder of the oligarchy that was also a plutocracy. 'Well, then, we are both orphans,' and he laughed softly, thinking that even God had been an absent father, impossible to please.

Knowing his bitterness and solitude without knowing them by those words, she continued to embrace him, and with a forefinger she caressed his ear and played with the hair of his temple. 'We should not be doing this,' he said.

'Tchaa,' she went, in the immemorial peasant manner, and with this one interjection dismissed centuries of clerical tradition and all the edifice of casuistry which keeps cold the beds of those who elect to follow heaven. The Cardinal was so taken by the force of her argument that he laughed again, abruptly becoming nothing more than a man in love with a woman. He returned her kiss.

In bed with the young Concepcion, moving together limb to limb, adrift upon some ocean where there is no more self and no more earth, where darkness and light are one and the same thing, where consciousness explodes at once violently and with tranquillity, Cardinal Guzman knew at last the gentle bliss of Eden. In the twilight aftermath of their love, hovering between sleep and death, he dreamed of nakedness in cool places. He dreamed that the sun became the moon, that God walked the earth in the guise of an angel, that there was a place where jaguars slept with fauns between their paws, that he and Concepcion lived alone in a world of fruit and birds, that somewhere one could awake in the dew and run without any purpose other than to rejoice in the body's ecstasy.

Sometimes he had been cruel to her during their time together; there had been the terrible fear of discovery that had led him to be curt and imperious with her when there was anyone else present, and there had been the crises of conscience that had caused him to strike her and call her 'the tool of the Devil' or 'Satan's paw', as though he could force her to usurp the place of Eve as the source of blame. There had been the time when, after a night of prayer prostrate before the altar, he had summoned her and dismissed her without explanation or compassion, so that she had fled away in tears and he had had to repent and send a messenger after her to bring her back.

But when the child arrived and became the scandal of the palace, he realised that the whole hierarchy of the Church knew of his affair and had kept silent for fear of his authority. He knew it by the way that people looked at him, by the conspiratorial manner in which they smirked when Concepcion entered the room bearing refreshments, and by the fashion that their expressions betrayed contempt whenever he took a moral stand upon an issue. He began to rely upon his office rather than his humanity in order to get things done.

The child was a secret delight to him that he could never own. When he placed his hands upon its head and called it 'my son', it was a pleasure to him that he could mean it other than figuratively, and he would dandle it upon his knee and allow it to tug at his crucifix with chocolate-plastered fingers. He would not object when a great string of saliva descended onto his robes, or when the child suddenly eructated vomit as children do. Concepcion said that when he was born, Cristobal was born laughing; thereafter he provided his father with happiness to outweigh his guilt and his anxiety, allowing him to experience another variety of affection that otherwise would have been denied him.

The couple settled into a relationship that was very like a marriage, except that it was unavowed and furtive. It survived through the years with its gentle routine of nocturnal assignations and meaningful glances, and it even survived the Cardinal's ever more frequent demonic visitations. When the devils arrived it would be Concepcion who would take him by the shoulders and steady him until the terror had abated, who would soothe him with motherly noises and bring him his crucifix to hold.

It was also she who dealt with his attacks of abdominal pain. The second one occurred a year after the first, and therafter they happened at least once every three months. She never understood (because he never told her) that the reason for his never consulting a doctor was that he felt, with a strange logic, that they were a punishment sufficient to cleanse him of his sins so that they were washed away. In this way they never accumulated so much that he felt he had to give up Concepcion in order to expunge them altogether.

So it was that she was making him fish cooked in dende oil so many years later, secure in the knowledge that she was with him for life. In any case, what would there be for her if she left? Prostitution and beggary? What would there be for young Cristobal? A job in the chrysanthemum-houses where one got skin diseases and died of tumours? A job polishing shoes in the streets and a dwelling place in the sewers? No, she was happy making fish in dende oil, and she would take it up to him so that he could eat it before Monsignor Rechin Anquilar arrived, and maybe it would do his stomach some good.

# 16 *In Which His Excellency President Veracruz Wins The General Election Without Rigging It Very Much (1)*

'Well, gentlemen, my term of office is rapidly drawing to a close, and it is no longer possible to temporise. Allow me to remind you of what you already know, which is that your jobs as well as mine are at stake, so let us have no fuel for rumours about cabinet splits and longshots for my office, OK?'

'Boss, this is not a good time for an election. The effects of the Los Puercos victory vote cannot be duplicated this time, because we have had no such further victories on account of having had no wars. We have no one against whom to declare a war at the moment, the situation is very bad.' This was Emperador Ignacio Coriolano speaking his mind at the meeting of the cabinet in the Presidential Palace.

'Emperador, how many times do I have to ask you not to call me "boss"? We are not in Panama now. Can't we declare war on East Germany? I am sure that would increase our grants from the United States, and the physical dangers would be very small.'

The members of the cabinet exchanged resigned glances; 'Your Excellency, may I remind you that East and West Germany are nowadays one country?' It was the Minister for Foreign Affairs, a huge, suave man in a velvet smoking-jacket, who had been humorously appointed to that office because his wife was Norwegian and his mistress was French.

His Excellency appeared to be disconcerted by this news. Wearily he passed his hand over his brow. 'Truly,' he said, 'one is so busy these days that one's job prevents one from keeping up with events. This must be the reason why the East German Ambassador no longer comes to official functions and has ceased to send me gifts of inedible sausages.'

'Why do we not just have the ballot boxes filled in advance, as we did last time?' asked Emperador, who for notorious reasons always smelled of anchovies.

'There was a scandal last time, when the number of voters turned

96

out to be three times the number of the population,' replied His Excellency, 'and in any case, I seem to detect that times are changing. I mean, these days one has to do it right. One cannot occupy the moral high ground against the coca people, and then go and lose it because of corruption scandals.'

'What we need is a few coups,' observed the Minister for Foreign Affairs. His Excellency appeared extremely shocked, and the Minister hastily added, 'I mean, Your Excellency, that undemocratic coups always increase the popularity of democratic governments. Is there no young colonel who could stage an abortive foco in return for a little something?'

'We've shot ourselves in the foot here,' interjected the Minister for Internal Affairs. 'Ever since we appointed General Hernando Montes Sosa to be chief of the General Staff it has become impossible to do things of this kind. He has established absolute discipline in the Armed Services and thrown out all the troublemakers. No one will do anything without his permission, and he won't do anything without ours.'

'Damn,' exclaimed the President, who had appointed the man for precisely the reasons that were now proving an obstacle. 'Maybe we can try the Communists.'

'There would be more chance with a Conservative,' said Emperador. 'There are fourteen Communist parties of different complexions now, and it is damned hard to find one of the old Stalinist school. They have all turned into soggy Liberals.'

'We are the Liberals,' said His Excellency stiffly.

'No one is suggesting that we are soggy, though,' said Emperador hastily. 'I suggest that we ask the Minister of the Interior to find a Conservative to do it.'

'I'll do it,' said the aforementioned minister, who was the token female in the political set-up, and had resolved to keep her place by being even more devious, mendacious, brown-nosed and calculating than the men. The people used to refer to her as 'Eva Perón' on account of her dubious antecedents and her penchant for populist escapades. She was to be seen almost daily in the newspapers, kissing stray dogs, weeping eloquently at the scenes of mining disasters, or shaking a proferred stump of the non-contagious variety of leper. 'But,' said Eva, 'why not simply pretend that there has been a coup attempt? It would be cheap, simple, non-dangerous. All one has to do is release a statement to the press, and then His Excellency can go on television and say something sobering about it, and then I can go on television saying how he heroically saved us by tackling the armed man in person, and then Emperador can go on television and say that it was the Conservatives. Then we can look at the polls, and if our popularity is high we can start the election immediately, but if it is not high enough we can declare a state of emergency so that we can delay a little . . .'

'Señora, if I may interrupt, I agree entirely with this notable plan, but I propose that we declare a state of emergency in any case, but still go ahead with the elections on the grounds that we cannot countenance even an emergency interfering with the due processes of democracy. I think that would impress the electorate most favourably.'

'Very good, Emperador,' said His Excellency, 'our slogan will be "Democracy is Safe in Our Hands".'

As it was decided, so it happened. The Ambassador in the United States went to a joke and novelty shop to purchase a packet of realistic adhesive bullet-holes such as one finds on the windscreens of the cars of the young men of that country, and sent them home in the diplomatic bag. His Excellency personally stuck them onto the presidential limousine, and appeared on television looking both calm and dignified. Eva Perón appeared on the news and, her eyes shining with admiration, explained how His Excellency had thwarted the gunman by wrestling the weapon from his grasp, whereupon the would-be assassin had taken to his heels. Emperador Ignacio Coriolano appeared on television to announce that in his opinion it was part of a Conservative anti-democractic conspiracy to eliminate the principal electoral asset of the Liberal Party. His Excellency announced a state of emergency and simultaneously proclaimed the election for the twelfth of June.

All at once the Conservatives, funded by industry and by covert donations from the Church, countered by erecting enormous placards all over the country. They depicted His Excellency and Eva Perón with cartoon bubbles coming out of their mouths. Eva was saying, 'What did we have in this country before we had candles?' and His Excellency was saying, 'Electricity.'

What was most discomfiting and wounding about this was that it was largely true. Out of the kindness of their hearts the Norwegians had constructed a miraculous system of hydroelectric plants that in theory would not only have supplied enough electricity to cater for the country as it was, but would also have been sufficient to power His Excellency's plans for industrial expansion. But there had been that business about the abduction of Regina Olsen during the time of the disappearances, which had caused so much diplomatic friction with Norway that when all the projects were completed the Norwegians had refused to stay behind and help run the power stations that they had built. All the indigenous electrical engineers had migrated to Brazil to help on the giant dam on the border with Paraguay, and would not come back to work on the pitiful wages offered by the government, and so the running of the turbines was left to people who would have had difficulty in wiring a plug and screwing in a lightbulb. Furthermore, there was a guerrilla group inspired by the Sendero Luminoso who were dedicated to bringing progress and the liberation of the masses, a project they deemed to be best achieved by the expedient of blowing up powerlines and pylons. In this way it was hoped that the proletariat could be brought forth out of the darkness by being plunged into it, and the power-cut became a way of life.

People very quickly realised that the redundant poles snaking their way over the landscape were marvellously suited to the building of bridges and water-towers, and that the cables were excellent for melting down and casting into statuettes for the tourist market in the capital. In this way the cables were exported, many of them, no doubt, back to Norway. The nation's lightbulbs were unscrewed from their sockets and used instead of bottles for target practice, and the flex in the houses ended up holding the doors onto people's cars. Electrical frigidaires and ovens became henhouses, and the turbines that were left were burned out by having nowhere to send their electricity. The great dams in the mountains settled into decrepitude, awaiting the *coup de grâce* in the form of an earthquake or a titanic explosion by courtesy of the guerrillas. The nation settled back into the comfortable routine of trimming wicks and keeping things cool in porous earthenware pots. Community life was maintained by the installation of televisions in bars and village halls, powered, as they had always been, by generators.

His Excellency caused to be erected some giant billboards of his own. They were in the style of socialist realism, and depicted a healthy-looking worker asking a blonde young woman, 'What should we have instead of Conservatives?' and the young woman was replying, 'Idealists.' The Conservatives continued this war of riddles by putting up more of their own. This one showed His Excellency in an Uncle Sam costume with dollars sticking out of his ears, his nose and mouth unmistakably streaked with excrement, and underneath a woman was asking a man, 'What should we have instead of an arselicker?' She was being answered by Lopez, leader of the Conservatives, dressed in the colours of the flag, who was saying, 'A Patriot.'

His Excellency was irritated to the core, and also outraged. He was outraged because everyone knew that the Conservatives were partly funded from Washington, and he was irritated because he had been intending to play the anti-gringo card himself, a sure election-winner if ever there was one. For three days he stormed about the Presidential Palace, smacking his fist into his palm and exclaiming, 'Damn, damn, damn,' until he suddenly had some good ideas all at once, and threw the whole party into a propaganda offensive.

# 17  *How Dionisio Inadvertently Started The Battle Of* Doña Barbara

Leaving his two black jaguars behind to be tended by Farides and Profesor Luis, Dionisio set off on foot to the little village of Santa Maria Virgen. Having learned to cover enormous distances of difficult terrain by walking slowly, he arrived there before noon and accepted a tinto from the people in the first house. 'How everything has changed,' he remarked to the old man who brought him the coffee. The two men looked along the street towards the plaza, and the old man smiled, revealing three crooked yellow teeth. In a voice cracked by tobacco and the thin air, the old man made an expansive gesture and said, 'Ay, ay, it is just as it was before, when I was young and getting girls pregnant behind the cemetery wall.'

Dionisio smiled. 'You were not so bad as that, viejo.'

'But he tried to be,' exclaimed the old man's wife, who had not been able to resist eavesdropping behind the door, where she had been hanging a string of salted fish.

The old man pretended to be exasperated; he waved his arms again, saying, 'Ay, these women, it is their vocation to hold out the prospect of pleasure, and then to deny it and delay it until you are defeated and go back to your goats.'

'You are an old goat,' she said. 'You belong with them.'

'To get back to the subject,' said Dionisio, 'I notice that the street is swept and the houses have been whitewashed. Even the chickens look healthy.'

'El Jerarca is dead,' observed the old woman, 'and that is the explanation. In the time of cocaine he was a plague all to himself. When we went back to chewing the leaves, everything went back to the way it was before.'

When Dionisio shook hands and walked away towards the choza belonging to the two girls, the old woman held up her hand and muttered, 'God bless the Deliverer.' Then she returned towards her husband and struck him across the side of the head. 'I never did deny you pleasure, after we were married.'

The old man said, 'We never were married.' Whereupon the old woman was silent for a moment's reflection. 'A good thing too,' she replied. 'I couldn't have stood being married to you all this time.'

Dionisio went to find his car, and discovered that it had been decorated with white flowers. He was looking at it wonderingly when the two girls came out. One of them touched his arm respectfully, and said, 'It is two years that you killed El Jerarca.' Dionisio sighed, half wishing that life could be rewritten. He kissed them both upon the cheek and said, 'I have to take the car today, and I fear that the flowers will soon be lost.'

Ines, the younger of the two, shrugged and smiled. 'That is in the nature of flowers.' She ran inside and brought out a slab of guava jelly wrapped in palm leaf 'for the journey', which he took with thanks. Rather than trouble the aged battery he cranked the car to life, and the girls cried 'Whooba' and clapped their hands at the aromatic cloud of blue smoke that shot from the exhaust and whipped away with the dust devils down the side of the mountain.

Dionisio drove into his old home town of Ipasueño and parked in the plaza. Behind him the road to Santa Maria Virgen was strewn with white flowers, an unexpected bonus for the trains of mules carrying alfalfa, bootlaces, clockwork toys, imitation baseball caps, and tambos of coca leaves compressed into cheek-sized wads.

In response to his fame Dionisio had perfected the art of inconspicuousness. It was not that he became invisible, as everybody said, but that he would walk in such away that nobody noticed his presence until after he had already gone, giving rise to the popular misconception that he was a ghost. He walked first to the Barrio Jerarca, and noticed that it had become shabby, but that the atmosphere of menace had disappeared. He paused beneath the lamppost where they had suspended Pablo Ecobandodo's body, and saw that the gilded church was peeling and becoming lopsided. He was pleased at such decay, because the splendour of its past had been created with coca money; it had been a shameful splendour at the price of human blood, and as everybody knows, the evils of the cocaine trade are not the consequence of poverty but of wealth.

He went to the police station and asked for Agustin. The young policeman came out and shook his hand, embracing him, and noting with pleasure that Dionisio still had Ramón's gun, saying, 'Dio', I really ought to take that back from you. It is police property, and so it is fortunate that I have not noticed it.'

'Nonetheless,' replied Dionisio, 'it brings you something,' and he removed the medicine-bottle cork from the barrel and shook out a thin cigar, giving it to Agustin. 'In memory of Ramón; it is for you, if you will let me use the police telephone for nothing.'

Agustin laughed wryly. 'I shall arrest you for attempting to bribe a police officer, and then I shall discharge you if you will come out and take a copa with me. The telephone is in there.'

Dionisio rang up the offices of La Oveja Blanca, 'publishers of books in the area of the countries of the Castilian idiom', immediately causing a flurry of activity by giving his name and asking to speak to the Sales Manager, who promptly came to the telephone, begging to be of service. When Dionisio explained that he wanted any surplus of good books that they had been unable to sell, remainders of old editions, editions damaged but readable, the Sales Manager, after recovering from his surprise, said that they had a large stock of *Doña Barbara* by Romulo Gallegos; 'We brought it out thinking that the copyright was finished, and then we discovered that a company in Venezuela still had the rights, and therefore we could not sell it . . . you want me to send one hundred copies to Ipasueña Police Station? Are you serious? . . . OK, you are serious, I apologise, I was taken by surprise . . . Yes, OK. I will send anything else there from time to time that is not cheap romances and other rubbish . . . respectfully, Señor Vivo, we do not publish any rubbish.' Then the Sales Manager asked for a little something in return, and Dionisio listened to what it was. 'Yes,' he said, 'it is alright with me if you use the slogan "Dionisio Vivo endorses our books", but you cannot use the slogan to endorse any rubbish . . . yes, I know that you publish no rubbish, but if by any chance you find yourself doing so, you cannot use my name to advertise it, OK?'

Agustin and Dionisio went to Madame Rosa's whorehouse to take a couple of drinks and reminisce about the old times when bodies kept appearing in Dionisio's garden when Ramón was still alive, when Anica was still alive. Then Dionisio went up to the cemetery and sat for a while by Ramón's grave, talking to him as though he were there. He placed one of the white flowers upon it and then went to visit Anica. He saw that the glass across the smiling photograph was cracked. He kissed the end of his fingers and touched them to the image. He placed two white flowers there, and then returned to Madame Rosa's to see Velvet Luisa, because he needed someone to embrace and to understand his emptiness.

# 18 *In Which His Excellency President Veracruz Wins The General Election Without Rigging It Very Much (2)*

Dr Galico was the father of the nation; his influence could everywhere still be felt, the presence of his ghost was palpable and pervasive. He alone had gone against the grain at the time when the leaders of the newly independent states were trying to outdo each other in the Europeanisation of themselves and their lands. It is commonly said that the Latin American is more European than a Spaniard, because a Spaniard is a Spaniard before he is a European. And the same goes for a Frenchman, who is French before anything else, and the same goes for all the other peoples of Europe. Latin Americans see Europe from the outside, as a whole, and so they are able to be true members of that continent without even visiting it.

But not Dr Galico, the foremost indigenist of his time. He encouraged the learning of Indian languages, and permitted no foreign trade of any kind, his aim being self-sufficiency and the avoidance of foreign economic domination. During his entire dictatorship of thirty-one years, three months and twelve days, not a single citizen left the country and only four foreigners came in, on condition that they never tried to leave. A botanist who tried to escape was hung from a tree in front of the palace and shot at until he fell to pieces small enough to be consumed by vultures without the necessity of further rending the remains.

No historian has ever been quite sure as to whether or not Dr Galico was an enlightened benefactor or a criminal lunatic, but this was never an obstacle to his posthumous elevation to national hero. Most national heroes of all countries have been criminal lunatics. He had the distinction of having beaten General Belgrano in battle, at dominoes, and at arm-wrestling, and had banned the study of the philosophy of William of Ockham on the grounds that there is no reason why there should not be limitless unnecessary multiplication of entities.

It so happened that Dr Galico had taken an Indian mistress as consolation for the religiously inspired reluctance of his wife, who would only co-operate on his saint's day. This Indian woman soon picked up as many airs and graces as a woman in her position does, and effectively became first lady of the nation. Dr Galico's impulsive use of his absolute power saw to it that even the cream of society swallowed their scruples and treated her with supreme respect and deference, not daring to refuse her invitations to come and bathe naked in the river before watching a corrida involving so many bulls that the streets flowed with blood for two days afterwards, permanently changing their colour in the process.

When Dr Galico died and had been safely interred in a soldier's coffin, society turned against Prepucia (so nicknamed on account of her preferred shape of hat) and she was forced to flee in ignominy across the frontiers. She found her way to Paris on board a ship in which the sailors exacted a cruel fee for her passage, and died there a pauper's death. Her bones were to be found in the cemetery at St Sulpice, and it was this fact that supplied His Excellency with an inspiration on that afternoon after the Conservatives had pipped him to the post in the anti-gringo stakes and he had been furious for three days. He too could play the patriotic card.

The very first thing that he did was to announce that he intended to change the refereeing decision in the World Cup, that had seen the national team knocked out in the second round. The Hungarian referee had spotted a handball designed to deflect a goalbound shot, and had awarded a penalty which duly landed in the net. Everyone in the entire world had witnessed the blatant attempt at cheating on their televisions; that is everyone except the loyal citizens of this country. A mood of aggrieved outrage swept across the land, girls wept, soldiers committed suicide, and stones hailed through the windows of the Hungarian Embassy. It was on this tide of bad feeling that President Veracruz surfed to his first patriotic *coup de maître*, by announcing that he personally was going to organise a mass petitioning of FIFA in order to have the decision reversed. Accordingly his party workers scoured the country from the depths of the jungle to the tips of the sierra, collecting signatures and marks, and in party offices until late at night the faithful forged further inventive signatures which upon close scrutiny would have revealed that many citizens were called Ronald Reagan, Princess Diana, Nikita Khrushchev, Luciano Pavarotti, Donald Duck, Chairman Mao and Bugs Bunny, living at such addresses as Bishop's Pussy, South Fork, Tiananmen Square, and the Sydney Opera House.

Conservatives defected in droves to the Liberal Party when the cubic metre of signatures was delivered to the Headquarters of FIFA by the Ambassador to the United Nations. Demonstrators took to the streets of the capital to shout 'Viva Veracruz' and to wave placards depicting him in the classic pose of the statues of Dr Galico, with one hand behind his back and the other clenched upraised in defiance of the world. His Excellency arranged for a debate very late at night in the National Assembly to discuss foreign policy with respect to Andorra, and sent out letters to every Liberal representative ordering them to be there without fail. As anticipated, no Conservatives arrived at all, and an emergency motion was passed unanimously, awarding His Excellency the title of 'The National Personification' for his championing of the nation's footballing honour.

The next thing that he did was to announce that henceforth his wife would be banished from the palace in working hours. On the television news he was seen explaining to the political correspondent that his love for his wife was so great that he found that her presence in the palace comprised a major temptation to be distracted from the business of state, and Madame Veracruz was seen explaining that, much as it grieved her to be parted from her spouse for even one minute of the day, she was consenting to the arrangement in the interest of good government. Naturally she continued to live in the palace, sit on her husband's knee feeding him with Turkish delight in exchange for favours for her friends, and draw him away at odd hours in order to experiment in sexual alchemy; but His Excellency had succeeded nonetheless in playing simultaneously the statesman card and that of the happy family man.

His Excellency was wondering what ploy he could implement next before he worked his masterstroke, when the Foreign Secretary arrived, excited and out of breath. 'Your Excellency,' he exclaimed upon bursting into the Presidential office, 'I have received a communication . . .'

'From the Archangel Gabriel, Garcilaso?' His Excellency put down the book he was reading about the sexual magic of the Order of

Oriental Templars. He was on the section concerning the homosexual practises of the secret degree, and his eyebrows had practically reached the back of his head.

'How did you know?' asked Lopez Garcilaso Vallejo, setting down his massively muscular bulk in the revolving chair normally occupied by the secretary.

His Excellency sighed with resignation. 'It has an inevitability about it. What is it this time, another message about nationalising the abattoirs? Really I cannot see the purpose of it. How is your dear wife and your pretty little French mistress, eh?'

'They are both well and at each other's throats as usual, boss, it was a mistake to put them both in the same house. Listen, the Archangel came to me, and do you know what he said? He said, "Everyone loves a stud."'

'"Everyone loves a stud?"' repeated his Excellency.

'Yes, boss, he said just that, and then I realised; it's God's own truth. If we let it be known that you're a stud, even at your age, everyone will vote for you, no horseshit.'

President Veracruz bridled. 'And what's this "even at my age" got to do with it? I can assure you that all is in order.'

'Proves my point, boss. You are a stud, and we should make capital out of it. We can put up posters "Vote for the Stud", it's a winner for sure.'

His Excellency leaned back in his chair. 'Garcilaso, it's brilliant, but perhaps we could go for something a little more subtle, no? And please do not call me boss; how many times do I have to ask?'

And so it was that 'Eva Perón' rang up the director of television news and current affairs, proposing a little deal. There was at that time a bill before the National Assembly called the 'Elimination Of Bias In The Media Bill', which His Excellency had dreamed up because he was convinced that all the media were either unreconstructed Communists or arrant Conservatives. He felt positively persecuted by the reportage in the news and in the exposé programmes such as *Did You Know?* and *The World Today*. His bill was designed to ensure that every time a case was made against him, one of his spokesmen should be consulted in order to balance it out. Almost everyone was opposed to the bill, and supported it at the same time. True, there were voices raised in defence of free speech and the ability of the public to judge for itself, but the real situation was that the Liberals were in favour of it because it would shut the Conservatives up in times of Liberal rule. But the Liberals were also opposed to it, because if the Conservatives should come to power they would undoubtedly use the measures of the bill to stifle Liberal criticism. The Conservatives supported and opposed the bill for the same kinds of reason, and no one was sure whether or not to vote for it in case the other side got elected.

The one faction that utterly opposed the bill in any form were the media themselves, since it would be utterly impossible to make current affairs programmes that were forty-five mintes long and contained everybody's point of view. Journalists regarded the whole thing as a cynical attempt at underhand censorship, designed to save the government from embarrassing revelations. Which of course it was.

Eva Perón's little deal was that the bill would be dropped 'in view of concerns about the constitutional right of free speech', in return for a documentary about His Excellency. She informed the director that the latter would be only too pleased to give him a list of potential interviewees. Meanwhile Emperador Ignacio Coriolano (or 'Emperor Cunnilingus the Insatiable', as he was more usually known) rounded up the many retired and active whores of his acquaintance, and briefed them thoroughly about what they could or could not say.

Thus it was that the nation was simultaneously scandalised and thrilled to hear glowing tributes to His Excellency's prowess, and was edified to discover that since his marriage this prowess had been solely at the service of Madame Veracruz, who spoke of it obliquely, coyly, and with a starry-eyed expression of gratitude and admiration. In this way His Excellency was able to play all at a stroke the family card, the defender of the constitution card, and the stud card. It remained only to play the patriotic card once more, bringing us back to the place where we began, with Dr Galico and his mistress Prepucia.

To put it in short, His Excellency arranged for her body to be brought back from Paris and laid alongside the Doctor in the pantheon. The body arrived in a military transport plane flying the national flag in yellow for the sands of the sea, red for the blood of the nation's martyrs, green for the forests, and blue for the sky. A guard of honour of mounted dragoons in shining cuirasses and thigh boots accompanied the gun carriage to the Presidential Palace, where His Excellency removed from the coffin the bottles of Chanel No. 5, the Napoleon brandy, the boxes of truffles, the book he had ordered describing the rituals of the Martinist Order, the Russian caviar, and the working model of a guillotine that chopped off the ends of cigars. He was placing the lid over the pathetic yellow bones and shrunken skin of Prepucia when he was summoned to the telephone to talk to His Eminence, Cardinal Dominic Trujillo Guzman.

The Cardinal said simply, 'Your Excellency, you cannot allow this sacrilege. The pantheon is hallowed ground, and the Church cannot permit that a man's mistress should be buried alongside him and his legitimate wife. It cannot possibly be allowed. The woman was not even a Christian.'

His Excellency, who had no time at all for the Cardinal, believing him to be little better than a scarlet-clad oligarch, brusquely told him, 'Your Eminence, I cannot talk to you now, but I will ring you back as soon as I can.' He put the telephone down and then asked for the Cardinal's file from the office of the Interior Ministry Internal Security Service. It was duly delivered, and His Excellency perused it with some amusement before returning the Cardinal's call.

'Am I to understand,' he asked, 'that whereas the Church does not permit me to bury a man's mistress in his grave, it does permit its dignitaries to have mistresses of their own and an illegitimate child or two? Am I correct in assuming that the Church permits embezzlement and nocturnal visits to brothels, admittedly in disguise? I seek your spiritual guidance, Your Eminence.' There was a long silence, and then the Cardinal hung up.

The funeral and burial were a magnificent success, mostly because a national holiday was declared that permitted the population to pour into the streets to cheer the gorgeous cortège, wave flags, become inebriated, and end up in the gutters and alleyways vomiting up the arepas and the empanadas that they had unwisely consumed along with the pisco. It was a winner, and not only for the stray dogs that cleared up the mess.

President Veracruz was returned to office with an enormous majority for the third time, and yet the ballot boxes were filled in advance only with enough votes to make up for the eighty per cent who never bothered to vote. The country's demographers noted with astonishment and perplexity that the number of votes was virtually the same as the number of registered voters, and agreed that times had changed indeed. The newspapers ingratiatingly led with the headline 'Democracy Is Safe In His Hands', and His Excellency decided to reward himself with a twenty-two month diplomatic tour of the world. He intended to find the tomb of Christian Rosencreutz, make love in the central chamber of the Great Pyramid (in order to rejuvenate himself), and in California he intended to have an operation that would enable him to achieve tumescence at will.

It is very likely that if he had not paralysed the administration of the country by his absence, then the events recounted here would never have happened. True, he left the government to his cabinet, but they never knew what to do, and took to consulting the United States Ambassador, who from time immemorial had always been nicknamed 'The Real President'. But no one in the country had the constitutional power to declare an emergency or to mobilise the Armed Forces, and the only guidance from His Excellency was a directive telegraphed from Italy that henceforth all citizens must wear a hat, so that they could doff it in the event of meeting him unexpectedly.

# 19 *Monsignor Rechin Anquilar*

'Shall I wipe that snot from your nose, Cristobal?' asked the Cardinal, and the little boy replied, 'No, it's all right, I'll eat it.'

Before His Eminence could stop him, Cristobal had spread the mucus on the back of his hand and removed it with one efficient sweep of his tongue. 'Yum,' he said. 'It's salty.'

'Cristobal, that is horrible, you really must not do it,' remonstrated His Eminence, and the little boy reflected a moment. Ingenuously he raised his eyes and observed, 'I saw a dog licking itself, that's not very nice, is it?'

'No it is not,' said His Eminence, amused, 'but they only do that because they have no sponges and soap.'

'Or hands,' said the little boy. 'Mama says that if I am bad I will be reborn as a dog, and then I'll have to lick myself, won't I? What do you think it's like?'

'Mama should not tell you things like that. When you die you go to heaven if you have been good, and to hell if you have been bad.'

Cristobal sent a toy car rattling across the polished tiles, and it collided with the leg of a table. 'O Jesus,' he exclaimed in his innocent treble. The Cardinal was shocked and raised his voice a little: 'Don't say that. God does not like people to call him when they don't need to. One day you will call him and he won't come because he is fed up with false alarms.'

'Mama says it all the time. She said it when I had that accident and she had to change my clothes, and she says it when you ring the bell to ask for something.'

His Eminence shook his head sadly, and Cristobal returned to his earlier topic. 'When I die I want to be a hummingbird.'

'Maybe God will let you be a hummingbird for some of the time when you get to heaven.' He paused. 'But you won't get there at all if you keep saying bad things.'

'Mama says that heaven would be boring. She says that all the interesting people go to hell.'

The Cardinal raised his eyes to the heavens and instructed himself to have a word with Concepcion. 'But if you go to heaven or hell you can't come back as a dog or a hummingbird, can you? So you must have been wrong about that.'

'You stay there for a bit, and then you come back as soon as there is a body waiting.'

'Your mama says that?'

Cristobal nodded sagely, and the Cardinal decided to change the subject. 'Will you clear up all these toys now? I am expecting a visitor and I don't want him to fall over and see all this mess. Put everything in a box and take it away.'

The little boy stuck his lower lip out in protest, and His Eminence said, 'That's how Indians point, by sticking their lip out, did you know that? Come on, I'll help.' His Eminence got down on his hands and knees and fished toys out from under the chairs, passing them to his illegitimate but dearly beloved son. Cristobal played briefly with each one before putting it in the big wooden box that His Eminence kept in a corner, covered with a cloth. The Cardinal returned to his chair and pulled out a handkerchief from beneath his robes. 'Come and sit on my knee a minute, Cristo'. Come and give me a hug.'

Cristobal climbed up the Cardinal's legs and kissed him wetly on the cheek. 'Are you my papa?' he asked. 'Everyone says that you are, except you and Mama.'

'I am your spiritual father,' said His Eminence gently, 'and I love you just as much as if I was your real father.' He stroked the boy's curls and squeezed softly at the back of his neck. 'Will you tell Mama that her fish was delicious? And will you tell her that I would love some of her tea that is good for my stomach? And guess what I can see?'

'What?' asked Cristobal, following the line of his father's finger. The Cardinal deftly wiped the boy's upper lip with the concealed handkerchief and said teasingly, 'I saw two horrible green slugs coming out of your nose, but now they are gone. What do you think of that?'

Cristobal looked aggrieved. 'Can I lick the handkerchief?' he demanded.

His father pulled a face and said, 'Certainly not. Now go and play in the gardens, and don't forget to tell your mama what I said about the fish and the tea.' He patted Cristobal's backside as he clambered down, and watched him run happily out of the audience chamber. He sighed and leaned back in his chair, intending to run over in his mind the things he was going to say to Monsignor Anquilar, but instead he thought about the sadness of being locked into a life that was nothing but unworthy compromise. In the distance he heard two gunshots that were the failed assassination attempt upon a visiting judge, and he went to the window. He spotted the group of pious widows before they spotted him, and he ducked back so that he would not have to bless them. The stench of urine was as bad as ever. There was a pall of smoke somewhere in the centre of the city where the coca cartels had blown up the police headquarters an hour previously, and he reflected upon the artistic way in which it blended with the first dark clouds of sunset. He practised what he was going to say when the press asked him to release a statement about these atrocities. All the usual words like 'inhuman' and 'barbarous' came to his mind, and he groped about for something more telling and original.

Concepcion came in with the medicinal tea, and he turned and smiled, 'Thank you, querida, just put it on the desk and I will come and drink it in a moment.'

'Ahorita,' said Concepcion, using the diminutive of the word 'now' that is used by everyone from mountainous regions. 'You have to drink it very hot, or it is no use.'

The Cardinal came to the desk and took a sip of the tea. It tasted exotic and bitter, but not unpleasant, and he took a deeper draught. 'Where do you find this?' he asked. 'It's not one of those barbarous country medicines is it?'

Concepcion shot him a reproving glance and said, 'Tchaa, I got it from the pharmacy,' thinking that on this occasion a lie would be tactful. The tea was made of coca leaves, yague, a drop of copal resin, some of her own urine, and desiccated llama foetus, with a little bit of ordinary tea thrown in to disguise it. She had got the recipe from the brujo up in the favelas that the Cardinal was trying to get removed.

'It does me good,' said His Eminence, 'you take good care of me.'

'I love you,' she said, and shrugged her shoulders to indicate that

that explained everything. They smiled at each other for a moment, and she gathered up the tray and left. 'She is like a cat,' he thought.

Very shortly afterwards, Monsignor Rechin Anquilar arrived, bearing a brittle smile and the gift of a missal inlaid with mother-of-pearl. As though by a flick of a switch, the Cardinal clicked out of his role as father and lover, and became every inch the primate. He grew stiffer, his movements more dignified and considered, and his smile more reluctant. He adopted a serious and apostolic air, and waved Mgr Anquilar to a seat with a balletic sweep of the arm and a slight bow. 'How pleasant it is to meet you,' he said, 'I trust that you are well.'

Mgr Anquilar nodded, and sat down without any discernible expression upon his face. 'I am late,' he said in his dry voice. 'It was because of the traffic jams. There has been another bombing.'

The Cardinal expected him to continue his explanation, to make lamentation about what terrible times we live in, or to say something more about the traffic, but Mgr Rechin Anquilar merely placed his hands upon his lap and looked at him in a vacant but direct fashion. His Eminence was to discover that Anquilar was taciturn and humourless.

'Read this,' said His Eminence, handing over the report of the Holy Office, 'but ignore the scurrilous attacks on the Church and the pieces composed by Communists.' His Eminence noticed that somehow Cristobal had left guava-jelly fingerprints upon it, and hoped that Anquilar would not notice and think it was him. He sat back and watched as the man read it carefully, flicking over the pages with the impatience of a man who is morally irritated. He took the opportunity to gather a first impression of he whom he was intending to appoint as the leader of the crusade of preaching.

He was a man so angular that he seemed to be composed entirely of polyhedra, and had the kind of nose that people assume to be Jewish but which in fact is aristocratically Spanish. His black habit concealed a bony body, and fell about him in such a fashion that it seemed to be a part of him. His Eminence read again his accreditation; he was forty years old, had a doctorate in Canon Law and another in the Theology of St Thomas Aquinas. He had lectured in France and in Uruguay, and was a noted authority upon the ontological argument for the existence of God. He had successfully evangelised the population of the Island of Baru, but had seen his work overthrown by a catastrophic outbreak of influenza caused by the arrival of a new missionary from Holland, and he was widely notorious for his inflexible orthodoxy. His report upon the Baru Island fiasco had concluded with the words, 'And so we find ourselves edified by the unshakeable belief that the islanders found their way to heaven earlier than they otherwise would have done, it being better for them to have died prematurely as Christians than at full term as heathens.' Here was a man who would jump at the chance to transform the nation.

'What do you think?' asked His Eminence when Mgr Anquilar had reached the last lines of the report.

'It is just as I would have expected,' he replied. 'The spiritual poverty of the people is everywhere evident.'

'I want you to do something about it,' said His Eminence.

'My life is already dedicated to that task,' said Anquilar. 'I hope that you have not found me deficient.'

'Far from it,' said His Eminence, rattled by the man's dusty voice and dry demeanour. 'My plan is to mount a crusade of evangelisation that will bring the lost sheep back into the fold, and I want you to shepherd it. I would expect you to submit accounts, but beyond that you would enjoy great autonomy. I expect you to gather together a band of men of great faith and resourcefulness who would be prepared to endure hostility and ridicule in order to bring the people back to God, and to send them to the most obscure corners of the land to drive out the Devil, so to speak.'

'So to speak?' echoed Anquilar. 'I take the Devil literally.'

'Indeed, indeed,' said the Cardinal. 'Now, will you take on the job?'

Mgr Rechin Anquilar reflected for a moment and then nodded. 'I will do God's will in the belief that it is transmitted via your office.'

His Eminence took this as it was intended, as a slight, since Anquilar had drawn attention to the distinction between a man and the office he holds. He stood up stiffly and extended his hand. Anquilar's felt bloodless, and he did not shake it for long. '*Dominus tecum*,' he said.

Anquilar returned his gaze as if through smoked glass. '*Et cum spiritu tuo*,' he responded, and the Cardinal watched him go with a sensation of apprehension in his soul. After putting his great design into motion he felt strangely empty. '*Kyrie, eleison,*' he muttered, and put his hands to his stomach. Either he was putting on weight, or his affliction was making his belly swell.

## 20  *The Battle Of* Doña Barbara

In Cochadebajo de los Gatos these was a plague of reading more insidious even than the great plague of laughing, the whimsical plague of cats, or the swinish plague of peccaries.

You could either borrow a book from Dionisio's by leaving a deposit for surety, or you could buy one outright. To this end he published a table of equivalents, setting out the price of books in the following form: 1 book = 10 mangoes = half a chicken or duck = 1 guinea pig = 20 apples = 4 pepino melons or 2 large ones = 6 grenadillos = 1 steak of llama, vicuña, sheep, pig or cow = 6 papaya (not too ripe) = 2 packs of large native cigars = 1 worn out machete ground down to make a knife = 8 roots of cassava = 3 kilos of potatoes or 2 kilos of sweet potatoes = the loan of a mule for two days = 2 decent-sized edible fish without too many bones = 3 bunches of eating bananas or 4 of cooking platanos. Any other offers at proprietor's discretion. NO YAMS, BREADFRUIT, ALCOHOL, STOLEN PROPERTY OR BULLETS.

Having the advantage of a fixed rate of exchange for real things rather than the floating rate of coin and paper representing something imaginary, this novel form of currency, unaffected by 200 per cent inflation as was the peso, almost replaced the latter and completely superseded those promissory notes issued by guerrillas in the past 'to be redeemed after the revolution'. With time Dionisio's table of equivalents became expanded to the point where it grew beyond anybody's power to memorise, and conventions arose, such as that an almost ripe tomato was worth a third more than a green one or one that was so ripe that it was only any good for putting in a Portuguese sauce.

Far worse than any confusion ever caused by the new currency was the furore caused by Dionisio's apparently innocent sale of all one hundred copies of *Doña Barbara*. In a town where television was an impossibility owing to the twelve-volt electrical supply and the absence of aerials, where the main source of stories was Aurelio's recounting of myths and legends and the reconstruction of memories in bars, the books filled a gap in people's lives that they had not hitherto perceived to be there at all.

A great hush descended, broken only by the braying of mules, the barking of dogs, the coughs and yowls of the jaguars as they ambushed each other, and the unrelenting drone of Father Garcia preaching to no one in particular in the plaza. The habit of literacy being unconsolidated, the hush lasted for an entire week whilst brows furrowed and lips silently repeated the text. Work stopped, or those working would cut alfalfa with the book in the left hand whilst the machete in the right swept aimlessly over the same spot. People read walking down the street, treading on the jaguars' tails and tripping over the kerbs, bumping into each other and forgetting to go and eat what their spouses had failed to cook because it had burned unstirred in its pot.

Even Hectoro read the book. He was convinced that reading was a habit of women and homosexuals, and so he bought it from Dionisio saying that it was for one of his wives. He buried it in the depths of his mochila so that nobody would suspect him, and he rode daily out of the city and around the upward slope of the valley. Hectoro wore a black leather glove on his rein hand, and for once in his life this hand held the book whilst the reins fell slack across the horse's neck. Hectoro read the book fiercely and with machismo, which is how he did everything; his moustache twitched, his nostrils flared at the moments of violence, and his lips uttered criticisms of Santos Luzardo for not giving Marisela the good lancing that she wanted. He burned his mouth on the cigar that was clenched in his teeth because he sucked it too hard when it was a stub and the Wizard had gone out to kill the hero, and he spat it out with an unmanly yelp, looking furtively around to make sure that there was no witness.

Hectoro read upside down, because when he was a child and his mother had taught him to read there had been only one book. His mother had taught Hectoro and his little sister at the same time, and he had had to peer over the top of the page in order to follow his mother's finger as it hesitantly followed the print.

But reading on horseback whilst the horse browsed the grasses proved to be an unmanning experience, owing to an unfortunate coincidence. Hectoro reached a phrase. It was 'the preliminary characteristic'. This phrase struck Hectoro as a real pansy phrase, a phrase worthy of the most effeminate, simpering homosexual. He bellowed with disgust at exactly the same moment that two chinchillas ran under the feet of the daydreaming horse. Startled by the terrible curse and the scurrying of the rodents, the horse reared violently and then kicked out with its back legs.

For the first and only time in his life Hectoro was thrown by a horse. He landed on his backside in an acacia, with the book still open in his left hand and a cigar still smoking between his teeth. 'Hijo de puta,' he exclaimed, 'this reading is dangerous business.' He drew out his revolver and shot the book through the centre where he had thrown it on the ground, and then he shot it again to make sure. It was for this reason that Hectoro was the only one who bought two copies of *Doña Barbara*, and for this reason that he changed his tune about reading. 'This is a thing for real men,' he declared, and from then on he read openly on horseback in the plaza, even though nobody believed he was really reading at all, since the book was upside down.

But Hectoro's experience was less bitter than that of the whole town, because there followed a plague of literary criticism, never a pretty thing at the best of times. It was an execrable time of 'guachafita', because everyone felt entitled to join in, even those who had not read it because they were illiterate and had had to listen to someone else's résumé.

The town divided into three factions: those who thought the book was unreservedly marvellous, those who believed it to be horse-manure, and those who thought it was part marvellous and part horse-manure. After everybody had finished the book there was a silence of two days whilst people thought about it and re-read certain bits. Felicidad re-read the end, where Santos Luzardo marries Marisela, in case she had missed any bits involving sex; she was disgustedly critical that what was obviously going to be the best portion had been missed out.

She had good reason to resent the lack of vicarious excitement. One day she had announced, 'I am eighteen years old now, and I am giving up whoring. I have grown out of it.' Radically opposed to chastity, she had set her cap at Don Emmanuel and had succeeded with a lamentable lack of difficulty, for he had always had a soft spot for her, mercurial, impulsive, beautiful and mischievous as she was. The trouble was that they were maintaining a separation at the time of the plague of reading. This was because one night he had eaten a pantagruelian quantity of Dolores' frijoles refritos with three eggs beaten into it. Any gentleman would have leapt out of bed and released the consequences harmlessly into the night air outside the front door.

But Don Emmanuel had an English sense of humour exacerbated by his attendance at a progressive English public school, and instead he held the covers over Felicidad's head and allowed the hurricane in his guts to belch forth uninhibited in a veritable tornado of inflammable and intensely malodorous gas. She writhed and screamed, bit and kicked, and then stormed out, vowing never to return, leaving Don Emmanuel helpless with mirth, tears streaming down his cheeks, convulsed and choking. Just now she was waiting for him to come and beg forgiveness, and she was missing him and his good points.

Misael and Sergio were intensely interested in the passages concerning the rounding up of cattle, and were in dispute over its realism. Hectoro was incensed by all the rustling and was in dispute with Josef about Santos Luzardo's reluctance to resort to bullets. Pedro, who had hunted in Venezuela, thought that the colloquialisms were all wrong, whilst old man Gomez who had been there before Pedro said that they were exactly accurate. The Mexican musicologist fell out with his best friends, the French couple Antoine and Françoise, because the former did not believe that it was realistic to expect Doña Barbara's character to change so much, and the two latter did. Ena and Lena, the identical twins married to the Mexican, pulled each other's hair out in a catfight because Ena believed that the author was unsympathetic to Doña Barbara's having been violated when she was fifteen, whereas Lena maintained that it was the author's sympathy over this and the death of Hasdrubal that made him imply that Doña Barbara eventually found salvation. Perhaps the only one who did not quarrel with her mate was Remedios, since her consort could not read, was contemptuous of stories, and was still confused about having been dead for four hundred years before Aurelio brought him back to life. Remedios thought that Doña Barbara was right to have been such a warlord, since that was all that a woman could do in a world raped to the core by men, and Consuelo insulted her vilely for this, saying that a woman should behave better than a man and not sink to his level.

The disputes reached such a peak that one day they developed into a riot, known forever afterwards as 'the Battle of *Doña Barbara*'. In this memorable fight in the plaza and on the street corners Dionisio's entire profit from the book was raided from his house and transformed into missiles. Doña Constanza started it by throwing a bag of flour at Misael, which missed and went all over Rafael. He riposted with a mango that bounced off her skull and splattered itself all over Tomás, whereupon Tomás poured his glass of chicha over his brother Gonzago.

One thing led to another, as things do, and soon the mêlée had moved out of Consuelo's whorehouse and into the streets, so that the jaguars scattered onto the roof-tops and growled in their throats whilst the people below argued the points of their literary positions at the tops of their voices whilst dodging half-chickens and grenadillos, launching their own papayas and skinned guinea pigs. Afterwards the jaguars came down and ate all the interesting bits, whilst the buzzards skipped amongst them competing with the dogs.

It is because of this that an amendment was made to the city's constitution. Under the paragraph which says 'In women, spitting in the street is not a sign of "gracia" and in men is not a sign of "machismo"', it says 'Fiction is not about anything real, and shall not be fought over'.

From this episode Dionisio deduced that the principle reason for religious schisms was that everybody derived their information from the same book. Having established this historiosophical point, he resolved never to sell large quantities of the same book at the same time. Farides and Profesor Luis were happy because the fight reminded them of the fiesta when they were married, and Don Emmanuel and Felicidad were reconciled because she got her revenge on him by jamming a mango in his mouth from behind. when he had opened it to shout encouragement to the combatants.

## 21 *In Which Cristobal Confounds His Eminence With Pertinent Questions, And Monsignor Rechin Anquilar Imparts Sombre News*

'I think it is very ugly in a pretty kind of way,' said Cristobal, burying his nose in the flower to see whether or not it smelled of anything.

Cardinal Dominic Trujillo Guzman and his illegitimate, unacknowledged, but beloved son, were in the courtyard of the palace, out of reach of the stink of urine and offal that wafted up from the river. It was a private world of flowers and vines, with its own fountain that refreshed the pool for a dozen enormous golden orf, and broke the sunlight into rainbows. The Cardinal would often sit down here with a book in his lap, moving around as the sun caught up with his patch of shade, and Cristobal would poke around in the flower-beds with a stick, marvelling at the hummingbirds that fiercely staked their claims to ownership of a bush or a creeper, or a stand of orchids.

'It is called a passion flower,' said the Cardinal.

'Mama reads books about passion,' observed Cristobal. 'It says "passion" on the front, and she won't let me read them, or even look at the pictures.'

The Cardinal smiled indulgently. 'This is a different kind of passion. Shall I tell you what the passion flower means?'

Realising that His Eminence was in one of his informative moods, Cristobal was indulgent in his turn. 'Yes please.'

The Cardinal pointed delicately with his forefinger, and the sun flashed from the ruby of his ring, something that Cristobal loved to see. It made the Cardinal seem glamorous as well as important.

'These five petals and these five bits which are called "sepals" add up to ten, which is the twelve disciples not counting nasty Judas Iscariot and St Peter who disgraced himself but made up for it later. This frilly blue bit that looks like hairs all in a circle is the crown of thorns that they put on Our Lord's head. These five greeny-yellow bits called "anthers" are the five wounds, and these three brown things called "stigmas" are the three nails. If you half-close your eyes and look at the leaves, they are like hands, and those are the hands of the bad people who persecuted Our Lord . . .' His Eminence wound one of the tendrils around a finger, '. . . and this is the whip with which they whipped Him. It was this flower that the missionaries used to convert the Indians, did you know that?'

Cristobal screwed up his nose sceptically. 'Being whipped with that wouldn't hurt very much, would it?'

'No, silly, it is supposed to remind you of the whip.'

'You said it was the whip.'

The Cardinal straightened up and sighed. 'The real whip was made of lots of bits of leather with lumps of lead in them so that it tears the flesh of your back away. They did it to make you die quicker on the cross, so they say, but some people took a week to die all the same.'

Cristobal pulled a disgusted face. 'And he died to make up for everybody's sins, so that all the sins disappeared and the Devil had to let everybody go out of hell?'

'Yes, child.'

'Why couldn't he just forgive everybody rather than go through all that?'

'He has forgiven everybody . . .' but the Cardinal trailed off, never having had to answer this question before, and anxious not to confuse the little boy with complex explanations.

'Mama says that you are always worried about your sins.'

'Everybody should be, Cristobal.'

'I'm not. If my badness is all forgiven, I can do as I like. I can throw stones at birds and not eat my fruit, and I can be rude, and pull girls' hair and not say my prayers and things.'

'God forgives, but I might not until I have sent you to bed with no supper and slapped your leg, so you can forget all about that.'

Cristobal smiled, exposing the quirky alignment of his milkteeth, and the Cardinal whipped out his handkerchief to arrest the flow of a new blob of green mucus. 'No, you cannot eat it,' said His Eminence, pre-empting the predictable request.

'I didn't want to,' said Cristobal, playing at being petulant. 'Mama says I should only pick my nose in private. She says everybody does, so I was going to wait. Why did they kill Jesus?'

124

'Because, my little Señor Curiosidad, He said and did things that got Him into trouble with the Jewish priests. We know that He was right, but from their point of view He was a heretic.'

'How do we know He was right?'

'Your questions are killing me, Cristobal. You are more full of questions than Mama's books of quizzes.'

'You don't know, do you?' said Cristobal with a triumphant gesture.

'Of course I know. I am a Cardinal. It is my job to know.'

'Tell me then.'

'O dear,' said the Cardinal, looking at the clock on the tower, 'it is your bedtime. You had better run along or your mama will be angry with us.'

Cristobal frowned and turned to go. 'And another thing. Why do you wear a dress?'

The Cardinal jocularly raised his hand as if to strike his son, and performed the familiar trick of converting the blow into a scratch on the head. 'To show that I am a Cardinal. Go on, off with you.'

Cristobal cartwheeled away across the lawn and pulled a face at His Eminence from behind the safety of a pillar. 'Diablillo,' called his father, 'get thee behind me.'

The little boy disappeared, and the Cardinal sat back in his chair and watched the hummingbirds. A few seconds later Cristobal's sticky fingers closed over his eyes, there was a giggle, and a mischievous voice said, 'See, I got behind you, and you didn't even notice.'

The Cardinal grabbed the boy's wrists and, holding him at arm's length, carried him screaming and kicking with delight towards the kitchens, where he handed him over to Concepcion. She grabbed his legs, and they swung him up and down until he was crying with laughter.

In the audience room an hour later the Cardinal was waiting for the appearance of Mgr Rechin Anquilar, who was supposed to be arriving in order to report upon the progress of the crusade of preaching. He was half an hour late, and so His Eminence crept to the window to see if the pious widows were outside waiting to catch a glimpse of him. They were, and so he ducked back, his intention of looking out over the city frustrated. 'I wish,' he thought, 'that

Concepcion would stop wearing lavatory rolls in her hair. It may be all the fashion with blacks and mulattas, but to me it is ridiculous. Perhaps if I say nothing, it will pass.'

The smell from the river contained something new. What was it? He tested the air with his nose. It was the smell of corpses. Perhaps that was why Concepcion had given him a new medicine to protect him from 'qhayqa', a disease of which he had never heard, and which she said was caused by the stench of death. No doubt something had been washed up on the banks.

Mgr Rechin Anquilar knocked on the door as he entered in order to draw attention to his presence, and came forward to kiss the Cardinal's ring. 'I am very late again, for which I apologise, Your Eminence. I have just seen a most sanguine thing, and that was what delayed me.'

'O?'

'Yes, indeed, I regret to say. The traffic jams are so bad these days, as you know, and there are many people selling things to the drivers of the stationary vehicles. I was in such a jam, and the car in front of me was a government limousine carrying the national flag upon the wing. And there was a man selling the latest Amado novel. But when the limousine drew level, the man dropped the books and drew a revolver and fired into it twice. He ran off, and there was mayhem.'

'Terrible, terrible,' murmured the Cardinal.

'I would have been on time, but my robes drew attention to me, and a traffic policeman demanded that I deliver extreme unction to the Justice Minister.'

'That is our third Justice Minister this year,' exclaimed the Cardinal incredulously. 'The work of the cartels no doubt. Is the poor man dead?'

'Yes, I am sorry to say, but one is tempted all the same to perceive the hand of God. The man was not only a Liberal but a secularist. Avowedly so.'

'Monsignor, one should not perceive any such thing in an assassination. I must reprove you.'

Mgr Anquilar maintained silence in order to indicate disagreement, and tapped his briefcase. 'Would you like to hear how our enterprise is proceeding?'

The Cardinal seated himself and indicated to the other that he should follow suit. The briefcase was opened, and a thin sheaf of paper extracted, which was then shuffled into order and placed upon the desk between them.

'Firstly, we have despatched missionaries in pairs to all those places indicated by the report of the Holy Office as being in need of spiritual renewal. The missionaries were volunteers who were then vetted by us for rectitude, zeal, and theological orthodoxy. In this way, Your Eminence, we were able to weed out those amongst them who were tempted by the prospect of a lengthy holiday.'

'Very good, very good. Most wise. Well done. And have they prospered?'

'I am afraid, Your Eminence, that most of them have encountered extreme hostility, amounting in some cases to severe mistreatment. Perhaps I could give you an example?'

'Indeed, I should be most interested.'

'We sent two fathers to Rinconondo, where there is a heresy which states that Mohammed was a reincarnation of Our Lord, who had returned in order to lose his virginity. They arrived in the town and proceeded to the plaza, where they preached a sermon against this belief. They then held an auto de fe, where they burned, amongst other things, several copies of the Koran, a Protestant Bible, a set of the philosophical works of Ortega y Gasset, a book by Paulo Freire that had belonged to the schoolteacher, and various different novels by Gabriel Garcia Marquez, who, as you know, has been associated with the atheistical experiments of Fidel Castro . . .'

'Monsignor, there should be no burnings of books. There has been no *index librorum prohibitorum* since 1966. We have no authority to burn books.'

'I understand that it was done on a voluntary basis by those who were convinced by the sermon, Your Eminence.'

'I see. Continue.'

'But then things apparently turned very nasty, and there was a display by some antisocial elements who stoned the fathers, beat them, and drove them out of the town.'

The Cardinal's brow knitted with concern. 'How appalling. What has been done about it? Were the police informed?'

'The police were apparently present, and turned a blind eye. We are contemplating sending in six priests next time, so that a repetition of this violence may be avoided, and we are adopting similar measures where other such unfortunate and ungodly incidents have occurred.'

'Very laudable, I congratulate you. It seems that you are admirably fulfilling our trust. Do not forget to submit your accounts to my secretary, and I shall see you again in two weeks. Until then, keep up the good work, and God go with you.'

Startled by the brevity of the interview, Mgr Anquilar gathered together his notes and left, feeling as though he had been slighted. Back in the audience chamber His Eminence spread his hands across his tautly expanding belly, and doubled over with the anguish. He heard the scuffling of leathery feet, the ribald shouts of laughter. He caught the metallic tang of the scent of ancient tombs, and he closed his eyes in order not to have to watch the rout of demons that mocked him in his torment.

Outside the intermittent but perpetual rain of the capital resumed, and the cadaverous perfume of the air was washed down onto the streets, where it filled the sewers and nauseated the population of discarded children who had found their home there.

## 22 *What Really Happened In Rinconondo*

Incandescent with righteous enthusiasm and insured against fallibility by the spiritual authority of the Church, Fathers Valentino and Lorenzo arrived in Rinconondo right at the beginning of siesta, when the sun of the llanos was vertically above and in a particularly unmerciful frame of mind. There was no breeze whatsoever, the birds were falling stone dead from their perches in the ceiba trees, and the cattle were wishing that they were elephants so that they could hose themselves down in the river. A confusing haze of dancing veils hovered over the red earth, and an engaging mirage of palm trees sprouted casually from the roof of the alcaldia. Nocturnal bats sortied from their roosts in the hollow trees and swooped along the surface of the ponds, risking suicide in the quest for water, and lemons ripened in minutes in the citrus groves. The fleas on the town's dogs hopped away into the shade, and the human inhabitants were overwhelmed with a lassitude very like a hangover. They had unanimously retired in order to snore away the afternoon in their hammocks.

Fathers Lorenzo and Valentino, despite the inferno, could not wait to commence their mission. They stationed themselves beneath a tree in the plaza, and began to ring a handbell in order to draw attention to themselves. When nothing happened, they rang the bell even louder, and started to clamour in unison, 'Hear the Word of The Lord, ye faithless, and repent.'

The mayor of Rinconondo stirred irritably awake. He blocked his ears with his hands, a movement that made him sweat profusely and which he immediately regretted, and tried to resume his dream at the place where he was about to undress Silvia, the winsome daughter of one of his policemen. But the terrible racket intervened once more at exactly the point when she inexplicably transmogrified into an iguana, and he sat up in his hammock and swore bitterly. He strapped on his holster and went into the neighbouring room, where his two policemen were similarly awake and cursing.

The three men crept swiftly down the street, ducking from one piece of shade to another, and emerged into the crushing light of the plaza at the same time as several irate citizens who had also suffered a shattering of their nerves and been aroused from their prostration. A guava described an elegant arc through the air and exploded gratifyingly against the habit of Father Lorenzo.

The mayor set his stubbled chin in determination and strode forward. 'We have a law,' he said, 'that there is to be no noise during siesta. Under this law I am empowered to ensure that you immediately desist, on pain of arrest for conduct likely to cause a breach of the peace, and I may also confiscate your bell and fine you.'

Father Valentino replied, 'We obey a higher law,' and Father Lorenzo, trying a different tack, said, 'Show me where this law is written.'

The mayor sighed, and gestured towards everyone present. 'It is a common law, assented to by everyone here, and it has no need to be written. Either be silent until after four o'clock, or I shall arrest you.'

The two priests, undeterred, and determined to show that salvation is of greater import than peace, looked at one another and with one voice defiantly resumed their chant. Father Lorenzo gave a loud peal of his bell, and jumped sideways as a bullet skipped off the earth by his left foot. The mayor pointed his pistol directly at them and announced, 'Until four o'clock you are under arrest, and your bell is declared confiscated and the property of the town. It shall be given to the school. And you are very lucky; if you had not been priests it would have been the death penalty.'

The priests were led away, protesting vociferously and prophesying hellfire, and were locked away for the afternoon in the schoolhouse. Here they sang hymns, said the rosary, and compared themselves to St Paul. When the doors failed to spring open of their own accord, their jubilant indignation turned gradually to boredom, and they began to take up the time by leafing through the books that the schoolteacher had spent years accumulating in order to form the nexus of a school library. Father Valentino read *Little Red Riding-Hood*, followed by a story about a porcupine who had lost his spines, and Father Lorenzo brushed up on his basic English with the aid of a venerable book that advised him upon the sense and usage of such sentences and phrases as 'Inclement weather for the time of year', and

'I am taking my dog to the vet.' Then they chanced upon the section that the teacher kept for herself, and discovered much to horrify them.

Rinconondo had been transformed many years before by the arrival of 'Syrians'; this word was used to denote anyone who was a trader originally from somewhere in the Middle East, and by extension had come to mean a muslim. The very first Syrian was a man appropriately named Mohammed, who had arrived with a handcart laden with leather bags, silver trinkets, and aphrodisiacs of doubtful provenance. He had at first puzzled the people by his manner of banging his forehead upon the ground when praying whilst facing east, the direction in which one commonly orients the head of a lamb before slaughter. They had been impressed by his robes and his statement that where he came from the llamas were twice as big. This boast caused some to suspect that he might be a Yanqui in disguise.

Then his wife and numerous relatives had appeared as if from nowhere, and set up a small colony of their own in one large house on the plaza. The people assumed that the wife must be disfigured because she always concealed her face, but Mohammed explained that the purpose of this was to spare her harrassment on account of her beauty, and to prevent other men from suffering the pangs of adulterous lust. Naturally, all the men began to long for a glimpse of her face, and as the years went by the veil slipped further and lower until the Syrians no longer noticed that it was absent and the male populace forgot their prurient speculations.

For the lack of a priest or an imam the purity of their faiths became diluted. The families intermarried and muddled themselves up; children were christened as Abdul and Fatima, some Islamic laws became incorporated into local custom, Lent and Ramadan became conflated, Christians made statuettes of the Prophet, and Muslims wore crosses about their necks. Some men took two or three wives, which made sense in view of the fact that they died younger and more often than women and were seemingly incapable of monogamous fidelity, and songsters incorporated muezzin-like wails and ululations into the garbled hymns handed down by their fathers.

All this was made infinitely easier by the fact that almost no one could read, which meant that it was only a matter of time before nobody could remember which story was about Jesus and which was about Mohammed; it was as if the wisdom of both were married seamlessly into one spiritual garment.

And then Ricardo the Goatherd received a visit whilst he was tending his goats near the waterfall. Ricardo was perhaps a little simple, or, to put it more kindly, a Holy Innocent. He was almost incapable of speech, suffered from a kind of palsy that gave him a violent twitch of the neck, and was in no way equipped to care for himself. But he did have a praeternatural gift for working with animals, and was thus assured of a vital rôle in that rural community, where dogs would one day unaccountably begin to chew their own tails, or cows would labour for days and bring forth prodigies with two heads and copious but redundant sets of genitals.

Ricardo was sitting in the shade eating a plantain fried in batter, when a shape began to form itself in the rainbow of colours created by the spray of the waterfall. He watched the vision out of one eye, and with the other he continued to guard the goats. The figure divided itself into three, and Ricardo could clearly see that it was Mary herself, flanked by two male figures, upon each of whose shoulders she had laid a maternal hand. 'Watch,' she commanded, and the figures of Mohammed and Jesus passed in front of her and became one. 'Listen,' she said, 'this is my son who returned because no man has understood love until he has known it in every form.' She made Ricardo repeat what she had said, and it was not until afterwards that he realised that his palsy had gone and he had spoken his first complete sentence.

Ricardo deserted his flock and ran into the plaza, his eyes glowing with healing and with the benediction of his revelation. His miraculous cure confirmed to one and all that his vision had not been the hallucination of a simpleton, and it took only a very little exegesis to work out (perhaps erroneously) that Jesus had returned as Mohammed in order to experience the love of women. The people erected statues beneath the waterfall depicting the event, which at the time caused some bad feeling amongst those Muslims who believed that one should not portray the human form, but which became eventually a popular local shrine where one might pray, meditate, or await minor miracles.

Fathers Lorenzo and Valentino found on the shelves of the schoolroom the teacher's clumsily typewritten account of the theophany, they found some Korans translated apologetically into Castilian, and they found a volume of letters by Camilo Torres, the priest who had embraced Marxism and become an instant martyr owing to a misplaced act of futile heroism. Clicking their tongues with righteous disgust, they made a pile of the books by the door, and awaited their release at four o'clock.

When the police came to unlock the door, the fathers acted with duplicitious humility. They asked for pardon, and begged to be shown the shrine by the waterfall. The mayor, in a more expansive mood on account of the cooling of the day, offered to take them there himself, and they duly admired it, offered up a prayer or two, and generally made themselves amiable and tractable. The mayor grew suspicious, but nonetheless arranged overnight accommodation for them in the alcaldia, whereupon the fathers declared their intention to call in on every house before bedtime, in a spirit of reconciliation.

They found very few houses with books, but in those where they found them, one or other of them would manage to spirit away the objectionable ones into the folds of their voluminous cowls. In this way they removed the volumes of Ortega y Gasset, several Korans, the Protestant Bible, the Marquez novels, and the book about teaching the poor by Paulo Freire. They furthermore collected the pile of books they had made in the schoolhouse, and hid the cache in their room in the alcaldia. Finally, before retiring, they visited the whore-house, where they found no dangerous books and, one presumes, attempted to reclaim a few lost souls.

The village awoke at dawn to the sound of inspirational preaching and the smell of fire. The villagers emerged with tintos in their hands and their brains still bleary from oneiric escapades, to find that the two priests were burning a pile of books at the same time as exhorting the town to repentance, and to renunciation of their common faith. This was insult enough on its own, but then people began to recognise their own cherished books charring in the pile, and Doña Sisimota arrived at full pelt from the shrine, announcing that the statues had been smashed to pieces.

The exhortations of the priests were interrupted by a wave of anger that expressed itself as a shower of fruit and stones. The fathers were seized, roped about the ankles, hauled over a branch, and beaten mercilessly with sticks and with the flats of machetes until the mayor

133

arrived to attempt to calm the situation. When he was apprised of what had transpired, he lowered the priests down from the tree and locked them once more in the schoolhouse whilst he consulted with the elder citizens as to the best course of action.

They decided on a traditional Quechua punishment, and made Fathers Lorenzo and Valentino carry rocks for the period of a week. With these rocks they built a small minaret at each corner of their church, and thus completed a project that had been mooted for several years. The fathers were then released, their faces smeared with mule manure and their cassocks full of fire ants, and they wended their sorry way back to the capital in order to report their outrageous treatment to Monsignor Rechin Anquilar, who decided on the spot to recruit squads of faithful laity in order to protect his missionaries.

On the anniversary of the appearance of the Virgin and her two companions to Ricardo the Goatherd, the statues at the shrine in the waterfall reportedly reconstituted themselves spontaneously, and most were of the opinion that now they were more supernally lifelike and serene even than before.

# 23 The Beast And The Three-Hundred-Year-Old Man

'He reminds me of Don Quijote,' said Profesor Luis, and Dionisio Vivio said, 'He reminds me of King Pellinore.' Those two have a kind of intellectual rivalry when it comes to drawing comparisons.

I remember that this was on a day when Aurelio was telling stories to Parlanchina. I hasten to say that I have never seen her, but Dionisio drew a picture of her and showed it to me; she is tall and very slim, with hair so long that it falls about her waist. She is quite exceedingly beautiful, and by all accounts is so delightful that she winds her father around her little finger, forcing him to tell one story after another. When this happens in the plaza everybody gathers around to listen, perfectly fascinated by Aurelio's ability to amuse the dead. Sometimes Federico is there as well, since he is married to Parlanchina in the other world, and I am told that she has a little child by him whom she suckles whilst she listens. Her ocelot, also invisible to me, torments the jaguars of the city by mischievously ambushing them, and it is a common sight to see one of our great animals rolling in the dirt to dislodge the little tigercat from its back, where it apparently clings tenaciously with its sharp little claws. When Federico arrives it gives great pleasure to his father, Sergio, the man who hires out his twin brother's skull for the purposes of sorcery.

It is to record such strange events that I keep this occasional journal, having resolved to keep a log of all things untoward that transpire in this city. Whilst I was still in the Army I was possessed by the desire to taxonomise all the hummingbirds and butterflies of the nation, but since I deserted and came here I find myself more fascinated by the marvellous reality of Cochadebajo de los Gatos, where I can forget all about being the famous General Carlo Maria Fuerte, and submerge myself in the life of this people whose beliefs and activities are more exotic than a morpho butterfly or an oropendola.

There are two facets to this people which mark them off from others; one is their capacity for love and the other is their mania for construction. But having said that, I realise that I might just as well have put 'their capacity for merriment and their thirst for knowledge'. It is just that their love affairs and their edifices and contraptions are perhaps the most obvious. It is certainly the truth that the pursuit of an amour is of infinitely greater importance to them than anything else, but to an outsider I daresay that the most immediately striking thing would be the labour of their hands. It is only when one has lived here a while that one notices that this latter is only something indulged in when having a break from the former.

The first sight that a traveller beholds when standing on the cliffs above the town is a map of the world. This came about in the first place when Profesor Luis did a survey and discovered that only ten per cent of the people knew where their country was. He was so alarmed by this that he decided to issue a Mercator projection to everybody upon a piece of paper, but came up immediately against the problem that paper is an extreme scarcity in these parts, and moreover the children grew rapidly weary of copying it out over and over. He went to Dionisio Vivo, and they resolved to construct a map of the world so large that lessons in geography could be conducted either in a boat or from the heights above.

There was at the western end of the valley an area of icy swampland butting onto the curve of the river, and it is in that place that the *mappa mundi* is now situated. Profesor Luis, old man Gomez, Dionisio Vivo, Misael, Fulgencia Astiz and numerous others who helped upon a casual basis, such as some of the Spanish soldiers that Aurelio brought back from the dead, first drained the swamp by cutting a channel that joined the river further down. This accomplished, they set to work digging out the oceans and piling up the spoil to form the continents. They then modelled the landscape to include ranges of mountains, and planted the whole lot with appropriately coloured flowers, green for fertile areas and yellow for deserts. All this was on a massive scale, taking many months, and at the end of it all they dammed up the chanel and allowed the 'oceans' to fill with water. But this was not all. Not only did Profesor Luis pole the curious around upon a raft, lecturing eruditely upon the various countries, but Aurelio somehow caused a shower of edible fish that populated the waters, and a flock of ducks took up permanent residence, providing us with delicately flavoured eggs. It is most impressive to climb up above and look down upon this cartographical masterpiece, and at night it is very calming to lie in one's hammock listening to the soothing conversation of the frogs.

Whilst upon this subject I should not fail to record the extraordinary achievement in rebuilding all the terraces up the mountainsides that had once supplied the city in Inca times. They did this by very cannily cutting up into bricks the alluvial soil that had buried the city during the time of its inundation, thus serving two purposes at once. Nowadays these 'andenes' are literally draped with vegetables, and those parts that have been harvested are used for sheep and goats which graze off the stalks. The people have also constructed a vast machine in order to reach the plateau below, and they have largely repaired every one of the old stone buildings; I am prompted to speculate that the spirit of the Incas lives on in these parts and has infected the souls of the people with monumentophilia, if there be such a word.

They also have a great liking for stories, which is probably why they spend so much time in the plaza. Here they may listen to the sermons of Father Garcia, who never fails to amuse people by his ability to levitate when involved in his narratives. These sermons consist mainly of complicated stories told in a vernacular and frequently racy style, and are usually about the doings of angels and devils. They seem to be designed to explain morals and the supernatural reasons for the world being as it is. Theologically his ideas are most heterodox, if not actually crazy, but the levitation trick convinces many of their truth, as well as the interesting blue nimbus that develops about his head.

In the plaza, too, one can overtly eavesdrop upon the tales told by Aurelio to his dead daughter, Parlanchina. It seems that he waits in the plaza for her, until she lets herself be known by playing a trick upon him. She runs away with his hat, or she puts her hands over his eyes and says, 'Guess who?' or she steals his coca gourd from his mochila. Aurelio reproves her, and then he says, 'OK, I will tell you a story, but only if you stop your pranks and listen.'

On the day when the three-hundred-year-old man arrived, he had already told three stories, the one about how the armadillo knitted his own shell and had to knit the last bits with looser knots in order to get it done in time for a party because he had got the date wrong, the one about the woman Sabare who discovered the culinary uses of salt, and the one about the woman who married a jaguar and supplied her village with meat until she became a jaguar herself, whereupon her ungrateful family killed her and became the cause of the jaguar's perpetual disillusionment. He was just commencing the one about the abused children who danced out of their village and went to the night sky, which is why one must never strike a child, when the stranger appeared at the end of the line of obelisks, crying at the top of his voice, 'Has anyone seen the beast? Has anyone seen the beast?'

As he drew near we could see that he was a scrawny individual mounted upon a sorry horse. He was clad in hessian sackcloth improvised into a tunic, his feet were bare in the stirrups, and he carried a long stave which he clearly believed to be a lance. He had long, thin grey hair and a beard of the same ilk, and his skin was saddle-leather brown from his years in the sun. His eyes were like black pinpoints, which made me think that perhaps he had been smoking marijuana, and when he spoke he did so with exaggerated gestures that reminded me of the villain in a melodrama. He rode up to us, interrupting Aurelio's tale, and glared down imperiously. 'Is the beast here?'

'What beast?' asked Misael, grinning from ear to ear and nudging Josef, as if to share the judgement implicit to all that here was a lunatic.

The man appeared perplexed. 'What beast?' he echoed. 'The beast that takes many shapes, but whose stomach rumbles like the sound of a pack of dogs running in the distance. Have you seen it?'

'That would be Don Emmanuel after frijoles refritos,' called out Felicidad, and everybody laughed.

'And where is this Don Emmanuel?' demanded the stranger. 'I must kill him.' Whereupon Don Emmanuel stepped forward, thrusting out his great paunch and his red beard, his eyes twinkling with humour. With a motion so fast that it seemed that we had not seen it, the stranger struck the unfortunate Don Emmanuel upon the side of his head with the stave, and the latter fell to the ground as though felled by lightning. Felicidad threw herself upon the assailant, dragging him from his horse, pulling out tufts of hair and and biting him so severely in the shoulder that he bled generously from the wound.

Once the mêlée had subsided and Don Emmanuel had returned to this world, sitting upon the ground ruefully rubbing his skull, we were able to listen to the old man, who apparently had often been the victim of such misunderstandings. 'The reason for my lamentable appearance,' he said, 'is that I am three hundred years old and cannot die until I have finished off the beast. I have travelled in that time many times around the world, even swimming the oceans, which always causes the death of my horse so that I have to buy another one, and I still have not found the beast.' He shook his head in a resigned manner, and the Mexican musicologist said, 'Surely, cabrón, it would be better not to kill this beast, and then you would live forever, no?'

The old man sighed and looked up somewhat patronisingly, as though the Mexican were incapable of understanding. 'I am more tired than if I were infested with hookworm,' he said, 'and I wish for the peace of death more than a young man longs for a woman. Can you perceive how wearying it might be to travel upon horseback for two hundred and fifty years, looking for the beast? I have had thirty-three horses, and every time one of them dies I am consumed with grief. All my friends are long dead. Is there a place to eat?'

Fulgencia Astiz, that fearsome Santandereana, took him to Doña Flor's, which is what Dolores calls her restaurant, and many others crammed themselves in there in order to satiate their curiosity. Dolores told them to eat or get out, but nobody moved, and we watched the old man eat two tortillas, three enchiladas, a chimichanga, a dish of sancocho, a dish of pumpkins stewed with chicken and sweetcorn, a whole pineapple, two guinea pigs, and the leg of a small vicuña. I need not remark that we were all entirely astonished, and he informed us that his digestive system, being three hundred years old, was most inefficient, and that therefore he was obliged to eat enormous quantities in order to be able to extract even a minimum of nutrition. He paid Dolores with coins from an old leather bag, these coins clearly bearing the head of King Pedro the First of Brazil. Dionisio took these up to the capital eventually, and came back with several thousand pesos for Dolores.

The stranger then mounted his horse and rode forlornly away in quest of his beast, having extracted from Aurelio the promise that he should be summoned if anybody ever saw it. I often dream of him fighting the beast, but I can never quite see exactly what the beast is. It is like a flurrying blur that screeches.

## 24 *Return To Rinconondo*

Abuela Teresa was a special person, and was the cause of the notice in the church which said, 'No rosaries, by special request of Our Lady'. When she was no more than twelve years old she had gone to the grotto of the three statues, and was at that crucial age when the sudden burgeoning of an adolescent's sexuality finds itself both expressed and assuaged by an access of religious fervour. She had fallen in love with Christ. He was forever before her imagination, clothed in glory but His wounds still bleeding, and she felt herself enclosed both by His enveloping feminine gentleness and His powerful masculine protection. Her face radiated serenity and contentedness such that her fresh beauty aroused no lust in men who saw her, and even at that age she possessed the extraordinary ability to love animals in a way that was entirely foreign to the community of peasants to which she belonged, a community which treated its beasts with casual cruelty at worst, and with exploitative indifference at best. In those days she had a capuchin monkey as a pet, which she used to carry on her chest, its arms about her neck in an embrace of perpetual affection, and its cheek against hers.

At the grotto she sat by the waterfall and detached the monkey so that she could say the rosary. It scampered into the branches of a flamboyant tree, and amused itself by plucking the blossoms whilst she closed her eyes, crossed herself at the crucifix, said the Apostles' Creed, and began the Our Father of the first bead. She was saying the second Hail Mary of the third bead when a silvery voice said, 'Teresa, please stop.' She opened her eyes and looked about her, saw nothing, and said the Glory Be. Having reached the bead at the bottom of the loop, she commenced the ten Hail Marys of the first mystery, but had reached only the second when the same silvery voice again interrupted: 'Teresa, should I have to ask you twice?'

Startled, she opened her eyes and looked up to behold a nimbus about the head of the statue of the Virgin, a nimbus so bright that it was impossible to gaze upon the face behind it. She shielded her eyes and trembled, but found herself unable to rise to her feet and run. 'I want you to know,' said the voice, 'that I would be very relieved to hear no more rosaries.'

Young Teresa could think of nothing intelligent or interesting to say, and so she asked, 'Why?' and instantly regretted her impertinence.

There came a profound sigh from behind the blaze of light, a sigh that seemed to express a weariness older than the world. 'How would you like it, Teresa, to listen to all that? Just imagine, for one complete rosary I have to listen to six Our Fathers, an Apostles' Creed, six Glory Bes, a lengthy litany, a concluding prayer, and fifty-three Hail Marys. Some people work their way through all fifteen mysteries, and then I have to listen to one hundred and fifty Hail Marys.'

'One hundred and sixty-five,' corrected Teresa.

'Quite so,' returned the voice, 'and it is more than I can continue to bear. Just imagine, Teresa, at any one time there are millions of people all over the world gabbling through this in indecent haste. It is like having one's head stuck permanently in a buzzing hive of angry bees. If you wish to say the rosary, please say only one Hail Mary for each mystery, and say it slowly and with attention.'

Teresa, never one to accept anything without question, protested, 'But, My Lady, it says on my rosary card that at Fatima you urged the world to say it, and it says that the rosary was given to St Dominic in order to combat heresy.'

There came another sigh out of the eight corners of the universe. 'Between you and me, St Dominic has much to answer for. Will you do as I ask?'

'Yes, My Lady,' said Teresa, still shielding her eyes against the ineffable and now pulsating effulgence of the light.

'And another thing,' continued the voice, 'I have a message from My Son. He says that you must learn to love Him not as He is, alone, but as you find Him in your fellows.'

From that time on, no rosaries were said in the pueblito of Rinconondo, and Teresa would look for Jesus in the faces of her family, in the broken teeth of itinerant beggars, behind the eyes of the mayor, in the artificial gaiety of the village whores, and in the embraces of the man who was to live with her all her life until he died shortly before her seventieth birthday. When this occurred,

Teresa bought another capuchin monkey from one of Don Mascar's peons, realising that such a harmless love would be sufficient to last her to the day of her own demise, bringing it to an end in a satisfyingly circular manner.

Teresa was sitting in the plaza shelling castaña nuts and feeding some of the kernels to her companionable monkey when Fathers Valentino and Lorenzo reappeared in the pueblo at the head of a ruffianly band of twenty men, most of them mounted upon mules or horses, and all of them armed with rifles and machetes.

Who were these men, and the thousands like them who swelled the ranks of the crusaders? This is something worthy of explanation, because it has been a puzzle to many who have looked back over these events and wondered how it was that a nation already so troubled by internal divisions and gangsterism should have succumbed to a revival of the interminable religious conflict that had plagued it for decades and been apparently resolved by uneasy constitutional compromises. In the past the Liberals had mercilessly slaughtered, tortured and raped in the name of the modern secular state, and the Conservatives had done exactly the same in the name of Catholic theocracy, the wars continuing so long that no one had ever known when one war was finished and another had begun. They were perpetuated until at the end of them no one could remember how they had started or what the initial objectives of the sides had been, so that the final peace treaty acceded to demands made by the Liberals that had originally been those of the Conservatives, and the latter insisted upon the inclusion of clauses which had originally been fought for by the Liberals. The only way to conceive of the possibility of such an improbable outcome is to understand that there was in the national psyche an atavistic lust for excitement and combat which sought irresistibly to express itself not so much in the interest of causes, but upon the slightest and most inexcusably infantile pretexts. The nation possessed the kind of mentality that would see no contradiction in invading another country in order to impose pacifism upon it. Coupled with this, one might discern a certain compulsive acquisitiveness that is so naive that it utterly fails to appreciate its own cynicism. An idealistic war would thus manifest itself as an orgy of theft that looted both the most insignificant possessions of the poor and the bodily integrity of the women. In such times the fear and contempt that men have for women explode into a cataclysm of rape and mutilation, and the lust for domination and extremes of experience leaves a trail of masculine dead who rot in the undergrowth, their testicles, heaving with maggots, in their mouths.

And so Fathers Lorenzo and Valentino had little difficulty in recruiting a 'bodyguard' that was bigger than they had expected and turned out to be too wilful for them to control, so that ultimately they had to resign themselves to its atrocities and console themselves with the thought that some evils are always perpetrated in the cause of a greater good. With the promise of plenary indulgence they found men who were prepared to leave the monotony of their wives' control, men who would forsake badly paid and gruelling employment for the sake of an adventure, men who were happy to act tough in the name of Gentle Jesus, Meek and Mild. The fathers would begin as leaders, and finish as accomplices for fear of becoming followers, which is exactly what happened to all the other priests who eventually found that their forces had congealed into a devastating plague of human locusts, at the head of whom was the dark and adamantine figure of Mgr Rechin Anquilar, who seemed to be everywhere at once, wheeling on his huge horse, the crucifix on its chain catching the light of burning huts and the red glow of the moon.

In the plaza the fathers rang their bell and called for repentance whilst their cohort of bodyguards lounged beneath the trees, replenished their water bottles from the trough, and some gathered sticks to make a fire with which they could cook some strips of meat, gaucho-fashion, upon the ends of their knives. The repetitive incantation drew the population from their houses, their eyes alight with amused curiosity and a certain wonder that the pestilential priests should have so imprudently reappeared after their previous humiliations. As before, a guava sailed through the air and flattened itself against the side of Father Lorenzo's head. But this time a shot rang out, and the leader of the ruffians stood up menacingly. 'Listen to the man preach,' he said, and he spat on the ground with an air of finality. The people listened.

They heard the fathers condemn everything that they held sacred. They listened as Ricardo of Rinconondo was described as a lunatic, as Mohammed was denounced as a heretic and polygamist, as their grotto was described as a pagan shrine of iniquity, as they were commanded to remove the minarets and reinstate the rosary upon pain of perpetual flame. At this point Abuela Teresa rose to her feet and made her way to the side of Father Lorenzo. Leaning upon her stick, summoning all the vehemence in her frail old body, her monkey clinging about her neck, she said, 'Young man, Our Lady commanded us through me not to say the rosary. Who are you to contradict Our Lady?'

Lorenzo shook his head with a devout and pious pity that was unmistakably redolent of educated condescension. 'It was not Our Lady, it was an apparition of the Deceiver. You have been misled, take my word for it.'

'It was Our Lady,' persisted Abuela Teresa, 'she spoke to me.'

'Have you any conception of hell?' asked Father Valentino. 'Is that where you wish to go? For that is what you must suffer, all of you, if you do not mend your ways. Throw yourselves upon God's mercy.'

Abuela Teresa looked up at the two priests and began to tremble with anger. Despite her rheumy vision she perceived in them a revolting self-righteousness, an appalling collection of unexamined certainties, a terrible spiritual hubris masquerading as gentle humility, and she was utterly repelled. As if by reflex she raised her stick and set about the clerics, who raised their arms to protect their heads whilst the villagers applauded and whistled, and even the bodyguards smiled with delight.

But then the leader of the ruffians spotted his chance to earn his eternal place in paradise, and decided to give his own lesson in theology. He strode forward and wrenched the stick from the old lady's hands, so that she fell sprawling to the dust. He bent down, removed the startled monkey from her shoulders, and, holding it under the armpits, he marched over to the fire.

The flames were by now copious and brilliant, and he turned around in front of them and raised the little creature aloft. 'Look,' he shouted, 'I will show you what hell is like,' and he suspended the monkey at arm's length over the tongues of fire.

A horrified silence fell over the villagers at exactly the same moment as the capuchin began to writhe and shriek. There was a momentary black burst of smoke as the soft grey fur singed away, and then the clinging miasma of burning flesh filled the plaza. The capuchin screamed like a tortured child, wriggled, attempted to pull itself higher in the man's grasp, grinned with agony and incomprehension, and choked in the smoke of its immolation. The leader dropped it into the fire. It stood up so that it was momentarily silhouetted, and then it collapsed into the conflagration, squirmed and twitched in its death throes, and charred into lifelessness.

The people stood, too amazed and horrified to act, paralysed by the horrible drama of the little monkey's death. But then a woman set up a long howl of anger and compassion, a man vomited upon the ground, and Abuela Teresa, consumed with a ferocious disdain and desolation, picked up her stick and went over to the fire to gaze upon the remains of her last companion as they shrivelled and shrank in their nest of flame. She raised her hands to her face, tears flowed out between her fingers, and then she knelt. She turned her head slowly towards the ashen-faced priests and said simply, 'I will be in heaven before you.'

She stretched out her arms and threw herself face-down in the flames before anyone could stop her, momentarily experiencing for the second time in her life a light brighter than the sun.

## 25 A Further Extract From General Fuerte's Notebooks

In the constitution of the city it states that 'It is strictly forbidden to procure abortion by hanging a woman upside down in a sackful of ants and beating her until she miscarries. But is it permitted to procure abortions by means of dried llama foetuses.' It also states that 'All visitors wishing to use the whorehouse must carry a certificate of clean blood from the clinic in Ipasueño', and that 'Anyone giving bad advice is responsible for what follows from that advice'. One might also find such items as 'This city disapproves of the Quechua practice of weaning babies by smearing the nipples with rancid guinea-pig fat', and poetical reflections such as 'Gold is the sweat of the sun, and silver the tears of the moon', and 'When the Gods weep, their tears become jaguars'.

The constitution came into being upon the premise that anyone could suggest anything to the informal council of the leaders, and would be accepted as long as no one could think of any objections. In the case of procuring abortion by beating a woman upside down in a sackful of ants, it was Leticia Aragon who heard of the practise and proposed its abolition. She is a woman who had been the lover of Dionisio Vivo when he was enduring a fit of madness in Ipasueño; having come to Cochadebajo de los Gatos in order to bear his child, they became lovers again when he regained his sanity. She earns her living by her extraordinary ability to recover lost property, which she finds in her hammock every evening before she climbs into it.

The clause about all visitors having to have a certificate of clean blood before using the whorehouse was proposed by Hectoro, and was the direct result of a sudden influx of curious tourists who were readers of *La Prensa*. This newspaper had mentioned a remark by Don Emmanuel to the effect that Cochadebajo de los Gatos was a 'magnificent submarine city of unmitigated fornication', and this had aroused great interest amongst a certain type of male reader. They had flocked to the city in droves, posing as traders, travellers, rich gringos, and ethnologists. Most of them bought clothing from the

Indian tribes on the way, hoping in this way to disguise the fact that they were mainly urban opportunists, and it was this invasion of ponchos, unplayed samponas panpipes, and those red hats with earflaps, that made it perfectly obvious that they were not the people they were wishing to impersonate. They shamelessly molested the young girls, became drunk, and lengthened the queues in the whorehouse to an extent that Hectoro found intolerable. On top of that, there was a wave of apprehension travelling across the country that the gringos had invented a new disease that made one turn purple, waste away, and die of any minor ailment that came along, and this made the whores especially reluctant to copulate with outsiders. Fortunately, most of the visitors could not stand the presence of so many jaguars, and left fairly quickly.

The one about bad advice was proposed by the Mexican musicologist who lives with the twins, Ena and Lena. This man may be a gifted musician and academic, and he is young and good-looking, but he is also a little long-winded and naive. One day a sports fiesta was held, with races, shooting holes in a hat, a tug of war against Cacho Mocho, a contest to see who could drag Antoine's tractor furthest up a slope backwards, lassoing Don Emmanuel from twenty-five paces, and various other events of greater or lesser machismo.

The Mexican musicologist had entered the one hundred metres race, and was very cocksure of winning it because he had been practising by running up the mountainside to his house. No one else had been practising because it was considered that a real man could triumph without so wasting his time and energy; there was also a general feeling that training was a form of cheating.

The Mexican was so smug that he was spending time in bars telling everyone what he was going to choose for his prize, which was a choice of three books from Dionisio Vivo's bookshop. He had already been in there to choose his books, and had asked Dionisio to set them to one side so that he could collect them after his victory. But Don Emmanuel set him up by taking him to one side and saying, 'Confidentially, cabrón, the secret of the one hundred metres is to let everyone else rush ahead and tire themselves out, and then, when they are exhausted, to put in a burst of speed and overtake them. All you have to do is to pace yourself wisely.'

The Mexican was very taken with this advice, and he thanked Don

Emmanuel and shook his hand. Of course when the race started, everybody except the Mexican flew off like bullets, and he came ingloriously last. So great was his rage that he tried to dunk Don Emmanuel's head into Doña Constanza's cauldron of guarapo, and had to be restrained by Misael and Josef. When he saw that everybody was laughing at him he kicked over the cauldron and stalked off home, where he sulked for two days before showing his face, and that was when he went to Remedios with his new clause for the constitution.

A further complication of the race was that although Capitan Papagato apparently won it, Aurelio, Pedro and Dionisio, all of whom enjoy social intercourse with the dead, claimed that Federico had won it by several metres, with Parlanchina coming in second. Sergio, since Federico is his son and Parlanchina his daughter-in-law, naturally supported this claim even though he was unable to say that he had actually witnessed the victory of the two spirits. There was quite an altercation about this, until Aurelio informed everybody that Federico and Parlanchina had decided that their weightlessness gave them an unfair advantage, and that they wanted Capitan Papagato to have the prize because the books were of no use to them since neither of them were able to read. This is why there is also a paragraph of the constitution that says 'People who are invisible to most of us should not use that fact to their own benefit', a clause that many of the uninformed have taken to be a rebuff to distant politicians.

Capitan Papagato has turned out to be an interesting case. It was he who proposed such eccentric inclusions as 'If tortoises had wheels they would go a lot faster', and 'Bats sleep upside down in order not to be confused with birds', and he has changed a great deal since he was my ADC in Valledupar. Back in those days he was conscientious and diffident, seeming to be married to the Army as I was, but when I returned from my captivity in the torture chambers of General Ramirez, I found that he had changed his name to Papagato, had four enormous black jaguars which had apparently been borne by my donkey, Maria, and had become a highly successful womaniser. When we deserted and followed the cats to this city, he took one look at Francesca and fell wildly in love, and who could blame him?

She is only seventeen, she is most vivacious and gentle, and she is pretty in the way that these girls are before they are ravaged by childbirth and travail. She has quite long and curly black hair, and one's eyes cannot resist following the curves of her body down past those pert little breasts and her flat stomach in order to come to rest at the apex of her thighs. One could pass quite a lot of time in a reverie, imagining how she appears when naked, and this, I fancy, is what Capitan Papagato found himself doing. I think that the most appealing thing about her is that the corners of her mouth have a small natural curve upward, which gives her a permanently smiling expression, but I would also have to concede that her heavy eyebrows perfectly set off her glowing brown eyes, and that, too, is very fetching indeed.

Capitan Papagato began to find himself outside her house on the slightest of pretexts, and very sensibly tried to make it look as though his real interest lay in befriending her father, Sergio. Every evening he would return to me and say, 'General, today she smiled at me twice,' or, 'General, today she wore a flower in her hair; do you think it could be a message?' and I would have to listen to all this and give him my opinion. I advised him always to take his jaguars with him so that their hands might cross in the process of stroking them, and to provide an unfailing topic of conversation: 'Are they well today? Are they not very big?' and so on. He reported that when their hands touched, she did not withdraw her own, and we took this to be an encouraging indication.

One day he came into my house with such a spring in his step that I thought he was likely to raise the thatch with his head, and it turned out that this was because he had found her in his path as he went out one evening for a stroll with the cats. Remedios told me later that she had seen Francesca tailing the Capitan, and then breaking into a run in order to circle him and find herself 'accidentally' in his itinerary. Naturally they took the paseo together, and things happened in such a rush that when they returned they had not only lips bleeding from kissing, but had decided to marry. Capitan Papagato told me that she was a little afraid of men because Federico's last words to her had been to the effect that she should be cautious of them, and she wished to honour this last request.

He went to ask Sergio for his permission, and was told that it was the custom to send a 'talker' rather than to ask directly. This talker has to be an older person who is respected, and of course I fell right into the trap and was obliged to take on the rôle. It is unbelievable how tedious this is. Whilst Francesca and her lover were out amongst the rocks amusing themselves, I had to act almost as though I myself were the suitor. Thus the first time I visited I was not allowed to mention the affair at all, and I had to sit there all evening drinking pisco and puffing in silence upon one cigar after another. On the second evening I had to do the same, except that at some point I had to say, 'Francesca is very pretty, is it not time to send her to a new home?'

On the third evening I had to say, 'Capitan Papagato is a very fine fellow; do you not think it is time that he was married to a respectable girl?' and on the fourth evening I had to bring up the subject directly by saying, 'Capitan Papagato and Francesca are making a great scandal by going out together, do you not agree that we should put an end to it and put them together in a house?' All this is strictly formulaic, as was Sergio's reply: 'How will he provide for her? Let him bring gifts to show that he has enough.'

Poor Capitan Papagato had to bring four sacks of maize, two of potatoes, a sheep, a pair of army boots and a copy of my pop-up book on the nation's butterflies before Sergio gave his consent to the betrothal. It seems that here it is normal to live together for some years before undergoing marriage, and that initially it is enough merely to become betrothed. Perhaps this is a relic of the way in which the Church tended to sanctify marriages that had already been contracted by indigenous methods.

Virtually all that I can remember of what happened next is that I had an excruciating hangover on account of three days of fiesta, and Josef told me that at one point I climbed onto the roof of Gonzago's house and urinated onto Misael's donkey. I pray to God that this is untrue. As for Francesca and the Capitan, I was told by Remedios that Doña Constanza had been told by Gloria that Francesca had told her that the Capitan is 'an absolute stud', and he in turn confided to me that 'Francesca is insatiable, thank God.' The two of them have moved into the house next to mine, and they have constructed a bed large enough to accommodate themselves and the four jaguars all at once, which means that the back room is one entire bed. They make such a racket during siesta that I have taken to having mine with my ears plugged with wax, but since Felicidad and Don Emmanuel are on the other side and Doña Constanza and Gonzago are opposite, I may as well give up the idea of peaceful sleep unless I move somewhere else.

# 26 *The Massacre At Rinconondo*

The mayor of Rinconondo appeared in the plaza with his two policemen at precisely the moment when hysteria had overtaken almost all the members of the assembly. He had been out at Don Mascar's hacienda investigating a suspected case of cattle poisoning, and had spent the most part of what should have been siesta wandering from one bloated corpse to another in the stupefying heat with a handkerchief over his nose. Since Don Mascar was to all intents and purposes the local caudillo, it stood to reason that he might have all kinds of enemies; a fired foreman, perhaps, or a peon who suspected that the indiscreet bulge in his daughter's belly was owed to the patrón. But one of the policemen had spotted the tip of a horn poking above the surface of the waterhole, and the conclusion was drawn that the cattle had indeed been poisoned, but by one of their own kind. Although it was not their civic duty to do so, the mayor and the policemen had assisted the peons in the objectionable task of removing the offending steer, and were now attired in clothes borrowed from Don Mascar himself, who had gratefully offered to have their own garments cleaned by one of his washerwoman. In such areas everyone understands the value of keeping relations sweet between the caudillo and the organs of law-enforcement.

And so it was that the three men arrived back in Rinconondo just as Abuela Teresa was being dragged by her feet out of the flames. There was a tight bunch of people gathered around her, so that at first it was not at all clear what was happening. They heard the terrible keening of grieving women, the angry shouts of men, and became aware that there were present a number of shifty and hostile-looking strangers who were very heavily armed.

The mayor stroked his stubble, summoned up his courage and his habitual air of decisive machismo, and waded into the knot of people. What he beheld at first was two priests kneeling beside the body of a woman to whom they were administering the last rites, and when he leaned over to try to discover the identity of the woman, he recoiled with a shock that struck him like a blow in the face. He saw a head that was without features. It was a bloody soup of liquids and livid flesh, studded with morsels of charcoal and smouldering wood; there were huge yellow blisters, and from the distorted mouth there came a groan that he had last heard when one of his men had been eviscerated by the horn of a bull during a fiesta. The crowd fell silent, as though suddenly attuned to his own astonishment. 'Who is this?' he demanded.

'Abuela Teresa,' someone replied. 'These bastards pushed her to it.'

'Is she dead?' he asked, and when Father Valentino looked up and said, 'No,' the mayor recognised him and realised that the two meddlesome clerics had returned and somehow caused more trouble. He removed his revolver from its holster and jabbed it vehemently into the chest of Father Valentino. His eyes sparked with fury and his finger twitched on the trigger, but he pulled himself back from the brink of murder and let the gun fall to his side. 'Have you finished absolution?'

'Yes. It will not be long now.'

The mayor looked down at the abomination at his feet that used to be one of the most revered elders of the pueblo, and impulsively he leaned down and put a shot through the old lady's forehead, in the centre, just above the level of the eyes. Never having done such a thing before, he was not to know that the back of the head would explode and embellish the feet and cassocks of the priests with a patina of blood and brain; but having done so he smiled grimly, wiped his forehead with his arm, and said drily, 'The river is over there.'

The two priests were horrified. 'You have committed a terrible sin,' stammered Father Lorenzo, 'may God forgive you for it.'

'Look to your own souls,' said the mayor, and he called his two policemen. 'Reinaldo, Aratildo, lock these two priests away, and then take statements from witnesses. I will have to make a report to the governor.' He walked over to where the band of crusaders was trying to make itself inconspicuous at the far side of the plaza. He saw that there were about twenty of them, and that they were a most unsavoury-looking bunch. He felt the hollow pangs of fear in his belly, but breathed deeply in, in order to swell his chest and appear larger and more confident. He reached into the breast-pocket of his shirt and took out a loose-leaf notebook with a pencil inserted into the spiral of the binder. He appraised the group with every appearance of coolness, and by intuition guessed correctly who their leader was. He pointed a finger at him and said, 'Name?'

'Emperador Ignacio Coriolano,' he replied, and his henchmen grinned.

'Ay, a cabinet minister,' observed the mayor sarcastically. He replaced the notebook in his pocket and took his revolver from its holster and raised it, taking up first pressure. 'To tell the truth, I do not care what your name is. But all of you will place your weapons on the ground in front of you, and then you will step backwards three paces.'

The mayor called over his shoulder to a group of men who were still inspecting with gruesome fascination the remains of Abuela Teresa, and they came forward hesitantly. The mayor repeated his order for the crusaders to drop their weapons, and his knuckle whitened on the trigger. Their leader glanced at his fellows as if to disown his cowardice, and tossed his carbine forward with a gesture intended to convey nonchalance, the rest of the men following suit. 'Collect the guns,' he said to the villagers, and then he addressed the crusaders once more. 'You will get them back in the morning if you care to stay with us.'

The invaders dispersed to the bars and the whorehouse, and the mayor locked their weapons in the same schoolhouse that had previously served as a temporary gaol for Fathers Valentino and Lorenzo. These two had in the meantime been questioned in the alcaldia by the two policemen, and had given a reasonably truthful account of the events leading up to the death of Abuela Teresa. An hour later, when the mayor had confirmed from the evidence of other witnesses that no prosecutable offence had been committed, he released the shaken clergymen on condition that they perform the funeral mass for the old lady. This the villagers would not permit them to do, and so they waited penitently until the body was in its grave and the people had dispersed before reciting the mass for the burial of the dead. Feeling defeated and ashamed, they went to the grotto of the three statues and passed the night in prayer, so that in the morning, hypnotised by the repetition of sacred formulae, they emerged just as full of righteous assurance as they had been before the tragedy in the plaza.

During the night three things happened that led to the inevitable débâcle of the following day. Firstly, the band of crusaders became very inebriated indeed, being far from home, shaken up by the events of the day, and anxious to prove their virility to each other. Secondly, the whores of the village would have nothing to do with them, which aroused them at first to anger and then to a desire for revenge that was intensified by drink. Thirdly, they forced open the door of the schoolhouse and took back their weapons whilst the village slept.

Shortly after dawn the people of the pueblo awoke to the sound of screams and oaths, and tumbled out of their doorways to behold a scene of such barbarousness that nothing like it had been witnessed by any of them since the time of La Violencia. The crusaders had invaded the whorehouse en masse, and had dragged the girls out by the hair. They were perpetrating such infamies on them that for a time no one seemed to know what to do.

The eight girls were being brutally violated in turn by the twenty men. It seemed as though each blink of the eye revealed a new horror. Here was a girl being raped at the same time as a man was holding her mouth open and another was yanking at a gold tooth with a pair of pliers. Here a girl was being pinned spreadeagled as a drunk stubbed a cigarette on her breasts and another man urinated over her face. Here was a girl who had been hauled upside-down over a branch and was being mercilessly flogged, so that the blood ran down to the ground and was flicked across the plaza on the backstroke of the bullwhip. Most terrible, the leader of the crusaders forced his shotgun barrels between the legs of the girl who had refused him, and pulled both triggers.

Someone mounted a horse and rode recklessly to Don Mascar's hacienda for help. Back in the village the mayor emerged in his nightshirt, but armed with his revolver. He shook his head as if to convince himself of the reality of what he saw, and was about to fire at the leader when a bullet in his chest flung him backwards. He died unattended, the most courageous and dedicated peacekeeper the village had ever had.

When Don Mascar and his men galloped into the plaza half an hour later, most of the girls were dead. It was a place where women became whores out of necessity or misfortune, and a whore could be one's sister, one's mother, or a sweetheart. Very little shame was attached to being a whore, and there was in that place none of that perverted logic of other countries where it is all but accepted that the prostitute is a natural target for violence. The villagers, heartened by the arrival of their caudillo, joined in the grim massacre of the evil men who had brought death to their peaceful homes.

Fathers Valentino and Lorenzo, alerted by the sound of gunfire, arrived from the grotto to find that the sweet scent of early-morning mimosa was drowned in a pall of cordite and the sticky, indefinable odour of blood. The girls had been taken into the whorehouse, and all the priests saw were the sanguineous corpses of their bodyguard being carried in hammocks out of the town. Horrified, they followed the proceedings. The villagers ignored them, oppressing them with the sensation of invisibility. They watched open-mouthed as the corpses were hauled into the branches of a giant ceiba tree, and left for the buzzards and vultures that had already gathered. Neither of them had ever before crossed themselves so often and with such mechanical rapidity.

At the end Don Mascar himself rode up behind them and said, 'Leave.'

'Leave?' echoed Valentino stupidly, and Father Lorenzo started to try to make a point. 'This atrocity . . .' he began, but he caught Don Mascar's eye.

Don Mascar was sixty years old and had been the unofficial lawmaker, employer, judge, jury, benefactor and avenger of the district since he was thirty years old. He had done some bad things in his time, but had never enjoyed the sour taste in his mouth afterwards, and so he had acquired the reputation for justice and reasonableness that had ensured the longevity of his reign. His finca took two days to cross on horseback, he had several thousand steers, and he possessed an invincible air of authority. He only had to look at a man disdainfully, and that man would shut his mouth.

Don Mascar looked down on the priests from the height of his saddle, and leaned forward on the pommel with his hands in order to ease his legs. 'I will preach you a sermon,' he said laconically. 'I am no philosopher, but I know this. Your religions cause wars and prevent marriages. There will be no peace on earth until every synagogue, every mosque, every church, and every temple is razed to the ground or made into a barn, and when that happens, no one will be happier than the Lord God Himself. Now leave, or . . .' and he pointed to the bodies adorned with clumsy vultures, '. . . I shall let you join your friends.' Don Mascar raised an eyebrow and moved his forefinger back and forth with exactly that gesture used by schoolteachers to dismiss a reprimanded child, and the two priests trudged away through the dust, unable to speak with one another for the horror at what had unaccountably happened to their band of the faithful.

A fortnight later in the capital Mgr Rechin Anquilar was fired with a new fury, and resolved to combine his crusaders into an unassailable army. He had just interviewed Father Valentino and Father Lorenzo, had heard that their bodyguard had been massacred for no apparent reason, and had put their report in a file that contained dozens of others that told equally sickening stories. All over the country it seemed that innocent missionaries were being brutalised and abused. There must be some kind of satanic conspiracy at work. He re-read the report of the Holy Office, and guessed that its epicentre must be Cochadebajo de los Gatos. Even the name of the place had a pagan ring to it.

Capitan Papagato and General Fuerte frequently experienced renewals of the unlikely friendship that they had forged after the latter's return from the torture centre at the Army School of Electrical and Mechanical Engineering. The General still suffered periods of debility arising from his terrible mistreatment in that place, and it was upon one such occasion, when the General was confined to his hammock with a disabling pain in his shoulders from the strappado, that Capitan Papagato and Francesca came round to keep him company.

The Capitan and his new wife sat tickling the ears of their accumulation of pet jaguars whilst the General tried hard not to breathe too deeply, and attempted to avoid gesticulation as he talked; he was beginning to feel like an Englishman. 'How do you find marriage?' he demanded of Francesca.

'It makes up for a lot of things,' she said. 'I missed Federico so much when he ran away and then got killed, and my uncle Juanito was killed too. It left a terrible emptiness that made me wonder how much I was still alive.'

'Federico, they say, got married to Parlanchina after he died. So says Aurelio.'

'I believe it,' said Francesca, 'and my father preserves Uncle Juanito's head with the hole in it that the Army put there with a grenade, but somehow that was not enough. Now I am happy.'

The General frowned. 'I am very sorry about that, you know. If I had known what was being done in my name by the troops under my command, I would have court-martialled a great many people.'

'It no longer matters, General. The Army gave me Papagato.'

Capitan Papagato smiled and reached out to stroke her hair. 'She is the prettiest woman that you have ever seen, is she not, General? All one needs in life is several overgrown black jaguars and Francesca, and one is content.' He paused: 'Permit me to ask, General, why did you never marry?'

'I am not a pansy, if that is what you are thinking,' said the General testily. 'I was married to the Army.'

'Was there never anyone?'

'There was,' replied the sick man, 'and as we have plenty of time, I could tell you about her, if you are disposed to listen.'

The two visitors nodded eagerly, hoping to hear details of great tragedy and lasciviousness.

The General's eyes misted over with memory, and he attempted to picture the face of the girl, but recalled only her smell.

'I was a lieutenant at the time, and I had had the usual experiences of a young officer, if you know what I mean.'

The Capitan nodded, and Francesca shot him a glance betraying some deeply jealous suspicions.

'I was posted to Cucuta, and really there was nothing at all to do. There was a bar there and about five brothels, but none of the inmates were worth a second inspection, if you forgive me for mentioning such things. On Saturdays there was a Jew who showed 'the latest movies' in the plaza, and they were a disaster. Absolute dross, and usually the skies opened just as we were getting to the end, so more often than not we never knew how the action resolved itself.

'One day I was at the movie, and I caught sight of a redheaded woman. She was about twenty years old, and I have to tell you straight away that I have always been crazy about redheads. Don't ask me why, because I don't know why, except maybe that when I was at school there was a little girl who was redheaded, and she smelled as sweet as hay. Maybe you don't know, but redheaded girls always smell the best. Sweet and clean. Like papaya and honeysuckle. There is something about the smell that makes me feel religious, God forgive me. And the worst of it is, that there are almost no redheads in this whole country.

'Anyway, I always knew in my own imagination that the woman I would love, the woman of my entire life, was going to be a redhead, and then I saw a beautiful redhead at the movie. I could not concentrate on one word of the dialogue from that moment, because I was looking at her. I had needles in my backside from seeing her.

'Afterwards I bumped into her on purpose, just to smell her, and she smelled even more beautiful than she looked. "I am so sorry," I said, "I have been unforgivably clumsy," and she laughed and said, "O, I forgive you." See? I remember her very words, that is how much she struck me down. Taking my chance I said, "May I walk you home?" and she said, "As long as you make nothing of it."

'I walked her home and I think she was impressed by the uniform, because the day afterwards I went back to her little house where she lived with her mother, and she waved to me from the window and invited me in. Not believing my good fortune, I went in, and in the light of day I could see that her hair was long and flowing, and it sparkled like new copper, it was so clean. She had green eyes, and already I was in love, and her scent filled the room so that afterwards I could smell it even on the arm of my uniform.

'I went back every day, and they fed me and asked me questions about the Army, and I tried to be as confident and worldly-wise as young men do. Soon everybody knew that we were courting, and other men stopped coming to see her, and her mother apparently thought that I was such a good catch that she let us walk about unchaperoned.

'One day I confessed my love to her, and she said that she felt the same way. I was so elated that I bought for her the biggest bunch of flowers you have ever seen. It was so big that it filled up the entire back of a jeep, except that I brought it to her across the saddle of a cavalry charger in full ceremonial order.

'Being a young man, you understand, I was motivated by adventurism of the sexual kind as much as by anything else' – here Francesca leaned forward with renewed interest – 'and I was ferociously bent upon doing what I could not help wanting to do, if you catch my meaning.

'But she was very rigid about it. There was nothing that she would consent to, not even reconnaissance or forward patrols. No pincer movements or covert operations behind the lines. Nothing. I was in a fever. Every night I could not sleep for thinking about you-know-what, and my imagination was running so wild that once the Colonel said to me, "You may dismiss, Lieutenant," and I actually replied, "Thank you, darling," as I saluted. I had not heard anything that he had said to me, and my troop did not turn out on parade as he had commanded.

'He called me into his office and made me explain myself. I took the bull by the horns and I told him the truth, and do you know what he said to me? He said, "Any woman will adopt a prone firing position if you offer to marry her."

'So that very evening I went down on my knees in the moonlight and asked her to marry me, and before you protest, let me tell you that I meant it sincerely and absolutely, as well as in hope of advanced supplies from quartermaster's stores.

'Do you know what she did? She practically dragged me back to her mother's house. She wanted to put a handkerchief in my mouth to stop me from inadvertently alerting her mother with my gasps, and she unbuttoned my uniform. I was thinking, "Thank you, Colonel, O thank you," and planning to buy him a big bottle of Scotch, and she pulled me down on the bed.' (Francesca at this juncture leaned forward so far that her chair tipped dangerously, and Capitan Papagato became embarrassed.)

'Naturally, I began to unclothe her, and I was in paradise. It was the smell, I was thinking, "Redheads are angels fallen to earth, and I am in heaven." My first disappointment was that her breasts turned out to be small like a ten year old's, and those round redoubts were in fact entirely padding made out of bags of pot-pourri, which accounted for the deliciousness of her corporal aroma. I thought, "Never mind, no one is so perfect that one cannot pass by a small deficiency," and I was so overwhelmed with, you know, desire, for want of an appropriate euphemism, that I launched an assault in open order on her Command Headquarters. She said, "No, no, let me turn out the light," and I was saying, "No need to be shy, I want to admire you." There was a fair struggle, I can tell you, all in complete silence so as not to awaken her mother, but I won. And do you know what I saw after that miserable victory?'

'No,' said Francesca breathlessly and somewhat unnecessarily.

'I saw that she was not a real redhead. Her real hair colour was black. And the disappointment and the sense of deception were so bitter that forever afterwards I have never been able to entrust my heart to a woman. And I never met too many more redheads in any case. And if I had, I could not have determined whether or not they were real redheads until I had already compromised myself.'

Later that evening Francesca popped back in to see the General on the pretext of bringing him a mango. She smiled coyly, hesitated, and asked, 'So you . . . did you do anything with her after all?'

General Fuerte smiled distantly and shifted to clear a dart of pain from his neck. His face brightened, and he tapped the side of his nose. 'My memory fails me,' he said, and he winked.

## 28  *In Which His Excellency President Veracruz Fiddles While Medio-Magdalena Burns*

There has been much argument amongst historiosophists as to what conditions must pertain in order for history to occur. There are those who argue for the neccessity of correct social conditions, and much energy is spent scrutinising the relation between the economic base and the cultural superstructure, and there are those who argue that history is a plastic medium in the hands of those who rise to greatness.

There has also been much argument amongst historians as to how the New Albigensian Crusade could possibly have occurred. From every angle it appears that such a phenomenon should have been utterly impossible at such a late stage of civilisation, when it was beginning to appear that there was so much peace that history had virtually stopped happening at all. Surely, the historians feel, mankind had already reached the stage when almost everyone recognised that no belief was so certain that it was worth killing for. Surely we had become sufficiently religiously mature not to have to bother about whether or not the Blessed Virgin was immaculately conceived, or whether or not one's neighbour believed in the literal resurrection of the body?

Such historians are possibly out of touch with reality, being insufficiently cynical about people's motives, because the New Albigensian Crusade, like all such outbreaks of puzzling fanaticism, was about venality and power as well as a certain unfortunate combination of circumstances.

In the first place it was unfortunate that His Eminence, Cardinal Guzman, was so anxious to save his own soul and then became too ill to understand what he had set in motion. In the second place it was impossible for him to have known in advance how Monsignor Rechin Anquilar would handle his accumulating power and influence, and we have to bear in mind that His Excellency, President Veracruz, was away on a world tour that had very little to do with the conduct of internal affairs. His cabinet were confused and at odds with each other throughout his absence, and in addition were more or less completely unaware of what was going on because events mostly occurred in the countryside of a land where politicians only took any notice of what happened in the towns, and especially in the capital.

The Armed Forces were in command of General Hernando Montes Sosa, Dionisio Vivo's father, and he was a man so conscientious and principled that he would not take unilateral military action without a Presidential directive, and one has to bear in mind that they were obsessively entangled in the cocaine wars of Medio-Magdalena, a fact worthy of explanation.

It all began with guerrilla groups that in the first stages of their activities were welcomed and supplied by the campesinos, who saw as their only hope of survival the establishment of a Communist state which would redistribute more equitably the profits of production. In the interim they hoped that the guerrillas would protect them against the Army, which at that time was under the command of General Ramirez, and which seemed to be little more than a state-funded organisation for the perpetration of rape and pillage, under the aegis of local commanders who were nothing other than rural satraps.

There was a brief honeymoon between the guerrillas and the peasants. To begin with, the first question demanded of a peon by a guerrilla chief was, 'How does your landlord treat you? Do you want us to sort him out?' and many a landlord found himself hung up by his feet and beaten, or hung up by his neck and disembowelled. The Army, either through incompetence, cowardice or discretion, made itself noticeably absent, and the guerrillas had a free hand to slot with immaculate precision into the place it had left vacant. Peasants were now raped and pillaged by guerrillas who demanded supplies and other privileges with the aid of unveiled threats that amounted to extortion and blackmail, and they killed the very same kinds of people as 'counter-revolutionaries' that the Army had used to kill as 'subversives'. There was soon an almost complete shortage of teachers, priests, doctors, mayors, and agronomists. The peasants went to their landlords and asked for protection.

These latifundistas, who had greatly cleaned up their act on account of their fear of the guerrillas, leapt at the chance to improve industrial relations, and appealed to the government to protect their peons. The government appealed to the Army, which just then was a little too busy to arrive in person (because of incompetence, cowardice or discretion), and so they sent supplies of arms in order that the peasants might defend themselves.

These new paramilitary groups enjoyed a honeymoon period. The guerrillas retreated further into the jungle and passed their time stinging with jiggers and acquiring fungal infections of the feet, and the campesinos rebuilt their fincas and schools, and went back to work. But the paramilitaries now had very little to do, their trigger fingers were itchy, and the taste of blood and the exhilaration of battle were fresh upon their tongues.

Providentially the cocaine lords moved in. As demand grew exponentially in the United States, they very logically expanded production by moving into Medio-Magdalena. They obtained huge tracts of land, and their men raped and pillaged in the time-honoured tradition, except that they did not repeat the mistakes of the guerrillas. They bought the services of the paramilitaries, who now formed death-squads that roamed the countryside liquidating the teachers, priests, doctors, mayors and agronomists who spoke out against them.

At this point the command of the Army passed to Hernando Montes Sosa, and he took swift action against the coca lords. The Army saturated the area, and immediately came up against one of the strangest alliances in the history of the world. The coca caciques and the most powerful right-wing landlords began to supply the Communist guerrillas with weapons to keep the Army busy so that they could carry on as 'narcotraficos' and exploitative employers in relative peace, and the paramilitaries now became allied with the guerrillas because the Army were trying to disarm them. The uncriminalised portion of the civilian population now hailed the Army as saviours, and it spent its time protecting teachers, priests, doctors, mayors and agronomists – those whom, in short, it used to persecute as subversives. This is not to say, of course, that certain renegade Army commanders did not take advantage of the situation in order to rape and pillage a little in their spare time.

And so it was on account of the mayhem in Medio-Magdalena that the Armed Forces were preoccupied at the time of a crusade of whose existence they were unaware, and were in any case unable to intervene owing to His Excellency's personal crusade for occult knowledge and push-button virility.

His Excellency lay in bed playing with his executive polla, which now had the extraordinary ability to be erected any time and for any period that the fancy took him. He had arrived at the hospital in California a month previously, suffering from fits of queasiness and apprehension. It is no light thing to voluntarily undergo an operation upon a vital piece of intimate equipment which suffers from no fundamental faults, and the mental image of a scalpel slitting dramatic cuts into his nether parts was not one to ease the mind. In fact, if it had not been for the persistent encouragement of Madame Veracruz, he probably would not have managed to face it, and would have checked himself ignominiously out of the hospital.

'O, Daddykins,' she would say in her most wheedlingly saccharine voice, 'just think of all the fun we could have and all the alchemy we could do,' and he would make a dubious face and wonder if all Panamanian wives were so enthusiastic. Certainly the Foreign Secretary said that they had the hottest tails in the world, but Emperador Ignacio Coriolano maintained that you could not beat a mulatta from Bahia.

President Veracruz had two hydraulic sacs inserted into the erectile tissue of his polla, a sac of fluid inserted into his abdomen, and a small pump mounted discreetly in his scrotum. The whole device worked with a system of automatic valves, and when he woke up afterwards the pain was excruciating. The gringo doctors filled him up with a veritable pharmacopoeia of painkillers, and for a week he sincerely believed that he had been the unwitting victim of an elaborate Communist plot to kill him, which was why he refused to speak to his wife. She went to New York and at the taxpayers' expense bought some alligator shoes for two thousand dollars which she could have bought at home for two thousand pesos, since the unfortunate alligator had really been a cayman.

After four weeks His Excellency was feeling better, and had begun to play with his new apparatus. He squeezed the little pump in his scrotum, and, miraculously, his polla rose and swelled. In fact he could make it swell so tightly that the sensation was arousing in itself, and then the blood rushed in and made it swell even more. He had not felt such tightness and tautness since he was sixteen and so desperate for appeasement that he could have done it with a pig, living or dead. 'Whooba,' he exclaimed, like a vaquero who has just lassoed a difficult calf, and then, 'Whooba,' again as he squeezed the pump the other way and his polla subsided gently like the sleepy head of a drunk. He pumped it up again and was admiring its impressive firmness when the nurse opened the door and came in. Hastily he covered himself with the sheet and blushed crimson. 'Enjoying ourselves with our new toy, are we?' she said, and His Excellency attempted to stand on his dignity. 'One has to ensure that one has had one's money's worth. I was doing it in a purely scientific spirit.'

'Scientists play with themselves as well,' remarked the nurse, and His Excellency was on the point of sacking her for impertinence when he remembered that he was in the United States. 'I came in to tell you that Señora Veracruz has telephoned to say that she will be coming to visit you this evening, and that you are to expect a present.'

'O, thank you,' he said, and discreetly squeezed the pump so that the erection would go away and allow him to lower his knees, which he had raised because his tumescent organ would have supported the sheet like a tentpole and the nurse would have noticed. 'I am sorry I disturbed you,' said the nurse, and she added confidentially, 'Everybody plays with it until the novelty wears off.'

Madame Veracruz came in that evening looking stunning. She had popped into the 'power room' in order to don animal skins and a horned helmet so that she might appear as Freya. She and His Excellency had by now worked through the Egyptian and Greek pantheons, believing that to make love dressed as a god and performing an intent visualisation at the moment or orgasm was an infallible way of achieving one's ends, and now they had decided to work through the Norse pantheon as well, having tired of Isis and Osiris, Ares and Aphrodite, Apollo and Kyrene, Set and Nephthys.

'You look wonderful, my dear,' he said. 'I am not sure that the long blonde wig is entirely necessary, though. I imagine it could become very itchy.'

'O,' she replied, 'I shouldn't wear so much nail polish either. I don't think they had nail polish. Look, I have brought you an Odin costume.' She unpacked from a small suitcase an eyepatch, a cloak, a large floppy hat, and two taxidermised ravens that had seen better days. She held them out. 'This one's called Hugin and you wear it on one shoulder, and this one's called Munin, which you wear on the other.'

'Let me try it all on,' said His Excellency, clambering out of bed and taking off his nightgown. He donned the cloak and the eyepatch, placed the hat on his head at an angle suitable for haunting gibbets, and tried to perch the ravens on his shoulder. They kept falling off, and one of them added a cracked beak to its list of injuries. 'I'll sew them onto the cloak by their feet,' said Madame Veracruz with a concerned expression.

'This is a wonderful present, my little pussycat, thank you very much. I am going to find out all about Odin so that I can assume his form effectively.'

'O, this isn't your present,' she said, and shyly she reached into the bag and produced a cylindrical object wrapped in cheerfully coloured paper. He reached out and took it, trying to guess at what it was. Madame Veracruz pulled a sour face at one of his suggestions. 'We don't need one of those now that we have your new thingammy,' she said.

His Excellency unwrapped it and found that it was a portion of branch. He looked perplexed and said, 'What is it?'

'It's a bit of branch.'

'Yes, but what is it for, this piece of branch?'

'It's a pet, silly.'

'A pet? What kind of pet is a branch? Shouldn't we have a parrot to sit on it, or something, and then we would have a pet?'

'It's the latest fashion,' she said. 'All over the United States people have bits of branch as a pet. You put it somewhere and you talk to it, or you can stroke it and it puts you in touch with your natural self. Even the President has one, and everybody is throwing away their pet rocks and their cabbage-patch children and their couch-potatoes.'

'Perhaps everybody is throwing away their dogs as well,' said His Excellency. 'Ay, these gringos, I will never understand them. I still think my idea was better.'

Madame Veracruz smiled coyly and looked at him with her most calculatedly fetching sideways glance. 'You will have to peel the bark off first.' Then she turned around and popped her head out of the door to check that no one was coming, came back in and said, 'Now let's play with our new toy. I want to see it work.' She parted his gown and began a countdown as he squeezed the bulb.

She was impressed. 'Daddykins,' she said, 'it's made it go longer and thicker. I just can't wait. Now make it go down.'

She watched it sink its head and resume its gentle repose. 'Not bad for a man of nearly eighty years, is it?' said His Excellency proudly.

'I want to try it,' she exclaimed, and she shot her hand forward and squeezed.

'Ay, ay, ay, Madre de Dios, qué puta de hijo de perra!' shouted His Excellency, grabbing her by the wrist and wrenching her hand away. 'For the love of God, that was my testicle.'

Madame Veracruz was abashed and guilt-stricken, and, attracted by the outcry, the nurse walked in just as she was bending down to kiss it better. It would be hard to describe accurately the nurse's impression of what it is like to see two Norse gods apparently engaged in a most egregious act of fellatio in a private hospital room; suffice it to say that she left precipitately, and shortly afterwards the faces of other nurses began to appear at the window at disconcertingly frequent intervals, hoping to witness either a repeat performance or something equally interesting.

It is sad to report that two days later His Excellency had to summon the surgeon and inform him that the apparatus was no longer functioning. This grave news was greeted by a resigned shake of the head and a scholarly smile. 'I am afraid that one of the valves has stopped working,' said the doctor. 'It happens occasionally. We will have to open you up and install another.'

Madame Veracruz made him go through with it, and it only cost the taxpayer a few more thousand dollars. Meanwhile, in Medio-Magdalena, the death toll reached six thousand, the situation became exacerbated because the coca lords recruited British and Israeli mercenaries, and more bodies bumped their way along the bed of the river Magdalena with their stomachs filled with stones.

Felipe Galtan, father of one of the three assassinated presidential hopefuls who had campaigned upon an anti-coca ticket, was quoted in *La Prensa* as saying that, 'Never in any country have so many tragedies happened at the same time.'

# 29  *Concepcion Buys His Eminence A Present*

It was the Cardinal's name-day, and Concepcion took Cristobal's hand and led him out into the thoroughfare in order to search for a gift. Name-days were always a problem to her because she had no salary to speak of, living off what was provided in terms of food and accommodation by the facilities of the palace. Normally she could go to the Cardinal to ask for money when she or Cristobal needed any particular item, but naturally she could not go to him in order to ask for money with which to buy him a present. She took a ring that was all that she had left of her mother, and sold it for a pittance to a 'Syrian' who persuaded her that it was not real gold; he gave her enough to buy more medicines from the brujo in the slums, and a present for the Cardinal.

'It is getting worse,' she told the medicine-man. 'His belly swells like a woman with child, and his mind is unclear so that one of these days I am afraid that he will not recognise himself in a mirror. What can be done?'

The brujo cast cowrie shells upon the mat at his feet, and squatted over them, furrowing his brow in the effort of interpretation. 'Does he still see demons?'

Concepcion nodded fearfully. 'It is very bad these days.'

The brujo took a deep draw of his cigar and blew the smoke over the shells to help them speak. 'He has a bad conscience.'

'He has always had a bad conscience, Master.'

'You should be careful of the child, Señora. Apart from his relentless picking of his nose, which will sooner or later cause bleeding and lead to an infestation of worms from beneath his fingernails, I think that there are going to be problems for him. Look, I threw the shells to ask about your man, and I got the configuration that means "Child".'

'It means nothing to me, Master.' Concepcion looked around the tin shack with its festoons of dried herbs and shrivelled llama foetuses. She shivered at the ekekko, the household god that guarded the doorway, and tried to avoid wondering whether or not its wild hair came from a corpse. It features were picked out in lines of cowrie shells, and its expression of amused and detached knowledgeability caused her to feel uneasy.

'I will put vilco in the medicine,' said the brujo, 'and it will make him much worse. He will see the demons more clearly and he will be more terrified than ever, so you must be prepared for that, and understand that I am causing a crisis that will get it all over with much quicker. Are you prepared for that?'

Concepcion's heart sank, and her face fell, but she said, 'Yes, Master,' in a low whisper that betrayed her trepidation. 'And what if he gets worse but is not cured afterwards?'

The brujo shook his head and stroked the grey strands of his beard. 'I will have to come to him and fight with the demons, and I might have to fight with him too, to shake his soul back into his body.'

'You cannot,' said Concepcion, 'he is a priest.'

The brujo laughed so that the lack of his front teeth caught Cristobal's attention and momentarily distracted him from swivelling his finger in his ear. 'I can come all the same,' replied the brujo.

'Thank you,' said Concepcion. 'Look, I have brought you some oranges and a chicken.'

'I cannot accept payment; my power would wash away in the rain.'

'It is not payment, it is a gift.'

'Then thank you, and Chango guard you with his thunder and Oshun preserve your beauty. Here is the medicine.'

Concepcion left the hut and went out into the mud of the favela. Across the floor of the valley could be seen the fair buildings of the capital, with the government blocks and the Hilton Hotel rising up above the colonial houses, most of whose façades had been replaced with plate-glass shopfronts. She could see the Cardinal's palace to one side, and noticed that the perpetual drizzle was drifting in that direction. She thought of His Eminence tutting irritably and moving his chair from the lawns and into the cloister.

On the mountainsides she saw the 'villas miserias', sometimes referred to euphemistically as 'new towns', that ringed the city and made visitors reflect that the wealth of the centre was somehow obscene by comparison. She stood for a minute and observed the section of it in which she found herself. A twelve-year old prostitute whose frequent coughs produced clots of blood that congealed around her doorway was waiting for customers who were too poor to pay her in anything other than plastic gewgaws and insults. A naked child was being washed in the rain by someone who might have been her sister but was probably an infant mother. A hydrophobic dog was being stoned from a safe distance by a small knot of drunks. It was reeling in circles, and any minute now it would fall over and consent to die. The cadaver of a cat lay in a mud-puddle, and a buzzard was circumambulating, working up a hunger. Higher up the slope a woman was wailing, probably because of a death or because of parturition. With his back against a shack, a man was defecating painfully with his trousers around his ankles. Cristobal watched with utter fascination. 'That man is doing a poo,' he announced, pointing.

'Everyone poos,' replied Concepcion.

'Does the Cardinal?'

'Even the Cardinal.'

'I bet he doesn't.'

She sighed and took his hand, beginning the long walk down to the glossy shops where she could find a present for her lover, where she would inevitably be tempted to splash out on make-up, on shiny sentimental ornaments of animals, on necklaces depicting the miracles of saints. Inevitably, she would finger these things, feel their solidity and weight in her hands, and put them back on the shelves because a shop assistant would be eyeing her suspiciously. Then a white person would come in, and the same assistant would rush up unctuously and ask, 'May I help you at all?'

In the Calle Bolivar she came across a stall that was selling records. Bored with her search for the unformulated present, she stopped and idly flicked through the cardboard squares. She found ones from the United States, depicting men with long hair like devils, their faces painted into masks like those of Indians; she saw that they were all scowling or angry. There were ones with blonde semi-naked women on them in seductive poses, whose hair was piled up exorbitantly on their heads and whose armpits were as hairless as a little girl's. There were pictures of groups of Negroes in sunglasses, their hair cut straight across the top so that the crowns of their heads looked like platforms. She showed one of the record covers to Cristobal. 'If you carry on picking your nose, you will end up looking like that.'

'Are they spacemen?' he asked. 'I want to be a spaceman, and when

I die I want to be a hummingbird.' He raised his arms and tried to flap them so fast that they blurred. 'Do I look like one yet?'

'Faster,' said Concepcion. 'At this rate you will only get to be a stork.'

In amongst the vallenato records Concepcion came across a record that from top to bottom and from back to front announced its own gravitas. It bore a bust of a man with downturned lips and an expression of dour disapproval. She scanned the foreign writing and found no exclamation marks; His Eminence always said that the mark of seriousness and good style in writing is the lack of them. In large black letters the cover proclaimed 'Beethoven: 3rd Symphony (Eroica)' and Concepcion marvelled at the incomprehensibility of it. She held it up to the stallholder and asked, 'Is this suitable for a serious rich man of high taste?'

'That is all it is suitable for,' rejoined the man. 'I have had it for ten years and no one has bought it.'

'I will buy it,' she said quickly. 'How much is it?'

The stallholder saw the light of hopefulness in her eyes and the poverty of her clothes, and was overwhelmed with charity. 'Take it,' he said. 'It was always yours and never mine. If you ever become ugly, then bring it back.'

She clutched the precious item to her chest and tried not to cry with gratitude. She would go back and reclaim her mother's ring from the Syrian.

His Eminence removed the wrapping from the present and was touched. 'I have not heard this since I was a young man,' he said. 'When I was nineteen I went with my brother, Salvador, the one who messed up at the seminary because of his taste in obscene poetry and then disappeared, and we heard this in Quito when we were in Ecuador. It was magnificent, and afterwards we came out in such high spirits that Salvador pretended to be Superman and he bounded along the street like an idiot, and I had the first theme running through my head for weeks.'

'You like it then?'

'I am delighted. How did you know I would like it?'

She pulled a wry face and said, 'I am not so stupid.'

She went away to the kitchen to make pichones con petit-pois, and shortly heard the strains of Beethoven drifting through the cloisters and corridors. She stopped extracting the entrails of the pigeon and stood perfectly still. Something made her leave her cooking and creep upstairs, where she sat on the floor outside the Cardinal's chamber, her arms wrapped about her knees. As she listened intently she began to weep without knowing it, and when the record was finished the Cardinal came out of his room and found her in the corridor with clean streaks descending her face where the grime of work had been washed away. She looked up at him and explained, 'Querido, it was so beautiful, it was like making love.'

## 30 *Dionisio Unexpectedly Acquires Two More Lovers On The Way To See His Family*

Dionisio shut up his house and went out to look for his cats. He found one of them at Josef's, where it was cadging panela from the latter's wife, and the other he located behind the Palace of the Lords, where it was nostalgically making the kind of scrape that it would have done in the wild. 'Venga, gatito,' he said, and the great animal looked up at him innocently with its huge amber eyes. 'Come along,' said Dionisio, 'we are going home.' The black jaguar hesitated dubiously, and then followed its master, cuffing the other cat playfully about the ears and biting its neck. 'It's time you two grew up,' said Dionisio, and proceeded to Sergio's house.

Capitan Papagato was there with Francesca, and everybody was admiring the nascent curves of her first pregnancy. Dionisio exchanged pleasantries upon the subject of children, and then he and Sergio went to the corral to rope the horse and saddle it. It had once belonged to Pablo Ecobandodo, universally known as 'El Jerarca', and was a spirited grey stallion that nowadays objected to being separated from its female companions and was therefore difficult to catch.

Today was no exception. Sergio tempted it with a grenadillo while Dionisio crept up with the bridle, but at the last second it pricked up its ears, snorted, and triumphantly departed to the far end of the corral with the grenadillo safely installed between its molars. 'Mierda,' they both exclaimed, and Sergio said, 'Why do you not command him?'

Dionisio was famous for being able to communicate directly with animals, but he shook his head and replied, 'It is all very well commanding him, but he will not obey. This is a truly Latino horse, amigo, and therefore he will work only when there is no choice. Believe me, he and I are old friends, and he knows that he is in for a long ride. Come here, caballo, or I will give all your fodder to a mule.'

The horse laid back its ears and showed its teeth in that typical equine expression that looks like a demented smile, and trotted briskly back and forth along the end of the corral. He bit one of the mares on the backside and stood still with satisfaction as the mare kicked out at him. 'We will have to lasso him,' said Sergio.

Nowadays most lassos are made of blue nylon rope, and the consequence of this progress is that horses are much harder to catch. The rope picks up permanent and intractable kinks that make it almost impossible to make a perfect loop with it, and furthermore it severely burns the hands if the horse should decide to run. But Sergio still used the old-fashioned kind that was made of twisted cowhide and formed generous circular loops, and with this he casually walked to within a few metres of the recalcitrant horse. The latter saw the lasso and shied back, so Sergio deliberately walked past him and made as if to launch the lariat at another horse. At the last minute he spun around and landed it neatly over the neck of the astonished stallion. 'He is not very bright, is he?' remarked Dionisio. 'He falls for that one every time.'

'Some people say that horses have no memory,' observed Sergio, 'but my opinion is that he likes to be caught. It is simply a matter of honour to appear to resist, and in this way a horse is very like a woman, eh cabrón? Except that no woman resists you, it seems.' Sergio clicked his teeth and smiled salaciously.

Once caught, the animal stood stock still as Dionisio placed the leather garra upon its back, heaved up the saddle, and then tightened the cinturon about its chest. As he put on the bridle the horse very deliberately stood on Dionisio's foot and shifted his weight. 'Ay, ay, ay,' exclaimed Dionisio, pushing against the animal's shoulders to make it move. 'Hijo de puta.'

Sergio laughed with his arms crossed, leaning back against the rails of the corral. 'It is not the horse who has no memory. He catches you every time like that.'

'He is one hell of a humorist, this horse,' said Dionisio ruefully, inspecting his already swelling toes. 'When I first had him he had no spirit at all, and now he is a trickster.' He mounted the stallion and shook the long hair away from his face. Sergio smiled up at him, thinking that he looked the very image of an Indian in an old Western, with the police pistol stuck into his belt, and the long-tailed shirt that served as his raiment. But in comparison to Dionisio the horse was very richly adorned, because it still wore the accoutrements owned by its previous master, the coca cacique, Pablo Ecobandodo, who had caparisoned it in leather studded with silver and emeralds. On a sunny day Dionisio could be seen coming from a great distance on account of the glittering flashes from his saddle, and this was another of the reasons that he was regarded with a kind of superstitious awe even by those who knew him well.

The jaguars followed behind the horse, swiping at its tail and dodging kicks, and Dionisio rode to the habitations of each of his women, calling upon Leticia Aragon the last. She was washing the first of Dionisio's children to live, and she smiled and turned her face upward so that he could bend down from the saddle and plant a kiss on her cheek. She held up the child for him to kiss, and he patted her cheek and cradled her for a moment in his arms. This child was Anica Primera, because he had thirty-two children, all of which were designated by their order of arrival. The boys were all called Dionisito and bore upon their necks the hereditary scar of the knife and the rope, and the eighteen girls were all called Anica, according to his wish. What all of these children had in common were the strikingly blue eyes of Dionisio, also to be found upon his ancestor, the Conde Pompeyo Xavier de Estremadura, and upon his father, General Hernando Montes Sosa.

It would have been quicker for him to walk, because he had acquired the Indian art of covering enormous distances over impossible terrain in very short periods of time. Aurelio and Pedro also shared this skill, and it was a terrible frustration for anyone to travel with them, finding themselves left behind by people who were apparently sauntering. Aurelio, of course, was capable of being in two places at once and knew the secret of flying off in the form of an eagle, leaving his body behind, empty-eyed and listless, and Dionisio too could give this impression by the speed of his ability to travel; but for some reason he felt today like taking the horse, and taking his time. Sometimes it is good to be ordinary.

It took him three days of riding to reach Santa Maria Virgen. In the evenings he would build a fire and wait for the jaguars to bring him a vizcacha or a cui to roast over the flames, and then he would throw stones down the mountainside for the pleasure of watching the cats chase after them in a feline caricature of football. When it became cold he would retire to his bivouac amongst the rocks and take up his guitar. First of all he would play his 'Requiem Angelico' in memory of Ramón and Anica, and sometimes the curious acoustics of the mountains would carry this eerie tune to distant hamlets where the conversation would stop and people would cross themselves in the belief that this was a song of God borne to them by special dispensation upon the airwaves of the celestial ether. Afterwards the sound of sobbing would float into the night as grandmothers remembered their stillborn children and spouses who had not embraced for years reached out to each other for consolation in the face of beauty.

Afterwards Dionisio would improvise more of his renowned musical palindromes which sounded the same forwards as they did backwards. He had begun to do this as a purely intellectual exercise, but had discovered that they possessed an hypnotic fascination caused by the puzzling reverberations of the suspicion of *déjà vu* in the mind of the listener. It was a feeling of the deepest and apparently groundless unease, which only disappeared when informed of the reason for it. With these Euterpean palindromes Dionisio felt that he was expressing all the anxiety of the age, and indeed he had made quite a sum of money out of them. They were enthusiastically transcribed by the Mexican musicologist who lived with Ena and Lena, and dispatched to Mexico City, from whence the musicologist's agent distributed them throughout the world.

When it became too cold for a musician's fingers to co-operate, Dionisio would settle into his blanket and think about the past before he drifted off to sleep. His dreams would continue the theme of his thoughts, and he would be back in Ipasueño drinking wine with Ramón and making love with Anica. Somehow he would be both in the past and in the present, and Anica would tease him about having so many women these days, and he would say, 'Bugsita, it takes that many to replace you,' whereupon she would laugh and say, 'But I am still here,' and he would find himself confused and unable to answer. Once she came to him in a nightmare as she had been left when she was murdered, and he awoke choked with horror at her lidless eyes, her lipless mouth, the bleeding apertures where her nose and ears had been hacked away. Sorrowfully she had held out to him his first child who had died with her in her womb. He lived all over again the

178

insanity and anger that had found only a small release when he had killed Pablo Ecobandodo in the plaza of the Barrio Jerarca.

In the morning he would awake encumbered by the luxurious jaguars with their desire for warmth and their sweet smell of hay and strawberries, and he would have to wrestle with them to shift them off. He would break some bread for breakfast and contemplate the mist rolling along the valleys. Sometimes he would climb towards a cloud so that the level sun could shine behind him, cast his shadow upon the vapour, and create an aureonimbus that decked him out as a saint. It would be a black shadow with an aura of rainbow lights that mimicked his every move and gave him intimations of a life to come, when he would live in Anica's world.

Generally he rode beneath the snowline for fear of chasms and out of respect for his horse. He would keep an eye out for avalanches and the onset of soroche, and sometimes he would squint against the sun in the hope of spotting condor vultures riding the updraughts of the thermals in their ceaseless quest for unmajestic carrion and ailing sheep. When he spotted an eagle he would wave in the suspicion that it might be Aurelio, and, when he was lower down where the maraña begins, he would do the same when he saw a hawkhead parrot, in case it was the spirit of Lazaro.

When he finally rode into Santa Maria Virgin it was midday, and he and the jaguars were covered in the fine white dust of travel. 'Hola,' he called to the old man and the old woman, and gestured with his hand in that lazy wave of peasants who wish to imply that all is right with the world and nothing is worth worrying about. They waved back, grinning through the gaps left by the absence of teeth, and he passed on to the house of the young girls who tended his car.

He tethered the stallion to the doorpost, left it to chew contentedly at the straw thatch where it hung down from the roof, and ducked through the doorway. Momentarily sightless owing to the dark, he called, 'Ines? Agapita?' and a voice from the kitchen replied, 'Is that you?'

'Of course it is me. Who else would it be?'

'That depends upon who me is. If it is not you, it might be someone else.'

'It is Dionisio,' he replied, 'I am on my way to see my parents,' and Agapita came in wiping her hands, with a shy smile upon her face. 'I knew it was you all the time,' she said. 'I was just wasting time whilst I finished rolling a tortilla.'

'You are growing so pretty that it breaks my heart,' said Dionisio. 'And how is Ines?'

She laughed at the compliment, and then a cloud passed across her face at the mention of her sister. 'She has been stupid,' she said. 'Come out and see.'

At the back of the house Ines was arranging macaw feathers around the windscreen of Dionisio's car. She glanced up as the two came out of the back of the house, gasped with shame, and ran off up the hillside with her arm across her face. Almost immediately she stumbled over a rock and fell sprawling. Striding forward, Dionisio went to where she lay and pulled her up by the armpits, only to find that she still held her arm across her face and would not look at him. He held her wrist and forced her arm away from her face. 'Look at me,' he said.

Very slowly she turned, and the first thing that he noticed was that her lips were quivering and her eyes were full of tears. The next thing he saw was that a diagonal chalky blotch had spread itself unevenly from her forehead to her neck, and his first thought was that she had been parasitised by some disfiguring fungus. Then he realised what it was and was shaken with anger.

'This is skin-whitener. For the love of God, Ines, how could you be so stupid?' He was so furious that for a second his hand was raised to strike her, but then he beheld her misery and his hand fell to his side. He turned to Agapita. 'Everyone knows that this stuff is a catastrophe. For God's sake, why has she done it?'

'It was for you,' said Ines. 'When she begins her bleeding and becomes a woman she wants to be one of your women, and she thinks that you will like her more if she is white.'

He was dismayed and astonished. He looked down at the girl where she lay sobbing. She had the beautiful dark skin of one who is an Indian with a little Negro mixed in for good effect, skin of the colour that many white women lie in the sun for weeks in order to achieve. His anger was unabated; he laid his own forearm alongside her own and demanded, 'What colour is this? Is it not darker than yours? Do you wish to insult me?'

Agapita put a hand on his shoulder and said, 'Be kind to her, she knew no better,' and Dionisio said, 'Does she still have that stuff? Will you bring it to me?'

Agapita went back into the choza and came out with the bottle. He took it from her and inspected the label. He memorized the name of the company that made it, and then hurled it away up the mountainside. The bottle smashed with a dull pop, and he bent down and lifted Ines to her feet. He rubbed his hand across her cheek and shook his head, 'You are very stupid,' he said, 'you were always going to be one of my women, I was just waiting for you.'

The young girl's heart leapt in her breast, and she smiled through her tears. A little smirk of mischief came to her lips. 'And Agapita?'

He turned to the older sister with surprise upon his face. 'You too?'

The girl shrugged, raised her arms a little, let them fall to her side, and said, 'Who else is there? All the men have gone to the towns.'

He raised his eyebrows and contemplated the fate that had conspired to make of him a responsible Don Juan. He noticed that his pet jaguars had climbed up onto the roof of the house and were sybaritically enjoying the sunshine after their days in the chill of the sierras. 'No more skin-whitener,' he said, and the girls shook their heads. 'Copy them, and lie in the sun until you have returned to your colour,' he instructed Ines, pointing to the cats.

'You will sleep the night with me on the way back,' announced Agapita, continuing her own train of thought.

Dionisio's next campaign in the pages of *La Prensa* was against skin-whitener, but even after he had succeeded in getting it prohibited, people continued to bring it in as contraband. Countless exploited women continued to despoil the velvet darkness of their skin at inflated prices in the vain hope of raising their status and their desirability.

But visitors to Santa Maria Virgen are sometimes shown a place on the mountainside where once upon a time Dionisio Vivo threw a bottle of skin-whitener, and there sprang up a purple lily blotched with white as a perpetual reminder to all races to set their own beauty at a proper value.

The abandoned children of the sewers were disappearing. The priests and nuns, the conscientious privileged, the good widows, the few socialists prepared to redistribute their own wealth, all found that the grimy children were evaporating away. Familiar faces at the soup-kitchens no longer appeared, and the number of ragged, rachitic little scarecrows begging at the entrances to the marbled shops and emporia seemed daily to diminish. Respectable housewives and anxious shop-managers breathed sighs of relief and said, 'I am glad that at last something is being done. It was a disgrace.' Shoppers no longer clutched at their wallets or repeatedly checked for that reassuring bulge in the backpocket that contained their credit cards, their driving licence, their cedula. Conversations no longer had to be made louder and more intense in order to avoid hearing, 'Help me, good señor, just a little change,' and one no longer had to look straight ahead and avoid turning one's head to see the pathetic faces with infected eyes and the matted mops of hair that almost visibly crawled with lice and ticks.

The mystery of the evaporation of the cloud of children was connected with another, simultaneous mystery. The river's stench became ever more intolerable until it was unbearable to live with one's windows open. The group of pious widows no longer stood on the riverbanks waiting to catch the blessing of Cardinal Guzman, but he was unable to enjoy the relief of their absence because the reek of deliquescence seeped even through the window-frames of the palace. He taped around the places where a draught might enter, and bought electric fans for his chambers.

The truth was that a little private enterprise had entered into the solution of the town's social problems. Vigilante groups of the right-wing lower middle classes had identified the dispossessed and forlorn children as the fountainhead that fed and renewed the ever-growing criminal underclass that was making life in the city impossible. The children grew up into the vandals who scratched one's car with keys;

they became the latchbreakers who crawled through lavatory windows and made off with one's new watch; they became the thugs who raped smartly dressed women on their own front lawns, and became the footpads who cut open the pockets of men who wore suits, stealing their grandfathers' silver cigarette-cases; they became the lounging and sneering youths who drowned out entire neighbourhoods with Yanqui music played on tape-recorders bought with the spoils of theft. At first the blackshirted vigilantes merely drove them back into the sewers, and beat them up when they caught them.

But then the owners of shops began to pay the vigilantes to keep the children away from their premises, believing rightly that customers would rather not enter shops at all than have to clamber over cardboard shelters and recumbent bodies, encountering the bewildered desperation in those huge brown eyes. The children sleeping above the central-heating ducts or sheltering from the rain in doorways were driven away by hails of truncheon blows, with insults raining about their broken heads.

But one thing leads to another. The lost children of the city now slept beneath the waters of the river outside the Cardinal's palace. They slept with their legs encased in concrete and their right hands missing, since a right hand was what one needed to collect the businessmen's bounty, and the sound of shots at night was put down to terrorist activity and the internal feuds of the coca lords. The police knew all about it, but did nothing because no one would have given them any thanks. The innocents slept and the crime-rate remained the same, because normally they would have died anyway at an early age, and the criminal underclass maintained its numbers thanks to the slums and the disaffected youths who fled the peasant life of the countryside and the uncomfortable scrutiny of the neighbours and the parish priest.

His Eminence was nauseated by the smell from the river and was paralysed by the fermenting agony in his entrails. These days he would be attacked at least daily by sudden pangs that maddened him and made him retch long strings of saliva that somehow could not be wiped from his mouth. The more his belly grew the less he could eat, and Concepcion resigned herself to making thin soups and cooling drinks. The perpetual dread of the next access of pain so distracted him that he could concentrate on nothing at all, and the burden of running the Church became increasingly laid upon the nervous shoulders of his new secretary, who would come with the aid of intense prayer to decisions that he hoped the Cardinal himself would have made, had he not been ill.

As if to crown his misery and his lifetime's accumulation of guilt, His Eminence now lived in the perpetual and visible company of his demons. Mgr Rechin Anquilar had come to visit him, to tell him that he was going to bring together all his missions into one vast crusading entity, and His Eminence had not been able to listen to him because the Contending Heads were biting at each other's necks under the desk. The Obscene Ass was winding his donkey's penis round and around the Monsignor's neck, the Smiters were crying out as they pounded the walls with cudgels carved from human limbs that rang with the mockery of gongs. The Litigators disputed so loudly and with such vehemence that he could scarcely hear the Monsignor's indignant words about the mistreatment of his missionaries. The Flaming Ones wrote in the air with fire the names of all his sins, and the Dispersers seemed somehow to fix upon his thoughts before he thought them, so that the words of his own mouth emerged as gibberish. Every thought that passed through this malign censorship, every thought that struck him as noble or true, was confuted by the Falsifiers. They would sit in front of him in a row upon the desk, their skinny legs swaying back and forth as if upon the point of detaching themselves from the rotund bellies with their huge spiral navels, and they would somehow prove with impeccable logicality that God was evil, that it was right to steal, that hell was a garden of Eden. His Eminence would dispute loudly with them, his voice ringing around the palace, until, his hands over his face, he would howl with anguish and kick over the chairs in order not to hear them, only to find that the Accusers could shout even louder from the inside of his own head, taunting him with his paternity, his veniality, his fallible humanity.

He achieved rest in the arms of Concepcion and in the company of Cristobal. It seemed that the demons could not penetrate the citadels of human love, and he would therefore stay in bed longer with Concepcion in the morning. He would send Cristobal to bed so late that the little boy would be puffy-eyed with exhaustion and have to be carried after midnight to his room, already fast asleep in his father's arms.

His Eminence found also that the demons could not withstand beauty. He could send them flying from the room in clouds of pungent smoke simply by placing the Eroica symphony upon the record-player, and they would return instantly after the last bar of the final presto. He played the record over and over, every day, until he knew each note of it by heart.

But one day he awoke from a light slumber in his chair when the record had finished, to find that the Falsifiers were sitting patiently in front of him. 'She was right, you know,' said the one with the eye consisting of worms. 'This music is like making love.'

'This symphony was originally named "The Erotica",' contributed the one whose sinuous tongue wriggled continually down in order to linger caressingly upon its own wrinkled pudenda.

'It depicts the sexual acts,' proclaimed the one who always assumed a professorial air, and whose long bony forefinger would lever out its own eye so that it could hold it aloft and see behind itself. 'And that is why we cannot stand it.'

His Eminence leapt to his feet and replaced the stylus of his gramophone upon the record. At the first chord the demons squealed and gibbered, clapped the palms of their hands to their ears, and fled through the walls to sulk and hide in the farthest corners of the palace.

His Eminence settled down to listen to the symphony, and became a prey to suggestibility. He furrowed his brow as he began to perceive the unchastity of the music. Dismayed, he went to the telephone to ask the librarian of the palace to bring him a copy of the score, if it could be found on the shelves of the long-unvisited musical section.

The librarian arrived, out of breath from the stairs, and handed him a yellowed and stained Henry Litolff edition that no one had previously perused in all its many decades of existence. His Eminence settled down with it and flicked through its pages. His first impression was that of amazement that anyone had ever written any symphonies at all. There was so much of it, and the composer must have had to hear every detail of the music as it unfolded in his imagination, adjusting it here and there in order to achieve intellectual and emotional effects, tinkering with sonorities, bearing in mind the ranges and limitations of different instruments. A symphony was a staggering achievement, enough to make one believe that the voice of God echoed in the mind of man.

The Cardinal put the record back to the beginning and tried to follow the score as the music unfolded. He found it difficult, even though he had learned some piano as a child, and he became lost on the third page. He sighed, and noticed with a start that there were two parts on the bass clef marked for 'fagotti'. Was that not the gringo slang for 'homosexual'? Could Beethoven really have written parts for homosexuals? He rang down to the library again and discovered that 'fagotti' were bassoons. He put the record back to the beginning once more, and followed the music with his finger.

Yes. The opening forte chords were very like the sudden arousal that one experiences upon catching sight of a beautiful and sensual woman, and then, 'piano', there was a period like the romantic wistfulness that one undergoes in thinking about her and imagining what one could say to her if only an accidental encounter might be arranged. There were violent triple chords like pelvic thrusts – could she be seduced already? – and then there were tripping violins just exactly like the teasing and fractional contact of slender fingers tickling the hairs of the perineum. Then there were more violent chords like pelvic thrusts, but perhaps they were really the tight embraces that one made during the first hugs of relief at the revelation of mutual attraction.

Sweat broke out upon the Cardinal's brow. The plaintive oboe at the beginning of the second movement portrayed indubitably the enervation of post-coital depression, when one somehow feels disappointed that the world has not been transformed as one had expected. Then at the bar marked 'maggiore', there began a new cheerfulness that signalled the return of tumescence. There were more great chords at the excitement of re-entry, but then somehow the erection failed, because it was too soon after the previous one perhaps, and there was a loss of confidence in the section marked 'minore'. But then the music cheered up again because the violins were sending shivers up and down the legs, because the woman was smiling salaciously and tantalising the man with excruciatingly exquisite foreplay, and then she was reaching under him as he made love to her, stroking his testicles so that suddenly he came. And this new 'piano' was the acute sensitivity of the penis after orgasm when one lies perfectly still, enclosed in her embrace, because one is afraid of the pain of withdrawal. 'Ay,' and the abrupt sforzando depicts the gasp of that withdrawal, followed by the muted collapse that is the sweet obliteration of sleep.

The Cardinal stood up to turn the record over, and tripped over his own feet, his mind whirling with the indecency of the symphony. With shaking hands he placed the needle at the beginning of the scherzo that introduces the third movement, and returned to his chair. He was no longer attempting to follow the music in the score, because he knew in advance what to expect. It was the merry exhilaration of waking up in the morning with a new woman in one's bed, and here was a crescendo at just exactly the moment when the warmth of her body imparts a refreshed and urgent erection. Here one is romping and playfighting with her, hitting her softly upon the head with the pillow, pinning her to the mattress in order to spread kisses all over her face and neck, wriggling against the soft mound of her pubis. Tickles and nibbles. A muting to lascivious caress. More slim, travelling fingers.

The fourth movement begins, and there is mischief in the pizzicato of the strings – what is she up to now? There is a surprising swelling of the music; she has squirmed against him and deliciously ambushed his penis, which is now inside her, and they are making love again with breath-catchingly brief increases of momentum, the emphasis upon the first beat of each bar because he is thrusting and resting, thrusting and resting. The Cardinal recognises his technique for avoiding premature climax. There is triumphant brass because he is about to come, and then there is quiet. What has happened? Has he come too soon after all? No, he has just managed to hold back because she is not quite ready yet. He begins again with little dips and thrusts. O God, it is as if the ring of her cervix is nibbling at the tip of his glans. There are crescendos and retractions; can he hold himself any longer? The Cardinal is on the edge of his seat with the drama of it, and then the presto begins and a mighty orgasm of terrific thrusts throws her pelvis into the air and she is clawing at the pillows and he is going as deep as he can so that it is as if he is disappearing inside her, and the bed skids upon the parquet, and they have thundered to sobbing contractions and the symphony has finished.

His Eminence rose to his feet and clenched his fist in the air like an aficionado who has just seen his favourite matador triumph over a brave bull. Then his hand fell limply to his side and he sank back into his chair. He leaned forward to lift the record off the player, and tilted it back and forth so that he could play with the light that reflected across it. 'Beautiful but evil,' he said, and he walked to his secretary's office. 'I want you to write to the Interior Minister, telling him that, in the interests of public morals, Beethoven's third symphony must be banned.'

The astonished secretary smiled nervously, 'Are you serious, Your Eminence?' and the Cardinal shot him a look of lordly impatience. He wrote it, but after much prayer, he could not bring himself to send it, preferring to spare his master the public ridicule, even at the expense of his own employment.

His Eminence proceeded to the kitchens and confronted Concepcion. 'Spawn of Satan,' he demanded. 'Why did you give me this record? Did you wish to corrupt me further? Did you think that I am so easily damned?'

She knew that his madness was becoming unmanageable, but she smiled brightly. 'You have worn it out with playing it, and now you tell me that you do not like it?'

His Eminence held the record out and with a melodramatic flourish he broke it over his knee. He spun the two halves across the room at her and turned on his heel to leave. In his chamber he was mobbed by howling cohorts of demons who clawed at his face and scornfully taunted him; he searched desperately for his Beethoven record so that he could banish them. In the kitchen Concepcion put her hand to her face and discovered that a jagged edge had sliced her cheek. She sat down at the table and felt herself go empty inside.

## 32 Dionisio's Continuing Adventures On The Way To Valledupar

Dionisio's car clattered and roared into Ipasueño, its exhaust having come off as usual on a hump in the road. He had to pass through here anyway in order to get to Valledupar, and he felt like calling in on Agustin and Velvet Luisa. He parked outside the police station, leaving the jaguars in the car with their heads poking out of their improvised sunroof; from this vantage point they swiped at unwary birds and low-flying butterflies, until their master came back out again having arranged to meet Agustin later in Madame Rosa's whorehouse.

He arrived there feeling sorry for himself and determined to confide in Velvet Luisa, one of the few women he knew who combined a warm intuitive understanding with a distinct lack of respect for his personal legend. She was sitting at one of the tables sucking an Inca Cola through a straw. He was admiring the elegant curve of her wrist as she held the bottle, when she looked up and smiled. She returned his affectionate hug and raised an eyebrow. 'Yes,' he said, 'let's go upstairs.'

Up in her room she slipped out of her dress and slid beneath the covers, holding out her arms to him. Out of habit, he undressed and got in beside her as though they had been married for years, having temporarily forgotten that he had only come in out of friendship. 'Those scars on your neck are still terrible,' she remarked, stroking them with her fingers and examining them at close range so that he could smell her distinctively musky aroma, 'do they still hurt?'

He ran his own fingers over the rope scar and the six-centimetre gash and replied, 'They itch sometimes. Do you know, Luisa, I don't know what Africa smells like, but I bet it smells like you.'

She smiled ironically. 'I don't know what it smells like either, but I can smell depression around here. Have you come to see Doctor Luisa by any chance?'

'Dios,' he said, 'am I so transparent?'

'Like glass, or perhaps more like a spider's web. So what's up? Come on, embrace me.'

He passed an arm around her shoulders and lay on his back, looking at the ceiling. He gathered his thoughts, reflecting that the cracks up there were like maps of rivers. 'Today two young campesina girls, they were zambas, offered themselves to me, and I accepted.'

'You find that depressing?' She chirred her tongue against her teeth to indicate impatience.

'Of course I do. I am not my own man anymore, I am a kind of public property. I have about thirty women already, and the only woman who knows me is you, and maybe Leticia Aragon. And the odd thing is that I used to have fantasies about this sort of thing, but now that I have it I do not appreciate it as I should. Why can't I be like a bull or a horse?'

'Because you are not a bull or a horse. What is the next question?'

'I thought you would understand.'

Velvet Luisa pulled a wry expression and replied, 'Listen, I do understand you, because I knew you before you became a legend, and I remember you when you were just Dionisio who came in and got drunk and sometimes managed to get it up when you were not too far gone. But these women, they see the man who killed Pablo Ecobandodo, who survived assassination and even survived his own suicide. They see your two tame jaguars that seem to understand you by telepathy, and they see the way that you have a detached look in your face. They realise that you are not just Dionisio who used to come in here with Jerez and Juanito and get drunk. They see the man who became famous for his letters in *La Prensa*.' She paused. 'I am afraid that you have crossed over the line between man and god, and now you have to live by different rules. Everyone knows that a god is different from a man; look how many lovers Chango has.'

'What are you saying, Luisa?'

'I am saying that you have duties beyond the duties of a man. These women choose you, it is not you who chooses them, and you have to live up to it. It's just the same with other things. You stood up to El Jerarca's evil, and that condemns you to stand up against all other evil in the future, because, as far as everyone else is concerned, you are the Deliverer. We need you to be like this, and you have no right to disappoint us. Ride a jaguar and you can't get off.'

He raised his eyebrows at the vehemence and conviction of her speech. 'And do you think I have changed so much?'

She toyed with his ear, and tugged it gently. 'You still don't clean your ears out often enough. It looks like an open-cast mine in there.'

'Thank God for you,' he said. 'With you I am no god.'

'Listen to my troubles now,' she said. 'You are not the only one.'

Guiltily he turned towards her and drew her against him. 'I am sorry.'

'My sister has gone off to Spain. Do you remember we had an agreement that I would work for three years to get her through university, and then she would do the same for me? It was what made being a whore bearable, knowing that it would end and there would be a better life afterwards. Anyway, she has gone, and I have been humiliated for nothing. The stars are burning at midday for me.'

He was shocked at Luisa's plight, and felt in the pit of his own stomach the emptiness of betrayal and disbelief. He saw that her eyes were watering and her lip quivering, and he held her even tighter, feeling the long curves of her naked body mapping themselves against his. She pulled away and sat up in the bed, wrapping her slender black arms about her knees. 'Do you know why women like you?' she asked, and he shook his head. 'It's because they know that you love them too much to hurt them, that is why.' Velvet Luisa pointed up at the crucifix on the wall and asked, 'Do you believe in all that?'

'I would like to,' he replied, 'but it is too difficult.'

She nodded in agreement and said, 'If the person hanging on it were a woman, then I would believe it.'

'Come to Cochadebajo de los Gatos. I could give up the other women. But not Leticia perhaps.'

'I don't want to. It is better to share you than to be owned.'

'Will you come anyway? You could breed animals on the plateau or something.'

She shook her head. 'I want to be educated. I will be a whore for another three years if I have to.'

'This job will kill you, as it kills everyone who does it in the end, and anyway, I am educated and now I know that it is not everything it is assumed to be.'

'I would like to be educated before I come to such a recognition,' she replied firmly.

'Do you have a pen and paper?'

'Over there,' she said, pointing vaguely towards the table.

He got up and sat naked at the rickety piece of furniture, writing. He handed her the leaf of paper and she read:

Respected Señor/Señora,

This person comes with my highest personal recommendation. She is intelligent, highly motivated, and very industrious. Over the years she has frequently worked in my employ, and I can certify that, given the opportunity, she will become a credit to any organisation that gives her an opportunity to prove herself.

Dionisio Vivo.

'You know I used to work at Ipasueño College,' he said. 'It is not university, but the place is not too bad. I am sure that the principal will accept my recommendation.'

'I like the bit about having been frequently in your employ,' she said, smiling, and then her brow furrowed. 'But it seems that a woman cannot avoid needing the help of a man. One is always turned by fate into some kind of a whore.'

'Do not be too proud, Luisa, everyone needs help from someone from time to time. Whether you succeed or not when you get there is up to you, so don't ask me to write any essays, OK? Are you going to carry on with . . .' He hesitated.

'Whoring?' she supplied. 'Not if I can find something better that pays just as much.'

'Look at that reference,' he said, 'it could be to anyone for anything, so use it to find a good job. They might take you on for something at the alcaldia.'

She laughed. 'The advantage of you becoming a god is that no one will refuse me for fear of divine vengeance.'

'I wish I had thought of it before,' he said. 'I suppose I was too wrapped up in myself.'

'Let's go downstairs and wait for Agustin, and then we can all get drunk to celebrate, just like old times.'

'Does Juanito still come here?'

'No, he married Rosalita. She finally got him, and now she keeps him under strict control. She has turned into a true cacafuego.'

He laughed. 'Poor Juanito, who would imagine Rosalita shitting fire?'

They went downstairs and found an empty table amid the smoke and the clinking of glasses. The brothel fell silent for a few moments as people recognised him and whispered to each other. Some of the whores came over and flirted with him a little, their dreams briefly flaring into arcs of flame, but went away again when it became clear that he was with Velvet Luisa tonight, and then Agustin came in and boisterously threatened to arrest everybody for the crime of being happy unless they each bought him a drink.

'You are getting like Ramón,' observed Dionisio, whereupon Agustin crossed himself at the memory and said, 'Ramón taught me that a happy policeman is the best prophylactic against crime. A happy policeman is a human condom barricading the womb of society against the infected and obscene ejaculate of disorder and dishonesty.'

'You really are getting like him. Are you sure that his spirit has not taken you over?'

'No, I am not sure, but I do know that one becomes just like the people one respects the most.' Agustin placed his cap on the table and undid the top buttons of his uniform. 'Now let us do some very serious revelling,' he said, and called to Madame Rosa to bring a bottle of pisco and an arepa, 'so that I have something substantial to vomit up later.'

At half-past midnight Dionisio reeled out of Madame Rosa's feeling as though he had been purified by his complete lapse of dignity, and with the strangest feeling beneath his feet. He sang at the top of his lungs until he staggered into the cemetery and barked his shin on a tombstone. 'Shit,' he said as he fell over, and he slept stupidly for a few minutes until the cold awoke him. Still singing, he found Ramón's grave and left upon it a cigar and a good lustration of rum. He found Anica's grave and lurched through the same little ceremony, singing softly to her a ridiculous improvised song composed of sentimental endearments. Then he wove his way out of the cemetery and became irretrievably lost somewhere up amongst the rocks and quechara trees of the hillside.

'You are the biggest lost thing I have ever found, capigorrón,' announced Leticia Aragon, shaking him awake from his stupor. He sat up in her hammock, rubbing his eyes and reflecting that he urgently needed litres of water in order to ward off a hangover. 'How did I get here?' he demanded. 'Where is my car? Where are the cats?'

Leticia shook her head. 'You know that what is lost always turns up in my hammock. The car and the cats must be where you left them.'

Cursing himself he climbed out of the hammock and instantly felt the rush of pain to his head. 'You stink,' said Leticia. 'Do not expect me to sympathise. And do you realise that your boots are full of squashed cigar butts and your feet are filthy?'

He inspected his feet and looked puzzled. 'Now I remember. I put my boots on the table and Agustin was using them as an ashtray. O, Dios, please do not tell Fulgencia that you saw me like this.'

'Punishing sin is God's business,' said Leticia. 'Why should I tell anyone?'

He looked up at her as she stood with her hands on her hips in the attitude of a critical wife. He saw that she had not yet brushed her black gossamer hair and that today her eyes were completely green. 'Emeralds,' he remarked, according to his habit of informing her of the changes of hue undergone by her remarkable eyes. 'Where is Anica Primera?'

'I put her outside so that she would not witness her father drunk. The False Priest is tweaking her toes out there by the axle-pole, and trying to teach her some Latin. He says her clothes wear out so quickly because when she was born her umbilicus was cut with scissors instead of a stone.'

He looked at her, smiled wanly, and then he groaned and massaged his temples, saying, 'Shit, now I have to walk all the way back to Ipasueño.'

Leticia softened a little. 'Well, just for once I have made you some breakfast.'

'When the Gods weep, their tears become jaguars,' said Dionisio. 'I think that I am about to weep tears of broken pisco and cañazo bottles.'

'Go to Aurelio and get an antidote. And if it kills you, do not come crying to me.'

'A wad of coca leaves is best,' he said, 'and a day's diet of water, God help me.'

## 33 *General Hernando Montes Sosa Confides In His Son*

Dionisio and his two jaguars arrived in Valledupar two days late, which would have surprised no one in that land of transportational mishaps and miscarriages. No vehicle of any kind ever departed on time, and if any had arrived at the designated hour, it would have irritated profoundly those passengers who would have had to have waited for hours for the arrival of those whom they were supposed to meet. The railways were so undermined by subsidence and so adorned with the spoil of avalanches that each train carried picks and shovels in the foremost carriage. Aeroplanes would take off with no clear idea as to whether it would be possible to land at their destination, and at airports the Regiment of Engineers would have to peel limpet mines from fuselages, defuse cassette-players and old-fashioned cameras, remove nails from tyres, and generally do their utmost to foil the attempts of guerrillas to liberate the passengers from life in the name of the people. This they did with the protection of talismans and frenzied crossings of themselves, it being the case that no one is more reliant upon metaphysical aid than bomb-disposal experts.

Ships travelling the mighty internal waterways of the Magdalena and the Paraná would ground themselves for days upon sandbanks caused by riparian deforestation, leaving the passengers with nothing to do except take pot-shots at manatees and caymans, fish for comelon with bits of string, and conduct short but intense affairs beneath the canvas of the lifeboats and in the gaps between the bulkheads. Sometimes all the alcohol would run out, and a collective hangover would settle upon those who believed in permanent inebriation as a protection against travel sickness, the stifling heat, and the relentless prickings of the mosquitoes.

It was true that some of the main roads along commercial routes had been macadamised and tarred, but the tarring always melted and caused discomfiting mirages which could force a driver to career off the road in the attempt to avoid Cartagena castle or an improbable mustering of storks. In places where the tar was unwisely thick one could find oneself sloughing to a halt, axle-deep in a glutinous soup, and in places where the land had slipped it was possible to find oneself briefly airborne.

But the road to Valledupar from Ipasueño was the good old-fashioned kind that was levelled annually by bulldozer, and for the rest of the year was free to deform itself into a whimsy of potholes and ridges. In one place a bridge had flattened itself under the weight of an enormous lorry, and now the cars and trucks drove intrepidly across the roof of that lorry, which had conveniently settled to exactly the right height in the gully below. A system of planks and wooden beams now rested securely upon the stricken vehicle, incorporating it into the structure in a masterpiece of economical improvisation.

So when Dionisio arrived in Valledupar two days late, no questions were asked; he had had to walk back to Ipasueño, find his car and his cats, and then weave his way down to the torrid plains before driving in a perpetual series of swerves to the town where his parents now lived. The journey had been filled with memories of Anica; here they had slung their hammock and made love beneath the stars, accompanied by the shrieks of monkeys and the metallic filings of crickets; here they had watched the little mechanical Negro of Puesto Grande sally from his niche and strike four o'clock upon the bronze bell outside the alcaldia; and here they had fed a cigar to a mammiferous goat and watched her contemplatively enjoying it.

The house was redolent of Anica as well. The spare room still smelled of her straw-like aroma, and at night it was possible to go in there when there was no moon and sense her waiting for him beneath the mosquito net, her eyes glowing with the anticipation and apprehension of love. Dionisio had therefore grown to understand that there was always some sadness in going home.

But Mama Julia and the General never seemed to change; they had not seemed to have grown older since he first remembered them. She still collected superstitions, tended wounded animals, and grew prodigious quantities of fruit. She still wore her hair in Carmen Miranda style, disapproved of her son's appearance and his attitudes, and she still had a secret passion for Cesar Romero which manifested itself in her perfect memory for the events of each of his films. The General still combined rectitude with an appreciation of extenuating circumstance, and had such a sense of history that to him anything new was merely a recapitulation of half a dozen ancient precedents. At the moment he was home from the capital, and was in the process of reading *The History Of The War Fought Between Athens And Sparta, By Thucydides The Athenian* in order to determine whether or not it could cast any light upon the struggle between the Armed Forces which he now commanded and the guerrillas, complete with their unholy alliance with the coca cartels and the paramilitary. He was greatly appreciating the funeral speech of Pericles, and did not come out to embrace his son until he had digested it.

Mama Julia emerged immediately, however, and launched into such a critique of his sartorial state that he felt bludgeoned into allowing her to sit him in a chair and shore away his prophetic head of hair. 'Ay, ay!' she exclaimed. 'It is disrespectful to Our Lord to look so much like him, and when are you going to settle down with a good plump woman and have children and a decent job? And you should wear a collar to hide those scars because no woman would want a man like that, and make sure she is from a respectable family. And why did you shave off your moustache when it was the one thing that looked distinguished about you? You could almost have passed for an officer, and some women like the tickle of a moustache when they are kissed, as long as it is not full of old food, which is very disgusting. And I do not care if you are famous, I am still your mother and I will have no disrespect, so stop smirking or I shall snip your ear and that will serve you right, and what is this I read in the paper that you have thirty women and squads of little bastards, forgive the word but what other word is there?'

'Exaggerations and lies,' replied Dionisio. Mama Julia paused in mid-flourish with a sceptical noise in the back of her throat, and then pointedly removed a very large hank of hair to indicate her disapproval. 'Mama, you are taking too much off, I shall get very cold up there in the mountains with such a radical tonsure.'

'Wear a hat,' she said, 'and why did you not tell us that you have written famous music? The first I know of it is when I hear it on the radio and then the Naked Admiral and his wife rush round saying, 'Did you hear it?' and wiping the tears from their eyes. Your father is very proud of you, God knows why, but if he has any sense he will never tell you. Stay still, I will not be blamed for making you bleed if you move, God help me with such a son, God knows why I love you, it is no easy thing for a mother these days. I want you to look at an ocelot I have that someone shot in the leg, and tell me what you think, and why is it that a man sees something beautiful and free and then desires to destroy it? Some things I will never understand.'

At this point General Hernando Montes Sosa came in, said, 'Ah, Dionisio,' and walked out again. 'He wants to talk to you later,' explained Mama Julia.

Dionisio still felt unequal to his illustrious father. The General had subverted the whole nation's expectations of the military by getting his appointment as Governor of Cesar ratified by plebiscite, and then, when he was made Chief of the General Staff, by insisting that all military activity should be subject to civilian political control. On a more personal level, Dionisio remembered vividly an occasion when he was a bumptious adolescent and had implied that his father was past it. The General had raised a contemptuous eyebrow and said, 'Give me your hand.'

Dionisio had extended his hand and the General had gripped it, interlocking their fingers. 'Now the other,' and he had given his father the other hand. The General had said, 'The first one on his knees is the loser.'

Squaring himself up to enjoy the humiliation of his parent, Dionisio had smiled confidently and exerted first pressure. The General's grip had tightened with excruciating force, and with a gladiatorial expertise his son's wrists had been bent backwards and he had been ignominiously brought to his knees before his father. The General had let go and marched stiffly away, straightening the waist of his uniform, and Dionisio had slunk off to his room in order to tremble, alone with his well-deserved mortification. Since that day he had been in awe of the General, who always gave him a feeling of being an amateur human being. Possibly he had travelled so wide of his upbringing in order not to have to be compared with him.

And so it was that he felt a little uncomfortable when, later that evening, he sat outside beneath the bougainvillaea of the reproduction of the Aristotelian peripateticon, and found that his father was actually confiding in him. The General said in his elegant Castilian, 'I trust, young man, that you have found me to be a good father. I have recently wondered whether in the past I have somewhat disprized you.'

Dionisio was greatly surprised, and replied tactfully, 'You merely put me in my place.'

'You mean I humiliated you?'

'The most humiliating thing was that you were beyond emulation, Papa, and that is why perhaps I was so rebellious.'

'What concerned me, Dio', was that you seemed always to be rebelling against what seemed to me to be upright and good, but since the episode of your campaign against Pablo Ecobandodo and his coca thugs, I have understood that your rebellion was mainly against submission to mores and codes which, in the last analysis, are somewhat trivial.' He paused for thought, and seemed to be admiring for a span the vast moon that was at that moment surging over the horizon. 'When it came down to something truly essential, you risked assassination and danger in a manner that was heroic. We feared for you at the same time as we swelled with pride. Now what I want to know is whether you feel that in my life I have been the equal of my son.'

For some reason tears came to Dionisio's eyes and he found it hard to speak; he had never seen or heard his father in a mood of this quality before. 'You seem to be speaking as though your life is over, you seem to be anxious to have a verdict upon it,' Dionisio replied. 'I think that you are not coming precisely to the point, Papa.'

The General stood up and walked to the edge of the paving so that his back was turned. 'Much of my life has been useless,' he said. 'I have been forty years in the Army, mainly doing very little of any consequence. It is only in the last ten years that I have found a role that justifies my salary, and all the rest is a blank that is filled with your mother and my children, and that is why I have asked you whether I have done well in that respect.'

Dionisio contemplated the question and replied, 'I have often thought about this, and I have come to the conclusion that everything that I am is owed to you. You were like a gun that fired me a long way off, but the aim was yours. If you are proud of me it is because your aim was true.'

The General smiled. 'I could have trusted you to come up with a metaphor that I would have understood. Did you know that a shell when it comes out of the barrel wobbles badly for the first part of its trajectory? And then it settles to a perfect arc? Perhaps your appalling behaviour when you were younger was your way of wobbling.'

'Papa, I still think you are avoiding your real point. What brings this on?'

General Hernando Montes Sosa said very simply, 'Since I became Commander-In-Chief the risk of my assassination has multiplied almost to a certainty. I am contending with numerous groups of guerrillas, four coca barons, and the risk of insurrection caused by appalling government that is the direct consequence of the absence of that idiot, Veracruz. There are also elements of the patrician right wing that would dearly love to end our little flowering of democracy. That, my boy, is why my mood has turned to self-examination. I would wish to die having lived meaningfully and well, that is all.'

Dionisio rose from his wicker chair and went to stand by his father. He put an arm around his shoulder and said sincerely, 'Papa, when you die your place in the pantheon is assured. Your soldiers love you dangerously well, so that it is indeed lucky that you are not minded to perform a coup. My sisters love you so much that it is a wonder that they ever married. I love you, and even my jaguars desert me when I am here. No man who lives amid so much love has lived for nothing.'

'You do not remember La Violencia, do you? No, you were only a little boy. I am afraid that it is about to happen all over again. Weak government, social chaos, perfect conditions for our proliferation of fanatics. Do you know what the Army did during La Violencia?'

Dionisio shook his head.

'It always arrived too late. We would go to the scene of an incident and find that the Conservatives or the Liberals had already been and gone, leaving behind them whole villages pillaged. Hundreds of bodies, not even the babies spared, not just killed, but tortured and hacked. It was an orgy of rape and sadism, and it proved to me that my countrymen are deeply sick with a morbidity of the heart. There was a bishop whose nickname was 'The Hammer of the Heretics' and he publicly encouraged the Conservative Catholics to go out and kill Protestants. And the Liberals, being secularist then as they are now, set out to kill priests and to violate nuns. That is the inferno which I foresee once more, and it makes my spirit bleed. Did you know that once the Inca sent to the Aymaras for their contribution towards the running of the empire, and they sent him their lice? Even before the Spanish it seems that our primary motive was contempt. In this land there is no tradition of toleration.'

Dionisio looked at his distinguished father abjectly hanging his head with foreboding, and felt his stomach sink. 'It seems to me that tolerance only ever prospers where people have grown weary of bogus certainties. With respect, that is why I rejected your faith and stopped going to mass.'

The General laughed ironically and replied, 'Between you and me, my faith is more of an instinct than a belief, but do not tell Mama Julia. Shall we take a little paseo?'

Father and son strolled about the grounds, reminiscing about each occasion that had prompted Mama Julia to plant a tree in its commemoration, and the General said, 'Do you remember Felipe? Anica's brother in the Portachuelo Guards? He has just become the youngest colonel in the Army. And by the way, I have made the acquaintance of the British Ambassador.'

'O, yes?'

'Yes, and he is very curious to visit Cochadebajo de los Gatos because he wants to see a genuine ancient city. He is a great linguist, you know; he speaks Hindi and four African languages, and so they sent him here where he cannot use any of them. Very British, I understand, to do that. Do you think I could bring him?'

'Of course, Papa,' Dionisio replied, unmindful of the possible consequences.

'We shall arrive at ten hundred hours on June the sixth,' announced the General, and Dionisio knew that he would, because his father was the only man in the country who operated not 'a la hora latina', but 'a la hora británica'.

# 34 *Cristobal*

His Eminence looked at the desk in his room and saw that it had become a rotten coffin through whose distorted boards there sprouted verminous cascades of ancient hair that waved like the tentacles of an anemone. There was no doubt that the grey wisps were growing apace and were winding about the furniture. A hank of it curled about his ankle and began to constrict it like a boa. He shouted, pulling his leg away, but the force reduced the casket to dust, and on the floor where his desk had been, there was now a cadaver watching him. The skin was shrunk over the bones like an Indian mummy, the hair was growing with the speed of a stream, and the amber teeth of the mouth smiled at him with contemptuous inanity.

As sweat poured down his face and a wild panic siezed his heart, a small black snake slithered out of the mouth, flicked like a tongue that removes sauce from the lips at the end of a meal, and withdrew inside with a repulsively slow sinuosity.

Shielding his eyes with his forearm somehow did not prevent him from seeing that the corpse was watching him. Shrieking at the top of his lungs did not shield him from the accusing curiosity of those bloodshot orbs with their black pinprick pupils.

There was a dry crack as the jaws unseized themselves and spoke. It was a harsh voice, more of wind and water than of flesh: 'Look.'

Cardinal Guzman, shaking in all his body, raised his tearfilled eyes and looked. It seemed that his study had melted away to nothingness, and all the world was smoke. With his right hand clutching his throat and his left groping for something to lean against while he retched against the fumes, he reeled about the room searching for a doorway back to reality. But there was nothing beneath his feet but baked earth and sandy dust, and there was no air to breathe. He tripped over something soft and yielding, fell forward over it, and sprawled. He stood up slowly, staring at his hands that seemed to seep blood, and realised that he had just embraced a young woman who had been hacked and carved with a machete. How pretty was her face! Behind the grime and the caked blood he could see full lips, delicate teeth, and black eyebrows that arched like those of an Arabian beauty. But her throat was slashed and bubbling with her last breaths, and she was holding out a book to him. He took it, and she sank back to die. He looked at the book and knew without examining it that it was a missal, its dark cover embossed with a cross, its pages rimmed with gold leaf. The smoke cleared with a change of breeze, and he was in a ring of brushwood huts, all of them aflame. Somewhere in the distance there were the gleeful shouts of the perpetrators of carnage, and the abject pleas of victims on their knees. He turned to run, but came up against what was the wall, invisible to him in the turbulent ordeal of his nightmare.

He staggered back, his hand to his forehead, and the Executioner came towards him. He saw the black hood with its glittering slits. His throat shrank at the sight of the colossal Negro whose naked torso was a knot of deep bronze muscle and proud sinew. He groped backwards, his hand once more seeking something to lean against, something with which to defend himself, but the Executioner stepped forward slowly, removing the sackcloth cover of the silver machete. 'Pay me,' said the Executioner, extending his left hand, 'according to the custom.'

The Cardinal looked down at the pink palm of that huge black hand, and noticed the craftsman's delicately precise fingers, the fingers of a potter or a carpenter. He looked at the thick gold bracelet on the wrist that bulged with purple veins, and he looked up at the eyes behind the hood. What did the eyes mean? Was there not a message in them? Surely the gaze of eyes was meant to convey some information? But the hood gave away nothing but impassive and final judgement, and the eyes were nothing more accessible than distant stars. 'Pay me,' repeated the Executioner.

'I have nothing,' said the Cardinal, his voice breaking into fragments and cutting his throat like shards of glass.

'Then give me your child,' said the Executioner, raising the silver blade high above his head, and spreading his legs for the strike.

Backing away, His Eminence felt the record player behind him, and was inspired in his mortal terror to try the one thing that always worked to drive away his demons. Sobbing with haste and desperation, his hands shaking and perspiring, he opened the lid of the player to fill the world with Beethoven, and there, revolving on the turntable, was the Obscene Ass, leering and gibbering. It cocked its head to look up at him, squawked with jubilation, removed the glistening glans of its penis from its mouth, wove it instantaneously and incomprehensibly into a lariat, and looped it about the Cardinal's neck.

His Eminence jerked back, but was drawn forward. His feet slipped beneath him, but still he was pulled, the demon working hand over hand to bring him in like a boat brought to harbour. He felt the soft muscular mass of the penis writhing and gripping, squirming and tightening, and his shrieks drowned in his throat as inexorably he found himself coming face to face with the Obscene Ass. Enveloped and enclosed in the foul breath of sulphur and pitch, his eyes closed tightly and his head turned away as far as could be reached. His Eminence lost the power to struggle. Tears coursed down his face with all the abandonment and desolation of utter defeat.

'Poor 'ickle boy,' gloated the Ass, 'kissy, kissy,' and the repellent creature inserted its tongue deep into the Cardinal's mouth. He felt that prehensile organ writhe and search in his gullet; he felt it dip and dive, roll lasciviously about his own tongue and cheeks, and felt his mouth engorge with the sticky saliva that tasted of shit and sarsaparilla. Vomit rose from his stomach and added its bitter burning to the nausea that had overwhelmed him. The Obscene Ass pushed him away and greedily swallowed the vomit in heaving gulps.

He fell back into the strong and patient arms of the Executioner. It was with gladness and sobs of relief that he felt the long silver blade draw slowly across his throat.

Cristobal came into the room dragging a tattered toy dog on wheels that played the xylophone as it moved. He let go of the string and stooped over the recumbent body of the Cardinal. He put his lips very close to the man's ear and said, 'Boo.'

Cardinal Guzman stirred, groaned piteously, and tried to rise up from the floor. A string of adhesive saliva seemed to attach him to it, and he tried to wipe it away with the sleeve of his cassock. 'You've been sick,' observed Cristobal matter-of-factly. 'Shall I fetch Mama?'

He looked up at his small son standing there with an expression of innocent concern upon his face, and Cristobal added, 'Why have you been crying?'

'I had a terrible dream, Cristobal,' replied the Cardinal, sitting up and wiping his eyes with his fingers. 'It was the worst dream I ever had.'

'But you weren't asleep. You hadn't gone to bed. My worst dream is that Mama leaves me in the market place and I get lost.'

'You poor boy,' said the Cardinal, stroking Cristobal's tight mulatto curls. 'I had my dream when I was awake because I am not very well.'

'Is that why you threw everything around, Papa?' asked the little boy, sweeping his hand grandly to indicate the broken furniture, the sheaves of strewn paper, and the record player that was lying on its side on the floor with the lid open.

'Promise you won't tell Mama. I'll get into big trouble if she finds out about all the mess. Why did you call me "Papa"?'

Cristobal smiled at his own cleverness. 'Because I am allowed to call you "Father" and that means the same as "Papa", doesn't it?'

A residual tang of bilious nausea glowed caustically in the Cardinal's throat, and instinctively he went to open the window. He took a deep breath and was assaulted by the poisonous stench of the river. He recoiled and shook his head.

'Mama told me that two countries went to war once because of a football match,' said Cristobal, searching through the day's events to find something that might prolong the conversation past his bedtime.

'People always go to war over stupid things,' replied his father. 'Do you want to sit on my knee?'

'You smell of sick, though,' complained the boy, wrinkling up his nose. 'I'll sit on your knee if you let me play with your cross. It's nice and shiny and it's heavy, and it's better than wood, and anyway, football isn't stupid.'

'Yes it is,' said the Cardinal, taking the Christus Rex from about his neck, and handing it over.

'Isn't,' said Cristobal with conviction, settling onto his father's lap, and ferreting inside his nose for any tender morsel that he might have missed during one of his previous excavations.

His Eminence watched Cristobal disapprovingly inspecting the disappointing harvest on the end of his finger, and felt a flood of affection cascade into his heart. 'I love you, Cristobal,' he said simply.

The little boy bounced in his father's lap, put his arms around his neck and kissed him wetly on the cheek. 'I love you too,' he replied, and then, 'if your tummy gets any bigger I won't have room on your lap anymore, will I? Mama says that you must have something growing in there. When I kiss you it feels all stubbly.'

His Eminence smiled, 'It's one of the prices you pay for becoming a man.'

'Getting fat?'

'No, silly, getting stubbly. And this isn't fat, it's a hurt.'

'Are you going to die?'

The directness of the question momentarily stunned the cleric, and forced him suddenly to contemplate a real possibility. Cristobal watched his face and continued, 'You're not allowed to die.'

Cardinal Guzman shook his head as though with pity, and squeezed Cristobal so tightly that the hug made his small son pull a face.

The creature in his lap squirmed and he looked down. But instead of seeing the beloved but forbidden fruit of his loins, he beheld the Obscene Ass wriggling there, with its coarsehaired ears, its enormous self-willed pudenda, its loathsome slavering tongue. It sneered up at the Cardinal, and in perfectly mocking mimicry of Cristobal's reedy voice, said, 'Give me another kiss, Papa.'

Appalled and outraged, the Cardinal stood up so suddenly that the beast fell to the floor. Summoning courage and intent from deep within his disgust, he picked up the monster, grasped it tightly despite its howls, and flung it out of the open window. As he did so he felt a painful tugging on his finger, and when he looked at his hand he saw that his ring of office had somehow been thrown out with the demon.

Cristobal hurtled through the air in what seemed to him to be an eternity of incomprehension and disbelief. He smacked into the turbid waters of the river with a blow that emptied his chest of air, and the gasp that wrenched his body drew in not air but the rank and slimy putrefaction of the waters, thick with the decay of the vanished children of the sewers. He drifted down ever more slowly, amazed and drowsy with the reverie of his gathering death, and briefly he brushed the hands that floated upward like weed, caressing him, and seeming forever to be reaching for the light, before he was taken up and carried away on the endless journey to the anonymous sea, still clutching in his hand the silver Christus Rex and his beloved protector's ring.

Cardinal Guzman turned away from the window, still gazing at the place where his ring once used to be, and beheld the Obscene Ass laughing at him from the armchair. He turned to the window, yelled, 'Cristobal, Cristobal!' took his head in his hands, and groaned as if all the grief of the world were his. He thought of diving after his son in the attempt to save him; but rationality asserted itself, and the thought struck him all at once that he had no way of knowing what had really happened. Perhaps he really had just ejected a demon that had simply re-entered. Perhaps all along the demon had been playing at being Cristobal. He went out into the barren stone of the corridors to search for him.

He went to the boy's room and found the bed empty. Cheerful toys in jaunty colours were scattered in disarray about the floor, and on the wall was the picture of Our Lord with his Bleeding Heart, competing for attention with pictures of football stars that Concepcion had indulgently cut from magazines. His pace quickening, Cardinal Guzman searched through the palace in all of the boy's favourite hideyholes and crannies, the same places that he could always be found during games of hide-and-seek. He went out into the courtyard where Cristobal liked to watch the hummingbirds and imitate them, his arms flurrying as he ran about exclaiming, 'Look at me! Look at me!'

With a dreadful certainty rising in his breast, the Cardinal ran back to his study, placed a chair against the window, and looked down into the waters of the river. He saw nothing but the broken reflection of the reddened moon and of the sodium streetlamps. He stepped back down, mopped the sweat from his brow, and caught sight of the small toy dog with which his son had entered.

Stupefied, numbed by self-hatred and contempt, desperate with remorse, he burst out of the room and ran for Concepcion's chamber. He threw open the door and flung himself to his knees. Caught in the middle of folding a dress and putting it in a drawer, she stood dismayed at this apparition of agony and repentance. With tears following each other down his cheeks, his voice breaking, he held up a quivering hand and looked at her imploringly.

'Christ have mercy on us,' he said. 'I think I have murdered Cristobal.'

A shaft of excruciating pain wrenched in his gut, he drew a sharp breath, toppled forward on his face, and lay still.

# Part Two

'It is given to no human being to stereotype a set of truths, and walk safely by their guidance with his mind's eye closed.'

John Stuart Mill

## 35  *In Which The Presidential Couple Enjoy The Delights Of Paris*

His Excellency President Veracruz skimmed through the dispatches forwarded from the Embassy, and felt himself notably free of homesickness. There had been an assassination attempt upon General Hernando Montes Sosa, which was being kept secret until the various branches of the internal security services had decided who had perepetrated it. The Service of State Information thought that it was the Communists, the Army Internal Security Service claimed that it was an admiral who wanted to be Chief-of-Staff in the victim's place, the Naval Internal Intelligence Agency said that it was a commodore from the Air Force, the Air Force Internal Security Agency thought that it was a disaffected army general, the Chief of Federal Police was convinced that it was a right-wing plot to blame the Communists and thus cause a backlash to their own benefit, the Chief of Provincial Police thought it had been done by a mere seeker of notoriety, the Chief of the National Gendarmerie believed that it was done by a lunatic, the Chief of City Police thought that it was the work of the CIA, the Foreign Ministry believed that it was part of an international conspiracy by MOSSAD, the Interior Ministry Internal Security Office thought that it was the KGB, the Ministry of Labour Surveillance Directorate blamed the Paraguayans because the General had clamped down on sources of cocaine coming in from that country, and the State Oil Company Industrial Security Operative had arrived at the conclusion that it was part of a wider plot by Muslim extremists and Mormons who wished to legalise polygamy. His Excellence noted that General Sosa was alive and well, and filed all the reports in the rubbish bin, his own opinion being that it was the work of the coca cartels. It was with greater interest that he read a letter from the French Ambassador, recommending spanking as an aphrodisiac, since it caused vasodilation in the appropriate regions of the body in both sexes; His Excellency pondered upon this, and then recollected that it had been he himself who had originally advocated this practise to the French Ambassador. He turned to a letter from the Finance Minister,

Emperador Ignacio Coriolano, saying that the National Debt was now at precisely the staggering figure that it had been at the end of Dr Badajoz' 'economic miracle'. Emperador stated that he was working with Foreign Secretary Lopez Garcilaso in the attempt to obtain fiscal advice from the Archangel Gabriel, and that the further missions to establish the whereabouts of El Dorado had discovered a cache of rusty muskets in a cave where they had been deposited in 1752 during an abortive rebellion. They had been sold to a Yanqui museum, and had raised half a million dollars which had somehow disappeared inside the international banking system. Emperador added, on a personal note, that he had bought a small aeroplane and was learning to fly.

His Excellency turned to a letter from the College of Heraldry (Baltimore), pursuant to his desire to adopt a suitable 'achievement' for his own use, and found himself intellectually entombed beneath an avalanche of quaint jargon; 'Erminois?' he muttered, 'A bouche . . . sable . . . mantling? Nebuly or invected? Fusilly, escartelly? Dieu et Ma Femme? Lioncels addorsed? Jaguars rampant regardant? Saracens salient?' He snorted with impatience and wrote the college a note which said, 'Just send me some pictures.'

His Excellency was not in a good mood. His special gringo device for ensuring automatic erections had taken much of the pleasure out of his life because, now that he could pump it up at any time in order to gratify Madame Veracruz, she made him do it even when he did not truly wish it. He would lie on his back watching her gyrations and her truly extraordinary and disconcerting facial expressions, and find his attention wandering. He made cracks in the ceiling into maps of mountains and roads. He fantasised about reuniting the countries of northern South America into Gran Colombia. He composed glowing obituaries for himself. He reminisced about his student days and his first dose of clap. He solved the National Debt by blackmailing the president of the United States and drilling all the way through the world into the Siberian oilfields. He recited in his imagination all the nationalist poetry he had learned by heart at school, and all the indecent playground rhymes afterwards. He wished he could read a book, and felt himself growing sore.

His Excellency's spirit was flagging. The thought of leaving the capitals of Europe behind him in order to return to the perplexities and prevarications of office rendered him deeply depressed, and he wondered whether it might not be possible to continue to rule from abroad. He read the letter from Cardinal Guzman accusing him of raising by black art the demons that tormented him, and he sighed. He read the letter from 'Eva Perón', saying that there were religious fanatics loose in the countryside, and he shook his head with despair at the same time as reminding himself that he must one of these days get around to giving permission for the Armed Forces to suppress them. Just now he would costume himself as Odin, and await Madame Veracruz, who would shortly be appearing as Freya, complete with her necklace of Brisingamen, her cloak of flight, and her horned helmet which was regrettably too large for her and tipped forward over her eyes at the moment of orgasm, just as had the headdress of Isis during their Egyptian period.

'Hello, Daddykins,' she exclaimed as she opened the door dramatically and revealed herself in all her Nordic raiment. 'Who are you today?' She looked him up and down and added, 'Not Odin again?'

'Yes, my little Pussycat, Odin again.'

Madame Veracruz had researched Freya thoroughly, discovering that that goddess was remarkably promiscuous, and so she had arranged for her husband to be sometimes her incestuous brother, Freyr, or one of the four dwarfs with whom she had slept in order to procure the necklace. 'I thought you could be Loki today, Daddykins, and play some naughty tricks on me.' She skipped forward daintily and kissed him coquettishly on the end of the nose. 'Look,' she exclaimed, opening her cloak of flight to reveal a freshly trimmed delta of Venus and a leather brassière with holes for the nipples. She performed a pirouette which swept the ashtray from the table, and fell theatrically upon the floor, holding out her arms to him. 'Go on, pump it up. What are we visualising today?'

'It will have to be the National Debt. Ever since we started concentrating on immortality the debt has been rising again.'

She pouted and said, 'But the National Debt is a big bore, Daddykins. Why don't we concentrate on our little daughter becoming a human being? And afterwards we can go to the Pompidou Centre and the Rodin Museum.'

'It must be the National Debt, Pussycat,' he replied, and he adjusted his eyepatch, pulled his floppy hat low over his face, and, with an extreme sense of apathy, reached into his cloak to pump himself up.

# 36 *Dionisio Receives Sad News*

Dionisio Vivo was sitting in his bookshop, studiously composing another of his celebrated musical palindromes. His head felt very cold where his mother had sheared away his hair, and he stopped frequently to scratch the scars upon his neck, which were itching in an ominous manner. Leticia Aragon always said, 'Whenever the scar of the rope itches, I expect good news, and when the six-centimetre gash itches as well, then I expect bad news,' and it seemed to be true that it always worked out in just that fashion.

Pedro the Hunter knocked at the door and entered with his milling pack of silent dogs, so that Dionisio's two jaguars felt obliged to leave the room in disgust.

'Hola, Pedro, have you come to take a copa with me? Sit down.' Dionisio pushed a chair in his direction with one foot, and Pedro made a gesture of polite refusal. 'Forgive me, cabrón, but these stacks of books make my mouth go dry and my palms sweat. Just imagine all the hours spent with a pen that could have been spent fishing or tracking a puma.'

'Puma skins rot,' observed Dionisio, 'but a book might last forever.'

'Not everything that endures is good,' riposted Pedro. 'Look, I was in Ipasueño, and someone gave me this letter to give to you.'

Dionisio took the proferred envelope and noticed that it was addressed simply to 'Dionisio Vivo, in Cochadebajo de los Gatos'. It was covered with grimy fingerprints and bore no stamp. 'I think it was given to you by a mechanic,' he said.

Pedro left, and Dionisio opened the letter to find that it was from Agustin, the policeman who used to collect the dead bodies from his garden in the company of Ramón.

Respected Friend,

    I do not know whether this will ever reach you in the absence of a postal service, but my experience has always been that a letter dropped in the street will sooner or later be picked up and passed from one to another until finally it arrives at its destination.

I thought that you would like to know that two days ago Velvet Luisa unexpectedly died of a sudden and very high fever. She was about to give up whoring and was going to come and stay with you before taking up employment at the alcaldia. But this, as you see, was pre-empted by misfortune.

I know that you were very fond of each other, and I put my arm around your shoulder even from such a great distance in order to express my sympathy for your sadness. At times like this I am filled with wistfulness because I know that in a country like France or Holland she would have been cured and still amongst us.

Your good friend, Agustin.

Dionisio read the letter twice, folded the paper in his fingers, and was filled with the sense of being an improbable survivor. He thought of Velvet Luisa's vibrant smile, her pointed breasts, the immaculate black silk that was her skin, and tried to imagine all that life shrinking and mummifying beneath the stones of Ipasueño cemetery. He thought of how she had been betrayed by her sister, of how one is so often a victim of circumstance, and his mind returned to the impossible image of Luisa as a corpse. He decided to go to see Profesor Luis.

Farides was in the kitchen as usual, and as usual Profesor Luis was standing in its doorway feeling guilty about her unshared labours. She smiled brightly at Dionisio as he came in, and Luis grinned sheepishly and raised a hand in greeting. Dionisio handed him the letter and asked, 'What do you make of this?'

Profesor Luis read the letter and reflected a moment. 'I think that it tells us to make the most of each other whilst we are here, because life is cheap and death arrives too soon.'

Dionisio nodded. 'Exactly. All my friends keep dying. And because of that, I am going now to find Leticia, to see what colour her eyes are today, and I am going to memorise it.'

As Dionisio departed, Profesor Luis turned to Farides and said, 'You had better take advantage of my offers of assistance, because when I am gone there will be no one even to stand in the doorway.'

Farides grimaced and handed him a guinea pig. 'Go outside and skin that, then.'

He took the limp rodent and commented, 'There must be some more pleasant task with which to evidence your love.'

'There is,' she replied. 'When you have done that you can empty the bucket in the excusado for once.'

## 37 *Dr Tebas De Tapabalazo*

Tertuliano Tomás Kaiser Wilhelm Tebas de Tapabalazo, a man who had travelled life apparently unburdened by the idiosyncrasy of his name, had spent his years as the foremost surgeon to the wealthy and the influential leading a double life. There was nothing he did not know about the afflictions of the affluent; he knew about the bloat and tenacious constipation of those who eat nothing but expensive cuts of meat and frivolous soufflés. He was fully equipped to deal with the imaginary gynaecological problems of aristocratic women who marry for money and influence, but who baulk at the fulfilment of marital rites. He could detect at one hundred metres the indiscreet and democratic onset of the clap, and would sensitively diagnose it as 'an unspecific melisma', in the satisfying knowledge that none of his patients would have heard of such a technical term for a melodic embellishment crammed with grace notes. He had mastered the art of palpating flesh that was interred deep beneath stupendous folds of fat, and he could visualise keenly the presence of portentous stalagmites of cholesterol in the arteries of unexercised hearts. He believed in the efficacy of pantagruelian quantities of garlic for purifying the blood, and in lofty and paternal intimidation as a specific against mental disorder and hypochondria. His solemn air, his mellifluous and tuba-like voice, his enormous face and cold hands, and the half-moon spectacles perched on the end of his nose, inspired fanatical confidence and devotion amongst his coterie of plutocratic patients, who always declared that Doctor Tapabalazo was expensive, but worth every centavo.

What they did not know was that Dr Tapabalazo was an improvident recycler of wealth. He lived in moderate style in the suburbs, amid a chaos of unreadable books. He loved old German volumes in gothic script, books from the East that were written in whirls and flourishes and were supposed to be perused backwards, books from China that were painted rather than written, books in Old Norse and Luxembourgish, and he collected them with an assiduity and

217

dedication that were a testament to his lifelong belief and asseveration that everywhere in the world there were meanings and connotations that were utterly mysterious. He could spend happy hours flicking through his collection, adrift in a sea of speculation and wonder because of the simple miraculous fact that most of the world did not speak Castilian. Nothing impressed him more than to see a foreign film on television, in which dogs obeyed commands in German or French. He would shake his head in surprise that even animals could intelligently comprehend foreign tongues of which he personally understood not a single syllable.

But the greater part of his very considerable earnings were spent on establishing and maintaining a string of clinics that stretched from the favelas of the capital to the remotest Indian villages of the sierra. His desk was covered with jotted notes that computed how many cases of leprosy could be arrested with the income from one case of overactive imagination treated with placebos and bottles of sugar syrup, how many cases of scabies or impetigo could be treated with the revenue from three prolapsed oligarchic wombs or four anti-distemper injections for the huge black jaguar that lived off Turkish delight, and which the President's wife disconcertingly referred to as 'my little daughter'. He calculated that the proceeds from operating on the Cardinal's growth would bring in enough funds to supply a thousand impoverished young mothers with contraception for an entire year.

When Cardinal Guzman was delivered to the hospital, vomiting and raving, his stomach cruelly distended, Dr Tapabalazo diagnosed cancer and paranoid delusions. The latter he proposed to treat later, with a course of severe criticism and acerbic remarks, and the former he would treat at once, but with little hope that his patient was not already riddled with secondary growths. He felt a glow of *schadenfreude* at having the Cardinal at his mercy, because he had been educated in a convent, and consequently was now a leading figure in the National Secular Society.

With his brow knitted and his spectacles in peril of sliding off the end of his nose, he placed his cooling hands on the Cardinal's belly, and closed his mind to all but the impressions that he received from his practised fingertips. The stomach was tighter than a snaredrum, and he had the intuition that much of what lay therein was liquid.

But a determined poke above the navel revealed that there was something solid and amorphous in there also. He inspected the thin face, the bony legs, the unpadded ribs, and knew without asking that for some time Cardinal Guzman had been unable to keep down his food. The afflicted man opened his eyes and jerked his body. 'I murdered Cristobal,' he said.

'Be quiet,' said the doctor sternly. 'You have all but managed to murder yourself. You should have had this treated months ago, when it first started. Did you think that God was going to make it better on His own?'

The Cardinal's eyes flickered and closed. 'It was my punishment.' A trickle of saliva meandered out of the corner of his mouth and found its way down to the pillow.

'I am going to do a laparotomy so that I can do a laparoscopy,' announced Dr Tapabalazo, relishing the inscrutability of his terminology, 'which means that I am going to cut you open and have a look. When I have sewn you up again and had a good think about it, I am going to cut you open again and put everything right. I would like to warn you that any of my patients who die are charged double, since the process of probate ensures that their capital becomes liquid.'

'You should let me die,' murmured the Cardinal.

'Between you and me, I feel very much inclined to,' jested the doctor, 'but it would be most unprofessional. Now, I am going to allow you very few visitors, so perhaps you will be so good as to tell me which ones you particularly want to see.'

'Concepcion,' whispered Cardinal Guzman, 'my cook. No one else.'

'Concepcion,' noted the doctor in his looseleaf book, remembering the lachrymose Negro woman who wore cardboard lavatory-roll liners in her hair in order to simulate Caucasian curls, who had knocked at the door of his office, and, her lips trembling, had asked him how her 'cadenay' was. He remembered his surprise when he had looked up this word in his dialect dictionary, and discovered that it was Quechua argot for 'spouse'. 'The dirty old hypocrite,' he had thought, reacting with the automatic prurience of secularists who have discovered clerical lapses and pecadillos.

Dr Tertuliano Tapabalazo rang for the anaesthetist, ordered his juniors to ready the operating theatre for a laparoscopy, and, whilst he robed himself in his surgical gown, made an invigorating cup of coffee with the aid of a bunsen burner, a tripod, and a fireproof conical flask. He drank the scalding brew in contemplative sips, thought about what he might find in the Cardinal's belly, and strode off down the corridor to see if his fears were to be confirmed.

# 38  *Of The New Albigensian Crusade*

In all times and all places the principal attraction of religions has lain in their licence to do evil; that this is so is amply demonstrated by the fact that as soon as a faith loses its militant aggressiveness, the number of its followers diminishes. A man who does evil in God's name and purportedly by His command becomes instantly justified, and the greater the evil he perpetrates, the more holy does he seem to himself. In the holy books of the world may be found precedents and even injunctions to delight the heart of the Devil, and both sides of any dispute find ample fuel for their fires within the mazes of contradiction that can be found therein. No proverb is more depressingly true than that which states that evil always pays good the compliment of masquerading as it.

Mgr Rechin Anquilar felt in his own heart that blaze of righteous anger and intellectual clarity that stems from the absolute conviction that God speaks and acts through oneself. In addition, the success of his early exploits served to increase his belief in himself far beyond the bounds of rational self-confidence, until he presumed himself to be upon such terms of intimacy with God that he ceased even to feel the necessity of prayer before deciding his courses of action. It was as though the Deity Himself were permanently perched upon his shoulder, whispering instructions into his ear that displaced the processes of thought and banished from his heart the mitigating modesties of compassion and uncertainty.

When he was a little boy, precocious, priggish, reluctant to share his sweets or lend out his catapult, slow to fight on account of cowardice rather than principle, Rechin Anquilar had escaped the vigorous beatings of the priests at school, and instead had become the victim of his fellows. He suffered from weak nasal bloodvessels, and it was a popular sport to whirl him by his feet in a vertiginous circle until the blood started from his nose and sprayed about in crimson droplets. He even learned to gain a kind of precarious popularity by cravenly volunteering for this treatment. Like all victims he turned upon those weaker than himself; he would tear off the wings and legs of butterflies. He once took the family cat and tossed it from a balcony, his heart thumping with guilty excitement, and was torn between relief and disappointment when the animal landed nonchalantly and sauntered away into the bushes. Once he nailed a lizard to a board and focused upon it his magnifying glass. Beneath the point of light that was the distillation of the tropical sun he watched the creature twist and writhe. The green flesh yellowed and began to smoke. Holding his nose against the reek of charring flesh, but his eyes wide with fascination, he witnessed the torment of the reptile. To his horror, it opened its mouth and shrieked. He had always believed that lizards were dumb, and this agonised vocalisation seemed to reveal all at once the animal's sentience and his own cruelty. He released it into the paraguatan bushes, and, instead of praying for its recovery, he fell upon his knees and prayed forgiveness for himself. He learned from one of the fathers at school that animals have no souls, however, and thereafter there was no dog or bird safe from his catapult. During the years of his priesthood he had discovered a similar pleasure in the humiliation of those who suffered his barbed and acerbic reproaches in the intimacy of the confessional; he was notorious for the severity of his penances, and became popular with those soured and vexatious women who in early middle age become spiritual masochists.

Mgr Rechin Anquilar had formed a formidable aquaintance with the writings of St Thomas Aquinas, being particularly cognisant of those sections which today are discreetly left out of all the anthologies, amongst them being the arguments in favour of the extirpation of heretics and heresy. He knew that to burn a heretic was an act of love, since this spared the victim the flames of hell hereafter, and he was one of the few Catholic historians who neither glossed over the activities of the Dominican Inquisition nor experienced a civilised retrospective shame on its account. This is perhaps why the new crusade recapitulated with such aberrant precision the atrocities of the original Albigensian crusade which destroyed the Cathar faith and the culture of the troubadours in Occitan France; perhaps it is coincidental that it also recapitulated yet one more time the ferocious destructiveness of the centuries-old struggles between Catholic

Conservatives and secular Liberals. Mgr Anquilar brought back La Violencia.

Perhaps what was most surprising about the New Albigensian Crusade was that it had not happened a hundred times already. This was a land divided between the followers of Santander, San Martin, Bolivar, Marx, Chairman Mao, Trotsky, Mariategui, the Roman Church, the would-be gringos, the Iberian nostalgics, all of them in their disparity sharing wholeheartedly in the Great Fivefold National Delusion. The first of these is that there are solutions to all the problems. The second is that only a strong centre can solve the problems. The third is that the strong centre must embody one's own views exclusively. The fourth Great Delusion is that heroic surgery is required, and the fifth, that the Heroic Surgeons must be oneself and one's cronies, armed with scalpels as big as machetes and amputation saws that run on gasoline and are designed for felling sequoias.

Central to the national mythology was the idea that the great historical struggles were simple conflicts of good and evil. Leftists, for example, excoriated the conquistadors and canonised the Incas, while for rightists it was obvious that the conquistadors were bringing civilisation to barbarians. To any informed outsider it was perfectly evident that both sides consisted of no one but cynical opportunists, and that this was largely true of all the other conflicts as well.

Mgr Rechin Anquilar, his missionaries, and the vast band of opportunists who called themselves 'crusaders', gathered together over a period of two weeks amongst the deserted classical ruins of the aborted Incarama Park, displacing the overflow of slum-dwellers and the colonies of wild animals, and confusing the gaunt and diseased fugitives of the cocaine wars who had set up bivouacs amongst the creepers, cracking the portentous stones with their cooking fires.

The demi-constructed replicas of the world's greatest monuments now resounded with coarse laughter and priestly incantations. The smell of roasting meat mingled with the aroma of olibanum and dittany of Crete, and the measured tread of sandals was drowned out by the methodical tramping of crusaders being drilled by ex-corporals into some semblance of discipline and cohesion. At this time they were still being referred to as the 'bodyguard', and not yet as 'the troops'. The capital's whores came out by the lorry-load to take advantage of the assembly of deracinated men, so that at night the encampments echoed unnervingly to the moans of purchased ecstasy, the shrieks of dissembled orgasm, the disputes about payment, and the dull thuds and muttered curses of customers fighting between themselves.

The clergymen, appalled by the sacrilegious intervention of mercenary carnality, at first sent the whores away amid thunderous and righteous storms of denunciation, but the resourceful ladies would merely creep around the encampment to re-enter it at a point of safety. They developed winning smiles, and when caught would say 'I am looking for my brother,' or 'Have you seen my fiancé?' Some even cobbled together garments that in the dark made them appear to be nuns, so that very soon the genuine nuns had to leave for fear of the frequent requests for 'French polishing', 'Mexican one hundred and eight centimetre fantasy massages', and 'Bolivian discipline'. The scandalised nuns at first appealed to Mgr Anquilar to temper the spirit of his bodyguard and prevent them from grabbing their breasts suddenly from behind, engulfing them in clouds of liquorish halitosis, and offering them a 'free one', or a 'pearl necklace'. But the self-styled 'legate' had no estimation of women of any variety, and his response was to deliver homilies, his most preferred being that, 'In God's work one must expect to suffer.' He was relieved when the nuns departed, and contemptuously tolerated the presence of the whores on the grounds that the moral imperfections of his men should not be an obstacle to the greater purpose of protecting his priests whilst they went about the divine labour of bringing salvation to the ignorant and the errant. When he caught his men with a whore, he would frown disdainfully, and admonish them to be truthful in the confessional and to be mindful of their souls. As the crusade cut its way through the countryside, the bedraggled camp followers became a fixture that even the priests learned to ignore.

One evening at the end of the second week, when Mgr Anquilar was sure that all his missionaries had assembled, along with their protectors, he sent messengers to announce that all should gather in the open space before the simulacrum of the Tower of Babel.

The Monsignor climbed to the second floor of the tower, and gazed with satisfaction over the host. The blazing torches made the upturned faces of the crowd redden in their glow and flicker, and he felt a commander's sense of pride and humility. Twice daily he had heard, as he sat in his accommodation in the gloomy and tenebrous reproduction of El Escorial, the majestic strains of psalms and hymns floating out over the picturesque ruins as his priests practised his army in their spiritual weapons training, and he felt himself scaffolded by the ancient warrior tradition of Joshua and David. No latter-day soldiers of Midian could withstand him. A chill of Holy Fire ran up his spine like the caress of an angel, and he raised his arms for silence so that he could speak:

'Brothers, throughout our sacred land there is a plague. This plague is a plague of disbelief, of false belief that imperils the health of Church and State. Our innocent children are brought up without the light of the Lord upon them, so that they will be bereft of salvation on the Last Day. How can we think upon this without sorrow and anger? This plague, this black plague that ravages our country, this cancer capable of corrupting the whole people, this evil that must be destroyed by recourse to steel, this purulent disease; if it proves itself refractory to a cure, the hour of the lancet has arrived. We, my friends, in waging Holy War against Evil, are doctors to our nation. It occurs that in setting a bone, in cauterising a wound, a doctor will cause pain to a patient in order to secure a greater good. Such doctors are we. We have God's sanction to be such doctors. Have we been supplied with provisions? No, but none of us starve, because we are divinely provided for. In poverty and obedience we set forth tomorrow in the morning, and the Lord will continue to provide for us as sign of His favour. Tonight we watch and pray. Tomorrow we march. The blessing of God be upon you all.'

The bodyguard, who had listened to this harangue and had endured the daily hymns with undisguised boredom and indifference, departed to their quarters to continue their revelry. Some of the priests watched and prayed, and a deputation of outraged local citizenry went to see the Chief of City Police, to complain that nothing had been done about the blatant brigandage of the campers in the ruins of the Incarama Park. Houses had been ransacked and local shops looted by bands of 'crusaders' supplementing what the Lord had in fact omitted to provide. Three girls had been violated brutally, and an old man killed and robbed of fifty pesos. Three policemen arrived two days later, and found nothing but litter and the corpse of a prostitute.

## 39  *The Spectacular And Wonderful Tapabalazo Teratoma*

'Gentlemen,' said Dr Tapabalazo, 'fetch your umbrellas, for we may be in for a shower. Stand by with the sucker!'

With a flourish that would have struck the ignorant as cavalier and downright dangerous, the doctor opened a short cut in the Cardinal's abdomen, and a small cascade of slimy liquid erupted elegantly into the air and fell back down again. 'An aroma fit for a perfumery,' commented the doctor, as a rank and stagnant stench like that of marsh water invaded every corner of the operating theatre. 'Hydrogen sulphide, methane, and general rot. How delightful. Now, where is our little vacuum cleaner?'

As the loathsome slime was pumped out, Cardinal Guzman dreamed that his brother Salvador had just stopped sitting on him in the garden of their parental home and had gone off to throw sticks for the family dog. 'It's no good telling me dirty poems in Latin,' he shouted after his brother, 'because I don't understand them,' whereupon Salvador looked over his shoulder and announced crushingly, 'You don't understand anything. You're so immature.'

Dr Tapabalazo waggled the siphon about inside the cavity, listening for the gurgles that indicated that what was being taken up was mostly air. He cast an eye over the large jar that was rapidly filling, and remarked, 'Just like snot with yellow bits and spots of blood! Most savoury. Think of the cooks who would give their lives to invent a sauce like that. A touch of salt, a pinch of chile, half a clove of garlic, a dessertspoon of cornflour. Perfectly delicious. An unparalleled accompaniment to delicately roasted veal!'

The siphon was withdrawn and he clamped the wound apart with locking forceps. 'Speculum, and plenty of light,' he demanded, and his assistants adjusted the overhead lamp, whilst another of their number handed him the speculum.

He bent over the recumbent body and gently inserted the instrument. He saw a thick mass of matted black hair. 'Gentlemen, we have here something quite rare and marvellous, that I have seen before only in textbooks, and which is definitely not malignant.' He invited them all to have a look, and one by one they inspected what appeared to be the kind of wig that is bought by Negresses to make it appear that their hair is straight.

'How did that get in there?' asked one of them, his eyebrows contorting with puzzlement above his surgical mask.

'All will be revealed in the fullness of time,' replied Tapabalazo, leaning again over the incision. He turned his scalpel so that the blade pointed upwards, and with the tip of the handle gently parted the hair.

Despite his years of experience and his consummate expertise, he was unprepared for what he saw. He started in astonishment and stepped backwards. He bent forward once more and verified that there really was a large and vacant eye looking back at him unseeingly from behind the wiry strands. He raised his head and said triumphantly, 'Gentlemen, we are truly privileged!'

'It is a teratoma,' the doctor informed the Cardinal later, 'and we will have to operate again in order to remove it. Fortunately it is not a true cancer, and my prognostication is that you will live a long life in good health.'

The Cardinal had awakened refreshed by the deep sleep and exhilarated by the oxygen of the revival mask. 'Is that necessary? I feel marvellous, and my belly feels very much less tight.'

'Of course it is necessary, my dear Cardinal. There is a very large growth in there, a growth of epic proportion, and I intend to pickle it in formaldehyde and present it to the university. It will be known as the "Tapabalazo Teratoma", and you and I will be immortalised. I am most profoundly grateful to you for being in possession of such a magnificent hereditary flaw.'

'Teratoma?' mused the Cardinal, who knew his Greek. 'Are you saying that it is some variety of monster?'

'Your grasp of etymology is most admirable, Your Eminence. This is most literally a monster in the truest sense. From now on I will have no truck with metaphorical or mythic monsters; they would leave me heartrendingly dissatisfied.' He looked down at the Cardinal through his half-moon spectacles, and smiled indulgently. 'It appears that we have a wonderful specimen of a growth that has been burgeoning inside you since the day of your nativity. It consists of a randomly assembled chaos of normal bodily components that have proliferated in an unstructured manner from a totipotential germ. I hope to find bones and teeth, bits of muscle and urinary and intestinal tract, nervous tissue, cerebro-spinal material, an ear if I am lucky. Permit me to become carried away! I hope to find sebaceous glands, sudoriparous, apocrine and eccrine glands, I anticipate non-myelinated and myelinated nerves, complete with perfectly formed perineuriums, I hope for ganglia of all descriptions, and ependymal and ventricular cavities thoughtfully provided with choroid plexuses. Perhaps there will be a hand or a foot, and, best of all, genitalia. My dear Cardinal, I have already found a great deal of hair and an eye, but I regret that the entity has already begun to regress and decay. Your abdomen was full of desquamation and the results of excretory processes, and I believe that both you and your improbable progeny have been progressively poisoned by it. Think of it theologically,' continued the doctor with an ironic glint in his eye, 'I am about to repeat the miracle of virgin birth, albeit by caesarian section. Parthenogenesis! A true miracle!'

The effects of this lengthy exposition on the Cardinal were not anything that the surgeon could have anticipated. The patient seemed to be utterly defeated, and appeared visibly to be entering the door that leads down the long corridor to death. 'Did you say that this monster has nervous tissue? Brain tissue?'

'That is nearly always the case. I believe that there is somewhere an example of a cerebellar cortex taken from a teratoma. One can find everything that one would normally expect to derive from an ectoblast, by which I mean that you can come across any feature of the human organism. It is as though one were to put an embryo into a mincer, and then grow it; it comes out with everything there, but arranged in the most haphazard manner. A real monster.'

'I cannot allow you to operate to remove it.'

'Good God, why not?'

'If it has nervous tissue and brain tissue, then it may possess consciousness, and to remove it would be to kill it.'

Dr Tapabalazo was both amused and horrified; 'My dear Cardinal, I doubt very much if it has consciousness. Even if it did, one regularly kills and eats animals, which undoubtedly are conscious and sentient.'

'We are talking of a human being, Doctor. We are talking of what amounts to abortion, which is murder. It were better to let me die with the creature within me, a natural death.'

'But this creature has no organisation of its elements! It cannot be conscious. And furthermore, it is dying already, as I believe I told you. And more than that, it is quite unviable on its own. Once I have severed the pedicle that attaches it to you, it could not possibly live; if it has a heart, then that heart would not work. It is not a human being but an abhorrent parasite that will kill you if I leave it in place. I cannot possibly agree to leaving it where it is.'

'How are you to know that it has no soul, Doctor? It is the soul that counts and not the arrangement of the brain. If it is dependent upon me for life, then it must be as God wills. I will agree neither to abortion nor euthanasia, as being contrary to the faith.'

Dr Tapabalazo frowned and sighed with impatience. 'In the first place, you have never been known before to practise your faith with such absurd extremism. In the second place, as your doctor, the ethical considerations lie with me and not with you. In the third place, Jesus Christ Himself permitted Himself to be taken and crucified in the full knowledge that this was about to occur, and therefore he committed suicide, which is also contrary to the faith. You will perceive, my dear Cardinal, that even the Lord Himself is prepared to make exceptions in matters of principle. I would add that if you do not allow me to operate, then you yourself are knowingly committing suicide in a cause that has no nobility to it whatsoever.'

Cardinal Guzman lay silent and pale, his lips moving soundlessly, perhaps in prayer. He said softly, 'I do not know anything anymore,' and two tears trickled down his cheeks from the outward corners of his eyes. The doctor held his hand, regretting deeply that he had told his patient anything at all about his affliction, and wishing that at least he had been less brutal. 'I should be kind even to cardinals,' he thought, and then said, 'I promise that after I have removed it I will try my best to keep it alive.'

A deep sigh of despair and resignation escaped from Guzman's lips, and he whispered, 'For the love of God, Doctor, I am only trying for once to do as I should.'

# 40 *In Which The Monsignor Encounters One Or Two Difficulties*

The crusade pursued its meandering, slow, and cumbersome way across the department of Cesar. For most of the time it was a disorderly rout that resembled an aimless biblical exodus, and indeed many of the priests found themselves in possession of a new understanding as to how it had been possible for the children of Israel to spend forty years crossing the tiny parcel of land that separates Egypt and Canaan, a journey that should have taken a few weeks at most.

It was not after all that Moses had been an incompetent mapreader or had not been able to discern his direction from the scintillation of the stars. It was not that the Divinity fell short in supplying that redoubtable patriarch with suitably prophetic navigational inspiration. It was not that the destination was simply unknown or undecided. It was not that the wheel had not yet been invented, necessitating the use of humans as pack animals. Nor was it due simply to a longstanding and disorientating amazement that the Egyptian army had been swallowed up by the Red Sea. It was not that the twelve tribes absorbed a phenomenal amount of time in worshipping the Golden Calf, or engaged in heated debate as to whether or not to return to the Pharaoh because of boredom on account of eating nothing but manna. It was due simply to the appalling difficulties that attend any attempt to move large numbers of people over a given distance whilst simultaneously keeping them supplied.

It became very clear almost as soon as the crusade departed from the Incarama Park that everyone would have to move at the speed of the slowest, or else it would presently break up into numerous parties of stragglers, wanderers and premature arrivers. There were three old and unpredictable trucks carrying camping equipment and general provisions, and to begin with Mgr Anquilar would send them ahead to a predesignated spot where he intended that camp should be set up for the night. But the drivers were never very sure as to whether or not they had arrived, and would generally keep on driving until they reached a likely-looking spot that they believed to be within range of one day's walk from the point of departure. In their estimates they were invariably optimistic, and after nightfall they would backtrack along their route until they met up with the crusaders, who were always in a cold fury on account of having been left with neither food nor shelter upon their arrival. One day Mgr Rechin Anquilar looked at his map and realised that he no longer had any idea where he was; coincidentally the truck drivers far ahead realised that they too were lost, and unanimously decided to keep driving until they found a buyer for their vehicles and the equipment therein, which explains why there is now in the region of Cesar a travelling circus which possesses numerous tents painted with crosses, and three elderly trucks which are still registered as property of the church, and whose roadtax is still conscientiously paid on an annual basis by a bespectacled clerk lost forever in the labyrinth of the Byzantine ecclesiastical bureaucracy.

'The Lord will provide,' agreed the priests, and, of course, He did, mediated by the peasants who found their fruit trees stripped, their pigs stolen, their horses and mules borrowed in perpetuity, their maize miraculously harvested overnight, and their tractors driven away and abandoned at whatever place the Lord chose beneficently to cause them to run out of fuel. The footsore clergy marvelled at this self-renewing miracle of the loaves and fishes, and the bodyguard was unanimously struck by wonder at the ease with which it was possible to obtain anything whatsoever by outnumbering any potential opposition by ten to one or more. The undesirable elements in each community were likewise struck by this, and joined in the crusade in such numbers that the necessity for pillage was constantly multiplied. All the more appealing to such thugs and brigands was the belief, disseminated by the priests, that the crusade would mean plenary indulgence and would count in God's eyes as equivalent to a pilgrimage. It would therefore be possible to commit any crime one liked, and still go straight to heaven faster than the flash of a machete on the day of one's death. No one is more naively pious than a brigand, and it was especially satisfying for them to feel that one could give free rein to one's baser instincts and yet be bathed in golden showers of divine favour nonetheless.

Thus there began an inexorable winnowing process, whereby those of greater theological and ethical sophistication and sensitivity found themselves unable to abide the depredations and coarseness of their fellow crusaders. Within days a tidal wave of unrest and moral outrage overtook those who had joined the expedition out of a sense of religious idealism, and who had wished to share the personal happiness and peace that had descended upon them after having made the decision to live their lives in imitation of a God that they conceived to be compassionate and merciful. These people were the kind that one can find all over the world, sentimental, helpful, rather lacking in self-esteem, diffident, but involved in projects that can include anything from teaching literacy and agronomics to peasants, to going shopping on behalf of the infirm and the elderly on Wednesday afternoons. When they marry they often find that their children end up as Buddhists, Quakers, or Baha'ists, and they do not mind because they believe that many paths lead to the one God.

Upon finding that the bodyguard was utterly impervious and even hostile to their docile reproofs, fending them off with bluff rejoinders that smacked unmistakeably of sarcasm and jest, these gentle people began to feel increasingly uneasy about being with the crusade at all. They formed deputations to Mgr Rechin Anquilar, and had the uncanny experience of hearing from his lips exactly the same kinds of remarks that they had received from the bodyguard, except that the Monsignor uttered them with chilling sincerity. Father Lorenzo was with one of these groups of the concerned, having discovered by eavesdropping upon the conversations of his bodyguard what was really going on, and he and several other priests and lay people approached the Monsignor deferentially one evening as he sat pensively upon his huge black horse, looking every inch the caudillo that in truth he was to become.

The Monsignor, who had recently begun to refer to himself as 'El Inocente' in honour of the pope who had called the original Albigensian Crusade, listened impassively to their complaints of rapine and larceny, and replied:

'Gentlemen, we are in the business of saving souls, and that is the most important thing, which should at all times be borne in mind. It has always been the case that many must suffer for the greater good. What does it matter if a pig is taken from its owner when that pig feeds those who are striving to save a thousand souls from the torments of the Pit? What does it matter if a woman suffers assault, when in the first place woman is responsible for the fall of mankind, and in the second place the immortal souls of a hundred other women may be brought before the gates of heaven? You tell me tales of murder, and yet apparently you have not considered that death is not a tragedy. We could kill everyone in the world, but no harm would come of it, for nothing happens unless God wills. You fail, señores, to see things *sub specie aeternitatis*.'

Father Lorenzo summoned up his courage and looked up at the zealous eyes of his leader. 'I and my fellows did not embark on this enterprise in order to increase the sum of human misery, we came to bring our fellow men to the knowledge of happiness in Christ, and –'

'We are talking about eternal bliss, not the little joys and sorrows of our temporal state, Father, remember that. Now I am afraid that I have plans to make.' He spurred his horse forward, leaving the company of the disillusioned to raise their hands in gestures of despair, shake their heads, and ask each other, 'What now?'

'We should go to the Cardinal,' announced Lorenzo. 'He would put a stop to all this if he knew.'

'I have heard that he is very sick and all but mad,' said another. 'I know someone who works in the palace.'

'In that case,' replied the priest, 'I shall go to the Monsignor and tell him that my conscience obliges me to return to the capital and inform the police of all that I have witnessed.'

It was the most courageous thing that Father Lorenzo ever did, and also the last. The Monsignor was in no mood to have his celestial mission thwarted by the secular authorities, and with righteous anger he deputed one of his bodyguard to cause the troublesome priest to vanish off the face of the earth and reappear two metres beneath it. This was the first of his many judicial executions, and thereafter they became ever easier and more frequent.

It was not long before everybody knew what had happened to Father Lorenzo, and the softhearted disappeared en masse, returning to their parishes to write urgent letters to the authorities. These letters were read with concern or disbelief, filed, and forgotten whilst more immediate administrative problems were attended to, and it

233

was not until Dionisio Vivo himself exerted his considerable influence that anything was done at all.

In the meantime El Inocente found himself beset by new problems caused by the left-wing faction in the body of men to which he had become accustomed to refer as 'my army'.

The Church, like most of those in Latin America, found itself divided neatly across the middle. There was the hierarchy, consisting of the ultra-conservative sons of the oligarchy, who promoted each other assiduously and controlled the allocation and use of resources, and there was the main body of the general priesthood. There had been a time when this latter was employed and paid mostly by the rich landlords (the latifundistas), and their mission on earth had been to counsel the poor to put up with their ordained lot and await their reward in heaven.

But ever since the Council of Medellin a great change had taken place, and nowadays the general priesthood overwhelmingly believed that to love one's neighbour includes helping him and taking his side in the face of injustice and exploitation. Some priests, such as Camilo Torres, even went so far as to take up arms and join the Communist guerrilleros in their hopeless 'focos' in the countryside, and many others found themselves able to read and agree with almost everything they read in *Fidel y La Religión*, a book by Frei Betto which, owing to the solitude of that continent, sold millions in Latin America and was ignored everywhere else. The radical priests and nuns who were so susceptible to this book considered themselves to be the new voice crying in the wilderness, preparing for the second coming of the Lord in the form of socialism, and they did not find themselves seeing eye to eye with Mgr Rechin Anquilar. This latter had his gaze fixed upon the next world, and was principally interested in cramming as full as possible the kingdom of paradise, whereas the former were chiliasts who looked forward to the kingdom of heaven on earth, and conceived of Christ as somewhat resembling Fidel Castro in demeanour, but with the soft and gentle eyes of Che Guevara.

These formidable idealists had their heads full of schemes of redistributing the wealth of the rich to the poor, which, if scrupulously carried out, would in sorry fact have given to each pauper enough money to buy three avocados per annum. They also wished to redivide the land, an experiment that once in Peru had caused the complete collapse of the rural economy, since the peasants had immediately reverted to unmechanised subsistence farming. Most importantly, these people had their eyes open and their ears perpetually pricked in the hope of hearing some new story that illustrated the oppression of the masses, and those involved in the crusade very soon found such dramas enacted aplenty before their very eyes. Such people act as the conscience of a nation, and they generally do not achieve power because they are pre-empted by concessions from those in authority, obliging them to look for something else about which to be outraged. But on this occasion no amount of protest seemed to awaken a spark of liberalism in the heart of Monsignor Rechin Anquilar.

The Monsignor found himself plagued by committees and delegations forming up outside his quarters every evening, pushing into his hands lengthy petitions and complaints signed by every one of their number. There were detailed eyewitness accounts of abuses and atrocities. He received elaborate and outspoken lectures from doughty nuns wearing battledress and enormous revolvers. He would gaze at them in angry silence, experiencing all the disdainful contempt that the autocrat feels naturally for conspiratorial gadflies, and would find amazement and disgust doing battle within himself at the mere idea that they had ever been accepted into the Church in the first place.

One day he summoned all of the radical clergy, and was obliged to wait whilst they held a vote amongst themselves as to whether or not they would go and see him. This was a lengthy process, since they had adopted the custom that all their votes should be unanimous, and therefore they would take many hours to arrive at a motion to which everybody could assent. Additionally, like all people who enjoy addressing each other as 'comrade', they were violently addicted to clauses, composites, sub-clauses, points of order, wordings of paragraphs, procedural formalities, and amendments of amendments.

After the discussion had raged for two days, Mgr Rechin Anquilar ordered his followers to strike camp, and when the exhausted committee emerged from their tent to go to see him in order to inform him that they had decided democratically not to go and see him, they discovered that there was no one left to go and see. They returned to their tent, and there they had another lengthy discussion about what to do next; but it took such a long time to arrive at a formula for a resolution upon which to vote in such a way that the outcome would be unanimous, that, once they had decided to rejoin the crusade, they had no prospect of finding it, since it was not clear where it had gone. Thus they returned to their clinics and their adult education projects in the slums, and the last chance was lost to save the crusade from becoming a plague. From that point forward, the only clerics left in the expedition were either fanatics or Holy Fools.

# 41 An Apocalypse Of Embarrassment Strikes The City (1)

'El Gran Azoramiento' (The Great Embarrassment) happened not least on account of an importunate plague of pigs. Periodically it occurred that migrant swarms of these small black creatures with their Indian files of jaunty little piglets would move from adjacent valleys in search of succulent novelties, and the city of Cochadebajo de los Gatos would awake to find itself occupied by a scavenging army. The pigs would root through refuse, shamelessly raid kitchens and foodstores, flirt outrageously with their domestic cousins who were twice their size, and unearth whole crops of potatoes from the andenes. A paroxysm of exasperation would seize the people and they would issue forth armed with sticks and guns to drive the creatures away.

But the pigs were evasive and cunning; when one attempted to kick them, they skipped adroitly sideways, and one would fall over. They left rank little piles in just those places where one was most likely to slip on them, and they most disgustingly displayed a predilection for consuming dogshit with an expression of extreme rapture on their shiny faces. One of them had most memorably once eaten a man's finger that had been severed by a machete.

Even the great cats of the city seemed to be confused by them; the cats had grown luxurious and idle, and were unable to select which one to pounce upon when there were so many from which to choose. Instead they swiped at them in passing or retired to the rooftops in search of peace, where no pigs could disconcert them by darting unexpectedly between their paws.

Hectoro would organise bloody massacres which involved all the men of the city, and most of the Spanish soldiers revived by Aurelio would take part, bloodlust being with them an even more powerful motive than desire. For days afterwards the aroma of roasting pork would drench the pajonales and punas of the sierra, and an invasion of buzzards and vultures would disgust the people more even than the original outbreak of swine.

The first time that this happened there was a terrible pestilence of trichinosis and hookworm shortly afterwards. Profesor Luis was kept busy for days injecting formalin into the runnels that crisscrossed the bodies of the unfortunate, and Aurelio was obliged to travel back and forth to the jungle in order to collect poisons and cibil that would kill the parasites from within. Everybody had to endure the inconvenience of wearing shoes and the nausea caused by Aurelio's medicines, which made one's urine stink of corpses, and thereafter everybody followed Profesor Luis' new addition to the constitution which stated that 'No pork shall be cooked on the bone, and it shall be cooked until it is nearly falling to pieces. It is also forbidden to attempt to cure parasites by the hitherto traditional method which only makes them worse; that is, by forcing children to eat the excrement of dogs.'

In the Andes each season of the year is reprised every day. When General Hernando Montes Sosa arrived in a helicopter with Mama Julia and the British Ambassador at precisely ten hundred hours on June the sixth, it was just turning from spring to summer, and the town was in a frenzy of despair because its elaborate preparations had been wrecked by a sudden influx of pigs. From the air it seemed to the General that down below there had been a catastrophic attack of St Vitus' dance, and from lower down he perceived that everybody was rushing this way and that in the attempt to catch what looked like particularly nimble small black dogs. When he dismounted from the helicopter he understood from the stench, from the squelch beneath his boot, and from the evidence of his eyes, that there had been a mass intrusion of wild pigs. Mama Julia glared balefully out of the door of the craft, and refused to come out. The British Ambassador exchanged his brogues for green wellington boots, and appraised the scene as being very similar to a prep school sports day or the opening of Harrods' sale.

Dionisio and the formal party of welcome were not only shy, but were crimson about the ears for the shame of what their visitors must have thought of the town. All were deeply conscious of the importance of the Ambassador, but most were entirely ignorant of the necessary etiquette. Dionisio shook his hand, and Sergio curtsied. Hectoro took the puro from his mouth, spat on the ground in a manner intended to be respectful, and said, 'Hola, cabrón, what do you want to see first, the Temple of Viracocha or the whorehouse?'

Misael doffed his sombrero, grinning dumbly from ear to ear. Don Emmanuel, who had laid special plans for the day, put on a perfect caricature of a public school accent, and said, 'What ho, old bean, frightfully spiffing to meet you.'

The British Ambassador raised an eyebrow and very coolly replied, 'Bertie Wooster, I presume,' whereupon Don Emmanuel bowed deeply, swept his hat from his head, and thus revealed the balding patch upon which Felicidad had painstakingly written at his instruction 'God Bless The Queen And All Who Sail In Her'.

The Ambassador raised the other eyebrow and twisted his lip sardonically. 'I wish you a speedy recovery,' he said, and passed on to shake the hand of the Mexican musicologist, who introduced him 'to my two wives, Ena and Lena'. The Ambassador looked at the smiling twins, dressed the same, and blinked hard. He shook his head as though to clear it of incomprehension, and double-checked that there were really two identical women before him who were married to the same man. His eyebrows rose to the top of his forehead once more, and he passed on to Remedios and Gloria, both dressed in khaki and armed with Kalashnikovs. 'Welcome,' announced Remedios, 'but your foreign policy stinks.'

'Gracias,' replied the Ambassador, who understood very little Castilian as yet, and was guessing as to the correct response. 'De nada,' said Remedios, who had always heard that the British ruling classes were unnaturally polite.

At this point Aurelio came forward and presented each of the visitors with the customary bags of coca leaves and lejia, the lime necessary to activate them. The General frowned but took his bag out of courtesy, as did the Ambassador, and Mama Julia, who had by now summoned up enough courage to descend into the flurry of pigs, whispered in Dionisio's ear, 'What am I supposed to do with this?'

'Round here they chew them,' he replied, and before he could prevent her, she had popped a wad into her mouth, and was saying, 'Mmm, is this some kind of spinach?' Throughout the day she surreptitiously sampled further mouthfuls, with results that will be revealed below.

'I must apologise about the chaos,' said Dionisio. 'We have had an unexpected invasion of wild pigs, but we are doing our best to get rid of them.'

'Never mind, my boy, you do your best, and we will try to ignore them,' said the General, snapping out of the path of a young boar well-armed with sharp little tusks that Antoine the Frenchman was attempting to chase away.

The party was taken on a guided tour of the town, with Profesor Luis learnedly discoursing upon it, and Don Emmanuel translating for the benefit of the Ambassador:

Profesor Luis: This is the temple of Viracocha . . .

Don Emmanuel (translating): This is our very largest latrine, which doubles as a whorehouse in bad weather . . .

Mama Julia: I feel marvellous.

Profesor Luis: This is probably our biggest and best jaguar obelisk . . .

Don Emmanuel: This represents Pachacamac's penis inserting itself into the resplendent pussy of the sky . . .

Mama Julia: I feel really marvellous.

Profesor Luis: This is the axle-pole with which we brought a giant reel of rope to the city . . .

Don Emmanuel: Here is our telephone system which operates on invisible wires . . .

Mama Julia: Oooooo, ay, ay, ay . . .

Profesor Luis: This is Doña Flor's Restaurant, owned by Dolores . . .

Don Emmanuel: This is where Manco Capac stayed for four days when struck down by amoebic dysentery . . .

Mama Julia: I don't feel hungry anymore, yahooha, oooooo . . .

Profesor Luis: This is where the line of the mud used to come to before we dug the city out . . .

Don Emmanuel: The shit came up to here during the last plague of pigs . . .

Mama Julia (singing): There was a lovely sailor boy who came from far Peru . . .

General Hernando Montes Sosa: For God's sake, my dear, what has got into you?

Mama Julia (singing): I said I'll drop them down, my love, I'll give it all to you . . .

General Hernando Montes Sosa: For God's sake, woman.
Profesor Luis: This is Dionisio's book exchange . . .
Don Emmanuel: This library houses a significant collection of early
  Byzantine pornography . . .
Mama Julia: La, la, la, I've forgotten the words, oo ah oo . . .

Dionisio was obliged to take his mother away and shut her in his
house, still hopping from one foot to another and remembering
snatches of naughty songs from her schooldays, and came back at just
the moment when the British Ambassador was beginning to realise
that Don Emmanuel's translation was a joke at his expense. His ears
became more and more flushed as his anger mounted and his
diplomatic sang-froid became more strained. 'What school did you go
to?' he asked suddenly.
  'Dartington,' replied Don Emmanuel, whereupon the Ambassador
said, 'That explains it; I thought you were an unusual species.'
  'And where did you go to?'
  'Eton.'
  'Excellent, excellent,' smiled Don Emmanuel, rubbing his hands
together and gleefully realising that his weeks of choir practice had
not been wasted. 'How do you know when a whore is full up?' he
asked.
  The Ambassador was astounded. 'I beg your pardon?'
  'She gets a runny nose,' said Don Emmanuel.
  The Ambassador winced and from that moment ignored his
compatriot as far as could be managed under the circumstances, a feat
that was made temporarily easier by the unanticipated non-coopera-
tion of the titanic lift.
  The General, Profesor Luis, the British Ambassador, and Hectoro
(still mounted imperturbably upon his horse) had all got onto the lift
and were descending towards the plateau. Profesor Luis was pointing
out to the General the features of the landscape, and the General was
feeling the profoundest admiration for the ingenuity of the construc-
tors of the lift, when it ground suddenly to a halt, leaving them
swaying in mid-air only half-way down the cliff. Profesor Luis
instantly became agitated, for his contraption had failed when carrying by far the most important person that he had ever met. 'I am so
sorry,' he repeated insistently, 'I am so sorry, I cannot imagine what

could have gone wrong,' and hopped from one foot to the other, mopping his brow with the sleeve of his shirt, and rushing from one end of the platform to the other, tugging futilely upon the massive ropes.

'Please do not be so concerned,' said the General, 'the lifts in the government building do this all the time,' and the British Ambassador, not for the first time, began to wish that he had not adopted a diplomatic career. 'Have a puro,' said Hectoro, offering each of them a cigar from the height of his saddle, 'it will help to pass the time.'

Up on the top of the cliff there was much consternation; no matter how much the people heaved and Cacho Mocho strained, the pulleys were locked. One or two people who suffered from the deeply ingrained national suspicion of machinery could not suppress their glee, and walked about saying, 'I told you no good could come of it; if God had wanted us to have lifts he would have created them Himself.'

Don Salvador the False Priest turned to Father Garcia and asked, 'Can you not levitate down there and then push it up to the top again?' And Father Garcia responded impatiently, 'No, I cannot. In the first place I can only do it when I am not thinking about it, in the second place I cannot push anything else up because there is no ground against which to stand, and in the third place it only happens when I am preaching and I could not concentrate on a sermon under these circumstances. You must ask Profesor Luis what to do, for the machine is his, and only he understands it.'

But Profesor Luis was half-way down the cliff and was unavailable for comment. Sergio suggested fetching Dionisio, but he could not be found because he had taken his mother on a brisk walk in order to try to work off the anomalous effects that the coca had had upon her metabolism, and so the puzzle was left to Misael to resolve, since his had been the idea of building it in the first place.

He clambered all over the pulleys and gantries, peering into the works in order to see whether or not their alignment coincided with his memory of it, and attempting to ignore the unhelpful suggestions of those down below. In the lift, Hectoro's horse trod heavily upon the foot of the British Ambassador, and Profesor Luis found himself unable to restrain the tears of his disgrace. He leaned against the side, his shoulders heaving, and General Hernando Montes Sosa felt obliged to pat him and make soothing noises.

Remedios decided to resume her habit of command, ordering everybody to solve the problem at once upon pain of her perpetual contempt, and at this point the Conde Xavier Pompeyo de Estremadura came forward, waving his sword dramatically and exclaiming, 'I have it, by God, I have it. We had such a machine during the siege of Arakuy in the year of Our Lord one thousand, fifteen hundred and thirty-one. We would merely wind it back a mote and then release it, by God.'

The Conde's idea was put into effect, and, as if by miracle, the lift jerked upwards and then resumed its long-delayed descent. The Conde leaned over the cliff, exultantly exclaimed, 'God's balls,' and swaggered amongst the crowd, condescending to receive their congratulations. He ran towards Remedios, his lover, in order to enjoy the admiration that was his due, and fell headlong over a pig.

'Are you well, my cadenay?' asked Concepcion. 'The doctor says that the operation was very good.'

She was standing at the foot of the bed, attired in her best floral dress, clutching a straw hat that, owing to her nervousness, was in danger of becoming kneaded out of shape.

His Eminence smiled wanly and beckoned to her to come and sit by him on the bed. 'Why do you have a black ribbon on your arm, querida? Did you think that I was going to die?'

She bit her lip, and her shoulders began to shake with suppressed grief. 'It is Cristobal,' she said, 'I can't find him, and it is all my fault.'

Deep concern passed over the Cardinal's face. 'What has happened?'

'When you fell on the floor I ran to the secretary, and then the whole palace was running about calling ambulances, and everywhere was confusion, and then I came all the way here on foot so that you would not be ashamed, and I asked the doctor about you, and afterwards I went out, and I was crying so much that a kind woman in the street put me up for the night in a whorehouse, and in the morning I remembered, "Cristobal!" and I ran back to the palace to find him, and I looked everywhere, but he was gone. I went to the police to ask about any missing children, and they told me they had heard of thousands, but no one knows where they are, and I thought, "Perhaps he has run away," but I could not think where he would go, and I asked all his friends if they had seen him, but nobody has.'

He took her hand and squeezed it comfortingly. 'Did you know that I had a nightmare that I had killed him myself?'

'You told me just when you were falling on your face, but I knew it was an illusion, like the time you came in and said that the Devil had challenged you to a game of chess, and the pieces kept changing positions on their own.'

'That will not happen any more,' said the Cardinal. 'It was caused by poison.'

She put her hands to her mouth in shock, and exclaimed, 'Who would do such a thing? You do not think it was my – '

'No,' he interrupted, 'it was not your cooking, and I was not blaming you. The doctor says that it was caused by the monster inside me. Apparently it was dying from its own poison anyway, but it poisoned me in the process. He said it was like very extreme constipation, when the poisons that should be ejected are reabsorbed into the body, and it causes delusions and madness.'

'What is this monster? Tell me about it so that I do not have to think of Cristobal.'

He pursed his lips and tried to think of a way of explaining it to her that she would find accessible. 'It was like a child that has been growing inside me since I was born. Perhaps it was even a twin that grew in the wrong place in my mother's womb. But it was a hideous freak, with everything in the wrong place, and the doctor says that it was the worst one that has ever been seen. He has given it to the university, and as soon as I am well he is going to take me to see it.'

'A child?' repeated Concepcion. 'And you a man? This is a miracle. How could you have been made pregnant like this? You have never . . .' She tailed off, too ashamed to continue. But the terrible thought could not be suppressed. She looked up and asked firmly, 'Have you been doing it with a man?'

His Eminence laughed brightly for the first time in months. 'Querida, I have not. It is just a miracle, a natural marvel, and it has happened in the past to other people.'

'You should use this in your writing to prove that Mary was a virgin, against the unbelievers.'

'I think it has to be the same sex as oneself,' he said, 'but otherwise that would have been a good idea.'

She smiled contentedly. 'You have never told me before that an idea of mine was good.' Then her face clouded over, and crumpled into tears. An awful longing welled up in her, a gap appeared in her soul, and she asked, 'What will we do to find Cristobal?'

'I am going to resign,' he said. 'I have plenty of private money. We will blaspheme when we want to, believe whatever seems reasonable at the time, and we will try to be happy. We will go away together and search the entire world for Cristobal. Come, give me a hug.'

She leaned down, put her arms about his neck, and laid her cheek against his. 'My cadenay,' she said, her tears flowing down over his face.

So it was that three weeks later the Cardinal, dressed nowadays in layman's clothes, along with Concepcion and Dr Tapabalazo, found himself amid the grisly medical collection of the university. Ouside the inexorable rain of the capital fell in its habitually noncommittal fashion, and in the courtyard outside, the students, dressed on account of an historical anomaly in military uniform, hurried to their lectures with the collars of their greatcoats turned up.

In the glass jars filled with cloudy formalin there bobbed the right arm of a famous general, yellow colons perforated like colanders, varicoloured cancers the size of tennis balls, enormous hearts taken from Indians living at high altitudes, foetuses without mouths but with genitals shamelessly attached to their foreheads, embryos with two heads, livers transformed to sponges by cirrhosis, the forlorn results of miscarriages, and the head of a man who had lived normally for years with an arrow straight through the middle of his brain.

'This is a metaphysical laboratory,' said the doctor. 'I have spent hours in here looking at all these exhibits, wondering how the universe must be in order for such things to exist.'

Dominic Guzman inspected a grotesque creature in a large jar, and pondered aloud. 'Nature's experiments, the Devil's miracles, or God's indifference?'

'Precisely, my dear Dominic. Look at the label.'

Guzman bent forward and read, '"The Tapabalazo Teratoma". This is mine?'

'It is ours now, and no amount of bribery or persuasion would induce us to give it back, I can assure you. We had to give it a haircut so that one can see some of the detail.'

'Is this your baby?' asked Concepcion, her eyes popping with horror and amazement. She crossed herself three times and said the last sentence of the Hail Mary.

What she beheld might at a distance have seemed to be a furry football that had gone out of shape. But a closer inspection would have revealed a sad and empty eye fixed motionlessly upon infinity.

Concepcion saw that the iris was of the same colour as that of the Cardinal. A portion of thumb stuck at a careless angle out from behind it, and a nodule projected from near by, at the end of which there dangled a tiny and useless foot. 'It was going to be a boy,' she said, pointing at the long pink penis that dangled from one side.

'It had a testicle inside, at the back,' said the doctor. 'We dissected the poor monster and removed the inside. Then we filled it again and mounted it like this. We found every kind of normal tissue, but all in the wrong places. Did Dominic tell you? We tried to keep it alive, but there was nowhere to attach the equipment to it. It actually had some signs of adaptation, with membranes growing around individual parts to protect them, but really there was no way to prolong its existence. When I look at this awful and pathetic thing, it makes me feel very sad. I feel a kind of acute compassion.'

'I always feel sorry for monsters,' said Concepcion. 'Even in fairy stories where the monster is bad and gets killed at the end, I always feel sad and I wonder if there was not another way. Did you keep any of the hair that you cut away?'

'Certainly I did. One can tell a lot from hair.'

'I would like some,' she said. 'When one loses a child, one should always have something to remember it by.'

Without questioning, Dr Tapabalazo went to a drawer and took out a folded plastic bag. 'Have all of it,' he said, 'since you have a good heart.'

Concepcion opened the bag and put in her hand. She felt the locks of hair between her fingers, lifted some out and scrutinised it carefully. She looked up and smiled at Dominic Guzman. 'I can tell it was yours. It even has grey in it and it feels the same. I shall keep it forever.'

They stood in silence looking at the misbegotten victim in the glass jar, and suddenly Dominic Guzman said, 'We should give it a name. I do not think that "Tapabalazo Teratoma" is a very sympathetic name.'

The doctor nodded. 'I am afraid that the students have already christened it "Attila the Hun", although for a while there was a fashion for calling it after different politicians.'

'It should be called "Dominic",' said the Cardinal, whose unspoken and melancholy line of reasoning was that he himself was the monster, and therefore it should be named after him. 'How the mighty are fallen,' he added.

Dr Tapabalazo, sensing his mood, put a hand on his shoulder and said, 'My dear Dominic, climbing down from an irksome pedestal is not the same thing as falling.'

At the palace the couple continued the business of packing up their possessions. Dominic Guzman sorted out the remaining administrative problems with his secretary, sent several Hebrew volumes to Dr Tapabalazo in token of gratitude, and steadfastly refused interviews with the hordes of hopeful pressmen who had gathered like vultures outside in the rain, their taste-buds tingling for the juice of scandal. In the newspapers he read accounts and retrospective assessments of his cardinalate with the strange sensation that none of it had anything to do with him, and he read articles about the growing public scandal of the bodies of children that turned up in the river. He and Concepcion suspected that somehow Cristobal had got out of the palace and been mistaken for one of the children of the sewers, but at the same time they maintained a persistent optimism that he was alive and that they would find him. They would talk about him for hours, each sentence beginning with, 'Do you remember how Cristobal . . . ?' and Concepcion gathered together his favourite toys so that she could give them to him to play with when he was found. In bed they would lie in each other's arms reminiscing about his sweet smell, his obsession with bodily functions and excretions, his alarmingly direct logic, his honey-brown skin and his huge dark eyes.

On the morning that they were to leave the palace in their new Brazilian jeep, Dominic Guzman looked into the mirror at himself and saw a man in the prime of his life, disturbed but not defeated by grief. He inspected the scar on his stomach, still livid, and noticed that he was even growing a little fat. He looked around the room and saw no sign of the Obscene Ass, the Litigator, the Contending Heads, or any other of the diabolical rout that had tormented him for so long. He went to the door for the last time and was about to close it behind him, when he heard a tapping sound. Intrigued, he went back into the room and looked around. The tapping came more urgently, from his left. He looked up and saw that at the window above the river there was a small bird hovering. They looked at each other in silence, and the bird tapped once more, as if with greater insistence.

He opened the window, not knowing what else to do, and the tiny and exquisite hummingbird darted inside. It seemed to be showing off. It flew backwards, upwards, sideways, looped in a graceful circle, shot across the room as though discharged from a pistol, and then, without turning around, shot back again. It settled on Guzman's hand and preened itself busily. He saw that it was a living sunbeam of iridescent colours; it was emerald and lilac, azure and cerulean, scarlet and viridian. He held it up to the light, and the feathers refracted through every colour of the spectrum. He held it, so rapt with its jewelled beauty that a choke arose in his throat. He took it back to the window and said, 'Little bird, you had better go.'

But the minuscule creature gripped tightly on his forefinger and would not be budged. When he tried to nudge it off with his other hand, it pecked him imperiously, squeaked defiantly, and sidled closer to him. 'O . . . well,' he said, and took it along to show to Concepcion. He raised his hand and said, 'We have been adopted.'

She looked at it wonderingly, and it performed an identical aerobatic display for her benefit before settling back on Guzman's finger. 'It won't go away,' he said.

'I will go and make it some sugar syrup,' she decided, forever practical and nurturing. 'It can drink from a cigar tube.' As she left the room she turned and said over her shoulder, 'Cristobal would have loved that.'

Down on the plateau the little party admired the citrus groves, the rice field, the guavas, yuccas, mangos, papaya, the splendidly enormous avocados, the irrigation ditches, the stewponds, the bridge across the river, and were just passing the platano plantation when they heard the sound of a violent struggle and someone being murdered amongst the bananas.

'Ay, take that,' they heard, followed by the sound of a wet slap.

'You bastard, ah; don't do that, oh.'

'No, no, no, ay, ay, ay.'

The members of the party exchanged glances, and Hectoro, anxious to prove to the Briton that here there was no shortage of machismo despite their Argentinian cousins' defeat in the Malvinas war, slipped silently off his horse, pulled his revolver, and crept through the luxuriant growth towards the scene of the brutality.

The dreadful shrieks and yelps continued until Hectoro surprised everybody by emerging with the ghost of a smile upon his lips. He removed the puro from his mouth, and whispered, 'You will have to help me, I cannot cope with such barbarism on my own.'

The General removed his automatic from his holster, Profesor Luis unsheathed his machete, and the British Ambassador reflected with a sinking sensation in his stomach that he was about to experience at first hand the legendary violence of this land. They followed Hectoro back into the green, rubbery verdure of the banana grasses.

After only a few metres of creeping Hectoro put his finger to his lips and pointed, and the party spread a little in order to peer between the greenery.

Doña Constanza, lapsed oligarch, and her lover Gonzago, lapsed guerrilla, had decided to take advantage of the occasion on the heights above in order to descend upon one of the smaller machines and cavort in private in the deserted paradise of the plateau. What the party witnessed was the two of them copulating ecstatically in an unfeasible position at the same time as splattering and smearing each other with a steadily diminishing pile of fruit. Gonzago was at this very moment licking the seeds of a grenadillo from her shoulder whilst, in between pelvic rotations, she was cramming a banana into his armpit.

Hectoro watched the lascivious display with undisguised enjoyment; the General watched it with a kind of detached amazement; Profesor Luis watched it with a horror of speculation as to what the British Ambassador must be thinking, and the latter was so overwhelmed with stupefaction that he failed to notice a deadly fer de lance drop onto his back and slither away.

Hectoro, being a campesino, was unable to enjoy such a splendid spectacle without some degree of participation; when the two lovers juddered to the end of their salacious earthquake and descended sideways to the ground, he leapt up crying, 'Whooba,' whipped his sombrero from his head, and waved it in appreciation. 'Mas, mas,' he shouted, 'queremos mas.'

Dōna Constanza and Gonzago started with comic surprise, looked up at the row of eyes peeking through the foliage, saw Hectoro jumping up and down waving his hat, and Dōna Constanza shrieked, leapt up, and disappeared into the plantation, leaving a trail of squashed fruit that had slid off her body. Gonzago stood up hesitantly, covered his nether parts with his hands, and bowed sheepishly. He grinned from ear to ear, looked around for an escape route, and disappeared in the same direction as his lover.

'Magnifico,' exclaimed Hectoro.

'I am so sorry,' said Profesor Luis to the Ambassador.

The General holstered his weapon, pulled a handkerchief to wipe his forehead, and the Ambassador noticed that the knees of his suit were symmetrically grey and wet where he had been kneeling in the clay.

Back at the top of the cliff the General attempted to revive the dignity of the occasion by personally thanking whoever it was who had solved the problem with the lift, but found himself frustrated because Dionisio had strenuously begged Remedios not to allow the Conde anywhere near his descendant. He was anxious to avoid lengthy and unbelievable explanations.

But the Conde was not to be so restrained; he shook off Remedios' firm grip on his arm and strode forward to introduce himself with a flourish as, 'The Conde Xavier Pompeyo de Estremadura, at your service, and God preserve His Catholic Majesty.'

'Extraordinary,' observed the General, assessing sceptically the anachronistic individual by whom he was confronted. The Conde was attired in the rusted remains of a half-suit of armour buckled over an Indian garment that puckered and bulged out of it at odd places. The cuirass was pierced with the holes torn by the bullets of Remedios' Kalashnikov, and on his head he wore a burgonet helmet, the rivets of whose peak were lamentably loose. It suddenly occurred to the General that numerous other men were also clad in scraps of ancient armour, and he blinked and shook his head.

'I have an ancestor of that name,' said the General, 'who disappeared in 1533 on an expedition to locate the lost city of Vilcabamba, and who founded the town of Ipasueño.'

'The very same,' exclaimed the Conde, 'and I claim from you your estate which is not yours until I have properly died.'

The General grew ever more perplexed and the Conde added, 'As your senior relative, it follows that you are obliged to yield before my authority, or I will slit your nose as I did with the Moor in Cordoba.'

'We shall talk of this in private later,' said the General diplomatically, and he beckoned to his son, who had been trying to creep away. 'Dionisio, come here and explain something to me.'

No amount of explanation over lunch at Doña Flor's could persuade the General that in fact that Conde really was the Conde, who had been buried beneath an avalanche of snow with fifty of his men on St Cecilia's Day, and been brought back to life by Aurelio in time to help with the disinterment of the city. Dionisio held out his hand and indicated to his father the Montes Sosa ring. 'He recognised his ring and demanded it back from me. Fortunately he only remembers things that happened several hundred years ago, and so he will forget that he was going to slit your nose. Remedios keeps him under control, I am pleased to say.'

The British Ambassador, who understood none of this intense Castilian discourse, was trying to kick out at the small pigs that had gathered beneath his feet in the hope of scraps, until he suddenly realised that he had been mistaken to ask for the Chicken of a True Man. When the essence of chile sauce sank its fangs into the back of his throat he choked violently and an uncontrollable stream of saliva descended from the side of his mouth onto the tablecloth. The brilliant red flush that transformed his throat and face into something resembling a salamander's was perhaps three-quarters Chicken of a True Man, and one-quarter shame at his appalling attack of lèse-majesté. Pop-eyed with pain, he picked up the water jug and drank its entire content at one gulp before realising that it contained aguardiente. Desperate at the onset of his inevitable inebriation, he broke out into a deluge of sweat. He managed to feed some scraps of his meal to the pigs, who ran out squealing, before his head descended slowly onto his plate and he slept like a baby with saliva still drooling into the remains of his meal. In his terrible stupor the urine ran down his leg into his wellington boots, and he dreamed of Dõna Constanza and Gonzago making love in a pool of vomit.

'Remedios,' said the General, oblivious of the Ambassador's plight, 'the name and the face are very familiar to me.' He ransacked his brains until inspiration hit him. 'It was a "wanted" poster, the leader of the People's Vanguard.'

Dionisio was petrified that the General would take it into his head to go out and arrest her, and he hastily interrupted the General's train of thought. 'The People's Vanguard was disbanded years ago after declaring peace, Papa. Are you enjoying your meal, Mama?'

Mama Julia, still smiling from the unusual effects of the coca leaves upon her unpractised psyche, nodded and replied, 'Yes, but he is not.'

They followed the direction of her glance, and saw all at once that the British Ambassador was negligently inert with his face in a pool of dribble that had overflowed his plate and was dripping onto the floor.

'Oh my God,' said the General, holding up the empty jug, 'He has drunk all of this. He must have thought it was aniseed-water.'

'We will have to make him sick,' said Dionisio.

'He has pissed himself,' observed Mama Julia inelegantly.

'Language, my dear,' remonstrated her husband, to which she replied unrepentantly, 'Well, so he has,' and she adjusted her plentiful hat to a new rakish angle. 'How do I look?'

'Today has been a terrible disaster,' moaned Dionisio. 'I was so hoping to impress you with our achievements. I will fetch Aurelio so that he can deal with the Ambassador.'

Whilst he was out a woman came in with a very little baby, and Mama Julia leapt to her feet in order to coo over it. It began to cry, puckering up its little face and punching the air with its arms and legs, and Mama Julia stuck a plump finger into its mouth in order to pacify it. 'Poor pequeñito's hungry,' she said.

'He is crying for lack of a name,' said the young woman. 'We have not had the ceremony yet.'

'And what will pequeñito's name be, then?'

'Dionisito Vigesimo. Is he not sweet?'

Mama Julia repeated the name innocently, and then straightened up suddenly. 'The twentieth little Dionisio? And who is the father?'

'Dionisio, of course, the one with the scars on his neck.'

The General raised his eyes to the heavens, and Mama Julia's eyes rolled in their sockets. 'What? How many does he have?'

The girl smiled contentedly and bounced the child on her hip. 'This is the newest Dionisito, and there are about twenty little Anicas as well.'

Mama Julia recovered instantly from the euphoria of the coca. She breathed deeply and said icily, 'You are not old enough to have forty children.'

'O there are hundreds of us.'

Mama Julia strode out of Doña Flor's with the General in hot pursuit. She tore the flowery concoction from her head and rolled up her sleeves as she ran down the street after her son, shouting, 'Come here you villain, you knave, you reprobate.'

She beat him about the head with her parasol whilst he shielded himself with his arms and a happy crowd of onlookers gathered around to urge her on. 'Hernando,' she cried, 'do something! He is no son of mine! Disgrace to the family name! Whoremonger!'

The General disarmed her and held her wrists whilst she struggled and yelled, until, in the end, she burst into tears in his arms and said, 'How can we afford forty presents for Saints' Days?'

'There, there,' murmured the General, patting her head, and then, to Dionisio, 'I will have a word with you later.'

The General was distracted by the appearance of Capitan Papagato and General Fuerte. Capitan Papagato had not been able to resist coming out to witness Dionisio's beating with the parasol, even though he was afraid that General Hernando Montes Sosa would recognise him as the deserter that he was. Dionisio's father indeed recognised him as the young captain who had changed his name in Valledupar to Papagato, and disappeared just after General Fuerte's assassination. He was about to open his mouth to say he-knew-not-what, when General Fuerte himself appeared at a doorway whilst attempting to chase out of his house a small pig that had come in unobserved and begun to eat one of his shoes. General Fuerte had resolved not to show his face that day, because Montes Sosa had once been his second-in-command, and he had faked his own death in order to desert the Army.

The two old friends caught each other's glance, and both stood still and silent, their mouths agape. Montes Sosa raised an arm and pointed, 'But you are supposed to be dead.'

'I am,' said General Fuerte, who straightened up and shot back into his house.

General Hernando Montes Sosa put his hands to his face and shook his head for a few seconds. He took his hands away, muttered something to himself, and said to Dionisio, 'You appear to have ghosts here as well as a harem.'

'Aurelio's daughter sometimes lives here,' said Dionisio, 'and she is dead. So is Federico, for that matter.'

The General sighed with extreme weariness. 'Please can we have the concert now, and get it over with? I just want to go home.'

# 44 *St Thomas Is Inspired to Mournfulness*

The insatiable heat of the plains ate into the souls of the crusaders and reduced their hearts to dust. In the sky, quivering mirages of Arabian armies fought interminable battles amid illusory skyscrapers and scenes of pastoral idyll. The metal seats of tractors caused third-degree burns on the callused backsides of peons, and entire furtive conversations drifted for miles with perfect clarity, shocking the sensibilities of susceptible widows. The vibrating haze transformed everyday objects into rare and wondrous things, so that black cats appeared to be bowler hats and metal baths were metamorphosed into monolithic hovering armadillos. In the fields the oppressed cattle were parboiled months before the date of their slaughter, enduring hallucinations horrifying and incomprehensible, and horses preferred to fall unconscious on the end of a lariat rather than be hauled out of the shade.

The bodyguard persevered because the cool of the evening would provide new opportunities for rampage, and the clerics were sustained by either their foolishness or their exemplary zeal. Monsignor Rechin Anquilar, habituated to the cool altitude of the capital, felt himself transported into a metaphysical world where nothing was solid. Objects seemed to flow like liquid, bellydancing before his eyes in a grotesque parody of seduction, and the screeches and groans of wild animals near at hand supplied him with intimations of the torments of hell. In this inferno of abstraction he would long for the cool nights in his tent, persecuted by mosquitos, but raptly attentive to the monologue of the Angelic Doctor.

Rubicund, as bald as an admiral, as tall and erect as a Prussian grenadier, but inconceivably corpulent, St Thomas Aquinas hunched in the tent with his shining pate vanishing into the folds of the canvas. Anquilar awoke one night, quickened by the sweet aroma of a fat man's perspiration, and beheld, in dark shadow, the massive bulk of the man he admired the most in all the world.

He sat up in his bed, rubbed his eyes, looked again, and enquired doubtfully, 'St Thomas?'

The dark shadow nodded, and replied, 'Do you have any conception of the boredom of death?'

'No, indeed,' replied the Monsignor.

'Take it from me, my son, take it from me. When I died on the way to the Council of Lyon, I thought, "Aha, now I will see the truth," but do you know what happened? I know not a jot more nor an iota less than when I was alive. Believe me, death is a disappointment. Now if you will excuse me, I have my usual appointment with Galileo, a most interesting man. He has a theory that matter is made of mathematical points and lines of no extension, and I, naturally, hold a more Aristotelian opinion. His view is heretical of course, because it endangers the doctrine of the Eucharist. I will see you tomorrow.'

On subsequent nights St Thomas appeared regularly at the same time to continue his disconnected flow of reminiscences, his colossal bulk occupying the space even on the other side of bed. In between each memory he would nod his head slowly, as if to say, 'Yes, that is how it was,' and the inebriation of immortality would cause his gaze to focus far behind the Monsignor, as though he were addressing him from a great distance. 'I startled the King of France once . . . I was thinking about a refutation of the Manichees, and I thumped the table so that the king jumped out of his skin . . . did you know that we had to write in abbreviations to save parchment? It was very expensive, you see . . . Albertus Magnus, my teacher, once he made a mechanical head that talked and talked . . . it was so irritating . . . when he died I could not stand all that talking, and in the end I had it buried under the corridor . . . I always felt guilty about that . . . He once said of me that people said that I was as slow as an ox, but one day the whole world would listen to my mooing. Wasn't that nice of him? I was kidnapped by my own family when I was young . . . I never intended to be a saint, you know, I just spent my whole life writing and eating . . . Albertus was a saint, but many said that he was a witch because of his marvellous inventions . . . Do you think that the dialogue is a successful way of writing philosophy? . . . Bishop Berkeley did it . . . He is still working on cures for constipation, and I say to him, "My dear Bishop, the dead do not suffer constipation," that is what I say. Did you know that recently my *Summa Theologiae* was produced in sixty volumes by some university or other? I keep revising it, and now it is three thousand volumes, and Bishop Berkeley says to me, "My dear Doctor, not even the dead will read it . . . indeed death is a futile business."'

'I have read the sixty volumes,' exclaimed Anquilar, 'I have many passages by heart.'

This was the first time that Anquilar had interrupted the Doctor in his many nights of melancholy reflection, and the latter paused, struck by astonishment. 'It is not worth it,' he said. 'I have completely rewritten it. When I was alive I had a revelation, and from that point I wrote nothing more on earth because all my words turned to straw, even the words I had already written.'

'But your works are the foundation and corner stone of the Church,' replied Anquilar. 'Without your work there is no doctrine.'

St Thomas shrugged dismissively, 'That's how it is.'

A dreadful suspicion formulated itself in Anquilar's mind: 'You are not St Thomas, you are a demon sent by the Prince of Darkness to deflect me. Get thee behind me, devil; go, or I will exorcise you myself, satanic heresiarch.'

The shade shook its head slowly, 'It won't work. I have come on your crusade to see for myself the results of my work. I have come to see you forcing Jews and Muslims to eat pork in public, to see you extinguishing enquiry and burning innocents who have more enthusiasm than intellect. I am watching you confiscate the goods of the poor and torturing women for fear of your own lusts . . . Did you know that my own work was forbidden in the University of Paris? . . . If I were Satan I would be a fallen cherub, because the cherubim are derived from knowledge, which is compatible with mortal sin. Gregory the Great says that Satan before he fell wore all the other angels as his garment, transcending all in glory and knowledge . . .'

'You are not St Thomas,' repeated Anquilar.

'Nonetheless, I will accompany you on your crusade for the good of my soul.'

'Do not come near me,' said Anquilar, crossing himself vigorously and muttering, '*vade retro*.'

From that time onwards Monsignor Rechin Anquilar received no more personal calls from the Doctor Angelicus. Instead the saint would wander contemplatively about the camp, the ruddy folds of his face reflecting the flames of the fires, his enormous body eclipsing the lanterns. Nobody saw him as he wandered sadly through the embers of incendiarised huts, stood upon hilltops to see the smoke of ruined pueblos, bent over the faces of broken children and ravaged girls, shaking his head with pity and resignation. Nobody saw him except Monsignor Anquilar, who wrote out from memory the saint's own words about heresy, and waved the paper in his face at every crossing of their paths. The saint would look at him wearily, saying, 'I have revised that passage.'

The incorporeal corpulent saint saw how it was that a regular pattern emerged from the wanderings of the crusaders across the llanos towards the sierras. They would reach a place outside a settlement and encamp there for the night. Early next morning they would process into the plaza, carrying banners and smoking thuribles. At their head would be El Inocente mounted on his black stallion, his face set with the zealous delight of doctrinal rage, and behind him would be the company of priests chanting the Veni Creator.

St Thomas, polymath and philosophical genius, partial empiricist and opponent of the Latin Averroists, would find himself taking notes like a schoolboy, taxonomising the varieties of outcome. In every place things always began well, because to all people the prospect of an impromptu fiesta was irresistible. People would leave the fields, having been fetched by breathless children, and pour into the plaza in anticipation of a great spectacle and formidable drunkenness and fornication thereafter. They would greatly enjoy the Monsignor's sermon of generalised denunciation, but would fall into perplexed silence when invited to reveal the doctrinal errors of their fellows. Someone would crack a joke, such as, 'Reinaldo believes that John the Baptist was really the Blessed Virgin,' and then the disorder would begin as the bodyguard swung into instantaneous retribution. In large towns the civil authorities would mercilessly and summarily expel the crusaders, and in medium-sized towns someone would go to beg the intervention of the local caudillo or the powerful latifundistas with their armed vaqueros and peons, who would arrive at the gallop and chase the marauders away, leaving the town with one or two dead and a sorrowfully aborted fiesta. These episodes increased the Monsignor's sense of outrage at the proliferation of satanic force in the country, and he would conduct impressive services of mass excommunication over the townsfolk at the nearest place of safety.

But in villages and hamlets where the number of crusaders was greater than the number of inhabitants, the Monsignor enjoyed greater prosperity and a richer spiritual harvest. In these isolated spots he managed to save many a soul by extracting from it a confession of orthodoxy and killing it before it had time to change its mind. 'Christ's faithful often wage war with unbelievers to prevent them from hindering the faith,' he would say, quoting St Thomas, or, 'With regard to heretics, there is the sin whereby they deserve not only to be separated from the Church by excommunication, but also to be severed from the world by death,' omitting for the sake of swiftness the procedure by which heretics were given two admonitions and lengthy periods of reflection even in the days of the Italian Inquisition.

Perhaps the most remarkable episode took place when the crusade came face to face with another crusade in the pueblito of Comédon.

In this land there is a kind of ecstasy derived from poverty and desperation that compels people to seek consolation and fulfilment in a pathological mysticism. With their eyes fixed resolutely on a future in a happier world, mighty throngs of people travel the countryside crucifying themselves in imitation of Christ, giving rise to tremulous orgies of religious awe in those who are spectators. In Comédon the crucifiers had arrived the day before the crusaders, and numerous hopeful saints were already perched on the top of telegraph poles in the hope of having food passed up to them by the faithful, in this way repeating the admirable ploy of Simon Stylites. Outside the village, twenty cadaverous men were flogged until blood sprang from their flesh, and were subsequently roped to crosses that they themselves had dragged across the countryside for miles. As they hung there, intoxicated by their hallucinatory flirtation with death and experiencing nightmarish visions induced by the heat and the impossibility of breathing, their fellows down below thrashed each other with exultantly rolling eyes whilst the villagers crossed themselves, prayed, wept, howled, and thrilled with that terrible voyeurism occasioned by vicarious agonies.

When the crusade arrived and happened upon these masochistic bacchanalia, it stopped dead in its tracks with unanimous astonishment.

This amazement was swiftly followed by an anger caused by having been completely pre-empted and out-performed; no villagers streamed to witness their procession, no one came out bearing tables to load with food, or knelt before the Monsignor to kiss his ring because they thought that he must be a cardinal. Instead the villagers turned their heads briefly to assess them as a minor distraction, and then turned back once more to watch the bodies groaning on the crosses and the flagellants drawing scarlet rivulets of blood from each other with bullwhips and flails.

Rechin Anquilar determined that the crucifiers were taking upon themselves the sins of the world in order to atone for them, so that the sufferings of others would be mitigated on the Dreadful Day. He determined that this was heretical since Christ had already performed this function by His own Passion, and he perceived a revolting blasphemy in what he saw. He brought everyone's attention to his own crusade by ordering his men to substitute nails for the ropes that attached the crucifiers to their crosses. The flagellants below, believing that at last the Day of Wrath was upon them, yielded themselves joyously to the bullets and machetes of the bodyguard.

The Angelic Doctor, revolving in his mind the many words that he had written on the essence of law, reflected ruefully on the many ways in which such dreadful practise could be derived from the pristine light of his own reasonable deductions. He surveyed the carnage and wished that no word of his had ever immortalised itself on parchment; 'Perhaps my habit of dictating to four secretaries at once militated against clarity of thought,' he mused.

## 45 *Don Emmanuel's Patriotic Concert*

The British Ambassador had, in the capable care of Aurelio, vomited up what remained in his stomach of the overproof aguardiente. His wellington boots had been emptied of urine, and he had been given a deep draught of a tincture that would restore him to something resembling a normal state of consciousness, if one discounted the rainbow-coloured lights at the periphery of his vision. He was carried in a chair to the site of Don Emmanuel's musical extravaganza, but had to stand for the first song, which Don Emmanuel proclaimed to be the national anthem of Great Britain. He lurched to his feet and leant heavily upon the General for support.

There was in Cochadebajo de los Gatos a peña. Most towns have such a music club, and they consist of whatever musical instruments can be found or improvised, played ad libitum at competitive volumes in whatever key or tempo each player wishes to select. The result is a cross-weaving of rhythms and tunes, random noises and shameless mistakes, that dwarf anything conceived by Stockhausen and which would knock into a cocked hat the drivellings of the most egregiously pretentious avant-garde jazz ensemble. The purpose of these cheerful assemblies of sousaphones, cracked French horns, taped-up bugles, home-made bamboo whistles, guitars strung with electric flex, and accordions with nothing working but sharps and flats, was to create new, wondrous, and strident levels of cacophony, and so to increase the impression of utter chaos at fiestas.

But the peña of Cochadebajo de los Gatos had been considerably tamed by the patient instruction of the Mexican musicologist, with the occasional help of Dionisio. The former had on this occasion been aided by Don Emmanuel, who had taught him some patriotic British songs, and also had instructed a choir of little children in the perfect pronunciation of the words.

These diminutive children now stood to sing the national anthem of Great Britain. There were twenty serious little faces framed by mops of thick black hair, that of the girls having been pulled into the tightest of bunches that stood out practically at right-angles from the sides of their heads. They were dressed in their smartest red and black ponchos with tassels, and now and then a shy smile would indicate that most of them were awaiting their second growth of front teeth, which is why the British Ambassador noticed that they sang with a charming lisp.

The band struck the first chord, faltered, and then regained itself. It launched not into 'God Save The Queen', but into the Eton Boating Song. Initially startled, the Ambassador then swelled with a pride like that of an old war horse at the call of a bugle. He began to sing along, but then, even in his altered state, he discovered that the words were unfamiliar. What he heard, sung breathily but in perfect tune by twenty seraphic little voices, was:

> 'My name is Cyril,
> I live in Leicester Square,
> I wear pink pyjamas,
> And rosebuds in my hair.
> Oh we're all poofs together,
> But nobody seems to care.
> Oh we're all poofs together,
> Excuse us while we go upstairs.'

A rapturous smile spread across Don Emmanuel's face as he witnessed the Ambassador's countenance betraying at first incomprehension and then outrage. The latter was still drunk enough to think that he could put things right by singing the correct words, and he waved his arms and sang, 'We all pull together . . .' so that the band, impressed by this display of patriotism, took up the tune whilst the children took up the refrain of Don Emmanuel's amended version and drowned out the Ambassador entirely.

'That is not the tune I remember,' observed the General to his son. 'Have they changed it?'

Before Dionisio could reply, Don Emmanuel stood before the assembly in the courtyard of the Palace of the Lords and announced, 'Our next little ditty is called "The British Grenadiers", and we hope that you all enjoy it as much as the last one.' He caught the Ambassador's eye, winked, and turned as the band launched into the introductory bars under the baton of the Mexican. Once again Don Emmanuel had improved the composition of the lyrics:

> 'Some die of drinking water
> And some of drinking beer;
> Some die of constipation,
> And some of diarrhoea.
> But of all the world's diseases
> There's none that can compare
> With the drip, drip, drip
> Of a syphilitic prick,
> And the sting of gonorrhoea.'

The Ambassador sprang to his feet to protest, and everyone else arose also to join in with what they assumed was going to be a standing ovation. The Ambassador gazed hopelessly at the politely applauding crowd, and faintheartedly joined in. Nor was the ordeal over until he had been subjected to an exquisitely harmonised twenty-four-stanza rendition of 'The Ball of Kirrimuir', plus 'Dinah, Dinah, Show Us Your Leg', cleverly converted into an interminable round. At the end of it all, when it was time for the policeman to make his customary speech, the Ambassador was in the pit of dejection, and he was slumped in his seat wondering how they had managed to stagelight the place in such wonderful colours with no apparent use of lamps.

The squint-eyed ex-policeman was just beginning to scratch the boil on the side of his nose in the effort of summoning up his eloquence, when from outside in the street there came the cry, 'Has anyone seen the beast? Has anyone seen the beast?' and the ragged stranger rode in on his skeletal horse. 'Ah,' said Dionisio to his father, 'it is the three-hundred-year-old man,' and he regretted it instantly when his father shot him a look of exasperation combined with resignation.

But Don Emmanuel, the stranger's last victim, took his chance and leapt out. 'There,' he said, pointing to the Ambassador, who was by now so depressed that his head was nodding on his chest. He awoke very briefly as the old man's stave cracked across his pate, and then lapsed into a perturbed unconsciousness in which Her Majesty The

Queen pirouetted coquettishly whilst declaiming obscene versions of 'The Boy Stood On The Burning Deck'.

The tumult resulting from the intervention of the old man effectively cancelled the speech of the policeman, whose rhetoric could not be heard above the mêlée of squealing pigs and flailing limbs. When the good-natured attempts of the crowd to restrain the assailant had petered out, it was discovered that the latter had been watching the fray from a safe perch upon the wall. Mama Julia's dress was torn, the General's impressive chestful of medals was askew, and Don Emmanuel was nowhere to be seen.

Just as the day was transforming itself from summer to autumn the citizens awarded the General 'The Supremely Elevated Order Of The Apparatus' for his services to democracy, and also to the Ambassador for coming, and for bearing so many sufferings as a consequence. The battered party returned to their helicopter, the Ambassador being carried in a hammock.

Standing by the aircraft, Mama Julia kissed Dionisio wetly on both cheeks, and the General embraced his son and said, 'Dio', this has been the most strenuous and bizarre day of my life.'

'Well, Papa, it is good to learn how the other half lives.'

'Thank God I am in the other half.'

'Where else can one eat pork every day?'

'In Saudi Arabia?'

The two men laughed, and Mama Julia said, 'I am beginning to get a headache; can I have another bag of that spinach?'

The General clambered into the craft and discovered that the pilot was fast asleep with a pornographic magazine on his lap. He gently removed it and beckoned to Hectoro to approach. He spurred his horse forward and the General handed him the glossy publication with the words, 'I suspect that you would enjoy this.'

Hectoro held it upside down, flicked through the assembly of splayed lovelies, pondered some of them seriously, and handed back the magazine. 'Forgive me,' he said, 'but for me they are not hairy enough, and most of them are white. Also, I am in the middle of reading another book.'

'I will have it,' said Misael, and the General tossed it down to him. He tucked it safely into his mochila, grinning so broadly that all his gold teeth caught the flashes of sunset, and the General said, 'Do not let your wife catch you with it, cabrón.'

In the morning, in the Montes Sosa residence in Valledupar, the British Ambassador awoke with the massed bands of the Brigade of Guards playing in his head, the bass drum being particularly to the fore. He put on his silk dressing gown inside-out, and his slippers on the wrong feet. Downstairs he went, encountering the General in the hall, where he was supervising the servants in their efforts to polish up the family collection of colonial weapons. 'I cannot remember anything from yesterday,' he said. 'Did I have a good time?'

'I do not speak English,' replied the General, saying the only English sentence he knew.

'I must have done,' said the Ambassador, and he went upstairs to dress. He was appalled by the state of his suit; it was filthy with soil about the knees, and the trousers distinctly smelled of childhood accidents. In the pocket he found a basalt phallus on a leather thong, beautifully worked with jaguars in relief, and he found a note scrawled on a morsel of dirty paper.

He took them downstairs and summoned up enough Castilian to ask the General what they were. 'This,' said the General, holding up the phallus, 'is the insignia of The Supremely Elevated Order Of The Apparatus, and the note says that everyone was very impressed by your boots.'

In Cochadebajo de los Gatos the reputation enjoyed by the British for magnanimity stems from the fact that the Ambassador, fearing that he must have done something disgraceful on his lost day, ordered a consignment of wellington boots of varying sizes from London, to be sent in the diplomatic bag. These he despatched to Cochadebajo de los Gatos, where they are still worn on splendid and special occasions, according to a strict rota laid down by the informal council of leaders.

# 46 *How Aurelio Became Himself*

It is I, Aurelio, who speaks, and General Fuerte who makes the marks. Already he tells me, 'Aurelio, talk more slowly,' and his pen scratches like a mouse. I say, 'Speak of what?' and he replies, 'Aurelio, speak of yourself, I am collecting information.' He compares me to a butterfly that is seldom seen, and I am pleased, but I do not show it because it is bad to smile when one is praised because that is the same thing as to praise oneself, which is a poor praise.

I am not myself, or to say it in another way, I am many at once within myself, because of my life, and it is for this reason that I talk to General Fuerte who is a white man. Before I became the third person that I am I did not talk to white people because when you look at them you could see that they did not exist. They had no faces, they were like alpacas, they were like cats who avoid and look away. When a white man looked at me he saw an Aymara, he saw my people but not myself, and I too, looking at him, saw only a white man. But I am three people now and I see well. I am one person for each race with whom I have lived, and these three are the one that is myself, and so perhaps that is a fourth, quien sabe?

It is true that I was Aymara, and it can be seen in my clothes, which are the imitation of a memory, because my original clothes were worn away. I have this wide white hat whose shape reminds me of Carmen's breast, and so there is another reason to wear it. I have this waistcoat of many strong colours and much gold thread, and my jacket is more strong colours, with woven into it in black the figures of a llama that has never been seen for hundreds of years because they all died.

But I will tell you that the Aymara are not a good people, they are not gentle like the Quechua, even whose speech is so gentle that it soothes like whispers. The Quechua are more hospitable than we, because once there was a fire, and the only survivors were the hospitable ones. Aymaras like to fight at fiestas, and I lost my own brother in a tinku-fight. I leapt over his grave so that I would grow old. His head was cracked with a rock in a fair wrestle. Also they are always drunk on lamp-alcohol, and they grow stupid from eating nothing but potatoes, and they stink because there is no water up there to waste with washing, because in those parts Pachamama's body is dying, and that is why you have seen me pour the first of whatever I drink upon the ground, because she is dying of thirst. And this is Inti's fault, Inti the sun, and the women wash their hair in their own piss for lack of water.

But it was not always like this. At the first, after Viracocha made us, there was only the moon, and up on the altiplano there were great lakes where now there is only salt and dust. We were a great people of plenty in the days of the moon, our empire was bigger than the Incas'. And there was another people there, worse than us, who were born of slime and lived by fishing, who returned nothing to Pachamama. We called them many names, we called them 'Munchers of Weeds of the Water' and we called them 'Monster-Livered', and they were an ugly people, stupid, filthy and idle, and now we are fallen and become like them.

'How did you fall?' asks General Fuerte, scratching with the pen like a chicken in the dust of the street, and I say, 'Do you want the story or what I myself believe?' And he says, 'Both, of course,' but perhaps the story and what I believe are both two parts of the truth. The story is that the sun came up suddenly one day and dried the lakes, and all the lands of Tiahuanacu about the Stone In The Middle, whose real name nobody knows, turned to salt. And there were twelve tribes of us all fighting each other, and then the Incas came and defeated us because we were divided, and they turned us into Quechuas, most of us. But what I believe is that we fell on account of Tunupa.'

'Who is Tunupa?' asks the General, and I say, 'I was going to tell you,' and he says, 'Excuse me.' Tunupa is the one that Misael calls Chango, except that our thunder is kinder than his. Tunupa in the first place lives in volcanoes. Tunupa had five men with him, and they were all alike. They wore white robes to the ground, they were bearded like this, like a bird's-nest, their eyes were blue and their skins were pale. 'They were white men?' asks General Fuerte, and I say, 'Probably not, because white men spread hatred, and Tunupa spreads love.' Tunupa told us not to get drunk all the time, and he told us to have one wife. He said, 'Do good, not bad,' and he told us to love each other and not to battle with each other, and those who believed him, he sprinkled water on their heads. But he annoyed the King by converting his daughter, and the King, whose name I forget but it will come back to me at a time when I do not need to remember it, he killed all the followers of Tunupa and drove Tunupa away. Nobody knows where Tunupa went. Perhaps he walked out over the sea and became the spume of it, perhaps he broke a bank with his canoe and floated to the sea from Titicaca, perhaps he became one with Viracocha, quien sabe? I believe we fell because we never loved one another, and we stayed drunk and fighting. I see you have a look of surprise, and I know that you think this Tunupa was the god Jesus of the Spanish, and the Spanish thought this too, and they treated us badly because they said that we had killed some saints, so that's that.

General Fuerte says, 'Tell me some more stories of your people,' and so I say, 'Have you heard about the monkey and the rabbit?' and he shakes his head and writes. Once there was a monkey, and he said to the rabbit, 'Do you find that when you shit, it sticks to your fur?' and the rabbit says, 'Unfortunately, yes,' and so the monkey says, 'O good,' and he picks up the rabbit and wipes his backside with it.

General Fuerte says, 'Is that a story of your people?' and I say, 'It is now, because I just made it up,' and you say, 'Ha, ha, now tell me more about yourself.'

I was one of the Aymara people who lived on the other side of the cordillera from the altiplano, which is to say that my people lived in plenty where Pachamama was not dying. But then the white people sprayed us with poison from the sky, and they shot at us, and they placed bombs under our paths which became thunder and lightning when you trod upon them, and this was because they wanted our land. And that was why we went our way, and I found my way down into the jungle. But before I got there I was struck twice by lightning, and that is how I became a yatiri, which is a brujo, except that in the mountains I had no one to learn from. But I am qualified by the lightning to dress in white and do divinations with the unborn of the llamas, and stick knives in the floor when a child is born and to bury the afterbirth to give it back to Pachamama in return for the child.

But in the jungle I learned to be the second person that I became, which is a Navante. They were a good people, and that is how I was able to compare and come to the conclusion that the Aymara are not good. The Navantes wrestle each evening, but in a friendly fashion, and no one is killed. It is very good. I had two wives, one after the other, and the first was stolen by the miners, and I never saw her again, and the second died because a white man came with a bible and he sneezed. That sneeze killed all my children and half of the people, and they all died of the sneezing fever, and so we killed the white man for the sake of the people, because sometimes one must do evil to do good. But we buried him with a cross and with his bible, out of respect, so as not to appear vengeful.

And in the jungle I learned to be qualified to be a paje, which is in Aymara a yatiri, which is a brujo. And do you wish to know how one learns magic? The General nods and he says, 'OK Aurelio, but no more silly stories about rabbits,' and I say, 'No, because magic is serious stuff.'

It happened because I saved the life of the sub-chief whose name was Dianari, and consequently my own life was saved by the paje of the tribe when I was dying from being oppressed by the jungle. I will tell you what the paje taught me. Everything has a song, did you know that? All things are cured by songs, but not without the exactly correct song, because each song is a path. Every animal has a song, and to learn the song one must become the animal, which is all very obvious. So to learn songs you take ayahuasca, which is very bitter, or you take shori, which is a vine. And to learn ant songs you let yourself be bitten by ants, and the fire-ant is the worst, with your neck and tongue against a tree, and you eat no food for four days except howler monkeys and songbirds. And you summon the spirits with a trumpet which is an armadillo tail, and you know if it is a bad spirit because it stinks worse than a corpse. And the paje, he dressed me in macaw feathers and necklaces made of snails, and he blew smoke into my mouth, and I learned that to each song there is a path and a spirit which is an animal, and I was completely naked. The spirits cure sickness, did you know that? I sing into the medicine, and the spirit enters it, and sometimes it is a water-spirit child with a baby's body and a fish's tail, and one can play a mouthbow too, twang, twang, twang, and that summons spirits like the armadillo-tail trumpet, and there are also the songs of the bamboo flute. And I learned to become many animals. I became a snow-egret so that I could learn to understand the white man, and I flew over his dwellings which are like sky-hills and I said, 'I would not live like a termite.' But my best animal is the eagle, it is my animal. I have flown to the end of the sky. Did you know that at the sky's end it sounds like pigs? I remember when my ears cleared and I could sing, and then I was a paje, and the song said, 'The harpy eagle is coming,' and then I was an eagle, and I learned useful information from the other birds. Did you know that the King Vulture is fond of rainbows? And the paje said, 'Now that you are a sorcerer, people will avoid you, because they will blame misfortune on you because of your magic.'

This was true in the end, because I could not cure the sneezing death, and that is why I left to live on my own and breed dogs. I married Carmen who is black, except that her hair was red before it turned white, and I became the third person which I am now, who lives with any people without trouble or loss of understanding, several peoples at once. And now I know how many kinds of magic there are. I have learned that there are priests who turn wine to blood and bread to flesh, in substance but not in appearance, which is a great mystery. I know that Pedro knows the magic of animals, and there is Dionisio who is a different kind of brujo all to himself because we made him that way when there was a candomble and all the saints gave him powers by dancing and singing.

So now I live down there in the jungle with Carmen and with my daughter Parlanchina who is dead and has a child so that I am grandfather to a spirit. She watches the paths in the jungle, she guards them, and she walks always with an ocelot who she loves and sleeps with, and she is married to Federico who is Sergio's son, and Federico is also dead, and he likes to watch the paths in the mountains. I say to Parlanchina, 'Watch out, Gwubba, a marriage cannot last when one of you is always in the mountains and the other is in the jungle,' and she says, 'But Papacito, you live in both places at once. Who are you to talk?' And I laugh, because it is true. I love Parlanchina with my whole heart and when I see her I want to weep because she is so beautiful, and she is like you, she makes me tell stories the whole time, but she does not write them down, she remembers them, and even so, she makes me tell them over and over.

I told her a story yesterday, do you want to hear it? Good. Here is the story.

Once a man went fishing, and he caught a giant eagle, and he thought, 'I will paint it blue and red,' and so he did. He took it to the top of a volcano to throw it in as a sacrifice, but the eagle objected, and he threw the man in instead. And that is the end of the story.

General Fuerte asks me, 'Is that an ancient story of your people?' and I say, 'No, it was a dream I had,' but maybe one day it will be an ancient story. Every story has to begin somewhere. Surely you have had enough of writing? And the General shakes his hand because of the cramp and says, 'Anyway, the pen is running out,' and I say, 'That is why memory is superior. It has no pen to run out.'

# 47 St Thomas Recalls

I used to be fond of quoting Augustine in matters of heresy, and now when I peruse his work I am forcibly obliged to reflect upon how it is that those of us who are connected directly with God and are enamoured of reason and law can deduce with such clarity propositions whose practical application can lead to such lamentable consequences. How easy it was to formalise the processes of Socratic dialogue into objections, answers, and replies to objections; how easily my mind flowed with my pen, co-ordinating and collating with edifying lucidity the sciences of Aristotle, the message of the Gospels, the commentaries of Saints Ambrose and Gregory, and even the illuminating writings of the learned infidels. How often I would retire late to my bed, a thousand quotations, precepts and precedents whirling in my head, and how often I would awake early in the morning with everything in perfect order, so that I would arise with a merry heart and set my secretaries to work, scribbling furiously what had been dictated to me in my repose! So great was the joy of my work that all care slipped away from me, and my mind dwelled not a moment even on the temptations of the flesh.

And now I have been drowned by the overwhelming presence of true flesh, in all its agony and valour, and daily I hear my own learned words on the lips of others who use them in perpetration of the Devil's work, as though all my caveats and reservations counted for nothing, as though my theoretical positions, achieved with such travail of reason, should be taken as truer than the Gospels and translated to brutality. How much better if my life had passed unremarked and unrecorded in the damp silence of the cloisters! How much better if all my work had mouldered unread in the fungal labyrinth of the University of Paris! I have heard a tale of Mohammed, that once, when called to prayer, he perceived that a cat was asleep upon his robe, whereupon he severed the end of his robe rather than perturb the cat. And yet this is the man in whose name have been committed uncountable atrocities, and now, like me, he walks unhappy in the paths of paradise.

I have seen such things! At the edge of a lake there were Aymaras who met there in silence each year with the purpose of waiting for the white man to go. These were butchered on the grounds that it is heretical to believe in the departure of the white man when their arrival had been willed by God, because otherwise it could not have occurred!

There was a young woman who was accused of having aborted a child. She was told that abortion was murder, and that murder was a mortal sin, and therefore she deserved to die, and therefore she would die. She protested her innocence vehemently and demanded proof, whereupon she was told, 'If you are guilty, then you deserve to die, and if you are innocent, then you will arrive in heaven all the sooner, so it will be good for you to die earlier than you would have done,' and she was abused by the bodyguard so that when they killed her she was in very truth impregnated, and the child died within her, and therefore an abortion was performed by the same people who condemned her for that sin.

And I have seen a man, who, in proof of his innocence, offered to throw himself from a high place, and with my own eyes I saw him float down from a steeple, only to be killed at the bottom on the premise that such miracles might only be performed by Satan's aid.

I have seen forgiveness bought at great prices by those who are rich and terrified, and I have seen lunatics throw themselves upon pyres rather than abandon their delusions. I have seen the intellectually modest informed that doubt is sinful, and summarily dispatched, and I have longed for the humanism of the ancients who declared that in philosophy all things are doubtful and open to question. And I remember writing somewhere that Jews should be spared because their faith bears witness to ours, but I have smelt the stench of glowing brands smoking upon the bodies of the innocent, and I have heard it laid down as law that writers, doctors, clerks and itinerant artists are all heretics by nature and inclination, and the doctors are killed and the heretics told that medical treatment is forbidden them.

In one place the people took refuge in sanctuary, and the church was burned down upon their heads so that even the orthodox

274

perished, and the Monsignor who knows my work so well smacked his lips and said, 'Where blessings come to nothing, the stick will prevail.' And afterwards he regaled his men with tales of the miracles of St Dominic, a man who has never been seen in paradise.

I remember in another place there was a town where all were dedicated to the faith of one Ricardo of Rinconondo, and it was a place where Father Valentino turned to the Monsignor and said with great anxiety in his voice, 'What do we do if they all convert?' and the latter replied, 'Do not worry, hardly any of them will convert.' They left it utterly destroyed, even though a negotiator had been let out on the promise of free passage, and then perfidiously slain. They went to dig up and burn the mortal remains of their saint, Ricardo, but they had been exhumed already by the faithful and carried away, sown up in the hide of an ox. And there was a Jew there, and someone proposed to spare him because he had been tortured, had converted, and had betrayed many others, but the Monsignor burst into the room, and he placed thirty pieces of silver on the table, exclaiming, 'For what price is Christ to be sold once more to the Jews?' and so they fabricated a charge that the Jew had cut out the heart of a Christian infant and then crucified it as a spell to destroy Christians, making him confess to it. There was also an old woman who was mad, distracted with grief because of the extinction of her family, and she came forward each day to denounce herself in the hope of death, but each day they sent her away in order to enjoy her torment. Then there came a day when she did not denounce herself, and so they arrested her and condemned her upon the evidence of her previous confession. She was thrown upon the flames like all the others, wearing a dunce's hat upon which was inscribed the names of all the crimes she had admitted.

There was another place built upon a prominence and walled about, where the inhabitants wisely locked the gates to exclude the invaders. But the bodyguard emptied the cemetery and slaughtered the cattle, and improvised trebuchets with which they launched the corpses over the walls, and then went their way in the hope that the townsfolk would die of pestilence. In that episode a priest was killed by a rock hurled by a woman from the walls, but I felt no grief, for which God forgive me.

Everywhere that this crusade processed it was the policy to

excommunicate upon one pretext or another all who owned property, so that progress was infinitely slowed by oxcarts groaning with chattels, and it became impossible to travel across the countryside. Everywhere the prospect of easy wealth encouraged the vicious and the dissolute to join the campaign. No one of that company had been given the right or power of excommunication, and in this respect I judge that there was a plenary exercise in cynicism. But what appalled me the most and most oppressed my soul was the absolute sincerity and conviction of the priests.

Would to God that I had never written, and my penance has been the infinite weariness of guiding away the dead.

# 48 *Of Concepcion and Dominic Guzman*

Dominic Guzman and Concepcion left the capital in their new jeep, trailed by a convoy of the press. They crossed the high plains, where the chrysanthemum houses sparkled in the sun as though innocent of the fate of the poor women who worked inside. They drove past the deserted and diseased greenhouse where Dionisio's greatest love, Anica, and her unborn child, had been butchered by the henchmen of the worst of the coca lords, and out into the rolling mountains of the Cordillera Oriental.

The cordillera disposed of the convoy. Desperate for the best pictures, those at the back overtook on blind corners and precipitate slopes. One jeep hurled itself over a chasm, another crashed head-on into a gaily painted bus laden with hopeful rural migrants, and a third slewed sideways on the scree of a landslip, so that all the vehicles behind it piled together in an inextricable tangle of bumpers and photographic paraphernalia. Soon there would be yet more tinselly little shrines at the side of the road, marking a death with candles, flowers, a statue of the Virgin, and a monochrome photograph of the deceased.

Beyond Tunja the world lost trace of the couple, who had turned from the main road and found a place to rest in a tiny pueblo near Arcabuco. It was a village that obeyed the old custom of maintaining a shelter for travellers, open-sided, but with a roof of woven palm, and with well-bedded poles from which to sling a hammock.

They sat on the front of their jeep eating bocadillo, the sandwich of invert sugar and guava that one buys carefully wrapped in the leaf of banana or palm, and watched the sun set on the snow of the peaks. The brilliant and scintillating colours reflected each other from one mountain to the next and back from the surface of the clouds until the whole sky was illuminated, and Guzman turned to Concepcion and said, 'Querida, it was watching the sunset that first made me feel religious.'

She licked the sugar from her fingers, and wiped them on the print of her dress. 'It is also watching the sunset that makes one cold.'

'I have a padded jacket for you,' he said, and went to the jeep, returning with a quilted coat. She inspected it, felt the material with her fingers, sighed, and said, 'I would feel like a stranger wearing that. I will go and fetch my poncho.'

Dominic Guzman felt suddenly like a failure. 'We two have never lived in each other's company, like a man and wife, sharing everything. I am afraid that I will be no good at it.'

He thought of all the things he had never done. He had never been to the market and shopped for her when she was ill. He had never asked her opinion, let alone conceded to it or compromised. He had never made a meal, cut wood, or swept the floor. 'I am very ignorant,' he said.

'Tchaa,' said Concepcion. 'Everything will be learned with time.'

'I only know about big ideas,' continued Guzman, as though he had not heard her.

'Anyone can have big ideas,' said Concepcion. 'I have some big ideas, and most of them I thought of for myself, and then I found out that others have thought the same, and then I found out that other people have big ideas that are exactly the opposite. And when I think about it even more, I decide that only small ideas can be true, and the big ideas are too big to fit inside anybody's mind, so there is no point in trying to have them. You know what my mother used to say, when I asked her a question like, "Why does God let babies die?" She said, "Pregunta a las mariposas." Go and ask the butterflies, because they don't know any better than anyone else.'

Guzman laughed and scratched the scar of his operation with a gesture that had become an unconscious habit. 'How should one live then?' he asked.

'We must give some more sugar-water to the hummingbird,' said Concepcion, following with her finger the shimmering little creature that was darting about her head delicately removing the grains of bocadillo from her lips, 'and we must give the bird a name, so that we can call it. I will put drops of honey on a list of names, and the bird will choose its own name.'

Until that point the pueblo had seemed deserted, except for two dogs, numerous chickens, and a vast sow that was fast asleep in a scrape of her own making. But as the world was on the point of darkness and Guzman was looking in the glove-pocket of the jeep for a flashlight, a small procession of cholos entered the village. On their shoulders they bore billhooks and spades, and accompanying them were weary little mules laden with stupendous piles of quinoa and alfalfa.

The villagers looked at them incuriously as they filed past, each one raising a hand and saying, 'Buena' tardes.' Guzman raised his hand in the customary gesture of blessing, but converted it diffidently into a wave of greeting.

'They are hard people,' came a voice from behind them that bore a distinctly Putumayo accent. 'They drink too much, they don't wash, they work without resting, they fight, they don't vote, and you can never tell what they're thinking.'

Guzman and Concepcion turned about, to behold a large black man with a shotgun, garbed in tattered clerical dress. His priestly shoes were coming apart at the uppers, and on his head he wore a straw sombrero that had frayed about the rim. 'Don Balsal,' he said. 'I am the priest, and those are my little flock. May I offer you something to eat? A little coffee? A bed for the night? I have a nice little hut.'

'We would be very grateful,' said Guzman. 'We had been reconciling ourselves to a night out in the fresh air.'

The priest hunched his shoulders ironically, and said, 'I can assure you that it will be just as cold in my hut, but at least you will not be disturbed by Olga.' In response to the couple's puzzled expressions, the priest pointed to the sow. 'Olga,' he said. 'She lives off the excrement of the villagers, since there is little else to feed her with. She seems to enjoy it, but I, for one, would consequently not enjoy her company out here. If she ever gets eaten we will all die of parasites, if we have not first died of something else. I haven't been paid for five years.'

Guzman flushed with guilt, and held his peace. He and Concepcion followed Don Balsal into his palm hut, and found themselves confined to a prison of darkness disturbed only by the sound of the priest moving about. A match flared, and a taper was lit that quickly filled the room with the noxious fumes of burning fat. The priest unceremoniously lifted a chicken from its nest on a shelf, and triumphantly produced an egg. 'Supper,' he announced.

Guzman went to the jeep and returned with a box of food, a small camping stove, and a bottle of wine. 'You can keep all this,' he said to the shadow that he had to assume was Don Balsal. 'I will buy some more tomorrow.'

Don Balsal lifted the taper over the box and whistled. 'Gold, frankincense and myrrh,' he said. 'I think I will keep the wine for communion, as I have always had doubts about having to use pisco and aguardiente.'

In the tenebrous light of the taper and of the stove, Concepcion showed Don Balsal how to make arepas with maize flour, eggs and dende oil. The latter was overcome with the simple delight of it, and exclaimed, 'Señora, blessed art thou among women! This is a skill that I shall pass on to everyone.'

'Why do you carry a shotgun?' asked Guzman suddenly. 'I would not have expected it of a priest.'

Don Balsal transferred his attention from the arepas and replied, 'Because it would be irresponsible not to. The coca people send out jeeps to abduct the little daughters of the peasants, and not long ago a party of religious fanatics arrived at La Loma and wiped out the whole village. What am I supposed to do? In places like this one is not just the priest, you know. One is the schoolteacher, the doctor, the Army, the police, the vet. There used to be a priest in every village around here, and now I am the last, so that I am always walking from one place to another. I even have to chew coca leaves like everyone else, just to keep going. I have written to the Cardinal many times.'

Concepcion put her hand over that of Guzman, as though by this gesture she could reconcile him to the history of his failure, and he said, 'I hear that the Cardinal has resigned, proclaiming himself unworthy of the position. Perhaps things will improve a little now.'

'I doubt it,' said Don Balsal. 'The only thing that will improve this place in the absence of good government would be if some rich benefactor moved into the district, secured some essential services, and provided some employment.'

'You might get some terrible caudillo who reduces you all to servitude,' observed Guzman. 'I hear that philanthropic landlords are few and far between.'

'There is no civilisation without good cooking,' said Concepcion. 'Eat these arepas before they go cold.'

'For progress we must have strength, and for strength we must have good food,' exclaimed Don Balsal, and he put a whole arepa into his mouth. He closed his eyes in ecstasy, like a Frenchman who has discovered a new and wonderful wine, and allowed the warm egg-yolk to trickle about the inside of his mouth. He chewed to release the flavour of the maize, and it seemed to him to waft about the inside of his head like smoke. 'I am going to get drunk on this,' he proclaimed happily.

Concepcion and Guzman slept soundly that night on the straw petate mats, using cushions from the jeep as pillows, and the padded jacket as a blanket. They awoke in the first chilly light of morning to find that they were sharing their warmth with Don Balsal's chicken, a fleabitten cat, and a shorthaired dog with one missing eye. Concepcion breathed deeply and said, 'The air is so clean that it hurts.'

'I bet that the river does not stink hereabouts,' said Guzman. 'I bet that one can drink the water from it. I am going to go out and have a wash in it.'

He was standing shivering in the freezing water, gingerly splashing himself, when Don Balsal stood above him on the river bank and said gravely, 'It is all right to pretend that this is the Jordan and that you are being baptised, but to wash upstream of a village is antisocial. You should go downstream where no one takes the water.'

'Forgive my ignorance,' said Guzman, hastily climbing out of the stream, so that his feet became instantly dirty again in the mud. He towelled himself and then looked up at Don Balsal, who was regarding his with an ironic eye. 'Father, can I make a confession to you? Where is the church?'

Balsal gestured expansively. 'The whole world is a church. You can make confession here.'

Guzman knelt in the mud before the priest, and began, 'Forgive me Father, for I have sinned . . .'

'With me you can leave that bit out,' said Don Balsal, 'let's get straight to the point.'

'I allowed my mother to die in an asylum, I caused the death of a priest by giving away his concealment to the security forces, I caused the death of prostitute and the death of her murderer, I closed many schools, I sold a cloister to be used as a supermarket, I impregnated my maid, I avoided blessing the pious widows, I have often treated Concepcion very badly, I destroyed a gift that she made to me, I have negligently lost my only son, and I have performed my duties poorly.'

'I didn't know we had any supermarkets,' said Don Balsal.

'I have sinned very grievously, Father.'

'Tell me, my son, are all these allegations against yourself true, or is this the assault of an irreverent sense of humour?'

'Father, it is true. Forgive me Father.'

Don Balsal looked down at him sternly. 'As a man, I say that you ought to be shot. As a priest, I forgive you. Go and sin no more.'

'Do I have no penance?'

Don Balsal scratched the stubble on his chin and glanced up at the sun as it lifted above the pristine snow of the sierra. 'Just do something useful with the rest of your life. If you say you have lost a child, go and find some others who need to be found. If you have taken life, then give life back. If you have sold what you should not have sold, then buy for someone else something that you do not need to buy.'

Guzman digested this verdict in silence, and then asked, 'Father, would you marry me to Concepcion?'

But Concepcion would have none of it. 'I am not mad,' she announced, when the idea was proposed to her later. 'If we were married legally by a mayor and religiously by a priest, you would only take me for granted. And as far as I am concerned, my cadenay, we have been married in fact already for many years, so that this idea is an insult. I will only consent to be married to you in the fashion of my mother's people, who always live together first, which is only common sense.'

And so it was that they mounted a hill, and Guzman listened as Concepcion proclaimed to the wilderness, 'I dedicate myself to the moon and this man to the sun. I will nourish him as I do myself, I will take the same care of him as I do of myself, I will give him the use of my fertility.' She turned to him and put her arms about his neck, 'There, my cadenay, we are married.'

'Don't I have to say anything?'

'No,' she answered. 'This way I am married to you, but you are not married to me, the same as always. That is how I like it.' She took his hand and laid the palm of it upon her stomach. 'You are a typical man,' she said, affecting an expression of resignation. 'It was not just your health that was restored by Dr Tapabalazo.'

An expression of incredulity passed over his face, and abruptly he fell to his knees, pressing his ear against her to listen for a heartbeat.

There is another story concerning Concepcion and Guzman. It tells how, having searched for Cristobal even as far as Cochadebajo de los Gatos, Guzman sold the estates that he had inherited, and at night scoured the slums and sewers of the capital for the forgotten children. How he saved some from addiction, prostitution, crime, and early death, and lost many others who could not resist being drawn back to the way of life that had clawed them into bondage. How he struggled with sceptical judges and corrupted mayors to arrest and imprison the policemen and the vigilantes who were shooting the children at night and lobbing grenades and poisoned food down manhole covers so that the sewers filled with tiny skeletons. How he petitioned President Garcilaso, enlisted the support of Dionisio Vivo and General Hernando Montes Sosa, raised money in London, Paris, and New York, and found himself back in the care of Dr Tertuliano Tomás Kaiser Wilhelm Tebas de Tapabalazo, who removed two bullets from his shoulder and another from his stomach. With paternal pride Dr Tapabalazo admired the tidy scars of his previous operation, and agreed to become a visiting doctor to the stately orphanage that had been opened near Arcabuco, with Don Balsal as its principal. Balsal would patrol the grounds with his shotgun, for which he now had some ammunition, and sprayed with buckshot several jeeploads of the coca hooligans who had turned up in the hope of abducting the little girls, until they gave up and never returned. The children roamed about the countryside, innocently doing things for which they would have been arrested in the capital, and some of them stayed on to become staff. The cholos, reluctant and suspicious, drifted in very slowly to grow vegetables that they had never seen before, and some of their children arrived unannounced in the classrooms, demanding in Quechua to learn how to read in Castilian.

Concepcion, happily the mother to uncounted children, including her own, grew old with dignity, planting flowers that would attract hummingbirds, and steadfastly continuing to refuse to marry Guzman, who, to the day of his death, never learned of the havoc caused by his first attempt to save the nation's souls.

# 49 *Parlanchina's Warning*

Carmen rolled out of her hammock before her husband. She had not slept very well because there had been something unidentifiable that had been worrying her. It was like an insistent voice, just out of earshot. Now that the sun was venturing above the horizon it seemed as though every animal in the canopy of the jungle was competing to express its joy and terror at the prospect of a new day's survival. A troupe of howler monkeys was whooping near by, a jaguar was coughing, the crickets were tuning up their sawmill, and flocks of scarlet macaws were flying overhead on their daily mission to the claybanks where they would swallow kaolin in order to counteract the poisons in their diet of bitter fruits.

Carmen revived the embers of the fire with a fan made of woven palm, and set a pot of coffee directly upon them. She squatted before it to warm her hands, and then sliced a plantain which she would fry for breakfast. She walked out of the hut and threw the skin to the sow, who heaved herself out of her scrape with a grunt, and bolted the food with appreciation. Carmen ran her fingers through her snowy hair in order to free it of the night, and went over to Parlanchina's grave in the clearing before the hut. As she rearranged the twigs and decorations, she talked to her daughter.

'Gwubba,' she said, 'how are you? And why do you come to Aurelio and not to me? Gwubba, I have been having troubles in my mind. Perhaps you would come to Aurelio and tell him what it is, so that he can tell me, and then I can know. Something is wrong because there is too much peace. Has the world stopped happening, or have I died, Gwubba?'

She contemplated the grave where the white bones of her exquisite daughter lay muddled with those of Federico and her pet ocelot, and out in the forest a bird called with a sound that could have been Parlanchina laughing in the days when she was alive and always talking too much. Carmen's eyes misted with the sorrow that had never left her even though she knew that Parlanchina had married

Federico in the afterworld and had borne his child. 'Without you I feel a terrible loneliness,' she explained to the grave. 'You were more like the sun and the moon and the wind than they themselves, and your hammock is empty, and your little cat does not chase butterflies and steal things from the meathooks.'

Carmen wept. If only the earth of the grave would heave up and Parlanchina rise laughing from the soil. If only she would stride through the trees with her hair brushing about her waist, imitating the calls of the animals and terrifying the patrols of the Jungle Rangers, with their burdens of backpacks and machine guns, and their terrible thirst for death. Carmen knew that Parlanchina still did these things, but only Aurelio could see her. Carmen could not help but take this as favouritism, even though Aurelio had explained the true reasons, and so she felt injured in the heart.

Carmen returned to the hut and took the coffee from the fire. She poured some into a gourd to let it cool a little, and fetched her little scrap of broken mirror from its concealment in the palms. She breathed on it and cleaned it on the fabric of the hammock, and then she tried to discern her face amid the pattern of scratches. She saw her white curls that had once been red, and the lines of age that had divided her youth into a quilt of a face. The lips that had been full and sensual now had grooves in them, and felt dry even when moistened with her tongue. Her eyes seemed to have lost themselves somewhere in the labyrinth of time, and looked back at her as though they belonged to another. The velvety blackness of her skin seemed now to have a pallor of grey. She gazed at herself for so long that her own image became incomprehensible, and she put the mirror away. She went over to where Aurelio lay sleeping and saw that time had reduced him also; he seemed smaller than before, and his long black Indian's hair caught streaks of silver in the light. She understood that she loved him even more now than in the past, despite his diminishment towards death, and she realised with surprise that he too loved her more than when they had been young together, and beautiful. More tears came to her eyes, because that is what happens when one suddenly perceives a miracle amid the commonplace. She settled down with her gourd of coffee and relit the cigar she had been smoking the night before. 'I am waiting for you to awake,' she said to her sleeping husband.

'Why do we still love each other?' she asked him as they breakfasted on the platano, and Aurelio licked the grease from his fingers whilst he thought about an answer.

'We have always sought happiness more than we have avoided suffering. And we have kept busy together so much that whilst we were not looking we have become each other's soul. Perhaps you have an answer to your own question?'

Carmen tossed some piassaba on the fire to revive it, and said, 'I love you so much that when I look at you I do not see your face.'

'It is bad to talk about it. It is better just to do it. I think that when you talk about love it is because you are afraid to lose it. Remember that I am an Indian.'

'I am black,' she said, 'and it is permitted for me to talk about it, and to be afraid sometimes. Will we do the coca today?'

Aurelio nodded, 'I have brought the shells.'

Carmen went to the little plantation because only women may pick the coca, and Aurelio built a fire because only men may calcify the shells. He had just placed them on the smouldering lattice of branches, and was sucking the end of his coca pestle when Parlanchina came up behind him and wrapped her hair around his eyes. 'Look, Papacito,' she exclaimed, 'it is night-time.'

Aurelio sneezed because the hair had tickled his nose when he inhaled, and Parlanchina protested, rubbing the pretended mucus on his shoulder. 'Have you come for a story, Gwubba, or have you come just to be a nuisance?' asked her father.

'I have come to tell you two pieces of news,' she replied, 'but you will receive neither until you have explained the coca to me.'

'Again?'

'Again.'

'It was Pachamama who gave us the coca and taught us how to use it,' began Aurelio, 'Pachamama who has many other names. She gave it to us so that we would stop being animals and become civilised. No one who does not have coca is civilised. Dionisio tells me that there were people who were called "Greeks", and they said that they were given wine in order to become civilised, and no one who does not have wine is civilised, so perhaps wine is the same thing as coca in a different form, who knows? When we became civilised we lived by the mountain of silver, Potosí, and we learned how to make things out of silver and became even more civilised, but then the Spanish came and took the mountain away, and offended Pachamama and made her weak, so that now there is less snow upon the mountains than before, and the lakes on the altiplano dried up and turned to salt, and the people who stayed became stupid and everyone else left forever. You understand that the mountain contained the people's spirits, and these spirits did not want to come out, because life is hard, and neither did they want to go back, because death is hard. When the Spanish took the mountain away, the spirits had to live in other mountains and my people became dispersed.'

Parlanchina sat upon the ground with her ocelot curled up in her arms, its feet in the air, and asked, 'Will you tell me more about Pachamama?'

'She told us not to wear shoes too often, because she liked to feel our feet upon her body. In the beginning she was the sea because that is all there was, and she remembered the future, and so it was that she gave birth to possibility. And Pachamama spun nine worlds, and this is why women spin in order to be like her, and this is why I turn when I am thinking, because I am spinning my thoughts. And Pachamama bled between her legs and became fertile, and her blood became gold, although it is also said that gold is the sweat of the sun, and she bore us so that we might take care of her as a child always cares for its old mother.

'And she gave us coca, which is why only women may cultivate it, and now I shall tell you about the poporro.' Aurelio held up his coca gourd, with its bulging base and long thin neck, encrusted upon the outside with the yellowed mixture of lime and crushed leaves. 'You may look at this and think that it resembles the parts of a man, and that is why only a man may use coca, but you would be wrong. This bulge is the womb of a woman, and this neck is her passage. It is this pestle which is the part of a man, because it goes in and out and works its magic on the inside. So women honour Pachamama by spinning, and men do so by pounding coca in the poporro. A man may not marry without this, for it makes him calm and fortifies him for work, so that he may care for his woman and not be tempted to strike her, which is a great evil, and that is why it civilises us. But when the white man takes coca, he takes out the essence, and becomes mad. And now the shells are ready; look, they are completely white.'

288

Parlanchina watched as Aurelio flicked the shells out of the cinders and scooped them into a large gourd with its neck removed. He poured water into it from another gourd, and the smoke of the chemical reaction billowed out. 'Pachamama showed us this,' he said. 'Without this lime there is no goodness in the coca. Now tell me your news.'

She teased him, 'No, I want another story first. Tell me how the jaguar got its spots.'

Realising that she was trying to keep him in suspense, Aurelio said, 'No, I shall tell you the story about the two worms. Once there was a woman worm who met her friend under the floor of my hut, and I heard them talking. One said to the other, "Where is your husband?" and the other replied, "He has gone fishing."'

Parlanchina screwed up her nose to ponder this story, and then realised that it was a joke. She took the paw of her sleepy ocelot and squeezed it so that the claws unsheathed themselves, and she reached over and scratched Aurelio's face with them. The ocelot growled in protest, pulling his paw away from Parlanchina's grasp. Aurelio took his daughter's nose in between two fingers and squeezed. 'Gwubba, I am not letting go until you tell me this news.'

She tried to bite the heel of his palm, and failed, 'Let go, and then I will tell.'

'Swear.'

'I swear it.' He released her, and she said, 'Federico is dying. Whenever I see him he is more faded than before.'

'Federico is already dead.'

'But he is dying all over again. What can I do?'

'He is dying because he is being reborn. One day he will go altogether, and you will know that he has come back to the world as a child. Perhaps the same will happen to you one day. Where is your child?'

'I left her with Mama in the coca plantation, because I want her to know her grandmother. Papacito, I am very sad.'

Aurelio stroked her cheek, and asked, 'What is the other news?'

'It is a message from the gods to the people of Cochadebajo de los Gatos. They say, "Build a wall, because we cannot help you."'

Aurelio was puzzled, 'Which gods?'

'It was Chango who told me on behalf of all the others.'

'But he is Santa Barbara, he is a god of the black people. Why should he tell me?'

'The gods are muddled up,' she replied. 'Chango says that there is a great evil in the land and that everyone is appealing for help to the saints and gods. He says that they will not answer both sides, because they would be divided against themselves, and therefore they will take no part. Chango says that he will not as a saint fight against himself as a god, and so he says to the people, "Build yourselves a wall," and he says to the other people, "Do not pray to me, I will not answer you." Pass the message on, Papacito.'

'I will, Gwubba, and you must do something for me. Show yourself to your mother; she is full of sorrow that only I can talk to you.'

Parlanchina tossed back her hair and smiled ruefully. 'I have tried, but she cannot see me or hear me except when she dreams. You must teach her to dream when she is awake.'

Aurelio sucked hard on his pestle and rubbed it against the neck of his poporro. 'It is not for me to teach her anything. For me she is like Pachamama. It is she who teaches. Go and learn from her how she may see you, and I will find out where Federico is to be born, so that you may visit him.'

She stood up and placed the ocelot upon the ground. It strolled away with its tail waving, and she began to follow it, but she turned and gave a small wave of her hand. 'Thank you for the stories, and do not forget the wall, because there is blood on the face of the moon.'

## 50 Sibila

'The gold of the world is the rot of the soul,' she said, and I woke up. I had been dreaming that I was in Ancient Greece. In the dream I was a rich and idle man, and I had a fine white robe. I was sitting on a hillside above the road, eating figs, when I saw a procession coming. It was a religious procession that was leading a bull to sacrifice at the altar stone, and everyone was singing and banging tambourines. I saw Sibila carrying the golden bowl, and immediately I took a fancy to her, the kind of fancy that can physically hurt. I think it was the childlike quality of innocence that was apparent in her odd way of being both clumsy and graceful at the same time. She was willowy and sinuous, she walked in an unconsciously beautiful manner, very straight in the back, and yet she had a permanent red mark on one side of her nose where she had walked into the edge of a door when her mind had been on something else. She was childlike in the way she made up words and sometimes muddled her sentences. If she could not remember a word exactly, she would use another that sounded a bit like it, smile as if begging one's indulgence, and pause to make sure that she had been understood. She would wave one hand and enquire, 'What was the word I should have used?'

In the dream I followed the procession to the sacrifice, and I remember watching as they cut the throat of the bull and Sibila caught the blood in the golden bowl. I was hiding behind a large red rock because I knew that no one was supposed to be present but the initiates, and I crouched there just willing her to come in my direction. Eventually I saw her coming. It was dark by now, and it was easy to grab her arm and put one hand over her mouth. I was a base character in that dream, and I began to paw at her whilst she struggled. I think I was trying to rape her, but she resisted so much that I took a bag of gold from my belt and spilled it on the ground. I said, 'Look what I will give you,' but she looked at me contemptuously, said, 'The gold of the world is the rot of the soul,' broke my grip, and ran off. In my complacency I could not believe that any woman could resist a man of my position and wealth, and then I woke up, feeling ashamed.

Do you believe in reincarnation? I never used to, but Sibila changed my mind, and now I think that the dream was about something that happened in a previous life. I think she never trusted me because she remembered by intuition that I was untrustworthy, and I think that she lived off raw fruit and vegetables because she was working off the guilt of all the sacrifices in Ancient Greece. I think it was my punishment to be given a crippled leg, so that I would be forced to be modest with women.

Sibila was always very sweet about my crippled leg. She never walked too fast, she stopped when I was in pain, and she always kissed me on both cheeks when we met, but all the same I always knew that she could only love me as a friend. Perhaps she also thought me too old, but definitely I was not attractive to her. It caused me some sorrow, but I loved her so much that I often bored her by staying too long with her. I could drink litres of tisanes and smoke many cigars in her little house, and even when she was bored with me she would still offer me more to drink, or an empanada to eat. I used to sing to her sometimes, and she used to sing as well, in her breathy voice, so thin and lovable. She liked to tell absurd stories about animals, and the thing she understood least in the whole world was why people enjoyed going fishing. I loved her so much that I declared myself one day, but I was not offended or surprised when she explained her position. To prove that she could love me as a friend, she invited me to see a film, when most girls would have said, 'I do not think we should see each other anymore.' I loved her so much that I was very happy just to be near her sometimes. She helped me to forget that I was a cripple. I would look into her grey eyes and feel that between us there was a direct communion of souls; it was because she saw me so clearly that she knew that she should not be my lover. I could not be trusted, you see, and she knew it by instinct, but loved me as a friend all the same. She was very noble. I would lie awake at night imagining that I was making love to her, and believe me, I know exactly what it would have been like, which is almost as good as having actually done so. If you do not believe me, it is because you have never loved anyone in that manner yourself. I had observed her moving, watched the fall of her clothes about her body, so many times that I knew precisely how she would have looked naked. Maybe there had been an incarnation when we really were lovers, and I was remembering it.

Sibila knew three languages, a very rare thing in Quintalinas de las Viñas, but there was always something about her that made her want to be somewhere else. She chose lovers with whom she knew that she would not remain, so that I felt safer in being merely a friend, and she loved to be left alone. When she was alone she would go to sleep or just do nothing at all. She felt guilty about not enjoying company very much and about looking forward to when visitors would leave. She once had a party and almost nobody came; this was because if you knew her well, you would love her utterly, but if you were only an acquaintance, then you did not feel like taking the trouble to respond to her invitations.

She used to like to disappear sometimes. She went to look at ancient monuments, great standing stones with holes through them, or strange archways standing in the forest for no apparent purpose. Once I went with her and we got drunk and smoked some marijuana together. She laughed more than I had ever seen before, sitting on the ground waving a loaf of bread and singing.

Once she went to Cochadebajo de los Gatos to look at the ancient Indian remains, and whilst she was there she heard Father Garcia preach. She had never been a good Catholic, and like me she never went to mass. I had a grudge against God for letting me be a cripple. When she came back she had a new light in her eyes, saying that she had seen Father Garcia levitate whilst he preached. She said that he had sorted out some intellectual problems for her by explaining that the world was created by the Devil, that we were all angels imprisoned in our bodies, and that to know this was the first step in reforming the world and finding our way back to our true nature. She told me that we could learn to pick up our fallen crowns and put on our robes of light. When she explained it to me her face lit up with a glow of beauty, and I fell in love with her even more. I was not sure if I believed in what she told me, but I loved her so much that I definitely pretended to, just to remain close to her. You see, she started to spread this new gospel herself, and I followed her around acting as a kind of assistant. She did not go to village plazas and preach, as itinerant preachers do. She used to go somewhere and just hang around in public places, and somehow she would accumulate people to talk to. I think that she made people feel intrinsically beautiful by informing them that in reality they were angels. Even beggars felt more confident. Old ladies would smile so happily that you could tell what they had looked like when they were young. She could make violent drunks recognise that they were betraying themselves, and she also scared them by saying that they would be reborn as armadillos and coral snakes. 'Behave like an angel, love like an angel, because you are an angel,' she said. 'Feel the ring of pressure about your head where once you wore a crown, and feel the silk against your skin that was your robe of light.' She took to wearing a cord about her waist to signify that she was bound to her faith, and people began to call her 'La Perfecta'.

The more that she created an immaculate simplicity in her own life, the more I yearned for her. But I was not good enough. I could not live off raw fruit and vegetables, and sometimes I would slip away and eat a steak so big that it had to be served on a wooden board. But my leg became much stronger from walking everywhere with her, and now I do not limp very much. I suppose that is a kind of miracle.

I do not want to give the impression that Sibila was a saint. She was not very austere, and she was like most women in that she could not walk past a stall that was selling sticky cakes. She liked to play games, and she did not disdain to join in conversations of a scandalous nature. She was also fond of cats. I think that most saints are probably either mad or obsessive or extremely disagreeable, but she was perfectly normal except that an inner light had switched itself on, deep inside her.

Then one day the Dominican terror descended on Quintalinas de las Viñas. Hundreds of them appeared without warning, before dawn, and the town found itself wholly taken over. They set up an auto de fe in the church, but first of all they announced in the plaza that on Sunday everyone would have to go to the church for mass, in order to hear an edict. Like most people, I went out of curiosity, but not before the town had had to endure two days of appalling rowdyism and random violence from the bands of men who were travelling as bodyguards to the priests. Most people had to lock their doors, a thing hitherto unknown, and all the women stayed indoors.

On Sunday the church was overflowing, and it seemed to me that our priest was looking very unhappy. He stumbled over the words of the mass, and he preached a sermon, very hesitantly, in which he talked about the trials of life, courage in the face of suffering, tolerance, and how we should emulate God in His mercy. We realised later that to preach this sermon must have taken great fortitude, but we all assumed at the time that his nervousness was due to having to preach in front of a Monsignor who was a legate.

At the end of the sermon the Monsignor arose from his seat and took the crucifix from the altar. He asked us to cross ourselves, raise our right hands, and follow him in a vow to 'support the Holy Office'. No one raised their hand, but then some of his bodyguard began to walk up and down the aisle, glaring at us in a threatening manner, and one or two timid souls raised their hands. The body-guard began to take notes of who had not thus responded, and were demanding our names, so that very soon we were all intimidated into raising our hands. When we were thus made to appear like school-children, the legate read out the oath for us to repeat, which we did with only half a heart and with a deal of mumbling.

Then the legate read out what he called an 'Edict of Grace', which listed an immense number of heresies, most of which none of us had ever heard of. It included things like reciting the psalms without the Gloria Patri at the end, circumcision, turning to the wall when dying, putting clean sheets on the beds on Saturdays, being Nestorians or Bogomiles, killing animals by cutting their throats, and God knows what else. It took half an hour for the list to be read. At the end of it he said that we had two days to discharge our consciences by coming forward to denounce ourselves or anyone else whom we knew to be guilty. He said that all taking advantage of this would be reconciled to the Church without punishment. Old Patarino, who has always been fearless of authority and a joker, immediately stood up and declared that he had been circumcised when young because of a tight foreskin. Many people giggled, and one of the bodyguard struck him on the side of the head and dragged him out of the church. It seems that they threw him down the well and stoned him to death as an unrepentant Jew and Christ-slayer.

In the face of this violence, many people stood up asking sincerely to repent, having divined correctly that it would be safer to denounce oneself than to have someone else do so out of a grudge or cowardice. There were some surprising confessions. One man said that he had taken soil from the grave of a bad priest to use in a spell, someone else said that he had a talisman made for him by an Indian brujo, and a woman said that she had prayed to Oshun for safer childbirth. The men of the bodyguard took their names, and the legate declared them reconciled. He then said that the following Tuesday there would be an Edict of Faith, inviting the denunciation of others, and that to effect this, everyone in the village would be questioned by him personally.

This legate, referred to with no apparent sense of irony by his followers as 'El Inocente', was a human devil. And I mean that literally. He seemed to be made of wood, he was so dispassionate. He was like a vulture. He was thin as a corpse, and his face looked as though it had been badly sawn out of a log. It had flattened portions like those you see in illustrations of Pinocchio. His voice was drier than leaves, and he rode a huge black horse. He filled us all with fear, and I went straight to Sibila to tell her that we must leave the town before hell broke loose. I had an intuition of it, as though I had been through it before, and remembered.

# 51 *Parlanchina's Lament*

I am undone by memory, I am not like a cat who loses her kittens and mourns for a day. When I was small there was a cat who had kittens, and one of the kittens I thought had too little milk, and I held it in a bowl of milk and it drowned, and I made a disaster out of my good intentions. And the mother cat, perhaps she did not even notice because she could not count, and perhaps she felt only a small emptiness and an absence at her dugs, but I wept with the desolation that she could not feel, and my guilt was terrible, and I asked Papa to punish me, and he stroked my hair and said, 'No, Gwubba, you punish yourself,' and I ate nothing but ants for a day, and I helped Mama with the cooking, which I hate, eating nothing of what I had cooked and eating only ants, and I begged the mother cat to forgive me, but she lay there with her kittens because every mother expects to lose a child. She looked at me with those big yellow eyes and I tore my hair because I had hurt her and she was hurting without any knowledge.

And now the stars are shining for me by day, and unhappiness is like a pain made of machetes and thorns. The taste of life is like piquia oil in the mouth, and perhaps I would spit but the bitterness would remain, and perhaps after all everything is for nothing, and I cry in the night like an owl and laugh without humour like the laughing hawk, and my soul flies hither and thither in confusion, and all I am made of is memory.

When I first saw you, my husband, sweet lover, my guardian, my dark fish swimming in the waters of my womb, you were handsome. You were like an old man, you were so serious, you were like a child, you were smooth and unmade. You were like a dolphin, strong and innocent, and how I loved you, lay awake at night for the thought of you, slept in the broad day for the sake of dreaming of you. I followed you in the forest and you never saw me, but in the not knowing of me you still loved me, and I was tempted. I tried to save you, but the jaguar killed you, and in death your soul rose up and the first sight of your dead eyes was me, and you said, 'Ah, I dreamed of you, and your name is Parlanchina,' and I took your hand, and at that time I was so young dead that I scarcely sprouted breasts, and nonetheless you loved me. And you took me as I took you, and we grew love as Papa grows his maize in the clearing, and our love was like a quebracha, hard and strong, and we became invincible. And on the praias and savannas, amid our bones whitening in the tomb, in the stone chulpas of the sierra, running above the topmost trees of the montana, I fell upon your body and our hunger was unfed with devouring. I remember your eyes grew wild and your lips swelled, and the waves would start at my feet and head and meet in the middle, and my toes curled so that sometimes it hurt me even when I was adrift on delight's canoe somewhere in the centre of a dark sun. 'Federico, Federico, Federico,' I said, and the name meant all things that I had ever meant, and, 'Ay, ay, ay,' I cried, and my happiness was such that I came out of the other side of happiness and began to weep, and you took my hair and wiped my tears with, 'I love you Parlanchina, I love you. You are beautiful like Yemaya. For this, death was not so bad, and the jaguar did me a favour, thanks be to all cats, and all the gods bless them.' And I was laughing as I cried, and I did not feel that I was dead, because this was life made better, like a knife that cuts sharper for the burning in Papa's fire.

And sometimes I would go up into the mountains and surprise you as you watched the paths, and sometimes you would come down into the jungle and catch me as I ran among the trees, and always we would mate like dolphins, twisting and rolling, calling and crying, and my breasts grew, and my belly swelled. I remember how you would run your hands and kneel before me naked, kissing my legs and the baby's door, saying, 'Come little child, your papa is calling,' and I would squirm, saying, 'Get away, get away,' and all the time you knew I was saying, 'Closer, I love you, come closer,' and you laughed and held me tighter, and the pleasure could have killed me.

And the daughter came in the night without my knowing, waking me up in my dreams, and there she was beside me before I had even woven a hammock for her, and she never cried, because she was born not to Parlanchina living but to Parlanchina dead, and Papa was happy, and you were her father, so proud to hold her that you scarcely gave me time to take her and feed her my body's milk. And now she can stand for a second and makes noises that could be words, if only they could be understood, and before my eyes you are fading.

I hug you and my arms embrace a nothing. I look in your eyes and they have no colours, they are dreaming. I kiss your lips and they have no response, like the lips of a man gone mad and disappearing in the jungle of his broken soul. Your mind is in fragments like the shards of huacos in a mountain tomb, I say, 'Federico, Federico, where are you? Speak,' and you blink and stand like an animal lanced with curare, and I do not hear even a sigh, and suddenly I think, 'Parlanchina, you have stopped existing when Federico's eyes have dimmed,' and Papa says, 'Be happy, Federico is being reborn,' and that is all nothing for me, for your child has no father and I am undone. I am shredded by memories, I am empress of grey seas of mourning, I shall weep rivers until the gods hear me and for fear of drowning grant my request.

Sibila did not want to leave. She pulled one of those comical faces of hers and said, 'But I have done nothing bad, and anyway, they are not the police.' At that point I realised that I should go to the mayor and persuade him to call the militia on the telephone. I went to the alcaldia, and there was a group of people outside it who had all had the same idea. Outside the building the severed wire of our one telephone hung down the boards, and inside there were screams. It seems that the mayor had attempted to arrest the legate, had been seized by the bodyguard, and was being questioned about his orthodoxy. His father had been a Syrian, and he did not have a chance. He was flayed alive and left to bleed to death in the sun as a example to us all. It was said he would not denounce anyone else. His corpse was the most horrible thing I had ever seen up to that time.

On the Tuesday we all had to go to church and listen to the list of heresies all over again, and we were made to swear the same oath to support the Holy Office. Our priest was not allowed to say the mass, and instead it was said by one Father Valentino, a man with the face of a simpleton. We were invited to denounce the heretics known to us, and told to go to our houses to await our individual summons; they had taken the list of inhabitants from the offices of the mayor where he kept them for the purposes of the census.

The town was crawling with priests and bodyguards, so it was difficult to walk about without being stopped and questioned. Many people went into their front doors and out of their houses by the back windows. I watched Sofia do precisely that from my own window, and run off into the trees. I do not think that she was caught, but I know of one woman who was raped to death by the bodyguard when they found her in a barn. I was too scared to flee, and I sat in my house waiting for the knock.

My name comes late in the alphabet, and so I was not to be

interviewed for some time. I could not sit still, and I began to prepare a meal, as though I could delude myself that everything was normal.

There was a knock on my door after sunset, and I assumed it to be the Holy Office. Trembling and terrified I looked through the cracks in the planks and saw that it was our priest, Father Belibasta. He was not a good man, in the sense that he had a concubine and two children, but he was a good man in the sense that he had an unblemished soul. I was relieved, and I let him in.

He was plainly frightened, more even than I was, and he said he had seen terrible things, and that I must hurry. I said, 'What things?' but he would not explain in detail. He said that people were admitting to things that they had not done, and were accusing each other likewise. He sat on my truckle bed with tears streaming down his cheeks, and he told me that he had seen such horrors as had never been seen. I will not tell you the names, because they will mean nothing to you, but for example he told me that one man had denounced himself for using contraceptives. Another had denounced his best friend for urinating against the church wall when he was drunk. A woman made a delation against her husband, saying that he had made her cook meat and onions on a Friday, and the husband said that she had once observed that St Maria Corelli must have been very stupid. Someone else was accused of saying, during a game of tejo, 'You will not win this game, even if God were on your side.' It seemed that neighbours were turned against neighbours, families against their own members, because they were being told that it was not enough to denounce oneself when fully cognisant of others who deserved to be arraigned. Father Belibasta said that statements were being extracted by force, and he asked, 'Where is La Perfecta?'

'Sibila is in her house,' I replied.

'Almost everyone has denounced her and yourself,' said the priest. 'With all that talk about angels and diabolical creation, it was inevitable. You must go to her and try to get out of this place. Please do not tell me where you will go, because my turn will come perhaps. I am going to try to gather my flock and lead them to a place of safety.'

I knelt before him and I asked, 'Pray to God to lead me to a good end.' I do not know why I said those words, but they came of their own accord into my head.

'God bless you, and make you a good Christian, and lead you to a good end,' he said, and he laid his hand on my head.

I have never felt so courageous, and it was love that did it. I was like a bird who hops within reach of an ocelot to lead it away from her chicks. I climbed out of the window at the back, and I circled the entire village in order to go behind Sibila's house. I was as stealthy and assured as a jaguar, and I forgot my crippled leg. It carried me as though it were healthy. I even stole a rifle from the side of a sleeping bodyguard, and I broke his head with the butt of it, I was so full of strength.

I tapped on Sibila's shutter, and at first she refused to come. But I begged her, and I told her to gather all the food in the house. There was a terrible shriek that floated out over the darkness, and that persuaded her. We went to live in the caves where we used to go and eat picnics on hot afternoons.

During that week I came to know her even more intimately. At night it grew very cold, and we used to sleep wrapped up in each other's arms, fully clothed, to keep warm. I can still smell her hair and feel the slenderness of her limbs. I was so happy. During the day we would look for wild fruit, and we would talk and talk until we lost our voices with laughing. I told her things about myself that I have told no one, and she told me all about every man she had ever loved. We made up stupid songs and sang them in rounds, tirelessly. I honestly believe that we would eventually have become lovers. I would look into her face and see her candidly gazing back, and that is how I know. I also know that she was an angel who was daily breaking further from her imprisonment.

I was growing accustomed to my newfound bravery, and every night I would creep back down to the village to see whether the barbarians were still there. I saw horrible things, even in the dark, because by night they continued the work of the day by the light of torches and vehicles. Many people were hanged. I heard the sound of pleading and wailing. I saw Gil. He was saying, 'I am innocent, I am not a homosexual,' but they castrated him and stoned him whilst he was tied to a post. I know that Gil was not homosexual, because he used to borrow money to go to the whorehouse. Who could have accused him? Guiralda, whose husband had died, leaving her pregnant, was thrown down the well, like Patarino.

Because my nose is slit and because I have lash marks all over my body, you will have guessed that I was caught. I was taken from behind by three men, one night as I was watching through the leaves. I could not run from them because of my leg, and when they grabbed me all my strength left my body, and I was like a child. They said, 'Ay, this is the cripple,' and they took me straight to the church.

In the church El Inocente was sitting behind a long table, looking more like a vulture than ever. At first he was kind to me. He pointed to the priest who had said the mass and told me, 'Father Valentino will defend you in this court. Did you know that you have been denounced, and that is why we have brought you here?'

I played dumb, and said, 'No, Your Grace. Who has denounced me?'

'We do not reveal the names of witnesses, to spare them from reprisals after we have gone.'

'Of what am I accused, Your Grace?'

'If we tell you that, then you may guess who has accused you. We require you to search your conscience. Were you at the Edict of Grace?'

I nodded, and he said, 'Then you have sworn a Holy Oath to help us. What do you have to confess?'

I searched in my mind for small offences, and I said, 'I do not often go to mass, and from time to time I have doubted that God becomes bread.'

This was noted down by another priest, and El Inocente asked, 'And do you have a confession *in caput alienum*?'

I asked him to repeat the question, and he explained that I should confess the evil I knew of others. I had a brainwave, and I named him some people who had already died and were out of harm's way. I said, 'These people went to candombles, and practised santeria, but now they are dead.'

'And are they buried here?'

I nodded again, and the list of names was handed to one of the bodyguard, who went out with it. 'You have more to confess, do you not?' asked the Monsignor, and I replied, 'No, Your Grace.'

'Put him *in conspectu tormentorum*,' said the vulture, and Father Valentino took me by the arm and led me into the room of the church where the priest robes himself. In there I saw whips and instruments made of iron, and a system of pulleys mounted upon a hook in one of the joists. I said to the priest, 'How will you defend me?' and he replied, 'There are four forms of defence. In the first place you can prove that witnesses are accusing you out of malice.'

'Who are the witnesses?'

He shook his head and said, 'It has already been explained that we cannot reveal the identity of witnesses. You may call favourable witnesses. You may plead extenuation, such as insanity, or you may resort to recusation, and that is something that I do not advise, under the circumstances.'

'What is it?'

'Objecting to the judge. Do you see this? This is the garrucha, or strappado. You are hauled to the ceiling and then dropped; it greatly agonises the arms and shoulders. This is the toca; you are tied down, a cloth is put down your throat and water is poured over it which soaks down the cloth and fills your stomach. How much it hurts depends upon how much water is used. This is the potro; it is a system of ropes that are wound upon a crank, and which cut into the flesh and crush the bones. If you do not confess, you will suffer until we are convinced that you have told everything.'

I went down on my knees and begged him. I said, 'Father, tell me what I have to confess.' He looked confused and fearful, which revealed to me that he was not a man like El Inocente, whose head was disconnected from his heart. He looked around to check that there was no one near, and he bent down to whisper, 'La Perfecta.'

I had already guessed that they wanted Sibila. My heart sank to my belly, and my head dropped to my chest. I looked at the instruments of torture, and I remembered the screaming I had heard, the flaying of the mayor and the castration of Gil.

In my life I had often thought about this kind of situation, wondering what I would do. From time to time I have toyed with the idea that I would be heroic and hold out until the end. But now I made excuses to myself. I said, 'I would be no worse than whoever it was who denounced me. What is the use of being hanged like the others?' I asked Father Valentino, 'What happens if I make full confession?'

'You will be spared,' he said. 'There will be punishment, but you will, if you abjure, be reconciled to the faith.'

'And Sibila? Will she be spared?'

He smiled at me indulgently and replied, 'When she confesses her errors, she will be spared.'

It was that statement that made up my mind. I reasoned that Sibila would confess and pretend to repent, as I was about to do. I thought that she would understand my cowardice and learn to forgive me, because she would realise that in my position she would have done the same. I went back to El Inocente and told him exactly where she was.

But I was not spared in the manner I had expected. In the morning there was an auto de fe, and El Inocente appeared dressed in purple for it. There were many there who were to be sentenced, and I was the last. It was hard to recognise many of my friends because of their mistreatment, and I felt ashamed that I was unharmed. Every one of us had all our property confiscated and given over to the Holy Office. I was taken to my house and they made an inventory of all my meagre possessions, down to the last spoon. They loaded the entire wealth of the village into carts and trucks, because they had found a heresy in every single person. The people who had confessed reluctantly had their eyes put out by the bodyguard, and they were tied to Father Belibasta by a rope. His eyes were left in his head, and he was told to lead them away through the country as a warning to others.

As for me, I was penanced. I was put on a burro and flogged through the streets. The people were supposed to throw stones at me. They were ordered to do so by the bodyguard, but no stones touched me. When we returned to the front of the church, one of the bodyguard took a knife and slit my nose. I am not telling you about what I suffered, because I cannot describe it and I cannot talk about it, and I cannot reconcile myself to it. Except that now I see justice in it if I think of it as my punishment for betraying Sibila.

When I was untied from the donkey, and I had been lifted from the ground where I had fallen, I was surrounded by the priests. They put on me the sanbenito, which is the shirt with a yellow cross on the back and front, and I was told to wear it all my life. I was told to go barefoot all my days, and I was forbidden to touch anyone. They gave me a wooden palette for shopkeepers to put my purchases on.

Blood soaked into my shirt and it ran down my legs. I thought that I was going to die, and my stomach felt as though it had caved in.

The Monsignor came forward and smiled at me benignly. He asked me, 'What faith do you embrace?' and I replied, 'The faith of Jesus Christ.'

He turned to the other priests and told them to rejoice. I swear there were tears of happiness in his eyes. He put his hands on my shoulders, said, 'Thanks be to God,' and kissed me on both cheeks.

# 53 *The Mexican Musicologist Recalls The Building Of The Wall*

I have lived here for some time now, and I never cease to be intrigued and amazed; the mania for construction seems never to abate, and this in a people naturally inclined to idleness and profligacy. The construction of the wall came about at the time when I had been down on the plateau and caught redbeasts. They crawl up one's trouser legs and burrow under the skin. Lucky is the man whose waistband is tight from prosperity or shrinkage, because then they stop and the upper body is spared. I had terrible sore spots that drove me crazy with itching, and I fell out with Ena and Lena because I thought that one of them had been unfaithful and come down with the pox. I went to Aurelio in high indignation, and he told me to block up the breathing holes with grease, and sure enough they died and I had an allergic reaction to the corpses and itched even worse. I went back to Aurelio and he said I should be grateful it was not warble fly, which reminds me that not long ago one of the horses got kicked in the eye and it went bad. Before long it was a mass of gruesomely writhing maggots and I believed the stallion would die, but Sergio removed the eyeball and cleaned out the socket with alcohol, and everything was fine except that the horse kept walking in circles for lack of vision on one side. Dionisio said, 'Never mind,' and he found a grey pebble and painted an eye on it with white paint. He put it in the socket and now the horse walks straight – how do you explain that? – but the eye appears most disconcerting when you see the horse like that.

Don Emmanuel bought the stallion and one day he rode up the hill on it and gave me a piece of paper, saying that it had a rare English Christmas song on it, and perhaps I would be interested in collecting it? It was very long because it increases by one line at a time for each stanza, and it is called 'The Twelve Days Of Christmas'. I give the last verse here:

'On the twelfth day of Christmas my truelove sent to me twelve twats a-twitching, eleven leaping lesbians, ten torn-off testicles, nine gnawed-off nipples, eight aching arseholes, seven convicted vicars, five choirboys. Four fornicators, three French whores, two shithouse doors, and my Lord Montagu of Beaulieu.'

Don Emmanuel sang it to me most tenderly in a fine baritone, and I confess I was extremely moved, saying, 'You should have sung it to the British Ambassador when he was here.' I do not understand the words because of the poverty of my English, but I have sent it to my agent in Mexico along with a transcription of the melody, with the hope that it might be incorporated in a forthcoming anthology of international traditional songs whose profits will go to UNICEF. Don Emmanuel is sometimes a most embarrassing man, but this time he has come up with something very marvellous. He has had another falling-out with Felicidad, and the town has been talking of nothing else. I wish they could conduct their affairs as blissfully as Capitan Papagato and Francesca; she has fallen pregnant again and is already beginning to waddle rather than walk. Everyone is surprised because she was still breastfeeding the first. I understand that their jaguars are having more kittens. Soon we will be overrun. I have had to reinforce the roof of my house because Lena says that the weight of the cats sunbathing at noon will otherwise cause it one day to collapse.

I was putting the finishing touches to the new beams and humming a tune that Dionisio taught me when General Fuerte arrived and kissed the hands of Ena and Lena like a true old-fashioned gentleman. Then he came to me and said, 'We might need your help,' and I said, 'Why? Has the three-hundred-year-old man come back and assaulted someone? Has the Conde finally split someone's nose? Has Felicidad broken a plate over Don Emmanuel's head? Has someone eaten a Pollo de un Hombre Verdadero at Dolores' restaurant?' And the General said, 'No, guess again.'

'Has Hectoro taken a fourth wife? Has the machine broken down? Are we fetching more tractors?'

And the General said, 'You are on the right track, cabrón. We are going to build a wall across the valley in front of the city.'

'What?' I cried. 'More labours?'

I was aghast because apart from helping to fetch the tractors I had helped Dionisio and Profesor Luis to build the great map of the world in the marsh, and I had had enough of breaking my bones and tearing my hands. I was even more perturbed when I discovered the reasons for the wall, and I ran down to the plaza, unable to believe my ears.

'Why should we build a wall because we have been told to do so by the purported ghost of Aurelio's adopted daughter?' I asked, and all I heard in reply was nonsense. Sergio said, 'It is because this time the gods will be unable to help us,' and I exclaimed, 'What do you mean by "this time"?' Misael told me, 'It is because circumstances have confused the saints.' Remedios said, 'We need fortifications,' and I demanded, 'Why? Are we to expect an invasion?' And Dolores the whore observed, 'Let the invaders be rich and horny, and I am content.'

Against this farrago of nonsense I was unable to make myself heard, what with Don Salvador the False Priest quoting obscenities in Latin and the Conde waving his sword about and declaring that he would bathe the invaders in rivers of blood, and Father Garcia solemnly explaining that the Archangel Sandalphon was deeply concerned for our safety. Don Emmanuel said, 'It will not do any harm to keep us all busy; one's hands should always be occupied,' and Felicidad spat on the ground and said, 'It is how your hands are occupied that grieves me.'

So we built the wall. I was glad for once of the conquistadors brought back to life by Aurelio. Normally they swagger about in their rusty armour, drinking to excess, tripping over the recumbent jaguars and causing distress to the women with their persistent oaths and molestations, and on top of that they have the vacant expressions of cretins and they dribble. Aurelio says that it is on account of their long freezing over the centuries and that we should be patient with them, but I have no tolerance any more. Except that now that we were occupied upon a military project that was comprehensible to them, they worked like slaves.

We brought enormous quantities of cement and sand from Ipa-sueño, which Doña Constanza paid for, and I lost count of the number of times we went backwards and forwards to Ipasueño with recuas of mules. I lost all the weight that I had put on since I had been cared for by Ena and Lena. We built up a wall three metres high and two metres deep that stretched right across the valley, with a gatehouse at the centre for ingress and exit, and a low arch to permit the flow of the river. We had problems at the ends because an invader could just have scrambled up the slopes and circumvented our battlements, and so we build it up along the mountainsides until it was so difficult to build any further that we reckoned that, if we could not go any higher, neither could anyone else climb round it.

Just when I believed that our months of toil were finished and I was thinking that there would be a great fiesta to celebrate, it was made known that the Conde had declared that in his long experience such a wall was useless without a moat, because one could bring ladders and grappling irons up to it. So the work began all over again, and we dug a moat in the silt and piled the spoil up against the wall so that the stone would be protected from missiles. Profesor Luis calculated the contours of the canal and it filled to perfection from the river just as soon as we lifted the wooden gates. Doña Constanza declared that she now understood that the canal to her swimming pool would have worked perfectly well if the work had been properly done. It appears that she has never been explicitly told that her pet project was sabotaged deliberately. To everyone else this is common knowledge and a reliable source of laughter.

'Fiesta time,' I thought, and was thinking up plans for a concert by the town band. I wrote a marinera and a jarabe in my head and was wondering who I could ask to make up a joropo dancing party, when Aurelio announced to all and sundry that he wished to conduct an experiment.

Aurelio is an Aymara, and for centuries his people were under the tutelage of the Incas. To this day every Aymara speaks some Quechua, the language imposed by the emperors. Aurelio said that he wished to see if it was possible to build walls in the ancient style, with polygonal blocks fitting so perfectly that one could insert not even a knife between them. He observed that it could do no harm to build the wall even higher. Hectoro proposed dismantling the temple of Viracocha and reutilising the blocks on the wall, but the man is a philistine even though he pretends to read so much. His book is always held upside down, and he moves his lips.

To my amazement there was general consent to this idea; Dionisio told me that all of them owed their very existence to Aurelio, and were willing to please him. It seemed that he wanted us to gather in the plaza by the axle-pole, and on the appointed evening we trooped down there, even Ena and Lena, who were reconciled with me by that time because I had apologised.

There were four great fires built, and Aurelio appeared dressed all in white, the colours of a witch amongst his people. He spoke to us, saying, 'In the days of my ancestors one made walls like this; firstly one poured a fluid over a rock to make it soft like clay, and one put it into place and fashioned it. Then one poured over it another liquid and it was made back into stone, and this is the cause that Inca walls are as they are. There is nothing I want you to do tonight except to stay here, for your presence alone will help whilst I bargain with the ancestors for the recipes.'

Having said that, he walked straight through one of the fires. A gasp came up out of the people because all of us thought that he would be burned. But he came out unscathed and walked straight through the fire opposite. We gasped again, but once more he came through untouched. He mumbled loudly the whole time, and he continued walking through the four fires, one after the other, until the miracle became veritably tedious. I amused myself by looking at the paintmarks on the moon.

Eventually he came for the last time out of the flames with his clothes covered in soot and the soles of his feet apparently smouldering. He coughed, and said, 'Thank you, that is all.'

With a strong sense of anticlimax we all went home, for it seemed as though nothing was to happen. But a week later Aurelio came back from the jungle with four mules laden with sacks, and he appropriated Dolores' cauldron that she uses normally to make guarapol at candombles. I do not know what grisly objects went into the concoction, because they all seemed shrivelled and without identity, but I went down to watch him once and saw him swig a mouthful of rum. He spat it over the brew and it caught fire most spectacularly. He also blew a great deal of cigar-smoke over it and pounded his coca-gourd relentlessly with that hypnotically rapid and deft delving of the pestle.

I was not there when he poured some of the fluid over a rock and made it plastic, but the General came up the hill and informed me of it breathlessly. I thought, 'O no, the work begins all over again,' and I was right.

The most immense boulders were levered off the mountainside and gathered from the plateau to be brought up in the lift. We had to construct a crane to raise the boulders up onto the wall, because we could not do it the traditional way, by making an earthen ramp, since the moat was in the way on one side, and there were houses on the other. Aurelio poured fluid over the rocks and we beat them into shape with shovels, and then he hardened them with another fluid. He was so pleased that even I, having worked my fingers to shreds and my muscles to leather, was glad to see him dancing in little circles with his hands in the air. Normally he is dignity itself.

And what do we have to show for it? A colossal defence made by request of a ghost to defend us against an implausible invasion that cannot happen in the modern world. But there were some good consequences. It blocks the wind that funnels down the valley, and one's clothes do not disappear any more from the washing line, and sail out over the plateau; all the rocks were gathered from the mountainsides, reducing the chances of avalanche, and from the plateau and the andenes, facilitating agriculture; it is good to stand on the top and watch the sunset; there are good fish in the moat and some very edible waterfowl; it proved definitively the usefulness of the tractors; and we had a formidable fiesta, after which Antoine and Françoise congratulated me upon the euphony of my two new compositions, and the town awarded me the Supremely Elevated Order Of The Apparatus for services to architecture and musical education. I was as drunk as a German, and I trust that my speech of acceptance was as witty and apposite as I think I remember it to have been. Ena and Lena giggle every time I mention it.

Josef died because a pregnant woman looked at him when he had been bitten by a snake. It was not Francesca's fault that she looked at him, because she had no way of knowing that they were bringing him up from the plateau in the great lift just as she was passing by to see whether or not she had caught any shrimps in the wicker basket. Nobody blamed Francesca, therefore, but for quite a while she felt deeply guilty.

Josef had been extremely unlucky as he swung his machete in the banana plantation. Normally a snake would have made itself scarce, but this one lay low until the machete gashed its flank, and, as if by reflex, it sank its fangs into Josef's foot and injected all its venom. Snakes are habitually parsimonious with their poison; they parcel it out carefully, innoculating their victims with just the right amount to paralyse them and begin the internal process of predigestion. Animals that they intend merely to scare away do not normally receive much poison at all, or just enough to make them more careful in the future. If snakes were humans they would be the kind of people who save up small coins and put them into investment accounts, eat chocolates only after lunch on Sundays, believe in swift corporal punishment to deter criminals, are sceptical about the value of social services, and give pocket handkerchiefs for Christmas presents. But Josef's snake was in a state of such rage and pain that it vengefully administered a legful of lethal anaesthetic, crawled away to die an embittered death, and was gratefully consumed by ants.

Josef turned very pale, so that his open black face became grey, and he sat down on the grass to await with mounting trepidation the traditional remedy. Sergio and Pedro the Hunter tossed a coin, and Pedro lost. He wanted to toss again, but Josef said, 'Come on, cabrón, I forgive you in advance. Let us just finish it.'

Pedro took his machete from its sheath and tested the edge for sharpness. A thin cut appeared in his thumb, and he knew that it was well-honed enough. Pedro was old, but very tall and lithe, and it gave Josef confidence to think that such a strong hunter, dressed in animal skins, a man skilled in blood, would be doing the job with well-practised hands.

'Close your eyes, amigo,' said Pedro, and Josef shut them so tight that he felt that they would pop backwards into his head.

Some say that bone-pain is the worst pain that can be experienced, and others say that it is childbirth or the pain of a heart that stops suddenly. To Josef the slice of the blade seemed to crash into him like a hurtling boulder or a bullet. He threw his head back with a jerk, and a scream that never emerged from his mouth filled his skull and then exploded into the rest of his body. Whilst he was submerged beneath this avalanche, too shaken to think or to feel, Pedro raised the machete high above his head and, with absolute accuracy, completed the amputation with a second blow.

Josef felt his stomach dissolve, looked at his hands to see them shaking like leaves in the wind, fought against his nausea, and vomited. He had never previously known that one could not only experience agony, but become it. Sergio quickly bound the stump tightly in a tourniquet twisted out of the sleeve of his shirt, and Pedro urinated into the bottom of his mochila in order to place it over the wound and, according to the old wisdom, keep it from infection.

Josef fainted ('It was from the heat, and not from the pain,' he explained later), and Pedro hauled him over his shoulders as if he were a slain brocket. He ran towards the lift, with Sergio running in pursuit, mopping his brow with the remains of his shirt and succumbing to a kind of sympathetic post-operative shock. Near the top of the cliff Francesca leaned over to admire the view, and inadvertently caused Josef to die. The latter opened his eyes to see a pregnant woman looking at him, and knew that it was all over.

In the city there was panic. Aurelio was nowhere to be found, since both of his apparent selves were combined into one self for the purpose of bargaining with the gods over the matter of Federico's disappearance, and Dionisio Vivo, who had the reputation of being able to deal with anything as long as it was spectacular, was in Santa Maria Virgen, making love to the two sisters who tended to the needs of his car.

Josef was brought to the whorehouse, since he wished to die in the same place as had given him the greatest happiness in life. His whole body was visibly swelling, and a great fever was breaking out on his brow. Remedios came in and said to Pedro, 'You will have to cure him; with Aurelio absent, you are the nearest we have to a snake-doctor.'

Pedro shook his head sadly and looked down into Remedios' incalculably brown eyes. 'I know only the secretos for animals. If Josef were an animal, it would be different.'

'Try the one for a horse,' suggested Dolores the whore in her smoky voice, 'the man is almost a stallion.'

Pedro knelt down and muttered into Josef's ear, but then he stood up and said, 'No spirits left me.'

'Try the one for a pig,' said Fulgencia Astiz, the leader of the fanatical women who had made a cult out of bearing the children of Dionisio Vivo, 'I hear that humans taste of pork.'

'I spoke once to a member of the tribe that ate the first bishop of Retreta, and he said that the word of his fathers was that the bishop tasted of veal,' offered Misael.

'Bishops taste different, everyone knows that. It is on account of their rich diet,' said Leticia Aragon, whose eyes were violet on this day.

'Forget it,' moaned Josef, 'just call Father Garcia. I am going to die because I saw Francesca looking at me.'

Outside the door came a wail of repentance and regret, since Francesca was out there, not wishing to compound his affliction by coming in and looking at him again.

Father Garcia entered in a hurry, fully armed with Holy Water, rum to serve as communion wine, and empanadas to supply the place of Holy Wafers. With him was Don Salvador, the False Priest, who bore his new parallel text of Catullus that Dionisio had found for him in the capital on one of his trips to see the editor of *La Prensa*.

'Everybody must leave,' announced Father Garcia, 'I am going to hear his confession.'

'I will confess in public,' said Josef, 'since I am not ashamed of my sins.'

'If you are not ashamed, then God will not pardon you and you will go to hell,' remonstrated Father Garcia.

'You misjudge God,' returned Josef. 'Before I sin I always go down on my knees and ask God how much He minds, and He has never prevented me.'

Father Garcia's lugubrious face lightened with a smile, and he said, 'Let us begin the confession.'

'I once fucked the niece of the policeman in Chiriguana after she had been sold to Pedro the grocer, and she was only twelve years old but she fucked like a rabbit, so I did it many more times. I threw a bottle of Anis Ocho Hermanos over Hectoro during the battle of *Doña Barbara*, which was a sinful waste of money and good liquor, and it stung his eyes. I once gave a spoonful of rum to a crying baby to make it shut up, and it nearly died. I stole a reel of barbed wire from the hacienda of Don Hugh of Chiriguana when we still lived down on the plain. I took an unbranded calf from Don Emmanuel and raised it as my own. I spent so much time thinking about dying that sometimes I forgot to live, and when I was very young I masturbated myself every day for three years until a woman took pity on me and made me into a man. Apart from that I have done only one or two bad things every day.'

Father Garcia absolved him and administered the last rites amid an increasingly oppressive atmosphere of piety and impending doom, and Don Salvador solemnly intoned the whole of Catullus' poem about the death of his Lesbia's sparrow.

Ten hours later Josef's fever was causing him periods of delirium, and his body was formidably bloated. He awoke from his dreams and beckoned urgently to Father Garcia, who leaned down to catch his words: 'In Chiriguana I paid Don Ramón the cura, for a proper burial in a coffin and three masses. Will you do it even though I have not paid any money to you?'

'I will do it on behalf of the Church,' said Father Garcia gravely, 'which has already received the money.'

Josef beckoned again and once more Father Garcia leaned down: 'Will I be able to fuck in heaven as much as I want? Because otherwise I wish you to arrange for me to go somewhere else.'

'A priest has limited powers of negotiation,' observed Garcia, 'but it is my opinion that if one could not fuck in heaven, then it would not be heaven, which is a contradiction in terms and therefore impossible. It would be a metaphysical oxymoron. That is something I learned from you, as it was always your opinion.'

Josef looked gratified, and then murmured, 'I have a last wish. I want to be buried with the rest of my leg, and I want to die drunk.'

Josef expired at midnight, deeply comatose from the rum, a puro cigar still smouldering between his fingers. Out of love and respect the people left him in the middle of the floor whilst they drank and whored, and others came in and out bringing burial presents. Dolores brought a bowl of Pollo de un Hombre Verdadero as tribute to his virility, Felicidad came in with tears in her eyes, leaving him the black sequinned stockings that used to make him drool and arouse him to ribaldry, Sergio brought him a decorated gourd from which to drink firewater in paradise, Hectoro brought him four pitillos crammed with the best marijuana, and Doña Constanza brought him her ancient copy of *Vogue* with the tantalising pictures of semi-naked white women in impractical clothing. Tomás brought him coca leaves to chew in case there were mountains to climb in heaven, Gloria brought him four bullets to commemorate his role in driving the Army away from the old village, and Pedro brought in a stillborn puppy from one of his hunting dogs, to help him in the celestial chase.

They buried Josef deep beneath the floor of the whorehouse so that he could listen to the familiar tumult and have copas of aguardiente poured over his resting place at moments of sentimentality and nostalgia. The burial was somewhat delayed by the absence of his lower limb, which Pedro and Sergio had left on the plateau in the urgent rush to bring him back up to the town. This severed item had been carried off by an opportunistic puma, and all that turned up in Leticia Aragon's hammock was the foot that the puma had detached to give to her cubs. It was intact but covered with the tiny pinpricks of their teeth. Eventually the eloquent and squint-eyed policeman whose niece Josef had pleasured had the idea of fashioning a wooden part to complete the corpse's anatomy, and thus Josef was consigned to the soil with all his presents, fully equipped for a riotous and fulfilling afterlife.

Josef's unjustly premature taking off had the consequences that from then on people who visited the plateau always smoked cigars with great vehemence, since snakes hate tobacco, and on their feet they rubbed a concoction of snakeroot, garlic, and sweet oil, which snakes find deeply offensive. The one was for protection, the other for revenge

On the night of Josef's death Aurelio called in on Francesca and found her weeping in the arms of Capitan Papagato, her husband. He closed the door softly behind him, and said, 'I have come to give you some news. When your child is born, you must not call him Josef, as you have been thinking. You must call him Federico, after your brother, the husband of my daughter Parlanchina.' He answered their questioning gaze with the remark, 'Some things are fate, because of the gods.'

He went out into the night and walked up the street. He stopped briefly by the axle-pole in the plaza and looked up at the stars. When he came into the sierra from the arboreal canopy of the jungle he was always startled into admiration by the immensity of the sky. He sat down and thought about how Parlanchina too had begun to fade away. These days she merely stood still by the path in the jungle, her beautiful long hair washing about her waist, her soft eyes empty and dreaming. He had seen that her child was fading also, and her capricious pet ocelot was curled at her feet, its vibrant spots and rosettes phasing in and out of focus.

Aurelio walked on to the door of Leticia Aragon, and knocked lightly. She appeared shortly, as naked as the snow, as if she had known that there was someone there who would not be astonished. Aurelio studied her beauty; her eyes were now sea-green, and her fine black hair fell upon her shoulders like a familiar caress. He suddenly wondered whether she had always been Parlanchina's mother, and was utterly smitten by a sense of the ineffable. Leticia smiled remotely and told him: 'I know that I am pregnant again.'

'It will be the first female child of Dionisio who will not be called Anica,' he said.

She nodded and invited him in, saying, 'It will help to free him.'

'And another thing,' added Aurelio. 'The girl will be born with a child in her womb, and this child will be born on a day before your daughter has ever known a man. But the father is Francesca's baby who has yet to be born, who will be called Federico. Do you understand?'

Leticia nodded. 'Oshun came to me in a dream as Nuestra Señora de la Caridad del Cobre. I will do as she said, and call the child Parlanchina.'

## 55 *Sibila Retrieves Her Fallen Crown And Dons Her Robe Of Light*

'O San Nicolas, who raised from the dead three children who had been pickled in a salting tub, O San Quentin, who spared a thief by causing the hangman's rope to break, O Santa Rita, who four times performed the impossible, O San Cosmas and San Damian, who could be harmed neither by fire, air, water, nor by the cross, intervene with Our Lady and Our Lord, that she may be spared. Amen. And God forgive me.'

This was the prayer that I prayed many times in my house during that night when I could not sleep for my pain, for my terror, and for my betrayal of Sibila. I am not religious by nature, and my words were as empty in my soul as they were unheard by God, but I prayed because there was no other recourse. I knew all the time that it was an illusion to pray, but it passed the night as I huddled sleepless in my room that had been emptied even of the bed. I had seen a vision of Hell, such as each generation sees it. My parents saw just these things during La Violencia, and their parents saw just these things during the civil war. It was the same play with new actors, and I asked the same question as my parents: 'What is wrong with us that we shit on paradise?'

I did not go near the church in the next few days because I knew that Sibila was there. I stayed in my house waiting for her to confess, be released, and come to see me. I practised the words that I would use to ask her to forgive me. I said them aloud, trying out the different ways, and I had nothing to eat, because they had taken even my food. But there was no knock upon the door. There was nothing except the silence of the afflicted, the squabbles of the vultures, the coarse jokes of the bodyguard, drunk in the street, the interminable chant of the priests in the plaza. There was nothing except the pain, which was like a hurricane roaring in my spirit.

Then after the days had passed there was the sound of chanting passing my house, and the priests went by, bearing candles and the green cross. I was already educated enough in their ways to know that tomorrow there would be another auto de fe, and my heart jumped in my breast as I understood that very probably it would be the occasion when I would know what was to happen to Sibila.

That night I prayed my prayer again until I had said it so often that I thought, 'Maybe I will weary the saints with my prayers, and they will concede to me what I ask,' and I slept. I had a dream in which Sibila and I were lovers. It was a cruel dream, because when I awoke I was happy.

At the auto de fe all the surviving children of the village were brought out. They made the children swear to attend confession at Easter, Christmas, and Pentecost, and to remain orthodox of belief. It was pitiful to see the chidren, streaked with dirt, the tracks of tears upon their faces, bruised, hungry, and orphaned. The Monsignor was in purple again, and there was a great censer burning in order to drown the stench of death.

When the children were led away, a tractor arrived with a trailer behind it. It was Patarino's tractor, and the trailer was piled high with bodies. They were not those of the newly dead. They were old and shrivelled, falling apart, with yellow bones and blackened skin. There was soil upon them, there were pieces of coffin plank, tufted pieces of scalp, hanks of brittle hair. Something connected in my mind, and I realised that they had dug up all the people that I had named as dead santeros, and perhaps many more besides. I could not help but look; there is something about the grotesquerie of death that fascinates. It was hard to make the connection between those carica- tures of humans, and the friends and relatives that they used to be. I actually felt a kind of satisfaction that my own parents had died during La Violencia and had been left to rot on the hillsides. Who knows if it was the Conservatives or the Liberals who killed them? But at least I knew that they were not exhumed and thrown into this tangle of cadavers.

The Monsignor and his priests withdrew into the church, and I watched as the bodyguard dug a deep hole in the ground and set a post into it. They piled it about with brushwood and faggots, and they began to throw the bodies onto the heap, limb by limb. They made jokes, such as, 'Ay, cabrón, how about this one for a dry fuck?' and, 'Ay, this one has no teeth. She was good for a blowjob, eh?' They put one of their number on the lookout for the priests, and they pulled all the gold teeth from the jawbones with pliers. They broke off the fingers to get at the rings. It made a desiccated sound, like the snapping of twigs, but you could see from the twisting and pulling that it was hard to break the tendons. Over the heap of bones they poured gasoline, and I knew for sure that they intended to burn heretics retrospectively, as if the dead had not already passed to judgement.

I had almost forgotten Sibila by this time. But then she was led out of the church behind El Inocente.

Perhaps I should explain that the priests themselves would not torture the prisoners or carry out sentences, and everything of a brutal nature was carried out by the bodyguard.

How can I speak of this? Did I tell you that the bodyguard were divided into clubs, and each club had its own methods? It seems that the ones who questioned Sibila were the Agatistas. That is to say that they recapitulated the sufferings of St Agatha. To me it is a blasphemy to do this, but I heard it justified. They said that to be a heretic was to insult the saints who had suffered for the true faith, and they inflicted the torment now upon those who truly deserved them, as an expiation. To me, this is a pretext.

Sibila was dressed in a black sanbenito painted gaudily with demons and flames, but it was soaked in blood. She could barely walk, and she was brought out leaning upon two of the bodyguard. Her eyes were half closed, her head lolled upon her chest, and with her arms around the shoulders of those two ruffians, her attitude reminded me perhaps of the deposition from the cross, and also of a Corpus Christi. Her hair fell forward about her face in the way that it used to do when she was concentrating on a book or making coffee, and I saw that blood was running down her legs to her ankles, forming dark pools in the dust of the street. She was all but dead. Believe me, my heart was bursting, but still I had no strength.

El Inocente stood before the table and gestured for silence. He preached a long sermon, of which I cannot recall a single word, but I can tell you that it was full of vileness, decorated and embellished to the point where one might almost believe that it was a noble speech. He read out a long list of those whose corpses were to be burned, and whose property was to be confiscated from their inheritors, so that there was no one in the village left with any possessions.

321

Then the Monsignor gestured to the bodyguard that Sibila should be taken, and I realised that they intended to burn her along with the corpses. They dragged her, trailing her feet, and there was a stream of blood behind her where she went. Do you know what happened to St Agatha? Her breasts were torn off with shears, she was rolled on broken shards, then on burning coals, and she died before they could burn her. But Sibila was alive, and she had suffered all those things. I began to weep, but my eyes were open; I was watching the consequences of my cowardice and treachery, and the consequence was that I was going to lose the one I loved in all the world.

The Monsignor went up to her as she stood bound amid the corpses and the stench of gasoline, and he said to her, 'Do you abjure? If you abjure you will be mercifully strangled before you are burned. What faith do you embrace?'

Sibila raised her head, and for a second I was relieved that she had not died, because that is what I had been beginning to think. She said in a voice that was feeble but very clear, 'I believe that the world was made by the Devil. I believe that when I am released I shall wear a robe of light and see the face of God. I believe that I was an angel.' She looked him in the face and continued, 'I believe that you were an angel.'

There was a peculiar emphasis in the way that she spoke the word 'were', an emphasis that seemed to imply that the legate was a soul lost forever. I know that he understood her because he was taken aback and did not know what to say. It was as though he had suddenly seen his own conscience in a mirror, and there was a long pause. Then he turned his back and walked away.

The men were lighting their torches when Sibila looked up for the last time, and she saw me. Her look struck me to the heart. It was not that she accused me with her eyes. It was that she saw my helpless tears, and pitied me. Sibila was feeling sorry for me, the one who least deserved her pity. I fell to my knees and clasped my hands so that she would know that I was begging to be forgiven, and she smiled as gently as if she had seen a child. It was a smile full of love, a smile with nostalgia in it, as though she were remembering me. She shook her head from side to side, as a parent reproves a mild misdemeanour, and I knew that she was saying to me, 'Why did you underestimate me by thinking that I would pretend to confess? Did you think that I would not stand up for the truth?'

Do you think that I am a shallow man, that I should be telling you of my feelings when it was Sibila who endured so much? I felt a rending shame that for so long I had pretended to her that I believed in her ideas. I had loved her, but I had deceived her. Do you think that she knew all the time? Do you think that she forgave me? Do you think it is possible that she was happy to die because she foresaw a better life, that she confessed on purpose so that she could die? Was I the instrument of her torment, or was she thanking me for being the means of her release? Can anyone sincerely wish to relinquish life?

I know that I loved life, cripple though I am, and I know that I loved it simply because she was a part of it. An insanity overtook me, and I threw myself forward. I do not know what I intended to do, but I think I meant to do two contradictory things at once. I wanted to release her, to fight to the last moment, because suddenly all my courage returned. And because my courage had returned, I wanted to die beside her. It seemed to be all I had ever wanted, a consummation, as the poet said.

I ran forward, but I am a cripple, and one of the bodyguard warded me off with a rifle, so that I fell down, and at that point they threw the torches on the pyre, and the priests sang the Veni Creator.

When the crusaders left, having torched my village of Quintalinas de las Viñas, one of them threw something down to me. He said, 'Hey, cripple, have a memento of your girlfriend.' I looked at it and knew what it was, because the crusaders had the habit of removing the private parts of women and stretching them over their pommels as trophies. I took it and put it on the cinders with the rest of Sibila, and I followed the crusaders at a distance, which was easy because they were moving at the speed of the carts that were laden with our possessions. Do you know what I did? In the night I cut the throat of the crusader who had done that foul thing to Sibila.

They are planning to come to Cochadebajo de los Gatos, Señor Vivo; I often heard them talking about it. They were working their way across the countryside, keeping from the towns for the sake of self-preservation. Señor Vivo, you must help our poor people, because you killed El Jerarca and everywhere you are known as the Deliverer. Have pity on the people as Sibila pitied me.

(a)

My Dear Son,

I am writing this in a terrible hurry at the aerodrome in Valledupar. There is no telephone service to Cochadebajo de los Gatos, and I have no idea how long this letter will take to reach you, and I am in despair at being so much isolated from you under these terrible circumstances.

I have to tell you that your father has been the victim of another assassination attempt. He was picking mangos in the orchard when someone put two bullets in his body from close range. I do not know if it was the Communists or the Conservatives, or the Liberals, or a faction in the Army, or someone from the Navy or the Air Force, or if it was someone from the coca cartels.

The General came into the house and fell at my feet, and we are taking him in a military transport to a hospital in Miami where he stands a better chance than in our own hospitals, where the surgeons are qualified only in carving joints of meat and prescribing lethal doses of poison for cases of mistaken diagnosis.

He is in good spirits and is more worried about who will assume temporary command of the General Staff than he is about himself. La Prima Primavera is coming to look after the house and the wounded animals. I will let you know as soon as we return from Miami, and in the meantime, pray for us both.

Your loving Mama Julia.

(b)

Dear Minister,

I am writing to let you know that I have heard eyewitness accounts of untold savageries committed by a band of religious fanatics who are terrorising the countryside on an arc that extends from the capital towards the mountainous regions of Cesar. It appears that they intend to finish their 'crusade' in this town of Cochadebajo de los Gatos from which I write.

It is imperative that immediate action be taken either by the police or the Armed Forces to end this terrorism, or else I foresee the possibility of yet another civil war inspired by religious intolerance. We in Cochadebajo de los Gatos have already made our preparations, but legal intervention by the state would be gratefully welcomed by us before I am obliged to resort to an exposé of governmental inaction in the pages of *La Prensa*.

Yours With Respect, Dionisio Vivo.

Copies to: The Ministry of Defence
The Ministry of the Interior

(c)

Dear Señor Vivo,

We thank you for your letter concerning disturbances of a religious nature in the countryside. We have been aware for some time of rumours about this, but have been unable to substantiate them. Several villages have been discovered to be razed and entirely depopulated, and so we have been unable to discover whether this was due to wars between local caudillos, the Communists, or the coca cartels.

You will be aware that we cannot initiate military actions without a Presidential directive. His Excellency is at present embarked upon a diplomatic mission abroad, and so we are without legal recourse at present. You, above all others, will be aware that your own father, who is Chief of the General Staff, is in hospital in Miami, and we are doubly incapacitated from a military point of view, especially as we already have heavy commitments in Medio-Magdalena.

We have decided that the only legal action possible is to send a detachment of the Portachuelo Guards on a 'live firing exercise' in that region. The commander of this 'exercise' will be confidentially briefed that he has the legal right of intervention, under the constitution, when this is requested by a local police commander in the interests of public safety. Accordingly we have appointed a 'local police commander' to accompany the exercise. The exercise will follow an itinerary from the capital to Cochadebajo de los Gatos. This is a vast tract of land, almost unknown to cartography, including swamps and forests, with only the most basic means of communication, and you will understand that from a military point of view the expedition is almost an impossibility.

I am afraid that this is the best that can be done within the legal framework that has been established between the Armed Forces and the executive for the protection of the democratic process. You will perceive for yourself that democracy is not always an unmitigated blessing when a strong hand is required.

You will be interested to know that, according to the office of Cardinal Dominic Trujillo Guzman, who is also in hospital, it is true that a 'crusade of preaching' has been authorised, but the office disclaims any knowledge of a crusade of medieval dimension and enthusiasm.

I wish your father, General Hernando Montes Sosa, a speedy and complete recovery from his wounds, and I trust that you will agree that we have done our best to deal with the matter that you have raised with us. I cannot emphasise too much that we are completely handicapped by the absence of His Excellency, President Veracruz, and many of us will no doubt be influenced by this during the next general election, which is at a regrettably distant date.

Please treat this communication as confidential, and, upon a personal note, may I say how much I have enjoyed listening to your musical palindromes on the radio? I have often speculated as to whether it would be possible to adapt one from Bach's Prelude No. 1 in C from *The Well-Tempered Clavier*.

I remain your humble and respectful servant,

Alfonsina Lopez,
For and on behalf of the Armed Forces and Civil Police Coordinating Committee.

(d)

My Dear Papa,

I have been desolated to hear from Mama that your worst fears have come true, and that at last one of the innumerable attempts upon your life has borne a bitter fruit.

I think that you should be reminded that you are the first Chief of the General Staff in the entire history of this country who has not been either a Fascist or a glorified caudillo, and therefore you have an absolute obligation to get well in a time so short as to be unprecedented in medical history.

The man who bears this letter will be of great help to you. Please treat him with absolute respect and hospitality, do not question anything that he tells you, submit to his treatments, however bizarre. I say this as a devoted son who in his time has had to obey many a paternal directive, and who on this occasion demands that the line of command be reversed for once. If you do as I say, I promise that I will keep my hair short for a year, and wear a suit whenever I am seen with you in public for the rest of my life.

Please extend my greetings to the British Ambassador when you see him, and tell him that his consignment of wellington boots continues to be much appreciated.

Your loving son,

Dionisio.


(e)

My Dear Son,

I write to you from my headquarters, sound in both body and mind, but infinitely perplexed.

In the first place, I understand from Alfonsina Lopez, the formidable lady who chairs the co-ordinating committee of the Armed Forces and the police, that you have seen fit to meddle in governmental business without the intervening neccessity of being elected and appointed to office. If you had not become the unofficial conscience of the nation through your splendid letters and articles in *La Prensa*, I would consider your letter to the Defence and Interior

Ministers to be blackmail. However, I am very glad that an 'exercise' has been inaugurated, and it is exactly what I would have done, given the absence of His Excellency. The capital is rife with talk of a coup, so great is the general disgust in governmental and military circles, but I am doing my best to circulate the idea of impeachment in order to reduce that very undesirable prospect.

Would you like to hear a story from your Papa, as in the old days? Good. Once upon a time there was a wounded general who had just returned from Miami, where he had been treated for gunshot wounds. He had been told to go home and convalesce, and was doing just that, sitting half asleep in a rocking chair beneath the beneficent shade of the bougainvillaea that grows exuberantly about the pillars and beams of the peripateticon, when there was an immense flutter of wings, a screech, and the scrape of talons clenching the joists overhead.

I looked up suddenly, hurting my wounds in the process, and thought that I saw a vast bird of prey sitting above my head, settling its wings into a comfortable position. But when I looked harder I saw a small Indian man in native dress sitting there instead. I do not know which sight would rightly be considered by an intelligent man to be more strange. My first thought was that it was another assassination attempt, and my second was that security about the house was still too lax.

The first hypothesis was confuted when the aforesaid Indian took a coca gourd from his mochila and began to prod and scrape inside it with a pestle, which he proceeded to suck with the air of a satisfied man. He caught my eye, and casually handed down a letter which, upon perusal, was revealed to be from my own unfathomable son. I read it with my eyebrows virtually at the back of my head, and with true Latin hospitality I invited the Indian down from his perch.

Adeptly he joined me at ground level, introduced himself as, 'Aurelio, husband of Carmen, father of Parlanchina, and true friend of Dionisio, arriving to perform a cure.'

I have never had to take orders from an Aymara before, but if the rest of his people are like him, then I am very surprised that they lost to the Inca and then to the Iberians. He may be a small old man with a wizened face and fascinatingly sparse facial hair, but he has the natural authority of a General Bolivar winning a battle whilst simultaneously in bed deflowering a virgin. Before I knew it he had me lying on the ground whilst he poked my stomach with his fingers and told me that I had been operated upon by ignorant butchers. He frowned and informed me that I still had a bullet inside me, and I told him that indeed a bullet was still in there because it was too close to the heart to render an operation upon it an acceptable risk. The Miami surgeons had told me that it had deflected upwards from a rib, and would present no great danger if left in place.

At that point Mama Julia came out, having seen me apparently prostrate beneath the hands of an apparent assassin. She ran up, ferociously brandishing a machete, and very shortly found herself tamely trotting away to fetch some rum and a cigar. I wish I had had the time to ask him how he managed to pacify her in such short order, because it has taken me over thirty years to achieve nothing of the kind.

Aurelio contemplated my stomach whilst blowing formidable clouds of tobacco smoke over it. He chanted in a low monotonous drone, swigged a mouthful of rum, and then blew it out suddenly in a very disconcerting jet of flame. Whilst I was still in a state of amazement at this trick, he abruptly dived at my stomach with his right hand, delved about in it up to his elbow, and then triumphantly produced a flattened and distorted piece of lead that looked exactly like a bullet that has been dug out of a sandbag.

I was turning this object over in my hand, when I heard the fluttering of wings once more and beheld no Indian where once an Indian had been. Instead there was a very impressive eagle arranging its feathers busily in the ceiba tree, whence it took off, circled high into the air, and disappeared in the direction of the cordillera. Your poor father looked down at his stomach and beheld his scars and stitches gone. Furthermore he later went for a medical examination and was bluntly informed that the evidence pointed ineluctably to the conclusion that he had never been shot. There was no bullet on the X-ray and there were no scars, so that I have had to send to Miami for photographs and medical certificates that prove that I am entitled to sick-pay, convalescent leave, and the medal for being wounded whilst on active service, of which I now have a growing collection.

Please thank your friend Aurelio for his remarkable treatment, and in future kindly bear in mind the psychological injury that can be done to an old man when his comfortable understanding of the metaphysical order of the universe is suddenly and violently shattered by small indigenous characters acting under the instruction of his own son.

Mama Julia sends her love and asks me to ask you what you would do to treat a porcupine that angrily launches fusillades of quills whenever approached, however tentatively.

Your loving Father,
General Hernando Montes Sosa, whose son apparently thinks that he can appoint himself to the rank of Field Marshal.

## 57 *In Which Felicidad's Gyrating Backside Provokes Hostilities*

Ines and Agapita arrived in Cochadebajo de los Gatos two days after the carrier pigeon that had been left with them by Pedro the Hunter. Footsore, dirty and exhausted, but overflowing with the righteous pride of a mission successfully prosecuted, they crossed the drawbridge over the moat, and went straight to the plaza, as by habit do all people who arrive in a town. They sat themselves down with their backs to the great axle-pole, emptied in gulps the last draughts of springwater from their gourds, and waited for Dionisio to pass by and notice them.

Everything had gone exactly according to plan. Dionisio had been right that the crusaders would avoid Ipasueño owing to the presence there of civil authorities, and would choose Santa Maria Virgen as the obvious place to 'evangelise' on the way to Cochadebajo de los Gatos. Accordingly the people of that pueblito had moved themselves and their possessions over the hill and into the neighbouring valley, leaving only the two girls to keep watch for the crusaders. When these latter arrived in Santa Maria Virgen, they found what seemed to be a ghost town, abandoned as mysteriously as the *Marie Celeste*. They also found numerous notices pinned up on the doors of the houses: 'No entry: purple fever, paludismo, and pneumonic plague' all carefully written by Felicidad in the flowing italic script practised by doctors, who are trained at college to believe that fine cursive handwriting lends credibility to their diagnoses and creates confidence in their prescriptions. Against the shed where Dionisio's ancient vehicle was tended, the girls had pinned a sign that said 'Quarantine Room', and at the first sound of the chanting priests they had crept over the hillside to inform the villagers before releasing the carrier pigeon and setting off in its wake for Cochadebajo de los Gatos.

The panic of the crusaders upon encountering a plague town which had apparently been evacuated did little credit to their faith. As though of one mind, they retreated in disorder and passed it by on the western side, thus ensuring that when they arrived in Cochade-bajo de los Gatos they would be utterly fatigued and unprovisioned.

On their first night outside Santa Maria Virgen, they found themselves the victim of an attack by the renegade spirits of the dead, who were in fact the villagers banging spoons on saucepans, whooping eerily, and rolling rocks down the mountainside onto the nests of bivouacs. On the second night, after a hard day's march from dawn to dusk in order to distance themselves from the mountain devils, they encamped upon a wide swath of grass that transformed itself miraculously into a freezing bog when it rained during the night.

'These are like old times,' said Hectoro, narrowing his eyes against the smoke of his puro as he peered out from behind the large boulder where he was concealed alongside Pedro the Hunter and Misael. Hectoro had dismounted reluctantly from his horse, and had tethered it farther round the mountain, but he still wore his creaking leather bombachos and his heavy-calibre revolver.

'These are indeed like old times,' replied Misael, who had blacked over his sparkling gold tooth in the interests of nocturnal camouflage, 'but it is a pity that on this occasion we have no snakes and alligators to put into their tents.'

'Aurelio's herbs will work just as well,' said Pedro, putting his hand into his mochila and scrunching the dried plants in his fist. 'I have seen before what happens when animals eat them.'

'We should just shoot them,' said Hectoro, 'and our troubles would be over.'

Pedro and Misael exchanged glances, mutually understanding that Hectoro had a carefully nurtured reputation for machismo to preserve. But he also had a sense of honour, and so, to deter him from rash action, Misael said, 'No, compadre, it is dishonourable to attack before one is attacked. And besides, a war is no good for anything unless there is some ingenuity in it. Otherwise what tale is there to tell afterwards? "We shot at them and they shot at us, and then we retreated and then we attacked." It amounts to nothing. It is better to be remembered for brains.' He tapped the side of his head to indicate intelligence, and winked.

'A man wishes to be remembered for his balls,' riposted Hectoro.

'It seems to me that the best plans require both,' observed Pedro, 'as tonight will prove.'

When night settled abruptly upon the encampment the three men were sound asleep beneath their saddle-blankets, with their sombreros tipped forward over their eyes, and only their ears awake for footsteps. Hectoro had mastered the ultimate masculine art of smoking whilst asleep, and a cigar smouldered between his lips at the corner of his mouth, its glow brightening at each gentle intake of breath. It would extinguish itself at a distance of exactly two centimetres from his lips at the point where the ash encountered the saliva that had soaked up from the tip. Hectoro believed that in this way he could ensure vigorous and satisfying dreams about heroic exploits, women, and the successful roping of steers.

Two hours before dawn the three men awoke at the same time, having agreed to do so beforehand, and took fortifying swigs from a bottle of Ron Caña in order to banish the impenetrable cold that could keep a man determinedly tucked up in his tent even when his bladder was weeping for relief. They pressed their sombreros down upon their heads, parcelled out Aurelio's jungle herbs, shook hands solemnly, embraced, and set off down the mountainside to their allocated corners of the encampment.

No one can say that their efforts were unrepaid. They watched with merriment as, in the morning, the crusaders attempted to control the horses and mules that had gratefully eaten the aromatic grasses from the outstretched palms of the three conspirators. The animals, enduring terrifying hallucinations about gigantic predators, kicked out and bit at any who approached. Mgr Anquilar's horse, mistaking him for a vulture with dubious intentions, threw him to the ground in an elegant arc that left him bruised and muttering blasphemies for which he would normally decree ten Hail Marys and two Our Fathers. Brother Valentino was taken for a large puma by a mule that tore the bridle from his hands and set off for the horizon. The army of holy warriors lost half of the mules that formed their recuas, and most of their horses, in the prodigious stampede that ensued from the animals' delusions of persecution, and were obliged to proceed to Cochadebajo de los Gatos carrying their supplies upon their own bowed backs.

Thus there augmented amongst the crusaders the suspicion that was never to leave them, that the divine favour was being progressively withdrawn, and only two factors kept them going. One was

Mgr Rechin Anquilar's insistence to the priests that the Lord was testing them and would judge them according to how well they met the test, and the other was the conviction amongst the soldiery that they would have to press forward to Cochadebajo de los Gatos, because if they turned back they would starve before they reached anywhere that could be pillaged. Never far from their minds were the prospects of the plenty of that city, with its beautiful and legendarily willing girls, and its pharaonic stores of food. Their own bedraggled and abused band of camp-followers they abandoned, leaving them behind to perish in the impossible cold of the night, the horizontal rain of the high places, and the perilous shale of the invious mountain passes.

Mgr Rechin Anquilar already hated the sierra. In the foothills he had looked down across a vast panorama of lushly vegetated hills and had received the impression of overwhelming femininity. The hills were like an abominable agglomeration of rounded breasts shamelessly naked to the suckling sky. Their fecundity and innocence reminded him of native women sunbathing upon a sandbank, unconscious or uncaring of their curves and mounds that made a man's hands twitch with the instinct to caress and to surrender. Higher yet there were gorges that he could not look upon without seeing that unfathomable wound between a woman's legs that made him shudder with disgust and fascination, and which at school he had learned from his peers would smell of fish, being full of intricate folds of slimy dark pink excrescences of fungal shape and texture. The vast and placid lakes set between the stony grey shores of the high valleys reminded him of those orders of contemplative nuns whose unbreakable stillness and serenity enraged his disputatious universe of words and expositions, and the vistas of wispy brown shrubs were unmistakably akin to the conformation of pubic hair. The sierra brought the Monsignor's deeply ingrained misogyny to a delirium of hatred as he cursed the mists that descended suddenly and, like a woman's reasoning, fogged the mind as much as the vision. All that intoxicated him was the conviction that here in the sierra he grappled daily with the wiles of demons. His sense of purpose clarified and grew until he was veritably a man who, like so many before him, would know no peace until he had drowned evil in its own blood.

When he arrived before those mighty ramparts of interlocking stone and found himself excluded by a drawbridge and a moat, he was the only one of the multitude who felt no sense of preordained defeat. He smacked his palm with his fist, jubilant at the thought of the last mighty battle with the legions of the dark, whilst his own legions, fractious, hungry, worn out and embittered, looked at one another and shook their heads with weariness.

There were no tables brought out, laden with food. There were no civil authorities declaring a fiesta, no gentle priest offering the use of the church, no pious widows kneeling to ask his blessing. There would be no impressive trials and executions, no women to violate and lacerate, no apocalyptic sermons, and no laying to waste and looting. There would be only the cold of the night and the long nothingness of day. A collective sigh of disappointment blew through their hearts, because before them lay only an impossibility, and behind them lay a retreat that would be nothing but a greater hardship.

As they stood before that monolithic wall they saw people begin to emerge from behind it and walk along the top, all of them women. They were Dolores and Consuelo, together with all the other whores of the town, who had arrived to do nothing other than to mock them in their misery. Dressed in their finest and richest clothes they paraded back and forth, swinging their hips and pulling ugly faces at them, as do schoolchildren. They stuck their middle fingers in the air in a graphic imitation of copulation, they thumbed their noses and protruded their tongues, and at the top of their lungs they yelled out obscene invitations and insults. 'Vamos, Commadres!' called Dolores, and all in a line they raised their skirts and displayed their unclothed nether parts to the infuriated and humiliated crusaders.

Suddenly there was a commotion as Felicidad joined her erstwhile sisters-in-arms. In front of them all she too paraded, caressing her own breasts lasciviously, licking her lips with her sly little tongue in a breathtaking display of what delights could be perpetrated by them. She stood sideways, flung back her long black hair, and pouted in a delicious caricature of the pose of models on the covers of men's magazines. She ran her hands up her legs, raising her hems to just that point where one yearns for more, and she blew sarcastic and contemptuous kisses with such salacious virtuosity that every man who watched her declared that they had shrunk back into their own souls as a snail seeks its carapace.

Felicidad turned her back on the warriors and priests, and it was as though, in the eclipse of her dark and vibrant beauty, the sun had left the heavens and the stars been extinguished. But she inched her skirts upwards with the coy expertise of a stripper, and stuck out her backside. It was the most rounded, most pert, most exquisite, most honey-coloured, most naked and velvet backside in the history of the world, and she was revolving it slowly, dipping with it, stroking it with her slender hands, looking backwards over her shoulder with an expression of desire so absolute that it could have melted candles and ignited tapers in every nunnery in the land.

One crusader felt his mouth go dry. 'My God, she is a furnace,' he said, with awe in his voice, 'I could leap into that and die.'

But Mgr Rechin Anquilar could no longer withstand the cruelty of that vision of an unobtainable but demoniac paradise. Furious with mortification, the honour of his manhood and the dignity and prestige of his station mortally offended, he grabbed the rifle of a man near by, raised it to his shoulder, and fired.

He missed, but the first shot of the war had been fired in Cochadebajo de los Gatos, and nothing could now recall it or prevent the conflagration.

# 58 The Council Of War And The Cripple's Atonement

The council of war was convened in the whorehouse on the same evening as Felicidad's adorable backside had narrowly escaped a horrible fate. 'They cannot send me out to infect everyone with clap, now,' she said, 'because in the first place I no longer have it, and in the second place I would be shot by the man who looks like a vulture, and in the third place I do not trust Don Emmanuel to be good whilst I am away. So I am staying behind this wall.'

Hectoro stroked his conquistador beard and said, 'We still have the two machine guns that we took from the Army. We should go up on the wall and blow away their balls, just like this.' He raised his hand and clicked his thumb and forefinger.

Dolores placed her glass upon the table so emphatically that some of the rum spilled upon it. 'You stupid men used up all the ammunition during the grand candomble and the fiesta aferwards. You took them up on the mountain and you were firing like madmen at nothing.' She spat onto the ground to indicate the immaturity and irresponsibility of men in general.

Hectoro looked at her and replied, 'A woman's opinion is of no account.' He saw Remedios glowering at him, and added, 'Unless she is Remedios, who is as good as any man.'

Misael passed his hand over his brow, and said with resignation in his voice, 'The fact is, compañeros, that we have very little ammunition of any kind. We used up most of it when we first arrived and were obliged to go hunting for meat, and we have never replaced it. We will have to be very careful of that which we have.'

'Where are General Fuerte and Capitan Papagato?' asked Remedios. 'Since they were soldiers, their advice would be valuable. Would someone like to fetch them?'

Pedro the Hunter rose from his seat. 'I will fetch them,' he said, very seriously, and in this way he showed Hectoro that it does not demean a man to pay attention to a woman. So great was his height, such a witness to his prowess were the animal skins in which he dressed, and so powerful was his dignity, that not even Hectoro would have questioned or ridiculed anything that he did.

'I have a request,' continued Remedios, as Pedro left the whore-house. 'I would like no one to mention to the Conde Pompeyo that those maniacs are the Inquisition. The very mention of the word makes him pale, since he remembers their confiscations and inescapable accusations from his own time. For his sake, I would like everyone to refer to them as 'the English', and then he will be as brave as a lion.'

'The English,' repeated the company, rolling the phrase 'Los Ingleses' around their mouths until it sounded familiar and applicable.

'What are we to do to beat the English then, compañeros?' asked Consuelo the whore in her smoky voice.

'We should charge out and slice them to pieces with our machetes,' said Hectoro.

'We should leave them alone until they starve, despair, and go home,' said Misael. 'They cannot get to us, and we have food from the plateau which we can bring up in the apparatus. There is no problem.'

Everybody nodded their heads and looked pleased with this strategy, since it required no effort and would disrupt no siestas. But Remedios shook her head so vigorously that she seemed to be flagellating her own face with her long and heavy ponytail. 'Listen,' she said, 'do you remember how we poisoned the Army in Chiriguana by leaving dead animals upstream in the river Mula? And Don Emmanuel told us to piss and shit in it, so that they all fell ill? Sooner or later these people would think of doing the same thing to us, and therefore we have to drive them away.'

'And also,' added Hectoro, 'there would be no justice in it and no satisfaction for us if we were to leave them alone.'

'We could merely abandon the town and go back to live on the plain where we were before, now that there is no danger there. We could move everything down in the apparatus of Profesor Luis, and when we are all down we could cut the ropes of the apparatus so that we could not be followed. In this way there would be no bloodshed, we could all go home as many of us have wanted to do, and the English would be left with nothing.' It was Misael who spoke, his gold tooth still blackened and making it appear as though he was missing a tooth entirely. 'We could work for Don Emmanuel and Doña Constanza as before, and everything would go in a big circle.'

'Doña Constanza would not like to return to her husband when she has a lover in Gonzago,' said Remedios.

'And besides, the plains are too hot, and everything happens by exaggeration,' said Hectoro. 'When it rains we are in a lake, and when it is dry we live in dust. Our crops are uncertain, there are coral snakes and vipers, sometimes it is so hot that we have to sit in the river all through siesta, and besides, the life here is good. We have a plateau that suffers no extremes, and here it is always the same temperature at noon. I for one do not want to leave, especially when it is considered that our former home has grown wild and is beneath the mud, as we were told by those who brought the tractors. We would have to start all over again.'

'Besides,' said Remedios, nodding in agreement, 'it is a matter of principle that we should believe what we want and live as we please. I for one did not fight for years with the People's Vanguard in order to end as one of the oppressed. Liberty or death!'

This vehement outburst drew a round of applause from all the customers and inmates of the brothel. Hectoro rose to his feet and proclaimed, 'Remedios has balls. Viva Remedios!' He sat down heavily, disconcerted by his own unusual lack of reticence.

General Fuerte and Capitan Papagato entered with Pedro, and sat down at the table on either side of the shade of Josef, who, ever since his untimely death, had emerged from the floor at precisely the same time every evening to sit motionless at the table where in life he had flirted with the girls, become helplessly drunk, and played at cards.

'What are we to do?' asked the General.

'We were hoping that you would tell us that,' remarked Remedios, raising an eyebrow in order to indicate disappointed expectation.

'It seems to me,' said the General, 'that no conflict can be won against a side that believes in what it is fighting for and whose morale is consequently high. We must find ways to demoralise them entirely, and to convince them that there is no recourse but retreat or surrender. At this point our tactics should be like guerrilla warfare, a stab here, a pinprick there. And whilst we are doing that, we can think up a grand strategy. We should not repeat the heroic mistakes of the Chaco War, or the Spanish Civil War, by charging out in frontal assaults.

'There is one problem,' said Capitan Papagato, 'which is that the wall keeps us from them just as it keeps them from us. It limits what we can accomplish.'

'The General is right,' said Remedios, 'as is the Capitan. I had not thought before that the wall would be a difficulty for us.'

Misael clapped his hands and stood up. 'I have the answer, compañeros. Who is the one who knows about pinpricks and annoyance? Who is the one who dreams up schemes to infuriate, and makes us all laugh? Who gave songs to the Mexican musicologist that turned out to be filthy, so that he received a rude letter from his agent in Mexico City?' He raised his glass: 'Viva Don Emmanuel! With his help we will defeat the English.'

'We will consult him tomorrow,' said Remedios. 'Who is keeping watch on the wall?'

'Antoine the Frenchman, the Mexican, and Doña Constanza,' answered Pedro.

'I hope that she is not with Gonzago, then,' said Misael. 'Because if she is, she will not be watching, but will be finding other ways of making love.'

During this discussion amongst some of the natural leaders of the community, a small drama was enacting itself, unknown to all except the protagonist and his victims.

He found himself a stretch of the wall in between Antoine's position and that of Doña Constanza, fixed a rope to an iron hoop, checked that his knife was secure in his belt, and let himself down into the icy waters of the moat. He clenched his teeth against the freezing of his muscles, felt a cramp coming on in his lame leg, and struck out for the opposite side, swimming with his arms and his one strong leg. He scrambled out of the water, sat there shivering with his arms wrapped about his knees, and thought about going back. He looked up at the stars and remembered the dream in which he and Sibila had been brought briefly together in Ancient Greece. He recalled the appalling spectacle of her martyrdom and the disaster of his dismal cowardice, and thought that he saw her face reflected in the tears that gathered in his hands. He kissed the reflection and tasted salt. 'If there is nothing hereafter,' he promised her, 'then soon

I will be with you in nothingness, and if there is heaven I will be with you there, and perhaps my leg will be healed, and you will forgive me.'

He crept towards the encampment of the crusaders, crouching down so that he could crawl, using his two hands as legs so that he could drag his helpless limb behind him. Panting, he watched the activity between the glow of the fires, and determined that the vulture's tent was the one in the middle. He understood suddenly that subterfuge would make him only more noticeable, and he stood up.

'I will walk like a normal man,' he told himself, and slowly he began to move towards the large tent where Mgr Rechin Anquilar held court to his priests, robed himself in purple for his judgements, and slept at night. 'Hola, cabrón,' he called to a man who was sitting by a fire, 'do you have a cigarette?'

'I have only three left in this godforsaken place,' replied the man.

'I will not trouble you then.'

Ambling so as not to betray his disability, he circled ever closer to his prey. He stopped suddenly with disappointment when he saw that outside the tent a man was standing guard. But then he continued to walk so as not to arouse suspicion of his motives. He made as if to go by the guard, but then turned, as with an afterthought. Remembering the last man's words, he asked, 'Do you have a cigarette in this godforsaken place?'

The man put a finger to his lips and pointed towards the tent to indicate that he should keep down his voice since the Monsignor was inside. The cripple came closer and leaned forward as if to repeat his request more quietly, but instead his hand lunged up from below and sent the curving blade of the knife up behind the ribs and through the heart.

The man crumpled sideways, clutching himself as though he had been punched, and the cripple threw open the flaps of the tent. The darkness inside it blinded him, and his confusion and fear paralysed him for a second as he understood that he had no idea where to strike. But the unmistakable croak of the Monsignor's voice came from one side, saying, 'Who is it? Valentino, is that you?'

'Yes,' he replied, attempting from memory to imitate the voice of the priest that he had considered a simpleton. 'Where are you? I cannot see in here.'

'Over here,' said the Monsignor, fumbling for a box of matches to light the lamp by his bed.

In the flaring of the match the intended victim looked up and saw a mutilated face that was familiar but forgotten. The two men held each other's eyes for a second, and then the Monsignor beheld the knife that was plainly dripping with blood. The Monsignor leapt from his bed, took hold of a pillow, and cringed away in the hope of fending off the knife thrusts with it.

He found that his eyes could now see in the tenebrous damp of the tent, and he clutched the knife in his hand more tightly. 'Do you remember Sibila?' he asked.

'Sibila?'

'The one you tortured and burned, remember?'

'How should I remember?'

'O yes, there were so many, after all.' He advanced with his knife until he was almost upon his victim. The Monsignor knew all at once the infinite terror of impending death, and his eyes rolled as he averted his head, whimpered, and pushed out the pillow to defend himself. He felt his guts churning and his bladder weaken.

But the cripple forgot his disability in the palpable bliss of consummated hatred and just revenge. He moved to dart forward, and fell.

The Monsignor threw down the pillow and broke from his tent. 'Assassin, assassin,' he shouted. In the tent the cripple rose to his knees, and more tears welled up from the immeasurable lagoon of the sadness that had begun as disgust at his own lameness, continued as the guilt of culpable dread, and now ended as abject failure. As the crusaders ran into the tent he looked upward to a heaven that may contain Sibila somewhere in its placid embrace, and cut his own throat.

## 59 *In Which Dionisio Humanely Miscalculates*

They found Don Emmanuel stark naked in his house, singing a beautiful Irish tune to the Mexican musicologist, who, having had his fingers burned before, was now sceptical of the provenance of most of Don Emmanuel's musical contributions. 'I will write down the name,' said Don Emmanuel, 'and you can check for yourself, It is called 'The London Derrière', see?'

'But London is in England, so how can this tune be Irish? And furthermore, I know that "derrière" means "backside" in French.'

'In English it means "Irishman",' asserted Don Emmanuel, feigning impatience and indignation. 'London is full of Irishmen. In fact it was constructed almost entirely by them, and all Englishmen have Irish blood. It is nothing suspicious.'

'Do not trust him,' advised Misael. 'He is worse than a drunk for false promises.' He turned to address Don Emmanuel, and indicated the others who had accompanied him. 'We have come for advice.'

Don Emmanuel grinned, scratched his rufous beard and then his pubic region, and said, 'I will give you all the advice in the world if only you can tell me why it is that the dingleberries excavated from my navel by Felicidad are always composed of blue fluff, when I possess no clothes of that colour.'

'This is strange,' said Misael, 'because truly I have found the same thing. Perhaps it is for the same reason that all vomit contains tomato skins even when none have been eaten.'

Don Emmanuel raised his finger in the air with an expression of enlightenment upon his face. 'Indeed you are very wise, for that must be it. Now what advice do you need?'

'We would like you to tell us some annoyances to inflict on the crusaders,' said Remedios, 'whilst we think of a strategy.'

'The best way to irritate those who are having a bad time is to have a good time oneself,' said Don Emmanuel. 'Having a good time is always the best way to annoy priests in any case. It horrifies them, unless they are Father Garcia or Don Salvador. We should hold a

343

fiesta, and that is my first advice. My second advice is that perhaps we should use the same tactic as we did with the army in Chiriguana. Hectoro and Pedro should go out each night and kill the guards.'

Hectoro and Pedro exchanged fearful glances, and Pedro coughed nervously into his hand. 'Forgive me, compañeros, but neither of us can swim, and we would drown in the moat. To tell the truth, water is the one thing that scares me. Otherwise I would go and kill all of them.'

'I likewise,' said Hectoro. 'My grandmother was a wise woman, and she said "beware of death by water".'

'In that case,' said Don Emmanuel, 'we should keep them nervous and pinned down by taking potshots at anyone who becomes a clear target. Once an hour, maybe once in two hours, one of you should go up on the wall and take a shot. More often than that, and they would become used to it, so that it no longer makes them unhappy.'

'Ay, ay,' sighed Remedios, 'what a pity that Federico is dead. He could shoot a mountain ranger from impossible disances.'

'Pedro is the best shot,' said Misael.

'I would be the best shot if it were not that I use only a revolver,' said Hectoro, bristling with wounded masculine pride.

'You are the best shot with a pistol,' said Pedro diplomatically. 'Everyone knows that, and I have often heard it said.'

'I have more plans,' said Don Emmanuel. 'You have all forgotten Dionisio. One of you must fetch him, and the rest of you must round up all the jaguars in the city.'

So it was that there ensued an episode of merry mayhem as the reluctant and self-willed cats were prodded off roofs with long poles, heaved from their owners' hammocks, aroused from somnolence by handclaps beside their ears, prised away from bowls of chocolate and guava jam, kidnapped from protective children and fond adults, and herded into the plaza in order to be addressed by Dionisio. Most of the voluptuous and gigantic creatures lay together in tangled heaps of glistening black fur and fell promptly asleep. Others paced back and forth, as though caged, and others still sat upon their haunches, their tails twitching and their mouths gaping in enormous yawns that exposed their pink gums and sabre teeth.

Dionisio arrived from his bookshop with his own two black jaguars, aware that for the first time his legendary telepathy with animals was about to be tested publicly. Virtually the entire populace of the city turned out to see what he would say to the cats; some said, 'He will speak to them in Castilian, except that the meanings will be in cat language,' and others said, 'He will speak to them in a language unknown to any of us.'

In fact the occasion was a disappointment for those who anticipated a grand and supernatural spectacle. Dionisio stood at the same spot where Father Garcia and Don Salvador the False Priest were wont to preach their gospel of procreation and renewal. He closed his eyes and thought himself hard into the mentality of the jaguar, until he could not imagine himself crossing an open space and his skin itched with botfly-worm. He knew suddenly how it was to pin down a turtle with one paw, and bite out a circular hole in the place where the front plate meets the back so that the flesh can be scraped out with the other paw. The focus of his mind's vision changed, so that it was not the single spot of the human but the horizontal slot of the predator. He knew abruptly the sharp twinge of defecating armadillo scales, and his own thoughts turned from the shadow castle of words into guttural grunts and bright unmediated intuitions. His tongue grew sharp and backward-pointing papillae, and his teeth knew the joy of crunching away in one bite the cranial cap of a peccary so that its brains could be savoured greedily. He stood, mesmerising a howler monkey with his golden eyes, until, branch by branch, it could not help but descend from the tree. He felt the rush of anger and hostility when, amongst the rich, damp, and fetid smells of the jungle floor, he detected the pungent spore of a rival male.

The part of Dionisio that was still himself then reminded him to think further into the mind of the Cochadebajo cats. He became lazy and tolerant, playful and affectionate. His mouth filled with saliva at the thought of chocolate, and his flesh was made of stuff invulnerable to bullets and the snares of man, as all animals must evolve to be if they are to remain upon the earth in the fullness of time.

'The cats are not listening,' said old man Gomez, pointing to the way in which the assembly of jaguars was persisting in its habitual way, playfighting, sleeping, or gazing raptly into empty space.

'Do not be stupid,' remonstrated Pedro, who was standing next to him, 'cats are always paying attention. Everyone knows this. They are perverse, and they like to play at deception.'

345

Dionisio felt suddenly that he was keyed into the world of the cats, and his own soul disappeared into an attunement in which he saw exactly what was to be done, knowing that the cats also would perceive it. He opened his eyes and said, 'Vamos.'

The sleek and massively puissant animals arose and stretched, their forepaws clawing the dust before them, and their muscles flexing. They looked at Dionisio expectantly, and turned to follow him to the drawbridge. When it was lowered, his own two jaguars rubbed their cheeks against his waist to mark him as their own as they did each day, and he started out with his feline army to take on the crusaders.

'Dionisio, do not go, please.' It was Leticia Aragon, her eyes, which today were the colour of lapis lazuli, fixed on a dreadful possibility, and her hair that seemed to be made of black spiderweb falling about her face. 'Do you want Parlanchina to be fatherless? And her child to be without a grandfather?' She indicated the compact hump of her pregnancy.

Dionisio put his hand on her neck and smiled softly. 'Leticia, you know better than that.'

'He has balls,' said Hectoro, as Dionisio left the city amid the sea of cats, which were now spreading out to advance like an old-fashioned formation of infantrymen. 'I never knew we had so many,' said Pedro.

'I love to see the waving of their tails when they walk,' said Remedios.

The crusaders looked along the valley and detected a glimmer of motion. It was as though the whole valley floor was a field of blackened wheat, with one solitary reaper walking in its midst. 'What is happening?' asked Monsignor Anquilar, coming to the frontline in response to the buzz of activity that was sending his men scurrying forward with their arms. He shaded his hand against the mountain light and exclaimed, 'The Devil is afoot. We are being advanced upon by the animal accomplices of hell.'

It seemed that no relentless volleys and fusillades could halt that inexorable advance. It seemed that no one could shoot down the one enormous man who paced forward in tune with the black beasts. When the company of cats were at a distance of one hundred metres, when they were stalking on their stomachs as their instincts dictated,

346

when the assault seemed inevitable and too horrifying to contemplate, the crusaders and priests threw down their weapons and ran.

Dionisio felt in his own muscles the primeval feline urge to give chase and leap, to rend and tear, to torture and to subdue. But he halted the line and called in the animals behind him.

'Why did you stop?' asked General Fuerte, who had been watching through the army binoculars that nowadays he used for ornithology. 'You could have defeated them utterly.'

They were sitting in Dionisio's house drinking tintos. His two cats were fast asleep on the rug with their feet in the air, and their sweet smell of hay and strawberries pervaded the room. 'They were already defeated,' said Dionisio. 'There was no need of bloodshed. There will be a great fiesta tonight.'

Indeed there was. The town band and choir played its entire repertoire of Don Emmanuel's bawdy English songs five times. It continued its retreta with vallenato dances, bambuco, and salso. It played Argentinian tangos, and the immensely turgid and lengthy national anthem, to which they bawled Don Emmanuel's rewritten and cheerfully obscene lyrics. Profesor Luis rigged up the gramophone to the windmill, and they wept communally to sentimental songs from Peru about desertion, premature death, and poverty. Doña Constanza became lewdly inebriated and had to be carried home by Gonzago and Tomás. Remedios sat with Gloria in the plaza and reminisced about their guerrilla days. Don Salvador the False Priest fell over in the whorehouse and hurt his shins.

Father Garcia went up on the walls to take a breath of fresh air that would combat the rising nausea of pisco in his guts, and found the Conde Pompeyo Xavier de Estremadura sitting alone on the wall. 'What are you doing, cabrón?' he asked.

'The accursed English have returned,' said the Conde, pointing a wavering finger along the valley. Father Garcia adjusted his eyes with difficulty and followed the sweep of the Conde's gesture. He saw a ring of fires in motion. 'Listen,' said the Conde, and Father Garcia heard the brassy tinkle of a distant bell. As the wind shifted he heard the monotonous incantation of priests and smelled the sweet aroma of incense. 'This is something in Latin,' said Garcia, his hare's eyebrows quivering with speculation. 'What are they doing?'

'You should know that,' replied the Conde, 'and you a priest. I saw this once in Valencia when there was a plague of incubi that molested the women at night. They are doing an exorcism.'

'But what are they exorcising? It makes no sense.'

But in the morning, when the town arose late from its merriment with a collective hangover which they intended to dispel with further medicinal doses of alcohol, there was about the place an eerie atmosphere of absence. People wandered the streets looking for what was missing without knowing what it was. Their puzzlement lifted, but desolation and confusion rose in their hearts, when they realised abruptly that all the cats had gone.

# 60 *Don Salvador The False Priest Reveals A Secret*

Father Garcia, who, as always, levitated from the ground when mystically illuminated or argumentatively emphatic, explained the disappearance of the cats thus:

'My friends, it is true that we were told that the gods and saints would not fight in this war because they are confused by it, and yet it is also true that our trusty and confiding cats have been exorcised from us by priests, as I saw with my own eyes when I was drunk but still rational, as the Conde Pompeyo Xavier de Estremadura will bear witness. How is this to be explained? Did the saints lie to Parlanchina, who gave their message to Aurelio to give to us? Did Parlanchina misunderstand them? Was it a demon disguised as Parlanchina?

'No, it was not. For it is true that the gods and saints have not intervened. Who has intervened then? I wish you to recall my teaching, which last night was proved empirically to be true. For I have told you repeatedly that this world is evil because the god that made it was evil, which is to say that God is in true fact the Devil. The One God who made spirit was not the God who made matter, as I have many times clearly explained. It follows that the priests who are encamped far up the valley are the unwitting accomplices of Satan, for they believe that they follow the Spirit Creator when in fact they follow the World Creator, who gave them many bad commands and wicked precepts. He set evil in their hearts, telling them that it was good. Where there was compassion he sowed brutality. Where there was merriment, festivity and joyful copulation, he sowed grimness, disapproval, and frigidity, because in this way he desired to taint love and tarnish happiness. He dressed his priests in black, for this is the colour of mourning, and their souls he shrouded in stone so that the ice of fanaticism froze out the light of reason and the exhilarating wisdom of conjecture. In this way was the modesty of speculation replaced by the iron cage of certainty.

The explanation is simple, my friends. The saints have refused to fight, and the Spirit Creator never fights, for he manifests His Love but not His Power. But the World Creator has not refused to fight, and therefore it follows that we lost the cats because of a ceremony of the Devil.

'But I have told you all before that the Spirit Creator has deemed it good to begin a new creation in ourselves, and we must not lose heart. We cannot lose our New World now, when it has only just begun, and therefore we must continue boldly, in the faith that what was lost shall through our courage and enterprise be restored. For you know that our cats were never true cats of flesh and blood. They were cats formed of angelic matter which is not the stuff of blood and bone, but is ethereal matter that has been condensed that it may manifest. This explains their love of chocolate and sweet things, and why otherwise they did not have to eat. They arrived mysteriously amongst us, unbidden, and now they have gone, but we shall not be dismayed nor deterred. *Deo Gratias. Dominus Vobiscum.* Amen.'

Hectoro rode up and spoke to him, face to face where he hovered above the ground. 'I hope, cabrón, that the Spirit Creator can restore terraces, because they are tearing down the stones to build barricades and are harvesting our crops so that they can eat them themselves.'

Father Garcia was so disconcerted by this information that his trance abruptly broke, and he fell to the ground, bruising his ankle. 'I have told you many times not to do that when I am levitating,' he said to Hectoro reprovingly. 'One day it may lead to a serious accident.'

What Hectoro had said was true. The crops of quinoa, pulses and potatoes were being pillaged by the hungry crusaders. General Fuerte stood upon the wall, peering through his binoculars, and passing the information to the people with him. Soon it was not enough that solely his eyes should witness the wrecking of the andenes that rose in steps high up the valley walls, and which held back the fertile mud that had been placed there during the original excavation of the city. His binoculars were passed from hand to hand, and the sense of outrage grew as it became clear that the crusaders were not only taking the food, but were transferring the stones of the walls down to the valley floor so that they could construct makeshift fortifications.

Pedro the Hunter appeared with a rifle. A wave of comment and speculation passed through the people, for Pedro hunted always with an ancient musket that was held together with wire, and whose ammunition he was obliged to make himself in an equally antiquated mould. But now he held Sergio's Lee-Enfield, the very same rifle that had once been stolen from his father by Federico when he had run away from home to take vengeance upon the Army. It was a legendary rifle, for with it Federico had killed the mountain rangers who had sought out the guerrillas in the sierra, and it was said that whoever used it was guided by the spirit of Federico, and therefore could not miss. Its range was greater than a modern weapon, its long barrel made it accurate, and its heavy ammunition not only pierced flesh, but shattered bones. There was only one box of .303 shells left, and Pedro had determined to make every bullet count. He lay down upon the wall, clicked the pillars of the sights upwards, and wound the knurled wheel to adjust them. He picked on a sturdy man who was standing still, directing the transfer of rocks. A silence fell upon the people as they awaited the crash of the weapon. Pedro aimed right to allow for the idiosyncrasy of the rifle, and fired.

General Fuerte swore afterwards that through his binoculars he had seen the bullet travel in a curve, waver, and disappear into the middle of the man's back. What the crowd saw was a tiny figure in the distance throw up his arms, wheel in a half circle, and fall upon his face. They saw the remainder of the crusaders scurry for shelter, crawling from one inadequate hiding place to another. The people of Cochadebajo de los Gatos clenched their fists and shook them in triumph: 'Bravo, Pedro. Viva, viva Don Pedro.'

From that time onwards the crusaders despoiled the andenes only at night when the moon and stars were sufficient, and during the day they hid behind their walls or marauded for the trustingly unattended flocks of sheep and goats in the neighbouring valleys and quebradas. No longer hungry, burning with irritation at their exclusion from the city, they cleaned their weapons and laid plans. One night, under the direction of Mgr Rechin Anquilar, they even waded out into the map of the world that had been constructed with so much fidelity by Dionisio Vivo and Profesor Luis, and shovelled into the water those parts that were not of the Roman faith. It turned into a shallow puddle of a pond, with only isolated patches of flowers where once whole continents had been represented; they had already eaten all the fish in it and consumed the wildfowl, and the loss of drainage now made their own camp into an unpleasant swamp.

'I wish to see if diplomacy may succeed where resistance fails,' said Father Garcia to the council of war, 'as does Don Salvador. After all, I was ordained a priest, and he looks like one. An appeal to brotherliness may be worth a try.'

'You are mad,' said Remedios. 'It is precisely the success of your ideas that has brought them here, it seems. Do you not remember what the cripple said?'

'I admit that it is mad,' agreed Don Salvador the False Priest, 'but I have a secret weapon at my disposal which may strengthen my argument.'

'A secret weapon?'

'Yes indeed, a secret weapon.' He nodded his head, smiling mysteriously.

'And what is this secret weapon, may I ask?'

Don Salvador shrugged his bony shoulders and made a helpless gesture with both hands. 'If I tell you, then it would not be a secret. And in any case, I am ashamed of it.'

'You are both idiots,' asserted Remedios.

Nonetheless the drawbridge was lowered and the two men ventured out. Father Garcia had dug out of his box what remained of his clerical garb, and Don Salvador had cut himself a new collar from white cardboard. The former carried with him a rosary in case he needed to escape, and the latter carried only his battered and beloved copy of Catullus' poems and epigrams. They walked with no conversation between them, the gaunt height and distinguished features of Don Salvador in peculiar contrast to Father Garcia's slight build and leporine face.

'We have come to negotiate with the man who calls himself El Inocente,' said Don Salvador to the group of surly and unshaven men who rose up to confront them as they passed the first line of makeshift drystone walls that served as protection against Pedro's bullets: 'I understand that he is your leader.'

The two men were brusquely searched for weapons, and made to wait, under guard. 'A more barbarous and short-tempered bunch of people have I never seen,' commented Don Salvador.

Very shortly, Mgr Rechin Anquilar approached. From a slight distance he saw something about the taller of the two negotiators that seemed both familiar and discomforting. His memory whirling, he came closer, and suddenly realised who the tall man was. His ears flushed with shame, and the colour rose in his face. He began to think of excuses and justifications for exceeding his remit, and the awful prospect of unfrocking and legal process loomed in his mind. 'Your Eminence?' he said, with incredulity in his voice.

Don Salvador smiled. 'Do I not look very like my brother, the Cardinal? We have often been mistaken for each other.'

Mgr Anquilar wondered if he was being toyed with. 'Your Eminence, what brings you to these parts?'

'I am Salvador Trujillo Guzman, the Cardinal's brother, as I have said, and I have something to tell you.' Don Salvador paused and considered his words, whilst the Monsignor continued to be confused and Father Garcia looked at him open-mouthed. In all their long friendship, in all their many discussions in which they had elaborated their doctrine, Don Salvador had never disclosed that his own brother was the head of the country's Church.

Don Salvador looked very directly into the Monsignor's eyes and said firmly, 'My brother has always been a very conservative kind of man, especially in matters of the faith. He could never tolerate my levity. But for all that, I always knew that he had more faults than I do myself. We are both dissimulators, but in my case it is very obvious and in his case he hides it even from himself. I have made my living as a false priest who fools no one, and he has lived as an ordained priest who has been careful to fool the right people in order to rise to prominence. Nonetheless I know that my brother has a good heart, and I am certain that he would never have authorised you to commit atrocities and barbarities in God's name, the name of the Church, or his own.

'I do not know what future you had planned for yourself after this escapade, Monsignor. It seems to me that a man like you has no future other than to be killed or to continue to pile horror upon horror. I cannot imagine you retiring to a cloister having tasted the exhilarating wine of bloodshed and generalship, can you? You have become a cacique, a caudillo – '

'Am I to understand that your point, when you reach it, is going to be that unless I withdraw you will inform your brother of my activities?' interrupted the Monsignor, his eyes glinting with malice and hostility.

'That is exactly my point, Monsignor. And I also require you to disband your army of marauders and savages.'

Rechin Anquilar put his hands behind his back and adopted a lofty demeanour that belied his trepidation. It was true that he had never given thought as to how he would return to a workaday life after the crusade; the contemplation of it gave rise to a tremor of dread in his heart, and he knew that sooner or later the details of the episode would emerge, that fingers would sooner or later be pointed at him. For the first time his faith in his mission wavered, and his imagination began to itch with the prospect of having to justify himself.

'My authority comes not from your brother, but from God. My aim is solely to spare souls the pain of Hell.'

'Personally acquainted with Him, are you?' asked Garcia. 'And why is it your business whether or not I go to Hell?'

'There is only one law,' said Don Salvador sententiously: '*Vivamus atque amemus.*'

'"Let us live and let us love?" Is that from the fourth Gospel?' asked the Monsignor, who was unable under any circumstances to avoid the temptation to fix correctly the attribution of a quotation.

'The Gospel according to Catullus,' said Don Salvador.

The Monsignor's attention seemed to wander. He reflected for a moment. He recalled the names of the two heresiarchs of Cochadebajo de los Gatos that he had read in the submission of the Holy Office, and thought simultaneously of a way of avoiding the story of his exploits ever coming to the Cardinal's ears. He raised his voice and addressed the crusaders who had gathered round.

'This man,' he said, pointing, 'is Salvador. And this man is the alleged "Father" Garcia. They are heretics, and the leaders of heretics. Kill them both, before they pollute this place any further.'

# 61 *Father Garcia Is Saved By St Dominic*

Father Garcia looked down at the severed head of his companion where it lay in profile upon the mud, and at the body that now seemed to have no identity, as though it were a part of a mannequin. He raised his eyes and looked at the man with the machete who was advancing upon him. He appealed directly to Monsignor Rechin Anquilar. 'Before I die I would like to say a rosary. As a Christian man, you cannot refuse my request.'

'You should prefer to confess,' said Anquilar, 'but say a rosary if it pleases you. There will be no harm in keeping the Devil waiting.'

Father Garcia crossed himself and recited the Apostles' Creed. He moved his fingers to the first bead, and, despite himself, he noticed that his fingers were trembling so greatly that the bead slipped his grasp. He recited the Our Father, and moved to the next bead. His knees began to shake, but he said the three Hail Marys and the Glory Be, bowing his head at the name of Jesus. Onwards his fingers moved, and, his voice quavering, he contemplated the first joyful mystery, that of the Annunciation. He said the Our Father, ten Hail Marys, and the Glory Be. A modicum of calm descended upon him, and he moved on to the second joyful mystery of the Visitation. He repeated the formula of the ten Hail Marys and the Glory Be, and proceeded to the mystery of the Nativity. Relentlessly his voice intoned the Hail Marys and the Glory Bes for the mysteries of the Presentation and the Finding In The Temple.

Father Garcia's plan had been that in contemplating the mysteries of the rosary he would become rapt, and this would enable him to levitate. He had never levitated to a very great height at any great speed, but was convinced that this could be done merely by intensifying his degree of concentration. But now he was finding that the prospect of imminent and bloody death was paralysing his soul. It was as if only the front part of his brain was operating, and all the rest of it consisted of an undifferentiated jelly of fear that could only repeat, 'I am going to die,' and which drowned out the pacifying monotony of his prayers.

He slowed his voice and tried to cover the Sorrowful Mysteries at a snail's pace. He looked around at the crusaders as they exchanged bored glances, looked at their watches, and fingered the shafts of their machetes. He tried to close his mind to them, and concentrate upon the Agony In The Garden, the Scourging, the Crowning With Thorns, and the Carrying of the Cross. He arrived at the Crucifixion with his feet still firmly upon the ground and a sense of utter despair burrowing in his heart.

Even a devout Irishwoman gabbling the rosary at a speed reminiscent of an express takes a very long time indeed to cover an entire rosary in one session. Even such a lady would rarely attempt more than five decades at a time, and Garcia was now beginning the eleventh of the fifteen. At Garcia's rate it would have been many hours before he finished, and he gave brief thanks in prayer to St Dominic for having decreed that each mystery requires ten Hail Marys and a Glory Be. He slowed his pace still further, and adopted the singsong tone of voice that he knew from experience could send a congregation to sleep.

On and on he droned, through the glorious mysteries. The Resurrection, the Ascension, the Descent Of The Holy Spirit, The Assumption. At last, his feet still upon terra firma, and his throat dry with panic and repetition, he arrived at the Coronation and embarked upon the concluding litany. He thanked St Dominic for having composed so many honorific epithets for the Virgin, and for having to say 'Pray for us' after every one of them. He reached the end of the rosary after five and a half hours, and, heavy with resignation, looked up.

The crusaders were all wandering about, chatting and joking with each other. The executioner with his machete was nowhere to be seen, and Monsignor Anquilar was discussing something with Father Valentino. It seemed that he had managed to dampen the bloodlust of his persecutors by means of the implausible length of his recitation. Seizing his chance, he began again at the Apostles' Creed, and sidled away behind one of the tents. From thence he darted to a section of wall, saying the Our Father. He set out briskly for the city, still reciting, and was half way there when he encountered

Dionisio Vivo, soaking wet, and striding towards the crusader's encampment.

'I came to rescue you,' said Dionisio. 'I was hoping that they would not dare to touch me because of that story that anyone who tried to harm me would receive the wound in their own body.'

'Pray for us sinners now and at the hour of our death,' said Father Garcia, who from now on would be forever unable to get the rosary out of his mind and speech, 'Thank you, Dionisio, Blessed art Thou amongst women. You know that the stories about you are all true, on Earth as it is in Heaven. You could defeat those bastards on your own, God is with you, Queen Conceived Without Original Sin, so why don't you? I suppose you got wet swimming across the moat. Did you see that they killed Don Salvador? I will never forget it, Mother Inviolate, it was the worst thing I have ever seen, Hail Holy Queen.'

'Come quickly, Garcia, they have noticed. We will have to run.'

Together the two men sprinted for the drawbridge, which had been lowered as soon as Dionisio had impulsively dived off the rampart into the moat. A bullet whined past Garcia's head as he threw himself panting to the cobbles of the street, and the drawbridge was raised. All he could see before his eyes was the scuffed toecap of an old army boot. He raised his eyes, and they met those of Remedios, who was standing above him with her hands on her hips, looking down at him disdainfully. 'Idiot,' she said.

'Remedios,' he gasped, 'Blessed is the Fruit of Thy Womb, Jesus.' He nodded, as from now on he always would when he mentioned that Name, and tapped his forehead smartly on the stones. 'Now and at the hour of our death,' he said, and passed out with concussion.

## 62  *The Discussion In The Whorehouse*

Father Garcia's words weighed heavily with Dionisio. Dionisio's reputation for miraculous invulnerability and extraordinary power, his title of the Deliverer, and his prolific paternity, had endowed him with a clearly perceived aura of praeternatural invincibility. The fact that his own father was chief of the General Staff, and that even cabinet ministers replied swiftly to his correspondence, seemed also to put him somewhere at the very centre of that vast civil power that enclosed the country in its umbriferous embrace. For most people the state was something to which they knew that they belonged, but which never impinged upon the lives that they led far out on the extremities of the frontiers or deep in the impenetrable interior. No tax gatherers appeared, no health and safety officers inspected the sanitary arrangements in mud huts; there were solely the local judges, quixotic and unpredictable police, and perhaps a deeply unpleasant encounter with the Army once every ten years. The state was simply an enormous machine that rumbled in the far distance, and one's only connection with it was the ability to remember the colours of the national flag.

But Dionisio's presence brought that of the state into focus, and he felt that the non-appearance of the Army, despite his appeal to the government, was a personal betrayal that also diminished him in the eyes of his fellow citizens. This redoubled the weight upon his shoulders of being the Deliverer, who could kill a man simply by touching him. He fell into a mire of self-doubt and fatalism, in which he knew on the one hand that he would be forced to go out on his own to drive away the crusaders, and on the other hand knew also that he might fail miserably and be killed. It seemed a very long time since, deified by his love for Anica and demented by her loss, he had gone out one morning and killed her murderer merely by touching him above the heart. 'I am becoming an ordinary man,' he repeated to himself, even though he had been told that when he had *gone out* with the cats to confront the 'English', he had been seen to grow to twice his size.

With a heavy heart, he went to the perpetual council of war in the whorehouse. When he came through the door, the brothel fell silent. He nodded to those who caught his eye, and went to the table. 'I have come to tell you,' he informed them, 'that I will go out and deal with them myself.'

'Bravo, Dionisio,' said Remedios, when the applause had died down, 'we expected no less. Nonetheless, we have decided against it.'

'There would be no satisfaction in it,' said Hectoro. 'If it had been a matter of inconveniencing us, and annoying us by wrecking the terraces, then perhaps we would say, 'Why not?' but now they have killed Don Salvador, who went out in peace to negotiate, and the whole thing has become personal.'

'Each of us wishes to participate in driving them out,' added Misael, 'and to ask you to do it would be to cheat ourselves of the opportunity to be tall and strong. I too am a man, as is everyone here.'

'I think that you are becoming confused,' commented Remedios, raising her eyebrows laconically.

'In that case,' said Dionisio, who had now begun to feel disappointed, 'I shall be at your service as you require it,' and he sat down next to the shade of Josef, who was contemplating fixedly the glass that was always placed before him in his memory.

'Now, what plans have we been able to come up with?' asked Remedios, who had assumed the role of leader by an accidental process that was clear to no one, but which nonetheless appeared inevitable.

'I had a plan,' said Profesor Luis, 'to disguise our tractors as dragons that belch fire. I thought we could drive them out at night with the lights on, painted like eyes, and I thought that we could put whistles on the exhaust so that they sound terrifying. But I have been unable to invent a flame-thrower with what I have available, and I can think of no way to protect the drivers from bullets.'

'I had a plan,' said Hectoro, 'to deliver them some of Dolores' Chicken Of A True Man. I thought of doing it in a huge cauldron, and sending it out as a peace offering. It has a delayed reaction, as

359

you know, and I thought that whilst they were running about clutching their throats and weeping with pain, we could come out and attack them. But then I realised that they would not eat it for fear of poison, and I thought, "What if I go out and eat some in front of them to prove that it is harmless?" but then I understood that they would shoot me down immediately before they ate it. Naturally I have no fear of death, but it occurred to me that I might be needed in the fight, and so I do not have this plan anymore.'

'Do you have to come to these meetings mounted on your horse?' demanded Consuelo the whore of Hectoro, puffing vehemently upon her cigar. 'You do not know how stupid you look with your sombrero crushed into the ceiling. And I am tired of cleaning up the turds of your horse.' She spat on the floor, disdainfully ignoring his baleful glare.

'I had a plan to kidnap one of them at night. One who knows their plans,' said Misael. 'But then I thought, "What if he swallows the plans, and refuses to shit them out?" So I thought, "We should threaten to cut open his guts to get the plans," and then he would shit himself, and we could get the plans like that.'

'With respect, cabrón, that is a very stupid plan,' said Pedro.

'I know,' said Misael, grinning so that his camouflaged gold tooth rendered his smile grotesque. 'It came to me in a dream, and that is the only reason I mention it.'

'It seems to me that we must come out and attack them,' said Hectoro.

'By God, I would like to slit their English noses,' interjected the Conde Pompeyo Xavier de Estremadura. 'I will take out all my soldiers, and we will hack them with our swords, pierce them with our pikes, blind them with our poignards, and leave their heads on spikes for the crows to feast.' He slammed the table with his fist, so that those seated at it had to jerk backwards to evade the runnels of spilled liquor.

'With respect, Conde, a frontal assault is likely to be bloody on our side, and leave them unscathed,' said General Fuerte gently. 'Such heroics would have no ingenuity, as Misael would say.'

'We could do it at night,' observed Hectoro, 'but then we would be likely to kill each other by mistake. Not that I am afraid, but I would not like to kill my friends, unless it were a matter of honour.'

360

'I favour an attack from behind,' said the General. 'It would be completely unexpected, and therefore very successful.'

A collective gasp of dismay arose from the company. 'General,' said Remedios, 'we would have to go down to the plateau, and then find a way back up by another route to get behind them. It might take weeks, and none of us knows the way. We could get lost and die in the wilderness.'

'We would have to go right up on the paramo before we could come down again,' said Misael. 'Have you ever been up there?' The General shook his head. 'It is so cold that one's balls retreat into one's body as far as one's throat, so that one cannot swallow. One's fingers become bananas. One's hair becomes encrusted with ice. The wind blows from every quarter at once and slides inside one's garments like the frozen fingers of a dead whore. The rain is sharper than knives and cuts the soul as deeply as the flesh. Sometimes it snows suddenly, and one is instantly buried, and sometimes the wind whips the snow from the peaks and one becomes blind. Sometimes one becomes blind from the light in any case, and the soroche comes down on you so that a terrible sickness strikes at the brain, leaving you reeling like a drunkard on the point of death from pisco, with your eyes popping from your head. At other times there are sudden mists that arrive from nowhere, and you breathe water, and you see not even your own hands before you, and all you do see are the shadows of the dead looming and lunging. We went through the paramo when we came to this place, and none of us wants ever to return.'

There was a lengthy and depressed silence as the people contemplated this familiar tale of the horrors of the paramo. Dionisio leaned forward. 'What if there is someone who knows of an easy route? Aurelio knows these mountains like no one else. If we asked him to lead us, surely there would be no problem. The General's plan is by far the best.'

'You should compromise,' said Josef, speaking with difficulty for the first time since his death. 'Some should stay, and attack when the others come from behind.'

They all looked with astonishment at the slow smile that was spreading across the grey face of the immobile ghost that had become as much a fixture of the whorehouse as the empty bottles and the spittle on the floor.

Remedios raised her hand to speak. 'Let us say that we adopt this plan, for the sake of argument. Nearly all of the women have children to attend to, so they should stay and defend the city. Most of the children are Dionisio's, so therefore he too should stay. The leader of Dionisio's women is Fulgencia Astiz, and she should stay here to lead them. I should go with the men because if I stay here I will argue with Fulgencia, and because I will prevent the men from doing anything stupid on the way. Also the Spanish soldiers brought back from the dead by Aurelio should stay here, because their long death has made most of them too stupid to do anything for very long, and the Conde should stay here to lead them, as is his right. When they hear gunfire, and see through the General's binoculars that we are attacking the English from behind, they should issue out of the city and also attack.'

'No one can withstand a campaign on two fronts,' said the General. 'Look at the examples of Napoleon and Hitler.'

'Bolivar could have done it,' said Profesor Luis.

'Do you see Bolivar out there with the English?' asked the General rhetorically, sweeping his hand in a dismissive gesture.

'This marvellous plan is all very well,' observed Pedro, sipping his aguardiente, 'but where the hell has Aurelio been all this time?'

# 63 Strategic Manoeuvres And
## A Pleasant Surprise

'If you wish to attack them from the south,' said Aurelio, 'then you would have to go back down into the jungle, where you would be bitten and stung, the way would be slow, and the weight of your packs would dissolve you in sweat and curses. Then you would have to go to the high place from where we once watched the flood pouring out over the plain. From there you would follow the same way as our first journey to this place.'

'Through the paramo?' asked Misael, shuddering at the thought, and Aurelio nodded affirmatively.

Misael put his hands protectively over his nether region. 'Let them not be frozen away,' he exclaimed.

'They will not have to be,' replied Aurelio. 'If you choose to approach from the north, you can merely go down to the plateau, go north to where the next valley comes down, and go up it. The slope is long and gentle. Near the top you may turn south up another valley that has a great torrent in it. It is another long but more difficult climb. Then at the end you may come over the ridge, and you will be over there.' He pointed to the right-hand end of the valley. 'I will come with you and show you the way.'

Aurelio had turned up inconspicuously, and had been found by Dionisio in the plaza, contentedly pounding the pestle in his gourd of coca leaves and lime. He had looked very surprised when reproached for his absence at a time of emergency, replying, 'I was harvesting chicle and smoking my rubber. I only came back to be here when Leticia Aragon gives birth to Parlanchina. I have left Carmen alone in the jungle when I should be planting maize.'

So it was that the men and Remedios gathered all the supplies that they would require for a short and victorious expedition. Profesor Luis' grand apparatus worked at night to lower down fifty mules, assorted armaments with ammunition, and the men themselves, leaving only the women, the Spanish conquistadors, and Dionisio Vivo. They leaned over the precipice to watch the expedition wending its way along the lush plateau below. 'Thanks be to God that the men have gone. We will have peace at last,' said Consuelo, wiping a sentimental tear from her eye at the thought of all that virility going into battle. Doña Constanza waved vigorously at a tiny figure that she thought was Gonzago, and Gloria waved at a similarly minuscule one that she believed to be Tomás. Fulgencia Astiz shrugged her sturdy shoulders, and went up to the wall in the hope of finding someone in her sights that she could shoot. Her Santander-eana soul was bristling with the pugnacious morbidity of her people, and as she lay down and adjusted her sights, she sighed with the satisfaction of true happiness. Her two children by Dionisio she sat beside her, so that they might learn at a precocious age the true intoxication and significance of death. The Spanish soldiers sat in the plaza, being harangued by the Conde in the name of the King of Spain, their vacant minds wandering away to distant campaigns, and becoming lost somewhere during the time of the foundation of the city of Ipasueño.

Down on the plateau the men already missed the practical and temperate climate of Cochadebajo de los Gatos, but were thankful that they did not have to descend into the jungle. They filled their mochilas with avocados, mangos, and papaya, and slaughtered two steers. The still-quivering flesh was cut into pieces that were wrapped in the leaves of palm, and handed out to each one as his ration for the expedition. Those who believed in such things drank the steaming blood from gourds, hoping thereby to acquire strength. Pedro poured blood over his own head and fixed white feathers in it as it dried in the sun, becoming inwardly, by this outward sign, quintessentially a warrior.

Through the verdant banana groves and orchards of guava they picked their way, past the irrigation canals that swarmed with fish and the larvae of mosquitoes, skirting the stewponds and rice fields, with their high banks and floodgates. Everywhere they saw as if for the first time the triumph of their own persistence and labour over the chaotic and disintegrating forces of nature, and everything that they saw strengthened their resolve to defend it even at the price of their own lives.

By evening they were half way up the first of the long valleys, and were already experiencing the milder air of a less exuberant clime.

They pitched camp on a raised and level spot, remembering from the past that to encamp at the bottom of a valley is to ask for a soaking in the event of rain. The rocks were stained red from iron, and high up on the valley walls were the abandoned mineshafts of the gold-loving Incas and the conquering Spanish. Below them stretched a prospect of palms, and above them there lay fallen rocks and spiny succulents unknown to botanical science, whose pink flowers seemed to be attended, every one, by quarrelsome hummingbirds defending their own tiny domain. They slept the night accompanied by the music of falling streams, the ache of their thighs obliterating the discomfort of stony beds.

The next day found them winding up the valley of torrential water. A thin mist of spume hung in the air, and in this place the hard hoofs of their mules slipped upon the watery rocks that glistened with the ears of fungus and yellow lichen, the film of green algae, and the absolute blackness of basalt. They followed an ancient path worn by feet that had not trodden those parts since before the time of Manco Capac, and they looked down upon the thunderous white flood, terrified by the mere fact of being able to understand why it was that one of the mules, stupefied and hypnotised, had leapt unprovoked into the abyss. They released their fear by whipping along the mules, with cries of 'Burro, burro,' that were lost in the rumble of water, and shouted with relief when it was time to turn and mount the ridge that would poise them for an attack upon the intruders who had despoiled their own valley and broken their abiding peace.

From their great height they were able to look down upon the town of Cochadebajo de los Gatos. Its antique stones and tilting houses seemed so small as to have been modelled by a child, and below them the campfires of the crusaders, with their thin plumes twisting in the breeze, seemed to be the very image of tranquillity and innocence.

'I could not stay behind,' said Dionisio. 'I was hardly needed there, since Fulgencia has everything organised like a German.'

'You came here on your own?' asked Misael, astounded, and unable to believe that anyone could have made this journey unassisted.

'I took a short cut,' he replied. 'I climbed up the cliff at the north of town, and came along that ridge. I am surprised that none of you saw me, because I could see you very clearly.'

'But the cliff leans outwards,' exclaimed Misael, crossing himself, 'Only the Devil could climb it.'

Dionisio poked him in the ribs good-humouredly. 'There is a kind of chimney up it that makes it quite simple, amigo. Nonetheless, I cut my hands, as you can see.' He held out hands that were a crisscross of cuts and tears, and Misael made a chirring noise with his tongue against his cheeks. 'You are loco,' he said, 'but welcome to the party.'

The men retired behind the crest of the ridge so that they would not be seen, and only Pedro and Remedios remained, to discuss their tactics, and to gaze speculatively upon the multitude below. 'How many are they?' asked Pedro.

'Maybe one thousand, maybe two. How does one judge?'

An unaccountable intuition stirred in Remedios' mind, and she raised her head. 'I thought I saw something move over there,' she said, pointing. Pedro followed her gaze, and he too saw something. It was not that he saw anything in particular; what he observed was more like a suspicion of stealthiness, a sly motion in the corner of the eye, that disappeared upon the first attempt at focus. Remedios thought that she saw a black frond waving as it slipped behind a rock. She called Dionisio forward and told him to come and see. 'Is that what I think it is?'

He placed the forefinger of one hand against the bunched tips of the thumb and forefinger of the other, and peered through the tiny aperture as he had been taught during his national service, when he had been involved in the futile expeditions against people like Remedios, always arriving after the guerrillas had already departed. He saw the tip of a black tail sway gracefully above a boulder, and flick out of sight. 'It is the cats,' he said delightedly. 'They hate to cross open ground, and so they are moving like commandos, or bandits.'

'If you can bring them here,' she said, 'then we are no longer outnumbered.'

Dionisio put his hands to his temples and uttered a silent call deep within. In the infinite void of his mind he heard a response, a deep and guttural cough, a growl.

Bounding over the rocks, oblivious to the fear of unenclosed spaces, the cats flowed in a velvet stream over the hillsides, almost comical in the abandonment of their leaping and their clumsy trotting, the only speed at which a cat loses its dignity and grace.

Into the camp they came, sniffing for their own people, hungry for sweet titbits, rolling over on their backs in the anticipation of the rough play that in men passes for affection. Dionisio's own two cats came and sat by him, cleaning their paws as if nothing had happened, feigning indifference, as if to punish him for his absence.

Father Garcia levitated in ecstasy for the first time since his friend Don Salvador had been so brutally and summarily cut down. 'See, see,' he shouted from his station above the mountain, 'I was right; the saints are not on the other side. *Jubilate!* Mother of Divine Grace, pray for us. I was right, I was right! Seat of Wisdom, pray for us, Cause of Our Joy, pray for us. I was justified.'

'Either that, or the exorcism was half-baked,' commented Hectoro.

'Which one is that?' asked Dionisio, pointing at a portly she-jaguar with a benign expression that was sporting about its neck a huge, exorbitant, and incongruous pink bow, spattered with mud, very bedraggled, but plainly made of silk. 'I do not know this one,' he said, 'and I know all the cats of the town.'

'Who cares?' said Remedios, and tartly she added, 'We should give the bow to Doña Constanza, since she enjoys such frivolities.'

They held their last council of war, and passed that night in the bitter cold of the uplands warmed by the voluptuous heat of the cats, soothed by their aroma of strawberries and hay, lulled by their sonorous and extravagant purring, and at last convinced that the unseen world had not turned its face against them.

Nonetheless, very few of them slept.

## 64  *The Epiphany Of The False Priest*

At the imminent prospect of battle one experiences a wild excitement that precludes rationality. But in the boredom of waiting for it, one's mood changes. The excitement transforms itself into a kind of thoughtfulness that is solitary, but which requires the reassuring presence of others; people offer each other cigarettes in low voices, and when they pat each other's backs, their touch feels the need to linger. Some write notes or poems that will be found upon them after the event of their death, detailing regrets and previously unacknowledged longings. Others pass the time dismantling, cleaning, and reassembling weapons that are already in immaculate condition. They pass handfuls of ammunition from one pocket to another, weighing up the best way to distribute it for ease of access. Others walk about with their hands in their pockets, smiling wanly, and with genuine affection, even at those who have always annoyed them intensely. Everyone looks at the world with a heightened acuity, as though perceiving for the first time the globular abdomen of an ant, or the porous texture of snow.

Just before the battle one's guts sink, and breathing becomes difficult. One is now in the kingdom of absolute fear, a place where fingers tremble too deeply to light a cigarette, and where the bladder needs urgently to empty itself every ten minutes. Everyone looks around for escape, knowing that it is impossible because everybody else is watching, and because ultimately one's honour is one's only inalienable possession. Some break down and weep into their hands.

All these stages were travelled through during the long night by those who waited upon the mountain. But when the word ran through the camp that it was time to go, then the last stage was reached, when the mind goes blank, one reacts without thinking, and in the surge of adrenalin one becomes almost a god.

There was long gulley down which they moved, out of sight, Remedios having learned, like the cats, the usefulness of broken ground. From there they fanned out amongst the rocks, crawling and creeping, until they spanned the entire northern flank of the crusaders, giving themselves clear lines of fire against an enemy which had anticipated attack from the front.

A volley of shots crashed metallically, and Remedios threw up her hands in exasperation; it had been agreed that no one should fire until she herself had loosed the first round, and as yet her finger had not even taken up first pressure on the trigger. There was the sound of a terse command, and a second volley rang out. She raised her head and gazed petulantly along her own line, but she saw no drifting clouds of cordite.

Dionisio tapped her on the shoulder from behind, and pointed over to the eastern slope next to their own in the north. 'It is the Army,' he said. 'At last they are doing something to aid us in this mess.'

Despite the previous help of General Hernando Montes Sosa in providing helicopters and engineers, Remedios still entertained deep suspicions about the Armed Forces against which her People's Vanguard had struggled for so long. On this occasion she irrationally begrudged their ability to arrive and begin firing without her permission. She raised her Kalashnikov to her shoulder and fired down at the developing mayhem in the camp below, whereupon her own people followed suit. Dionisio tapped her on the shoulder again, and shouted in her ear, above the cacophony of the fusillades, 'I am going to make contact with them.'

Remedios fired again, and said angrily, 'Just tell them whose war this is.'

Taken by surprise, the 'English' down below were scurrying to their tents to fetch weapons, were attempting to run towards the city to get out of range, or were desperately seeking protected vantage points from which to return fire. Mgr Anquilar, demented with the exhilaration of a conflict which he genuinely mistook for Armageddon, wheeled upon his prancing and rearing black stallion, holding aloft his silver crozier, and shouting snatches of the Old Testament that were concerned with Samson's slaughter of the Philistines and the defeat of the troops of Midian.

Meanwhile Dionisio renewed his reputation for fearlessness and invulnerability by crossing the open hillside that separated the Army from the men of the city. With his two black jaguars following at his heels, the thin soil spitting about his feet where the crusaders' bullets struck, he fixed his eyes upon his destination, and walked at an even pace, his fatalism greater than his fear. Afterwards the soldiers were to say with amazement in their voices that he had seemed a huge man, the absolute blueness of whose eyes could clearly be remarked at half a hundred metres.

He passed behind the first soldiers to where he surmised that he would find the commander. He saw a tall man, approaching thirty years of age, whose blond hair and erect carriage reminded him of someone from his past, who was giving instructions to a sergeant with elegant sweeps of the hand that were clearly indicative of a tactical decision. The sergeant ducked away, and the officer raised binoculars to his eyes to observe the enemy. 'Felipe,' said Dionisio, approaching him from behind and putting his hand upon his shoulder.

The officer lowered his binoculars and turned. His eyes widened with incredulity, a huge smile broke over his face, he threw his arms wide, exclaimed, 'Dionisio!' and enclosed him in a deeply felt embrace. 'Shit,' said Colonel Felipe Moreno, 'I never thought I would see you again. What the hell are you doing here?'

'I live over there in that city,' said Dionisio, pointing towards Cochadebajo de los Gatos. 'My father told me that you were now the youngest colonel in the army. Congratulations.'

'For what it is worth,' replied Felipe, 'I may be a colonel, but they sent me on this expedition with only one other officer, a perfect idiot with a block of wood where his head should be, and they have given me one company where I should have had three.'

'Are these the Portachuelo Guards?' asked Dionisio, pointing at the earnest figures in khaki who were oblivious to all but their task of selecting their own target and firing at will.

'Yes, thank God. If they had been conscripts they would have deserted months ago.'

'Listen, Felipe, we must talk later. I have to tell you that on that slope, as you probably realise, we ourselves are attacking. Soon the women will come from the city and attack also, so do not shoot at them. Our plan was to run down and attack them with machetes when and if our ammunition runs out, since we do not have much.'

'You people have balls,' commented the officer.

'That reminds me, our leader is a woman, Remedios, and she wants to be in charge, since this is our struggle more than it is yours.'

Felipe raised his eyebrows and smiled in the aristocratic manner that seems to be universal amongst the officer of élite corps around the world. 'Very well,' he said, 'we will fix bayonets and charge when we see you advance. My men have never had any genuine practice in it, and I cannot see the people down there lasting for very much longer in any case.'

As he crossed back to his own lines with bullets streaking past his head, Dionisio could think only of the time when he had gone reluctantly with Anica to a bar in Valledupar. With them had been her brother, whom he had hated on sight for his good looks, his self-confidence, and the mere fact that he was a successful young officer in the proudest regiment of the Army. Dionisio loathed the Army because of his national service; he hated the obsession with details, hierarchy and formality. To him it was a hideous expense in a country starved of the means of life. He remembered with a wry smile how, in a couple of hours, he had become so close to Felipe that afterwards Anica had complained of not having been able to get herself heard all evening. The memory of that occasion warmed him, but the picture of Anica toying with her glass as the two men discussed democracy also opened up an incurable wound in his heart. He knew suddenly why it was that he took no precautions against the bullets.

'The officer is under your orders,' he said briefly to Remedios, and he went to call all the cats together, determined not to repeat his previous mistake of succumbing to his principled humanity.

The Spanish soldiers under the leadership of the Conde Xavier de Estremadura, the lover of Remedios, and Fulgencia Astiz at the head of the women, emerged from the city and crossed the drawbridge. They separated into two columns, since the Conde had refused to be commanded by a woman. She had disdainfully riposted with a remark to the effect that she would do anything rather than rely upon a man. Despite their altercation, they were now beginning their advance upon the enemy, from the very side from which an attack had been originally expected, but which had now become the enemy's rear. But they covered barely more than a hundred metres, for two reasons.

In the first place they came upon those who had fled towards the city in order to escape the inferno of crossfire at the far end of the valley. Cowardice on the part of the enemy had never entered into the strategic calculations of the council of war, and for a minute Fulgencia was both outraged by it and nonplussed. But it was not long before the Spanish soldiers were poking their rusted rapiers into crevices and hiding holes, and the women were heartlessly firing into the backs of those who were fleeing once more for their own lines, or attempting to scale the unsupported mud of the andenes in their attempt to escape.

In the second place, a cloud billowed down from the peak above the city, and another swelled simultaneously from the valley to the south. Down they rolled, obscuring everything, leaving freezing droplets of condensation upon the barrels of the guns, and enveloping the world in a grey and sodden twilight. 'Shit!' yelled a voice that was plainly Hectoro's, and another that was Misael's said, 'Do not worry, it will lift in a minute. It always does.'

'Cease fire,' shouted Remedios redundantly, since everybody had already stopped shooting at what they could not see.

But it would not lift. Instead it rained. A conspiracy of vapour funnelled cloud upon cloud in a stack that could be clearly seen from the dappled sunlight of the jungle by Carmen as she stabbed the soil with her planting stick of quebracha, and dropped three grains of maize in each hole; one for the gods, one for the birds, and one to eat. The combatants beneath this incontinent deluge shivered and suffered, wrapping their ponchos about their bodies, pulling down the brims of their hats, but becoming more soaked than if they had dived into a lake stark naked. Remedios stood in the relentless downpour, shaking her fist at the mountains whose unpredictability she had previously loved, her face streaming with tears of fury and frustration. It was the first time she had wept since she had found her own brother dead amongst soldiers that she herself had helped to massacre, and only the third time since, as a tiny girl, she had seen her own parents butchered during La Violencia.

'I knew it would rain,' came Misael's voice. 'My ankle was hurting.'

'You should have said so, cabrón,' came the voice of Pedro.

At the very centre of the impenetrable fog a tiny bright light coalesced and grew. It pulsed, diminished, and abruptly exploded to a great yellow fire that seemed to fill the space above the valley. It flashed to a brilliant silver incandescence, and slowly sobered to a steady golden glow. The head of Don Salvador the False Priest filled the vibrating emptiness of the light, and a murmer of awe rose above the leaden plashing of the rain. Father Garcia fell to his knees, as by instinct did all the others who saw, and the countenance of Don Salvador broke slowly into a glorious and ironic smile. It seemed for a second that the effulgent smile was on the point of transforming itself into Don Salvador's unmistakable laugh, but it settled back and illuminated his kindly face more even than the natural light of the vision itself.

By the time that the vision imploded upon itself and disappeared inside its own infinitesimal point of origin, the women had retreated to the shelter of the city, Dionisio's carefully marshalled cats had absconded to the caves, and the battle was already won, even though it rained pitilessly for another two hours and no one could see further than the contents of their own imagination.

# 65 *The Pit*

'It was the best thing I ever saw, when you came to attention in front of Remedios, saluted, and asked permission to stand down your men,' said Dionisio.

'It was entirely right,' answered Colonel Felipe Moreno. 'I hope she did not think it was sarcasm.'

'Certainly not,' said Dionisio, bringing over another tiny cup of thick black coffee. 'She could see that you were perfectly serious. Here is your tinto.'

'Thank you. These jaguars are quite remarkable,' observed the officer. 'I have never seen anything like them. I would expect to have my throat torn out by creatures like these, and yet not only are they as tame as kittens, but you have hundreds of them here. How do you feed them?'

'These two like to eat chocolate. They remind me of Anica in that respect.' He leaned down and tickled the whiskers of one of his cats, so that sleepily it pushed him away with one paw.

'I think the best thing was when that infernal rain lifted, and we saw all those bastards floundering in the mud,' said Felipe, chuckling. 'I was so surprised.'

Dionisio laughed at the memory. 'In retrospect, I suppose it was perfectly obvious that the terraces would slide down the first time it rained. It was absolute folly to suppose that one could remove all the walls to make fortifications without causing that to happen. The odd thing is that none of us had anticipated it either. To tell you the truth, we were all very disappointed that it was the mud that defeated them. It gave us no chance to satisfy ourselves by winning through our own efforts.'

'There can be no doubt that we would have wiped them out. They were facing assault on three fronts, and were already defeated. Are you serious that you want to keep the prisoners? I would be quite happy to take them away and deliver them to the civil authorities.'

'The ones that Hectoro has not shot. Yes, we are serious. We are going to make them rebuild the terraces, and that will give us the satisfaction. After that, who knows? It will depend upon the council. Hectoro will want to execute them himself with his revolver, the Conde will want to slit their noses with his own sword, and perhaps Don Emmanuel will want to make them listen to some of his jokes.' Dionisio became suddenly serious. 'Felipe, why did it take the Army so long to deal with them?'

The officer sighed, puffed out his cheeks, raised his eyes to the heavens, and shook his head. 'That is a sore point,' he said. 'First of all the whole thing had to be processed through the bureaucracy of the Interior Ministry, who wanted the police to do it. Then it went through the Defence Ministry. Then it went back again. It appears that at that point your father, General Sosa, kicked a great many backsides, and passed the task on to my divisional commander, who organised it, having to bear in mind all the requirements of the unrest in Medio-Magdalena. Are you getting the picture? I was told, "They started in the Incarama Park. Now get on with it." I had no logistical support and no other information. We had to follow our own noses, cadging supplies from garrisons along the way whose quartermasters were the very epitome of obstreperousness and ignorance. All quartermasters are like that, so it was no surprise. Dionisio, we have done a forced march of several hundred kilometres through places that do not exist on maps, without vehicles. We picked up the tracks of the enemy numerous times, but they never seemed to be following a plan. They were zigzagging about, backtracking, going sideways, and God knows what. We always missed them. We saw plenty of what they did, mind you, and the stories I can tell you, you would not believe. It was horrific, and that was precisely what kept us going. We spent hours looking at maps trying to predict where they would go next, and we performed outflanking movements by the dozen, but they never behaved in a predictable way that could be called rational. Then one day we came across a priest. His name was Father Belibasta, and he was leading a group of people who had had their eyes put out by the so-called "crusaders". It was he who told me that the destination of the crusade was Cochadebajo de los Gatos, and I said, "Where the hell is that?" He told me it was in the mountains behind Ipasueño. Of course I was born in Ipasueño, and I

375

had visions of my father being blinded, or worse. We marched to Ipasueño and found nothing, so at the police station we asked the way to here, and they sent us to Santa Maria Virgen, where for once the people were glad to see the Army. One of the villagers came with us, and we came upon the enemy as night was falling on the day when you yourselves were up on that ridge waiting to attack. We deployed under cover of darkness, and from there you know what happened.'

Dionisio whistled. 'Quite an epic, Felipe. I had been seething with fury that the Army were doing nothing. Was the policeman at Ipasueño called Agustin? He is an old friend of mine.'

'I did not ask his name. He told me that he would arrest me if I farted in Ipasueño.'

'That sounds like Agustin.' Dionisio hesitated, and then asked, 'Did you see anything unusual in the sky during the rainstorm?'

The Colonel shook his head. 'Should I have done? I could see not even the end of my own nose.'

'I was just wondering, that is all.'

'Shall we go and see how things are going with Mgr Rechin Anquilar?'

The two men left Dionisio's house, and ambled through the streets of Cochadebajo de los Gatos. The town was a shambles of empty bottles, vomit, half-eaten empanadas, abandoned and dented musical instruments, and the sprawling bodies of those too overwhelmed with alcohol to move. Felipe surveyed the desolation, and bent down to pick up some bright red underwear, which he conscientiously hung upon a nail outside the door of a house. 'That was one hell of a fiesta,' he said. 'None of my men have ever known anything like it. A whole week of victory celebration!'

'Your men have become very popular,' replied Dionisio, 'possibly because they are very tall and polite.'

'We take no rabble in the Portachuelo Guards,' said Felipe, proudly.

They passed the axle-pole in the plaza, which now sported Misael's sombrero at the very top, endowing it with a raffish appearance, and left the city by the drawbridge. Just outside the walls, on the other side of the moat, had been dug a deep and muddy pit. On either side of it a heavy beam had been set upright, joined by a cross-beam, from which there hung a large bag knotted from a fishing net. In the bag there seeped and putrefied some of the bodies of the crusaders who had been killed in the battle. The stench was already nauseating, and the contents of the net, with its tangle of limbs, its gallery of colourless eyes and distorted grins, its gaping of suppurating wounds, was obscenely aflutter with the quarrels and avarice of the moth-eaten buzzards and vultures that adorned it.

Down in the pit, stark naked and gibbering, Mgr Rechin Anquilar fluttered his hands and wiped futilely at the loathsome effluent of bird dung and dripping decomposition that oozed upon his body from above, streaking him from head to toe with its varicoloured, clinging, and odious slime.

Felipe held a handkerchief over his nose and read once more the sign that someone had pinned to one of the uprights. It read simply: 'El Inocente'.

'I know that this is poetic justice,' said Felipe, 'but it still seems barbarous to me.'

'Do not concern yourself,' said Dionisio. 'The stench is already so bad that soon the city will not be able to stand it any longer. The point is that if a man wishes to wallow in death, he should be made to wallow in it properly.'

Felipe looked down pityingly upon the erstwhile warlord, who was at that moment searching for fallen maggots in the grey sink of the pit, and cramming them into his mouth with accompanying sighs and grunts that were hideously reminiscent of a gourmet's delight over a fine new sauce. 'By the time that you get him out, he will be completely mad.'

'He already was,' replied Dionisio. 'He is no madder than Father Garcia, but Garcia's madness is not pernicious or poisonous. This was a madness that seems to have been attained by following a line of perfect reason from a dubious premise, which makes him responsible for what he did, don't you think? Also, he was in love with death, and if you look at him now, you will see that he is perfectly content.

It was true. The Monsignor was consuming his maggots with all the absorption of an ape cracking its own lice. 'I sentence you to perpetual happiness,' said Felipe, mimicking the sombre tones of a judge.

The sun began to set above the mountains, casting the world

suddenly into chilliness and twilight with the speed of its descent. Violet, yellow, and crimson rays began to spread across the sky, sparkling upon the reflecting snows of the peaks. Felipe looked down once more, and the gashes upon the Monsignor's head reminded him of a question that he had meant to ask. 'Dionisio, how do you explain the eagle? Remember? When he was trying to ride away on that great black horse, and he had managed to get away from the mud. I was just about to shoot at him when the eagle came down suddenly and attacked him so that he fell from his saddle. Why would an eagle do that? How come it was so big?'

Dionisio thought of Aurelio, and replied, 'I have no idea. A quirk of fate perhaps? Maybe the eagle had a chick near by.'

'Maybe.'

'We had better go back to the city,' said Dionisio. 'It becomes dark here very suddenly, and it has gone cold.'

'Will you give me this man?' The voice came from behind them, and they turned with surprise. In the semi-darkness they saw the silhouette of a vast man, a monk, immensely tall and upright, with a girth so great that no one would have known how to embrace him. The gentle light of the sunset glowed upon his hairless pate, and his solemn face was set in folds that gave him the air, not of grossness, but of modesty and gentleness. 'This man is, so to speak, a child of mine, and I would like to take him.'

Felipe looked at Dionisio and said, 'I for one think that he has suffered enough.'

'I should put it to the council, but if you take him, then everyone will think that somehow he managed to climb out. He would die naked in the mountains, anyway, and no one would regret his escape.'

Felipe put his hand on Dionisio's shoulder and said very sincerely, 'Legally I should take this man away and have him tried, and to tell the truth, I would have taken him with me when I leave with my men, whether you had liked it or not. But I have been thinking of the repercussions. There would be riots and demonstrations by the ultra-conservatives in his defence, and that would lead to a backlash, and then we would once again have all the fanatics running about shooting each other, and we would be back where we started, with La

378

Violencia. It would be better if this were lost to history, if it disappeared unaccountably.'

'You are right, Felipe,' said Dionisio eventually. 'The important thing is peace.' He addressed the vast man: 'Take him, but first tell me your name.'

'I am Thomas, and I promise that this man will go naked forever.'

The two friends watched as the monk unbound the long chord about his belly and lowered it into the pit. They heard him calling to the Monsignor, 'Take hold and I will haul you up, my son.' They saw the slippery scramble out of the pit, and the solicitous way in which the monk took his charge to the river to wash away the traces of the quagmire of death. They heard the whining protests of Monsignor Rechin Anquilar, struggling and flailing, demanding to be returned to his hole beneath the corpses, as he was carried bodily away beneath one arm of the striding colossus of a monk.

It was because of this that only two people in the city were surprised to hear in the morning that El Inocente had died of exposure in his pit, sometime during the coldest night that any of them could remember.

# Epilogue

## 1

'O no,' I said, 'You cannot both be pregnant again. The house is just not big enough, and one of the cats has had another litter. I can't believe it. When am I supposed to do my music?'

'At the same time as you always do,' said Lena, putting on her sly smile that utterly disarms me, 'in the evening, sitting on the doorstep.'

'You can borrow Antoine's tractor and build on another wing,' said Ena. 'You know he still comes to listen to you playing the guitar. I caught him sitting behind the wall. He can pay you for the entertainment by helping you.'

'Soon this house will be the size of the temple of Viracocha,' I said, and Lena kissed me on the end of my nose. 'Don't you love us any more?'

Ena put her hand down my shirt, and I felt the familiar terror coming over me. Lena took the cigarette from my mouth and stubbed it on the tiles beneath her foot. 'We had better go to bed,' she said, 'before Don Emmanuel comes round and plays any more jokes on you.'

All the children seemed to start crying at once, and one of the cats bit the strings on my guitar so that one of them broke with a slap and a twang. 'Can't I have another cigarette?' I asked, but we went to bed anyway.

## 2

Your Eminence,

We of the Holy Office, both before and after the resignation of Cardinal Guzman, have for a long time felt that our institution has been of little value. Since submitting our report to Cardinal Guzman, for which service he at one time rewarded us with the accusation that we were 'Communist subversives', we have had no precisely defined role, and there has been no indication that one would ever be found for us. Cardinal Guzman's principal concern was with doctrinal orthodoxy, whereas ours was with the laxity of our own clergy, and the quality of pastoral care. As far as we know, no action was in any case taken after the submission of our report.

We therefore welcome your decision to abolish this office and release us to return to our diocesan duties, and we also congratulate you upon your appointment to the cardinalate.

### 3

'One of the strange things about history,' said Profesor Luis to his class of dark-eyed little children, 'is that it has long periods of idleness, and then makes everything happen all at once. In that respect it is like you, since none of you have given me last week's homework, and you are all going to give it to me tomorrow, without fail. Or else.'

### 4

'I have a letter from my father,' said Dionisio to Profesor Luis as they sat with their feet on the table, ready to remove them ashamedly when Farides peeped out of the kitchen. 'He says that it was not the Communists or the Liberals or the Conservatives who were trying to assassinate him. It turned out to be a lunatic who thought that my father was not the real General Hernando Montes Sosa.'

Profesor Luis smiled. 'Who did he think the real one was, then?'

'It was not a "he". It was a woman. She thought that she herself was.'

'The world is full of them,' said Profesor Luis. 'History is more or less entirely a catalogue of the actions of lunatics.'

'Here's to the end of History,' said Dionisio, raising his glass. The two friends clinked their glasses together, drank their toast, and sat together in a reflective silence.

'Here's to no more lunatics,' added Profesor Luis.

### 5

Capitan Papagato lay in his immense hammock with his four pet jaguars, clutched his stomach, and was appalled by the terrible pain of his wife's labour. Francesca hung onto the rope that was suspended from the roof, and squatted over the pit lined with palm-leaves, where she would drop her baby when it was born, and where later the afterbirth would be buried.

The Capitan heard the joyful hubbub of the birth, and Francesca came over bearing a little bundle in a shawl. She put Federico into the Capitan's arms, and said, 'It's all right, Papagato, you can stop hurting now because it is all over.'

The Capitan wiped the sweat from his brow with his sleeve, and said, 'My God, it was like shitting a cannonball.'

On the other side of the street Leticia Aragon, like a Russian doll, gave birth to an exquisite child which itself contained a tiny foetus. Aurelio, Carmen, and Dionisio gazed in wonder at the new child, because her black hair flowed down to her waist and her deep brown eyes gazed back at them with the glow of recognition. Carmen asked permission of Leticia, and held the baby to her own bosom. She looked at Aurelio and said, 'It is our little Gwubba. Parlanchina has come back to us.'

Dionisio felt a choke of emotion rise in his throat, because when he looked at Aurelio he realised that it was the first time he had ever seen an Indian weep.

Carmen took the child and laid her in the crib which she would share with Federico until they were old enough to share a bed, since they were long married already in the other world. Aurelio put in an abandoned ocelot kitten that he had found mewing upon a jungle path, and later Leticia fed both Parlanchina and the kitten, one at each breast.

## 6

'Has anyone seen the beast? Has anyone seen the beast?' called the three-hundred-year-old man, as he cantered over the drawbridge upon his rachitic horse. 'Has anyone seen the beast whose stomach rumbles like a pack of dogs, taking many shapes, and devastating the land? Has anyone seen the beast?'

In the plaza the ancient man's horse fell forward upon its knees with exhaustion, and he leapt clear of it just before it trapped his leg by rolling over to die. 'Ay, ay, ay, my thirty-fourth horse,' wailed the old man, tearing at his hair and raising his eyes accusingly to the heavens.

The people of the city gathered around in delight as the three-hundred-year-old man displayed the pyrotechnical virtuosity of his grief. He beat the ground, he kicked his horse in the hope of reviving it, he ululated and gesticulated, until at last he remembered himself and asked bathetically, 'Has anyone seen the beast?'

'The beast came here, but unfortunately we killed it ourselves, since you were not here to do it.' It was Pedro who spoke.

The old man's shaggy eyebrows quivered, and a trail of saliva emerged from the corner of his mouth. 'You killed the beast? But I cannot die until I have killed it myself. I have searched for three hundred years. What will I do?'

'You can continue to live,' said the Mexican musicologist. 'If you cannot die unless you have killed it and we have killed it already, then it follows that you will live forever.'

'Ay, ay, ay,' lamented the old man, running in small circles, 'I have lost my thirty-fourth horse and I will live forever.'

'Do not worry, viejo,' said Pedro. 'Our beast did not have a rumbling stomach, so perhaps it was the wrong one, and you will still get your chance.'

'The wrong one? The wrong one? I pray that it was so, or I will live forever with my horses dying beneath me.'

'We have the beast's horse, and you are welcome to it,' said Remedios. 'I for one want no souvenirs of him in this city. Would you fetch it, Hectoro?'

'I will fetch it,' said Hectoro stiffly, 'not because I was told to do so by a woman, but because I had already had the idea for myself.'

Hectoro came back with the great black stallion and handed the rein to the old man. His eyes opened wide with rapture as he stroked the shining flanks and raised his hand to prove that it was the biggest horse he had ever had. He unsaddled his dead mount and tried to transfer it to the new, but the saddle was plainly too small. 'Never mind,' he said happily, 'from now on I will go bareback. Is there still a cantina here? I could eat a thousand pigs, complete with teeth, trotters and bones.'

'Doña Flor's?' said Don Emmanuel, mindful of the beating he had received from the old man when he had been mistaken for the beast.

'Yes, Dolores still has Doña Flor's. If you want a good meal you should try the Chicken of a True Man.'

7

On the day that the last traces of red paint vanished from the face of the moon, Dominic Guzman and Concepcion entered the end of the valley and saw before them the city of Cochadebajo de los Gatos. They had left their new jeep at Santa Maria Virgen with Ines and Agapita, where they tended it with as much concern as they lavished upon the car of Dionisio, except that they were charging forty pesos a day to the strangers.

'This is the place,' said Dominic Guzman, and they began the long walk between the terraces that rose high upon either side, and which were now once more draped with vegetation.

'Salvador, Salvador,' cried Father Garcia, looking up from *The Book Of Mormon* which he had found in Dionisio's bookshop, and was now reading avidly as he sat upon a sunny rock outside the city. He left the book and sped towards the couple, embracing Dominic Guzman and kissing him upon his cheeks with the rapidity of a harpsichord continuo.

Concepcion looked both astonished and amused, and Guzman, mistaking the name for its meaning, said, 'I am nobody's saviour.'

'He thinks that your name is Salvador,' explained Concepcion. 'You know, like that brother you are always talking about.'

Father Garcia, so excited and pleased that he could not make sense of himself, turned and ran back to the city, waving his arms and shouting, 'The False Priest has returned! Salvador is with us! Virgin most prudent, pray for us!'

'False Priest? Salvador?' repeated Guzman, dumbfounded.

Naturally the confusion was eventually resolved, but not before Guzman had been embraced and kissed by everyone in the city, including a troupe of pretty whores who embarrassed him mightily in front of Concepcion by referring to exploits of which he genuinely had no knowledge. Very soon it seemed perfectly reasonable that the brother of the False Priest should have arrived because he was searching the entire world for his son, and had heard that there was a great wise man in Cochadebajo de los Gatos who could peer beyond the veil to help him.

Aurelio looked at the minute and iridescent pet hummingbird that was sipping honey from Concepcion's lips, and said gnomically, 'Why search for something that is not lost?'

8

His Excellency President Veracruz arrived exhausted at the Presidential Palace. It was true that Madame Veracruz had been greatly rejuvenated by repeatedly making love in the Great Pyramid, but he himself had not, more especially as the overuse of his apparatus had finally caused it to expire with fatigue, rendering it necessary for him to arrange another trip to the United States as soon as possible. He was, despite this disaster, overwhelmingly pleased to be back home.

Mme Veracruz, however, was not. She had sulked and wept on the aeroplane, thrown a tantrum at the airport, and in the limousine had demanded to be taken at once to Paris, because, 'Here there is no civilisation.'

His Excellency went up to his office and found that nothing had changed. His secretaries were still filing their nails and talking to their boyfriends on the supposedly secure telephone lines, and his revolver was still in the drawer of his desk. He sat down at it, and discovered with annoyance that the ink in his pen had dried in such a way that no more could be sucked into it with the squeezy rubber tube.

He was shaking it vigorously, with a perplexed expression, when one of his secretaries came in and said, 'You had better go, Your Excellency, or you will be late.'

'Late? For what?'

'Why, the impeachment of course.'

'Impeachment? Whose impeachment? What are you talking about, woman?'

'Your impeachment,' said the secretary sweetly, 'for dereliction of Presidential duties as laid down in the constitution. At the Senate House at two o'clock.'

His Excellency was apoplectic. He waved his arms, his face reddened with rage. 'At two o'clock? What about siesta? What about the trade credits I got from Andorra? Impeachment! They dare to impeach me when I am not here?'

'They impeached you because you were not here, Your Excellency.'

'It's the fucking Conservatives,' he shouted, throwing his pen to the floor and kicking the desk.

'It was an all-party motion,' replied the secretary in a mistaken attempt to soothe him.

'My own party, too? *Et tu Judas*?'

'*Brute*' corrected the secretary, retreating from the room for fear of the blotting-pad that was being aimed at her head.

Madame Veracruz threw herself into the room in a whirlwind of hysterical shrieks and imprecations. 'Our daughter's gone, our little daughter. Disappeared! Ay, ay, ay, ay, ay!'

'You mean the cat has deserted us too, you cretinous woman! How many times have I told you that I cannot be the father to a black cat?'

'But Daddykins, you saw it when it was born,' wailed Madame Veracruz, her maquillage so reconstituted by her tears that her face had taken on the appearance of a painting by the late Jackson Pollock.

A tearful and repentant chambermaid entered the room from the door that led to the presidential suite. 'I am sorry, sir,' she said, 'it was a month ago, and I had just put the new pink bow around her neck as Madame Veracruz told me to do every day, sir, and I brushed her and gave her some Turkish delight, as I was told, sir.' The maid kneaded the duster that was in her hands. 'And then I looked round and she had gone, sir. We searched the whole place, sir, and we even told the police and the Interior Ministry, but no one saw her, sir, and we had to give up.'

The maid shrieked as Madame Veracruz threw herself across the room and wrenched out a large hank of her hair whilst slapping her face resoundingly. 'Slut,' she howled, 'whore of a bitch of a pimp's cocksucking mother of a whore!'

Madame Veracruz turned her attention from the maid and dramatically tore down the curtains. She overthrew the Presidential desk, bit His Excellency's restraining hand, and flung herself from the room amid a tempest of howls and recondite obscenities that had not passed her lips since her days as a 'hostess' and 'actress' in the Panamanian strip-club.

His Excellency heaved a sigh that embodied every scrap of bitterness and resignation in the world. Desperate for a morsel of peace and quiet, and worried lest the affliction that he had picked up in Cairo might reassert itself during the impeachment hearing, he made his way to the highest lavatory in the land and closed the door.

It was wonderful. As usual, Beethoven played gently in order to drown out the intestinal rumbles of his executive bowels. He took off his trousers because when he was a little boy a jet of urine had once squirted under the rim of the seat and discomfitingly wetted his underwear where it had lain crumpled about his feet, and he sat down wearily. He had the reassuringly familiar thought that one of these days he must get the seat upholstered, or an electrical warming-coil installed.

'I was very right and wise,' he said to himself as his intestines released more of the malodorous and sloppy aftermath of his visit to Egypt. He began to feel equal to the task of facing the impeachment, and commenced to compose long and noble speeches in which he defended his lengthy absence on the grounds of the national interest, to the gentle and arpeggiated rhythm of the Moonlight Sonata.

He consigned the paper to the pedal bin and stood up to flush the chain. He was rewarded with a dry clanking noise that left the evidence of his activities entirely undisturbed. He pulled again, with as little result.

No president in the world, even one facing impeachment, feels able to leave evidence such as there lay in that lavatory bowl; it would have been so demeaning as to be even more unacceptable than to be caught naked in a public place with a little boy on the end of one's virile member. Even assassination would be preferable.

He scratched his head and wondered how it was that a cistern might dry out, even from disuse. He lowered the protective cover of the seat and climbed up on it in order to peer inside the reluctant tank and find out what was amiss.

Although a tall man, he could not see very well, and he went up on his tiptoes, lifting the scrolled and gilded metal lid. He leaned back to bring the flex of the light a little closer, and very suddenly the flimsy cover of the lavatory gave way beneath him.

Down he plunged. His feet slid with unerring accuracy around the bend at the bottom of the bowl, and he fell backwards, knocking his head violently upon the tiles of the floor. When he awoke, he found his feet jammed and his knees compressed together in the hole in the cover. He attempted to raise himself up, but his backside was not upon the floor and his stomach was too weak to cope with the athletic contortions involved in such a manoeuvre. He put his fingers to the back of his head, and found a portentous lump burgeoning upon his occipital bone.

Throwing pride and dignity to the winds he began to yell, at first with stupendous vigour, but thereafter with a forlorn and pitiful hopelessness caused by the fact that the sound system was now thundering and reverberating with the last movement of the Choral Symphony.

It would not be until Madame Veracruz ran out of places in which to weep that she would be inspired to do so in the lavatory, on the other side of whose rococo door she would discern the despairing whimpers of her husband. He would finally be released by four smirking members of the palace guard in spiked helmets and full ceremonial dress, too late to attend the first of the impeachment hearings that were eventually to bring Foreign Secretary Lopez Garcilaso Vallejo to the presidency.

Garcilaso's term of office was to be marked by his unusual dependence upon unminuted interviews with the Archangel Gabriel for advice, by the publication at the state expense of an omnibus edition of all his pseudonymous works upon the occult, and by the unprecedented proliferation of exotic foreign women with unpronounceable names living and cavorting in the many chambers of the palace.

But prior to all these momentous events the outgoing president lay in the lavatory vanquished by Beethoven, immobilised, with his own oily and fetid excrement lapping about the scrawny bones of his shins. Altogether it had been a most inauspicious week for His Excellency President Enciso Veracruz.

# A SELECTED LIST OF CONTEMPORARY FICTION AND NON-FICTION AVAILABLE IN VINTAGE

| | | | |
|---|---|---|---|
| ☐ | THE DUMB HOUSE | John Burnside | £5.99 |
| ☐ | THE LUXURY OF EXILE | Louis Buss | £6.99 |
| ☐ | AFTERNOON RAAG | Amit Chaudhuri | £5.99 |
| ☐ | A STRANGE AND SUBLIME ADDRESS | Amit Chaudhuri | £5.99 |
| ☐ | WITH CHATWIN | Susannah Clapp | £6.99 |
| ☐ | BAUMGARTNER'S BOMBAY | Anita Desai | £6.99 |
| ☐ | GAMES AT TWILIGHT | Anita Desai | £6.99 |
| ☐ | JOURNEY TO ITHACA | Anita Desai | £6.99 |
| ☐ | A SKIN DIARY | John Fuller | £5.99 |
| ☐ | HERE ON EARTH | Alice Hoffman | £6.99 |
| ☐ | ORIGINAL BLISS | A.L. Kennedy | £6.99 |
| ☐ | MY BROTHER | Jamaica Kincaid | £6.99 |
| ☐ | THE UNDERTAKING | Thomas Lynch | £5.99 |
| ☐ | SNAKES AND LADDERS | Gita Mehta | £6.99 |
| ☐ | THE WAY I FOUND HER | Rose Tremain | £6.99 |

- All Vintage books are available through mail order or from your local bookshop.

- Please send cheque/eurocheque/postal order (sterling only), Access, Visa, Mastercard, Diners Card, Switch or Amex:

☐☐☐☐☐☐☐☐☐☐☐☐☐☐☐☐

Expiry Date:_____Signature:_____

Please allow 75 pence per book for post and packing U.K.
Overseas customers please allow £1.00 per copy for post and packing.

**ALL ORDERS TO:**

Vintage Books, Books by Post, TBS Limited, The Book Service, Colchester Road, Frating Green, Colchester, Essex CO7 7DW

NAME:_____

ADDRESS:_____

_____

_____

Please allow 28 days for delivery. Please tick box if you do not     ☐
wish to receive any additional information

Prices and availability subject to change without notice.